PLAYING DEAD

By the time Hank and I reached her, Maisie had grabbed Adriana's wrist and then placed two fingers on her throat. She kept her fingers there for a long time and then slowly looked up at us, her face pale in the harsh sunlight.

I noticed a dark red patch was spreading from Adriana's chest to her collarbone—a concealed packet of fake blood, I decided. They call them squibs in the movie business. The actor presses her hand to her chest and the thin plastic packet explodes, leaking blood everywhere. The blood looked frighteningly real as it trickled down her neck and then spilled onto the grayish sand around the pond.

"Hank—" Maisie said, as he knelt down next to Adriana in the sand. I noticed her eyes were blurring with tears and her voice was trembling. "She's not unconscious. I think . . . I think she's dead."

Other Talk Radio Mysteries
by Mary Kennedy

Dead Air

REEL MURDER

A Talk Radio Mystery

Mary Kennedy

AN OBSIDIAN MYSTERY

OBSIDIAN
Published by New American Library, a division of
Penguin Group (USA) Inc., 375 Hudson Street,
New York, New York 10014, USA
Penguin Group (Canada), 90 Eglinton Avenue East, Suite 700, Toronto,
Ontario M4P 2Y3, Canada (a division of Pearson Penguin Canada Inc.)
Penguin Books Ltd., 80 Strand, London WC2R 0RL, England
Penguin Ireland, 25 St. Stephen's Green, Dublin 2,
Ireland (a division of Penguin Books Ltd.)
Penguin Group (Australia), 250 Camberwell Road, Camberwell, Victoria 3124,
Australia (a division of Pearson Australia Group Pty. Ltd.)
Penguin Books India Pvt. Ltd., 11 Community Centre, Panchsheel Park,
New Delhi—110 017, India
Penguin Group (NZ), 67 Apollo Drive, Rosedale, North Shore 0632,
New Zealand (a division of Pearson New Zealand Ltd.)
Penguin Books (South Africa) (Pty.) Ltd., 24 Sturdee Avenue,
Rosebank, Johannesburg 2196, South Africa

Penguin Books Ltd., Registered Offices:
80 Strand, London WC2R 0RL, England

First published by Obsidian, an imprint of New American Library,
a division of Penguin Group (USA) Inc.

First Printing, June 2010
10 9 8 7 6 5 4 3 2 1

For Kristen Weber

ACKNOWLEDGMENTS

Thank you to Sandy Harding for her wonderful editorial skills, her kindness and her sense of humor.

Kudos to the entire Penguin art department and marketing team for all their hard work and creativity.

I'm grateful to my friend and fellow author, Mark Bouton, for answering my endless questions on crime scene investigation, forensics and law enforcement.

Thank you to Bob and Jill TenEyck for being my cheer leaders, for loving every single one of my books.

And I'm deeply grateful to Alan, my husband and computer guru, for his design skills and his technical expertise.

Chapter 1

Something was horribly wrong.

I knew it before I opened my eyes, before I saw the faint pinkish-orange light seeping in between the "Faux-teak" blinds that shutter my bedroom windows. It was barely dawn, yet I could hear someone rattling around my condo, moving from the hall into the kitchen.

I instantly slammed into Def Con 1. I sat straight up in bed, pulse racing, nerve endings tingling, skin prickling at the back of my neck. An icy finger traced a lazy trail down my spine and I crept out of bed, yanking my arms into my favorite terry bathrobe.

I was gripped by a fear so intense, I could hardly breathe.

A home invasion? *Call 911!* I reached for my cell phone, then realized with a stab of despair that I'd left it in the kitchen. How annoying. Not only was I going to die, I was going to die because of my own stupidity, just like the heroine in a Kevin Williamson flick. Never an ideal way to go.

I could only hope there would be enough of my body left for the police to make a positive ID. Maybe the pale blue bathrobe, decorated with goofy yellow ducks, would give them a clue. My roommate, Lark Merriweather, always says that no one over twelve years old would be caught dead in it.

Or alive, for that matter.

I tiptoed to the bedroom door, my heart lodged in my throat. I felt the beginning of flop sweat sprouting under my arms as I cautiously turned the doorknob. At least Lark would be spared. She was away for the weekend, visiting friends in Key West. But where was my dog, Pugsley? He'd been sleeping at the foot of my bed when I'd drifted off to sleep watching Letterman. Had he been abducted? The victim of foul play? I couldn't face life without Pugsley. Rising hysteria!

And then I heard a familiar voice.

A breathy, smoke-filled voice, early Kathleen Turner. My shoulders slumped with relief and I shuffled out of the bedroom, my pulse stuttering back to normal.

In the kitchen, I found both good news and bad news awaiting me.

The good news was that there was no sign of a crazed serial killer, no ax murderer.

The bad news was that my mother, Lola Walsh, was back in town.

In my condo, to be precise. She must have let herself in with her key sometime during the night and now she was padding around my living room, talking on her cell.

"That would be just fabulous, darling, fabulous! How can I ever thank you?" A pause and then, "Oh, you naughty boy. I'll have to think of something, won't I? But will your wife approve? You know what they say, 'what the mind doesn't know, the heart doesn't feel.'" Her tone was lascivious, bordering on high camp, and I had to stifle a grin. She turned around and flashed me a broad wink.

Lola was on full throttle, charming someone with her Marilyn Monroe "happy birthday, mister president" voice. Lola's an actress, although she's having trouble finding parts these days, because she's "of a certain age," as she likes to say.

According to Lola, the Hollywood establishment has been hijacked by the Lindsay Lohans, the Hannah Montanas, and the Lauren Conrads, long-legged ingenues who edge out classically trained actresses like herself. Although God knows, she tries her best to stay in the game.

Sometimes she tries too hard.

Today, for example, she was wearing a spaghetti-strapped tank top with a pair of red and white Hawaiian-print skintight capris. Her considerable assets were spilling out of the tank top, making her look like a geriatric version of a Hooters Girl.

Age is "just a number" to Lola. A flexible number. I'm thirty-two, and ten years ago, Lola listed her age on her resume as thirty-eight. As far as I know, she's still thirty-eight. Don't try to do the math; it will make your teeth hurt. And her head shot is a sort of reverse Dorian Gray, since it makes her look younger than I do. She often introduces me as her sister, which would probably have me in analysis for years, if I didn't happen to be a shrink by profession.

"You're awake!" she said, flipping the phone shut and enveloping me in a hug. Her voice was warm and breezy as a summer's day. "Maggie, you'll never guess who that was," she added playfully.

"Nicolas Sarkozy?"

"Oh, don't be silly. He's married to that supermodel, Carla Bruni. C'mon, try again."

I gently untangled myself from her embrace and made tracks for the coffeepot. I always set everything up the night before, so all it takes is a quick push of the ON button. That's all my sleep-fogged brain can handle first thing in the morning. A nice mug of steaming dulce de leche to start the day. I was still feeling shaky with adrenaline and took a couple of deep, calming breaths.

"Mom, you know I hate to guess." She made a little moue

of disappointment and I sighed. I knew I had to play the game, or I'd never be able to drink my coffee in peace. "Okay, Daniel Craig called. He wants you to fly to London and have drinks with him at Claridge's tonight."

"Nope." She giggled and clapped her hands together. "Although that certainly sounds like fun. I love his movies and he's a major hunk."

I smelled the coffee brewing, my own extra-caffeinated version, and greeted Pugsley, who heard my voice and came racing in from the balcony. Pugsley is the furry love of my life, a three-year-old rescue dog who understands my most intimate thoughts and feelings. He's the next best thing to a soul mate and gives me what every woman craves.

Unconditional love and a ton of sloppy kisses.

Plus he's game for anything if it makes me happy. How many guys can you think of who would curl up on the sofa with me on a Saturday night to watch *Marley and Me* for the third time?

Mom's voice pulled me back from my reverie.

"Guess again! Who called?" She held up my favorite WYME mug and dangled it just out of reach. WYME is the radio station that I left my Manhattan psychoanalytic practice for—I host a call-in show, *On the Couch with Maggie Walsh*. It has a small south Florida market, and strictly a bottom-rungs-of-show-biz operation, but I love my job and I don't miss those New York winters.

"Mom, I swear I don't know." I sank into a chair at the kitchen table and put my head in my hands. I said the first Hollywood name I could think of. "Aaron Spelling?"

"Don't be silly. He's already passed," Mom said crisply. "It would take James Van Praagh to reach him now."

"Then I give up."

Mom shook her head. "You give up way too easily." She paused dramatically. "Okay, that was Hank Watson on the phone." She waited for a reaction, her blue eyes flashing with excitement, her magenta nails beating a tattoo on the table. "*The* Hank Watson." She raised her perfectly plucked eyebrows for emphasis.

She released the mug and I immediately crossed to the counter and poured myself a hefty cup of coffee. Ah, sweet bliss.

"Hank Watson!! Director Hank Watson," she added, shaking her head in exasperation. "Don't you watch *Access Hollywood*? What in heaven's name do you watch? The History Channel? C-SPAN?"

"I take it he's a film director." I sipped my coffee, enjoying that first quick jolt of caffeinated energy flooding my system.

"Not just any film director." Her voice was gently chiding. "He's a master of the horror genre. Didn't you ever see *Night Games*? Or *Highway to Hell*? And what about, *A Night to Forget*? He won the Okaloosa County Film Festival award for that one."

I frowned. These all sounded like B movies that probably played to three people in Kentucky before going straight to video. Only one name rang a bell. "*A Night to Forget*? Was that the old flick about the *Titanic*?"

"No, that was *A Night to Remember*," she said with heavy patience.

"Okay, tell me about Hank Watson. And the phone call." Pugsley jumped into my lap hoping for a piece of croissant that didn't materialize. Unless Lark had picked up some "bakery," before she left town, Puglsey and I were both going to be stuck with a healthy breakfast. Kibble for him and high-fiber cereal for me. Blech.

"Well, brace yourself, darling. Hank made me an offer I couldn't refuse. Your mom's going to be a movie star. Again." She sat down across from me, her cornflower blue eyes dazzling.

"A movie star?"

"It's a speaking part," she said, backpedaling swiftly. I raised my eyebrows. "No, it's not an under-five," she added quickly with a toss of her head. "It's a small role, but you know what they say . . ."

"There are no small roles, only small actors," I parroted.

She grinned. "I've taught you well." She smiled approvingly. Some of Mom's recent roles have been the dreaded "under-fives," meaning she had fewer than five lines of dialogue. As an "under-five," she's relegated to lousy pay and the tiniest of bit parts. Last month she was a waitress in a Georgia barbecue joint ("Do you want hush puppies with that, hon?") and just last week she played an emergency room nurse ("Get the crash cart! He's flatlining!")

In an industry rife with rejection (ninety-eight percent of Screen Actors Guild actors are unemployed at any given time) Mom has learned to never turn down work. You never know when another part will come along and the competition is fierce. Five hundred people can turn up to audition for a two-line role.

"Tell me about the movie."

I rummaged in the pantry, found a five-day-old Entenmann's crumb-topped coffee cake, and zapped it in the microwave for exactly five seconds. Then I cut a hefty wedge for each of us. Fiber has its place, but you can never go wrong with Entenmann's. Breakfast of Champions.

"Well, you know Hank and I go way back," she began. "Years ago, when I was getting my feet wet in Hollywood, Hank was making a name for himself as a director."

"So the two of you started out together?" I broke off a corner of coffee cake for Pugsley who was beating a staccato on the floor with his tiny feet. He wolfed it down and gave me one of those intent stares that pugs do so well, his dark eyes riveted on my face.

"In a way," Mom said cautiously. "I'm much younger than Hank, of course."

"Of course." I plastered a nonchalant look on my face. According to Mom, she's younger than everyone in Hollywood, with the possible exception of Dakota Fanning. "So he wants you to fly out to Hollywood to work on his latest flick?"

"No, something better! He's going to be filming part of the movie right here in south Florida, in Cypress Grove. How perfect is that? He got a really good deal from the Florida Film Commission, and he can't wait to start shooting here. You know, the sunlight, the ocean, the scenery—this place is paradise for a cinematographer." She was as giddy as if she'd taken a hit of Ecstasy. "Just think, Hank and I will be together again, just like in the old days."

"I'm happy for you, Mom. What's the movie called?" I wanted to take a peek at the *Cypress Grove Gazette* that was spread out on the table, but I knew Mom was on a roll and I figured I'd better play along. I couldn't imagine anyone shooting a movie here, but I decided to take Mom's word for it.

Cypress Grove is a sleepy Florida town, north of Boca, not too far from Palm Beach, and a pleasant ride to Fort Lauderdale. As the Chamber of Commerce says on their welcome sign, "Cypress Grove. We're near every place else you'd rather be!" I never could figure out if that was said tongue-in-cheek. Maybe, maybe not.

"The film is called *Death Watch* and it stars Adriana St. James. It will be wonderful to work with her again. I haven't seen her in years, you know."

I frowned. "Adriana St. James? Mom, I thought you loathed her. How can you stand to be in a movie with her?"

"Oh, that was nothing, a mere creative difference of opinion." Mom reached down to pat Pugsley, her face melting into a dreamy smile. "You know how it is with us theater people. One minute we're discussing Larry Olivier and *Hamlet* and the next we're arguing over whether or not Jeremy Piven really had mercury poisoning when he bailed out of that David Mamet play." She gave a wry little laugh. "It doesn't mean a thing, darling. It's just the artistic temperament shining through. We're bound to clash from time to time. We always kiss and make up."

"Mom, you told me Adriana dumped a very large Caesar salad in your lap at Chasen's one night. She claimed you were sleeping with her husband. The whole story was on Page Six."

"Oh, yes, the Caesar salad." Mom frowned. "You know, I never did get that stain out of my Chanel suit. I had to donate it to charity. Just think, some poor homeless person is probably wandering around Rodeo Drive, wearing a vintage Chanel with a really big stain on the skirt."

"Mom, I don't think homeless people spend much time on Rodeo Drive—"

Lola cut me off with a wry little laugh. "Well darling, no one could seriously believe I would sleep with her husband. What a dreadful little man! The funny thing is, I was probably the only woman in Hollywood who *wasn't* sleeping with Marvin." Mom chortled. "He had so many girlfriends, he made Warren Beatty look like a celibate monk."

I took at peek at the *Gazette.* Nothing on the front page about the film. I quickly riffled through the sections: local, business, arts-and-entertainment. Zilch. I'd have to call Nick, my reporter pal, the moment I got into work.

"The movie deal isn't a secret, is it. Mom? Because there's nothing in the local paper about it."

"Well, maybe not in *this* paper," she said. "Hank said the news is hitting the *Hollywood Reporter* today. And the *L.A. Times* and *New York Times.*" She reached over and tapped the *Gazette* with a manicured fingernail. "You're living in a

time warp, sweetie, a time warp. I wonder when the news
will make it to this burg?"

I strolled into WYME show around noon, with plenty of
time to call my favorite reporter, Nick Harrison, at the Gazette. I waved to Irina sitting at the reception desk, before
heading down the hallway to my cubbyhole of an office.

Irina is our beautiful blond receptionist, straight from
Sweden. Irina is doing her best to master the English language, but she's making slow progress. Puns, humor, and
slang expressions go whizzing over her head, which leads to
some embarrassing gaffes and a few double entendres.

Today, she was chatting with Big Jim Wilcox, our sports
announcer. "So I said to Gustav, I can't go back to square
zero, no way! It's time to fish or get off the pot."

"Time to fish or get off the pot, that's a good one." Big
Jim chortled appreciatively. He was peering over the reception desk, hoping to catch a view of Irina's impressive
cleavage. Big Jim spends a lot of time hanging around Irina,
laughing outrageously at her comments, letting his eyes skim
lustfully over her body.

But this time Irina was too fast for him. She jutted her
chin, folded her arms primly over her chest, scooting her
desk chair back several feet from the desk.

"Is Gustav your boyfriend?" Big Jim asked. He was ogling
her, with his tongue practically hanging out of his mouth like
Jim Carrey in *The Mask.*

"Boyfriend?" Irina gave a sardonic laugh. "No, not boyfriend; he is landlord. He is . . . how you say, filthy old man.
He is at least forty years old. I would have to be cuckoo to
be interested in old man like that."

"Oh. I see." Big Jim's face flushed and he backed away. I
knew Big Jim had hit the big four-oh at least five years ago.
"Well, that's very interesting, Irina. I better get back to the

sports desk now," he added, beating a hasty retreat. It was obvious how his mind was working. If Gustav was a "dirty old man" at forty, that made Big Jim—out of the running!

Score one for Irina. Zero for Big Jim.

Vera Mae, my producer, scurried out from the control room to meet me in my tiny office. "Hey girl, did you have a good weekend?"

I tossed my oversized hobo bag on the desk and riffled through the listener mail. "Lola's back in town." I arched an eyebrow, waiting for Vera Mae's response. "Need I say more?"

"Oh Lord," she said, sinking into my visitor's chair. "And I have the feeling she has more on her mind than shopping at the Sawgrass Outlets." Vera Mae patted her towering beehive, which she'd lacquered like a Ukrainian Easter egg. My producer hails from Georgia and she's of the firm belief that "the higher the hairdo, the closer to God."

"You're not going to believe this, but she told me she's got a part in a movie being filmed here. Some schlockmeister flick called *Death Watch*. Have you heard anything about it?"

"A movie? Being filmed here in Cypress Grove?"

I nodded. "Someone named Hank Watson is the director. Lola actually has a speaking role."

"I haven't heard a thing about it. We could check with Cyrus. He's still head of the Chamber of Commerce, far as I know. If there's any filming going on, he'd be sure to know about it. "

"Good idea." I gave myself a mental head-slap. Of course, Cyrus Still, the station manager at WYME, would know about *Death Watch*. I'd talk to Nick first, and then Cyrus.

Vera Mae reached for a pack of cherry Twizzlers I keep in my desk drawer and helped herself to one. Vera Mae has been trying to give up smoking since I joined WYME a few months ago and she's going through at least twenty Twizzlers a day.

"We could do a show on it, you know? Maybe you could interview the stars, or you could even do a remote broadcast from the set? Cyrus would like that. Ratings are down this month." She lowered her voice. "He thinks we need to jazz up the show a little, get some exciting guests, some more controversial topics. I think he's gonna bring it up at the next staff meeting."

"I'm not sure what he expects me to do. It's not like we're going to lure any big names to WYME," I reminded her. "How bad are the ratings?" I asked after a moment. I hated to ask, but I had to know.

"Well, you know how you and Bob Figgs on the *Swine Report* used to have identical ratings?"

"I sure do. We always tie for last place." Bob Figgs calls himself a "radio personality" in all his publicity; so I do, too. It was embarrassing to see my show, *On the Couch with Maggie Walsh*, linked with his.

Vera Mae leaned closer and whispered, "I hate to tell you, sweetie, but Bobby's inching ahead of you."

"Ohmigod, you're kidding!! I'm losing out to a show about hogs?" *And to think I left a nice, cushy psychoanalytic practice in Manhattan for this*, I added silently. *What was I thinking?*

"It looks that way, hon."

"If we can't change the guests, maybe we should change the title," I suggested. "*On the Couch with Maggie Walsh*. It doesn't really pop, does it?"

"Now, I wouldn't go messin' with the title. You know Cyrus loves that title. He thought of it himself. He thinks it's sort of cute and sexy."

I rolled my eyes. "He probably doesn't even know it's a reference to Freud, a play on words."

"It is?" Vera Mae put her Twizzler down to stare at me. "Well, butter my butt and call me a biscuit. What's Freud got to do with it?"

"Freud used to have his patients lie on a couch while he analyzed them. He thought it helped them free-associate as he delved into their unconscious."

"Well, you got me on that one, girl. Sounds mighty impressive, though. I don't think you should change it."

At that very moment, Kevin Whitley, our college intern, popped his head into my cubicle.

He's annoyingly cheerful, as effervescent as a club soda.

"Hi there, Dr. Maggie."

Kevin is barely twenty but he dresses like someone forty years older. Today he was sporting Larry King suspenders, a Matlock seersucker suit, and wire-rimmed glasses. Bizarre.

Worse, I noticed he was squinting at a sheaf of papers that looked vaguely familiar. Oh God, the Arbitron Ratings "Maybe if you have a sec, you can explain something to me." He gave a wide smile, showing a large number of teeth, which gave him an unfortunate resemblance to Eeyore.

"Sure, Kevin. I'll certainly try." I flashed a helpless look at Vera Mae, who raised her eyebrows. Maybe she knew what was coming.

"Dr. Maggie, what does it mean exactly when the Arbitron Ratings says your show has a minus twelve? How could you have a negative number? I'm afraid we haven't covered that yet that in broadcasting school." His toothy grin never wavered.

"A minus twelve?" I shrieked, pulling the papers out of his hand. I forced myself to take a deep, calming breath. I stalled for time, even though the numbers were right there in front of me. "Well, Kevin, a minus twelve means . . ."

"Yes, Dr. Maggie?"

"It means not only is no one watching my stupid show, but twelve people are marching outside, picketing the station and throwing rocks!" I snorted in disgust. "That's what it means."

Kevin's face crumpled and he put his fist to his mouth, his eyes wide with shock. "Dr. Maggie! Bite your tongue! You shouldn't be saying things like that."

"She's kidding," Vera Mae said quickly. "Kevin, why don't you go check and see if the coffeepot is turned on in the break room. I filled it with hazelnut decaf this morning, but I may have forgotten to turn it on. You know how the announcers get antsy if they don't have their morning joe."

"Sure thing, Miss Vera Mae." Kevin grinned and loped off down the hall like an obedient border collie, glad to have something to do.

"Could my show really be a minus twelve?" I asked, aghast.

Vera Mae gently took the papers out of my hand. I hadn't realized I was holding them in a death grip; my knuckles were white and I was hyperventilating. "Maggie, you're gonna have an aneurysm if you let this stuff get to you. I'm worried about you, girl."

"I'll be fine, Vera Mae." I gritted my teeth and tried to come up with a game plan. I had to increase my ratings, but how?

"Well, first off, you can't be telling Kevin things like that," she chided me. "Even in jest."

"It wasn't said in jest," I said tightly. "I was dead serious."

"Well, it's not a negative number," she said, peering at the sheets. "See, look right here; it's a tiny bit better than you thought." She flipped to another page and pointed to a column of numbers. I was listed right under Bob Figgs, the King of Pork. It wasn't a negative twelve after all.

"It's still bad." I let out my breath in a slow whoosh.

"You're right, sugar; there's no way to put a good spin on this. We need something to boost these numbers. A movie would do the trick. Let me get right on it. I'll make some calls. If no one's covering it locally, maybe we could get an exclusive interview with some of the stars. The first thing we need to do is find out who knows a dang thing about the movie. We have to start at the top."

"I'm going to put in that call to Nick at the *Gazette*," I said. "And I might even call that AP stringer up in Boca."

"I know something that's a lot quicker." Vera Mae grinned. "I'll just call Wanda at the House of Beauty. If there's a movie company comin' to town, she'll know about it. There's not much that gets by Wanda." She heaved herself out of the chair and grabbed a couple of Twizzlers for the road. She tapped her watch and gave me a meaningful look. "You can't spend too much time frettin' over this; you need to go through some of that listener mail."

I nodded grimly. "I'll get right on it."

Chapter 2

"Hey, Maggie, what's up?"

Nick Harrison's voice came racing across the line. Nick and I have been friends since I first arrived in town and he interviewed me for the *Cypress Grove Gazette*. Nick covers arts and entertainment, but he'd love to be an investigative reporter and he's angling to get into a bigger market like Miami or Atlanta.

"I need to pick your brain."

"Slim pickin's," he teased. "What can I do for you?"

"Any news about a movie being shot here? *Death Watch*, by a director called Hank Watson?" I heard Nick typing in the background.

"How'd you hear about it?" he asked idly.

"My mother has a part in it. But she doesn't know the start date and I'm wondering if it's legit."

"If it's Hank Watson, it's probably legit. Probably one of his straight-to-video epics. I bet it's an indie, though." He sounded preoccupied and I heard more tapping in the background. A long beat passed. "Okay, here it is. *Death Watch* is legit, and filming is supposed to begin in Cypress Grove this week, maybe as early as tomorrow. The film company should be rolling into town late today. Gotta run; I'll keep you posted."

O-kaaaay.

A few minutes later, Cyrus Still, the station manager, handed me a press release and asked me to start plugging the movie on my show. So now it was official.

"How did Cypress Grove ever persuade Hank Watson to come to town? I figured he'd rather shoot exteriors in Boca or Palm Beach, or maybe even Key West."

Cyrus grinned. "In this business, connections pay off, Maggie. Big-time. Not many people know this, but Hank and I went to Ohio State together."

"You're kidding!"

"Yeah, it sure beats all. Hank went out to Hollywood and I guess I missed my chance because I fell in love with small town radio. Oh well, you know what they say, woulda, shoulda, coulda. Can't complain; I've always been happy here. Maybe I'm just a hick at heart."

It's true, I suppose. As Irina always says, Cyrus is a "big wheel in a little pond."

Cyrus paused, helping himself to a Reese's peanut butter cup from the jar I keep on my desk. "When I heard that they planned to shoot in south Florida, I called up the production office out in L.A. and got the name of the location manager, Eddie Kosinski It turns out that he was looking at Manalapan and a couple of other places in Palm Beach County."

"Manalapan? Interesting." I knew that Manalapan and Lake Worth were popular with cinematographers. *Body Heat*, the steamy flick that launched Kathleen Turner's career, was shot in both those cities. I still was amazed that a film company would want to come to a little boondocks town like Cypress Grove. I wondered if Cyrus had an ace up his sleeve.

"And that was all it took? A phone call?"

I was stunned by his initiative. It was totally out of character. In many ways, Cyrus has a lot in common with Pugsley. They both enjoy long naps, are addicted to junk food, and try to get as little physical or mental exercise as possible.

Cyrus nodded, pleased with himself. "Well, luck was with me. It turns out Eddie went to Ohio State, too, so I sent him some digital shots of the town and the beach. I guess he liked what he saw." He reached for another candy. "Plus we offered them a really sweet deal. A lot of the stars will be staying at the Seabreeze Inn, and we're picking up the tab. Figure it's a small price to pay for all the free publicity we'll be getting. The town will be flooded with tourists."

"Tourists? Yes, I suppose it will." I thought of Vera Mae's views on tourists: *If it's tourist season, why can't we shoot them?* Vera Mae likes the cozy, Mayberry-like feel of Cypress Grove and wouldn't be thrilled that a gawker invasion was in the works.

"You know, my mom has a part in the movie," I said idly, flipping through my phone log.

"Really?" Cyrus stopped chomping on the peanut butter cup long enough to look surprised. "You could have her back as a guest on the show, if you want. I remember the ratings were really good that time she cohosted with you. In fact, they were through the roof."

"I remember," I said, trying to keep the edge out of my voice. How well I remembered Lola's guest appearance on my show! A guest had canceled at the last minute and Vera Mae had come up with the bright idea of Lola cohosting the show with me.

It was a success for Lola and a disaster for me. The listeners remembered Lola from her soap opera days and she practically hijacked my own show right out from under me. All the calls were about Lola's soap opera career and everyone wanted her advice on life and love. *On the Couch with Maggie Walsh* had morphed into *Lola Walsh: My Life in Soaps.*

"So do you want to schedule Lola for next week? Maybe do a special show on her first day on the set, something like that?"

"Sounds good. She'd like that." Total understatement. Correction. She'd *love* that.

Vera Mae bustled by, carrying a stack of newspapers— probably the *Miami Herald*, the *Sun-Sentinel*, and the *Palm Beach Post*. Even though we're a small town market, Vera Mae is always on the lookout for news stories featuring visiting celebrities, authors, or other people who might be interesting show guests.

She waited until Cyrus ambled off before darting into my office and plunking the papers on my visitor's chair. "Well, I guess you heard the news." Her expression was glum. "It's really gonna happen. Wanda gave me the lowdown on *Death Watch*. They start shooting here tomorrow and that means the trailers and trucks will be rolling in this afternoon. And they even hired Wanda as a part-time hairdresser on the set! That girl is over the moon." She heaved a sigh.

"You don't sound too happy about it," I teased her. "Maybe this will finally put Cypress Grove on the map."

"Maybe," she said slowly. "It'll mean a lot of tourists. What if we end up like Key West?"

"Key West?"

"Yeah, can you imagine a bunch of people running around town in parrothead hats, looking for Margaritaville?"

I bit back a laugh. "I don't think Cypress Grove will ever be that famous, Vera Mae. Maybe it'll all turn out better than you think."

"I wouldn't count on it," she said morosely. "Hollywood's comin' to town, and there's not a gosh darn thing we can do about it."

Chapter 3

"Can you believe it?" Mom asked me that evening, flashing her pearly Hollywood teeth. "Tomorrow is show time." She was dancing around the condo clutching Pugsley as she swayed to "Go Your Own Way" by Fleetwood Mac. When the song ended, she finally returned Pugsley to the sofa and sank onto a kitchen chair.

Lark, my roommate, had returned earlier in the day and had cooked a big pot of veggie fettucine alfredo for dinner.

Lark was ladling out the pasta when Mom clutched her hand dramatically to her chest. "Oh, that Stevie Nicks. I could have been in her shoes, you know. I would need extensions, of course." She picked up a lock of her platinum hair and let it fall back softly to her shoulders.

Lark and I exchanged a look and I thought I detected just the hint of an eye roll. Lark is slim and petite with choppy blond tresses that give her a young-Meg-Ryan sort of look. She has a sweet, pixiesh face and is the kindest person I've ever met. She's much too polite to ever challenge Lola on her flights of fancy and she either deftly changes the subject, or says something flattering.

At twenty-three, she hasn't been beaten down by life and has a sunny optimism that is at odds with my own rather cynical personality. Her favorite movie is *Forrest Gump* and mine is anything by Woody Allen. I think that says it all.

"I can just picture you in a rock band, Lola," she said loyally. "You'd be terrific."

"Yes, sometimes it's like a knife in my heart to know that I could have been up there on stage with Lindsey Buckingham." She gave a heavy sigh, and Pugsley gave a little yip of concern, trotting over from the sofa.

He's incredibly sensitive to human distress, and he's also a big fan of Lark's pasta.

You decide.

"It's all right, Pugsley," Lola said, reaching down to pet him. "Opportunity knocks but once, as they say, and this is a brutal business."

I felt another stroll down memory lane coming on. I sat down, fortified myself with a hefty slug of Chardonnay, and tossed a tiny chunk of French bread to Pugsley. He opened his mouth like a sea lion and swallowed it whole.

"Mom," I began, "you're not really suggesting that you could have joined Fleetwood Mac, are you? You can't even carry a tune. I thought you auditioned for a music video once and the director said you were tone-deaf."

"Well, he had to say that, didn't he, my dear?" She leaned over to Lark and winked. "He had already picked out a girl for the role, you see. Some sweet young thing caught his eye, and I didn't have a chance. He was blind to my charms."

"That's awful; so unfair," Lark said staunchly. She patted Lola sympathetically on the arm. "You can't let it get to you, though. I believe in karma, Lola, and I bet that girl never went anywhere with her career. You've probably had a lot more success than she's had."

Lola hesitated, her cornflower blue eyes flickering down to Pugsley. "Oh well. She did all right, I suppose. In fact, she's made something of a name for herself in the music business."

"Really? Who is she?"

"Beyoncé."

Beyoncé?

Lark raised her eyebrows, her lips twitching. Lola has a vivid imagination and some of her show biz stories are so over-the-top, one can only smile.

"Give me the rundown on your schedule tomorrow," I said briskly. "You're going to meet with Wardrobe and then do a quick line rehearsal?"

"Yes, that's right," Lola replied, returning to Planet Earth. "I'm going to have to wriggle into my Spanx if I want to squeeze into my outfit. I told the wardrobe mistress I was a size four. What was I thinking?" She eyed the big ceramic bowl of veggie pasta, as if angling for a second portion, and then sipped some iced tea instead.

"I'm sure you'll be fine," said Lark, ever the optimist. "Then what?"

"Then I have a quick run-through of my lines with Hank. We're doing a table reading. I already have my sides, so I'll have to go over them tonight."

"Your sides?" Lark looked puzzled.

"They call them sides," I explained. "They don't bother copying the whole script; they just give you the pages with your lines."

"That's great that you didn't even have to audition," Lark said.

"I know; I was very lucky." Lola smiled. "I think Hank has seen enough of my work that he knows I can deliver the goods. I expect to have my entire role memorized by tomorrow."

"Won't it be sort of odd, though, not knowing how the story ends? I mean, you only know your own lines. How will you figure out how your scene fits into the whole picture?"

This was my cue to start clearing the table as Lola explained the mysteries of the film business to my wide-eyed roommate. Lola conveniently left out the fact that each of the principals has a copy of the entire script. It's only the bit players who are given sides. Their roles aren't crucial to the story line and they're strictly supporting actors. Far be it for me to rain on her parade, so I kept quiet.

I busied myself at the sink, glancing out the sliding glass patio doors to catch the spectacular sunset. The sun was like an orange lollipop as it sank slowly into the horizon, splashing the sky with paint-box colors: gold, flame, and burnt umber.

Cypress Grove, my own little piece of paradise. Tomorrow it would be open to the world.

"Lola, sweetie, is that you? Dahling, you look fabulous. Absolutely fabulous!"

Lola and I were chatting with one of the grips on the *Death Watch* set the next morning, when Adriana St. James descended on us. Lola was due for a table reading in half an hour and I'd tagged along, hoping to score an interview with Hank Watson for WYME later in the week.

"Here comes the barracuda." Lola ducked her head close to mine and whispered," Purple alert, dear. Purple alert!"

Purple alert? I remembered that Florida lifeguards use purple flags to warn swimmers about dangerous marine life in the area.

"Barracuda?" I mouthed.

"You'll see. Or maybe a Portuguese Man o' War," she added vaguely. "They can attack you from thirty feet away, you know. That's how far their tentacles reach."

At that very moment, Adriana's tentacles were inching dangerously close to us. She elbowed her way through a group of gawking extras, and then paused to hop nimbly over a tangled maze of electrical cables. Her face was flushed and her smile was amped to the highest power.

"Kisses, kisses!" she shrieked, grabbing Lola by the shoulders and planting noisy air kisses on both cheeks, European style. I nearly choked on the cloyingly sweet wave of Jungle Gardenia that enveloped me. It seemed to hang over Adriana like dank yellow smog over Los Angeles. I know it's a popular fragrance, but it always reminds me of Fruit Roll-Ups.

Lola and I practically break out in hives from just a whiff of it. I staggered backward as if someone has just zapped me with an entire can of Glade air freshener.

"Nice to see you again," Lola said in a strangled voice. Her eyes were watering and she scrunched up her nose as if she was trying her best not to sneeze.

I started to edge away from the noxious fumes when Adriana noticed me, pulled back, and did a comic double take. "Ohmigod! Lola"— she lowered her voice to a shocked whisper—"this can't possibly be little Margaret Anne! Good heavens, she's all grown up! In fact, she's more than grown up; she's positively mature." She tossed me a snide look. "Yes, I would definitely say mature." She drew out the word "mature" and looked solemn, like a CNN anchor reporting an outbreak of swine flu.

Adriana peered into my face and then let her eyes slide over my body like a buyer at a horse auction. I wouldn't have been surprised if she'd slapped me on the flank or done a quick check of my rear molars.

So now I was mature? Oh God, the dreaded M word. Lola winced before flashing me a knowing look, her expression telegraphing, "I told you so."

If I was "mature," then that meant Lola was beyond mature—she was OLD. So old she was practically a leftover from the Ming dynasty. Or a centenarian worthy of a birthday shout-out from Willard Scott.

In Hollywood-land, saying someone is "mature" is the kiss of death. Anyone who reads the casting ads in *Backstage* or the

Hollywood Reporter knows that "mature" actresses often find themselves doing ads for Depends and denture cleansers.

"I don't really use Margaret Anne anymore. I go by Maggie now," I said, sticking out my hand. Adriana ignored it and crushed me to her spongy bosom. It was like being trapped between a pair of giant water balloons.

Like Mom, Adriana was decked out like she'd bought her entire wardrobe at Wet Seal. She was wearing skintight white capris and a gauzy blue halter top with a black Victoria's Secret bra peeping through, and she was tottering along on four-inch espadrilles.

"I just can't believe it," Adriana said, still squinting at me in the bright sunlight. It was only nine o'clock, but the day promised to be a real south Florida scorcher, and I could feel a thin layer of perspiration coating my upper lip.

Adriana, on the other hand, was hermetically sealed inside a heavy coating of Max Factor Pan-Cake makeup (Tan, #10), looking like she'd just escaped from Madame Tussaud's. I doubt she could sweat, even if she wanted to.

"Maggie darling, it's hard to believe, but I haven't seen you since 1970," Adriana said smoothly. "You were just a little slip of a girl back then." She gave a small catlike smile and I noticed the skin around her eyes didn't move at all. Botox? Juvéderm? "You must have been what? About ten, I think."

She thinks I was ten years old in 1970? Yowsers. Either Adriana was no math wizard or she was getting in a quick dig at Lola.

"I think your numbers are off, Adriana. In 1970, I would have been an ovum," I said sweetly. "Not even an embryo." I could hear a stifled snicker from Lola followed by a long asthmatic wheeze. "I'm only thirty-two,"

"Really?" Adriana sniffed. "Funny, I could have sworn . . .

oh well, it doesn't matter, does it? Are you here auditioning for a role, dear?"

"I'm not an actress—" I began, but Lola cut in swiftly.

"Maggie is something of a local celebrity," she said proudly. "She's a psychologist and she has her own talk show on WYME. She's here on assignment." She stepped out of the way as a gaffer hurried by, lugging a pair of heavy Klieg lights. They were doing exterior shots here at Branscom Pond, a tiny park on the outskirts of town, but they still needed artificial lighting to get the right effect.

"Oh, my goodness, a radio celebrity; how lovely for you." Adriana looked flummoxed for a moment. Or she would have looked flummoxed if she could have found some way to raise her eyebrows. "I had no idea you were media."

Media, the magic word.

Media opens the door to a world of freebies—free mimosas, complimentary tickets to sold-out events, and invitations to A-list parties. The only downside is that you have to interview people you have absolutely no desire to spend five seconds with, and you have to pretend they're fascinating.

"I'll have my peeps call your peeps and arrange an interview." Her tone was regal, as if she was granting me a papal audience. I nearly laughed out loud, thinking of what Vera Mae would have to say about being referred to as a "peep."

Adriana pulled me out of the sun into a shaded area near the craft services table. It was crowded with cast and crew members wolfing down coffee and doughnuts. The tantalizing aroma of industrial-strength Hazelnut wafted over to me and I found myself longing for a caffeine hit.

"You can stay and have lunch with us, can't you, dear?" Adriana was clutching my upper arm with her blood-red talons. Lola was right, there really was something predatory about her. She lowered her voice. "I prefer to eat in my trailer, but

Hank wants us to pretend that we're one big happy family"—
she made a little moue of disgust—"so we're all going to
share a picnic lunch together at noon. I think he's taking this
democratic thing too far, but it's his call."

She gave a snarky smile worthy of Leona Helmsley. "Everyone eating together, can you imagine? The principals, the
leads, the extras, forced to socialize as if we're equals."

Oh my, yes, very Leona Helmsley, maybe even early Marie
Antoinette. She stopped to fake smile at a gorgeous guy
strolling by with a clipboard and a headset. He was wearing
a *Death Watch* T-shirt, so I guessed he was a techie. Probably working with the crew, waiting for his big break.

"Sounds like fun," I said politely.

"I'm sure I won't get to eat a single bite; I'll be hounded
for autographs every second. The price of fame, I suppose."
Adriana heaved a weary sigh. "As my dear friend Larry Olivier used to say, 'it goes with the territory.'"

"Hmm; yes, he was quite right." Lola permitted herself a
very small eye-roll.

"And tell me, Lola, what role are you playing? Is it an
under-five?"

"Of course not!" Lola practically quivered with indignation. "I have the fifth female lead, I play a high-powered real
estate agent, Roxanne Clark."

"Roxanne Clark? I don't recall seeing that character in
the script."

Lola's lips tightened, but she forced a smile. "It's a rather
small part, but I think Hank will probably expand it once we
get rolling. I heard there's been some dialogue problems and
the script has already gone into rewrites. So this might not
be the final draft." Lola waved the sides in the air as if she
were swatting away a particularly annoying gnat.

"Interesting," Adriana said, inspecting one of her fake nails.

She seemed supremely bored, now that the conversation had veered away from her.

Lola was undaunted. "In fact, I want to discuss it with him at the reading—"

"Oh, look; there's Mitch, the cinematographer," Adriana cut in. She pointed to a wiry guy with a deep tan who was frowning at a startling array of cameras and lighting equipment. "I've got to remind him to use the rose gels; honestly, you can't trust these people to do anything right. I heard Liz Taylor used to carry her own set of gels with her. Smart girl; no wonder she always looked so terrific on camera. See you at lunch!"

Chapter 4

I waited until Adriana galloped out of earshot before turning to Mom. "Rose-colored gels? Are they anything like rose-colored glasses?"

"Even better, darling. They can knock off quite a few years—they're very flattering to mature faces." She squinted up at the white-hot Florida sun and gave a little sigh. "Natural light can be brutal, if you're over eighteen."

"It looks like Adriana is trying to plead her case with Mitch." The actress and the cinematographer were locked in a heated discussion in front of the craft services table. "And it doesn't look like it's going well," I added. Adriana was gesturing wildly like a demented mime and Mitch was avoiding eye contact with her, munching on a doughnut, his expression tight.

"Adriana's never satisfied with the lighting," Mom said, glancing at the pair. "She makes life hell for the tech people. She'd like them to shoot her through a wall of Jell-O, if it were possible. It's the only way they're going to get that hazy, out-of-focus look she likes."

"How's my favorite leading lady?" A fiftyish man with a graying beard suddenly appeared from behind us and grabbed Mom in a crushing bear hug. "You've still got it, babe," he added, drawing back to look at her.

From the way her eyes sparkled, I figured this had to be the famous Hank Watson. He was wearing faded jeans and a Lakers T-shirt, and he moved with an air of easy confidence.

"Oh Hank, you're such a tease." Lola smiled up at him, and I noticed she kept her arms looped around his neck.

"I'm here to whisk you away to a table reading," Hank told her. "We can catch up on old times over lunch."

"I'd love that." She gave him a saucy smile and then remembered that I was standing there like the proverbial third wheel. Oh yes, the Mature Daughter. Hmm. How was Lola going to handle this one? I wondered for one crazy moment if she was going to try to pass me off as her younger sister. No, I'm not being paranoid. She's actually done this from time to time, and as a shrink I can tell you that past behavior is the best predictor of future behavior. Of course, she'd already revealed my true identity to Adriana, so I suppose that ship had already sailed.

Lola went for the direct approach.

"Hank, sweetie, I want you to meet someone very special; this is my daughter, Maggie. She's a psychologist," she added proudly.

Hank flashed me a high-beam smile and we shook hands. No air kisses, thank God. He was quite attractive in an older-guy sort of way and I could see why Mom was so taken with him.

"Hey, good to meet you, Maggie. I'm a big fan of your mom; we go back a long way."

"Well, not *too* long a way," Lola teased him." I was practically a child when you cast me in the role of Maria in *Luigi's Daughter*. I remember you were afraid the role might be too sophisticated for me." I bit back a smile. Mom was forty-five years old when she played the ingenue role in the straight-to-video art flick.

Hank was giving me a speculative look and I wondered if

this was the best time to hit him up for an interview. "A psychologist," he mused. "You know, we might have a job for you—" he began.

"I'm a radio talk show host, not an actress," I said quickly.

"But you're a real psychologist, right?" He turned to initial some papers a production assistant shoved at him.

"Well, yes, but—"

"Ever do any forensic work?"

"That was Maggie's specialty when she started out," Lola said, clasping her hands together. "You should see the people she dealt with—psychopaths, convicted felons, all sorts of low-lifes." She gave a delicate little shudder." I never could understand why she wanted to do that kind of work instead of having a nice Park Avenue practice."

"So why did you do it?" Hank seemed genuinely interested. Most people's eyes glaze over when I talk about psychology, so I try to say as little as possible about my former career.

"I know it's hard to believe, but I really liked the rough-and-tumble of courtroom work, facing off against trial lawyers, working with prosecutors, that sort of thing. And I got a kick out of getting to know detectives and CSIs. I learned a lot from them—I had all the theories, but they had the real-life experience in crime solving." I paused. "They taught me about lie detector tests and how the perps can beat them and how to interview criminals and keep your cool. If you show fear, you're through." I wondered if I was saying too much, but Hank was listening intently and suddenly he snapped his fingers.

"Maggie, you're exactly what I'm looking for," His river-green eyes dazzled with excitement. "I need a forensic consultant on the set. Someone who can get inside the head of a psychopath, and tell us where we're getting it wrong and where we're getting it right."

A consultant on a movie set? Cyrus would be thrilled and maybe it would help my ratings. But would I really be any help to the production? "Look, Hank, I've never worked on a movie set before, and I'm not sure I can—"

"For heaven's sake, Maggie, you don't have to be Dr. Henry Lee," Lola cut in. "You just have to help Hank make the scenes a little more realistic. It's not rocket science, you know."

I could see Lola was getting impatient with me. I tend to approach new situations cautiously, and Lola is just the opposite. She likes to act quickly and impulsively. She's also way more decisive than I am. She's a big fan of the adage: "Lead, follow, or get out of the way."

Hank locked eyes with me. "I know you can do it, Maggie. We've already gone through five script revisions, and I'm still not happy with it."

"What sort of problems are you having?" I felt a little frisson of excitement. It might be fun to get back into forensic work, even if it was just a Hollywood version of it.

"Some of the interrogation scenes are a little rough, and the dialogue needs some work. Plus we've added a scene where the psychologist interviews the suspect in his prison cell. This is the kind of thing you could really help us with."

"Maggie, say yes!" Lola urged.

"At least stay and meet Sandra." Hank's green eyes were pleading. "I know she'd be thrilled to talk to a real-life forensic psychologist."

"Sandra Michaels?" Lola asked. "I saw her name on the call sheet."

Hank nodded. "She's playing Dr. Rebecca Tilden, the psychologist who solves the zombie killings. If Maggie can stay for lunch, I'll make sure she has plenty of face time with her. I know she'll have a million questions for you," he said, turning to me.

I raised my eyebrows. Zombie killings? Oh God, what was I getting myself into?

"So what do you think? A couple of hours a day on the set, working as a consultant? We're an indie production, so we don't have a big budget. We could swing a thousand dollars a day and it should only take a couple of hours. Would that work for you?" Hank was staring at me, waiting for my reply.

Yikes. A thousand dollars for two hours of my time?

This was no time to dither, and Mom answered for me.

"She'll take it," Mom said firmly.

And just like that, I was in the movie business.

I made a quick call to Vera Mae at WYME to tell her I'd be tied up on the *Death Watch* set for lunch but would be back at the station in time for my afternoon show.

Vera Mae is a big fan of crime shows—*CSI*, *Law and Order*, *Criminal Minds*, and most recently, *The Mentalist*. Just as I'd expected, she was thrilled to hear that I was going to be a consultant on the set.

"We need to tell Cyrus right away," she said firmly. "He'll be wanting to do some promos, and maybe you can even do some live interviews from the set."

"I can certainly ask," I promised. "Things are pretty busy here, though. I'm not sure how much time the actors are going to have to give interviews."

"Oh for land sakes, Maggie, that's a load of hogwash. Have you ever known an actor who didn't love to talk about himself? Believe me, they'll make the time to talk to you." She gave a knowing laugh, and I guessed she was thinking of Lola.

"I suppose you're right," I agreed. "I can run the idea by Hank during lunch, or I can talk to their press person, if they have one. It's a low-budget indie production, so I'm not sure."

"Try to get an exclusive," Vera Mae suggested. "But it may be too late for that. Once word gets out that a movie company's in town, the entertainment reporters will be on that set like white on rice. But maybe you can jump the gun and get some good interviews in the can. Do you have your little tape recorder with you?"

"Yes, but—"

"You never bought batteries for it," Vera Mae said.

"Guilty as charged." Vera Mae knows me too well. I've been carrying a tape recorder around for months. It has a WYME logo slapped on it to make it look official, but it's just a prop, since the batteries are dead.

I always take my own notes on a mini legal pad. I try to be unobtrusive, because subjects tend to freeze when they see me wielding a pen and paper. I noticed the same thing when I had my psychoanalytic practice back in New York; clients would clam up whenever they caught me writing down anything.

I was heading over to the craft services table for a glass of iced tea when I spotted Nick Harrison from the *Cypress Grove Gazette*. So Vera Mae's prediction about a media blitz was right on target.

Nick is a good-looking guy, tall and athletic looking with a boyish smile and dirty blond hair worn on the longish side. There's enough of an age difference that he thinks of me as an older sister, not potential date material. Today he was wearing what I call Cypress Grove casual: a snowy white golf shirt, neatly pressed khakis, and Reeboks.

He was juggling a paper plate filled with doughnuts and Danish pastries in his right hand and a jumbo-sized coffee in the other. Like most reporters, Nick can't resist the lure of free food—offer him an Oreo cookie, and he'll follow you anywhere.

When he saw me, he gave a sheepish nod. He balanced

the paper plate on top of the coffee cup and I watched, fascinated, as he reached for a sugary bear claw.

"Having an early lunch?" I teased him.

"Actually, this is a snack. I'm having lunch with the cast and crew in half an hour. I've managed to score an interview with one of the cast members."

"Really? I've been invited to lunch, too. Who are you seeing?"

Nick and I always trade information—we often cover the same stories, but we're not really rivals or even competitors. After all, we work in different media and we use a lot of the same sources. I met Nick when I first came to town and we've been friends every since. We've sat through loads of boring civic speeches and rubber-chicken dinners together at the Cypress Grove Press Club and shared a lot of laughs. He's cute, laid-back, and young enough that there's no temptation to have a romantic relationship.

I held his coffee while he flipped through a tiny notebook he always carries. "Sandra Michaels, the formerly fat actress."

"That's what you call her—the formerly fat actress?"

"That's what the tabloids call her. Not very nice, is it?" Nick had an adorable smile, complete with a Mario Lopez dimple. "Do you know anything about her? They gave me a press packet but I haven't had a chance to read it."

"All I know is that she plays a forensic psychologist. It's a major role, maybe the second female lead. I'm not sure. I'll be meeting with her today as well." I filled him in on Hank's offer to be a consultant on the set and he gave a low whistle of approval.

"Wow, it sounds like a sweet gig."

"I hope so. Lola talked me into it." Nick grinned; he knows how persuasive Lola can be. "You seem to know more about Sandra than I do. What's with the 'formerly fat actress' bit?"

"She used to weigh over two hundred and thirty pounds

and her acting career was in the toilet. Then she slimmed down through a really intensive diet and exercise program. She's writing a book about it and I think there's even a TV deal in the works. She told *Access Hollywood* she's lost a hundred pounds."

"A hundred pounds? That's impressive." Back in Manhattan, I saw patients who were "emotional eaters" and it was hard to get them to lose even ten pounds. "And she did it all on her own? That's really amazing."

"She claims she did it through sheer willpower, no pills or surgery." He peered at his notes. "According to *USA Today* she said she knew there was a skinny person trapped inside her, screaming to get out."

"Hmm. A skinny person screaming to get out?" I gave a little snort. "I wish I could say the same. I always feel like there's an entire Sara Lee cherry cheesecake outside me, screaming to get in." I paused, watching a pair of grips setting up long picnic tables under a grove of straggly palm trees. Some shiny silver catering trucks were rolling in and I figured they were getting ready to set up the noontime picnic.

"Anything else?" I prodded Nick.

Nick raised his hand to shield his eyes from the blinding sun. "Here's a little gossip piece from TMZ. It seems Sandra and Adriana St. James are archenemies, but I'm not sure why." He scribbled a quick note to himself. "I need to check that out."

"I think you may get your answer at lunchtime. The first thing that struck me is that half the people on the set can't stand Adriana. It's going to be hard to find anyone to say anything good about her."

I thought of her snarky remarks to Lola earlier that morning. She certainly wasn't angling for the Miss Congeniality prize with that acid tongue of hers, and those jabs about my age.

"I can't believe you're really a psychologist," Sandra said half an hour later. "It's so exciting, I've never met one before."

We were sitting side by side on folding chairs at lunch, which seemed to be a Paula Deen southern barbecue served buffet style. I had to pick my way past piles of barbecued chicken and blackened ribs to fill my plate with french fries, hush puppies, and corn bread. Carb city, but everyone else seemed to be enjoying it. I bet I was the only vegetarian on the set. I'd added a scoop of coleslaw as a vegetable along with some limp lettuce that was intended as a garnish.

"No ribs?" Sandra said, staring at my plate.

"Vegetarian."

"Oh," she said uncertainly.

Sandra was mid-forties, probably a decade younger than Adriana, and had flowing blond Stevie Nicks hair plus a wide Julia Roberts smile. She dressed young, but her body was toned and she could carry it off. She was attractive in a sort of flashy, in-your-face kind of way, just like one of the Real House-wives of Orange County.

She looked eerily young in the bright Florida sunlight, almost Photoshopped, from her gleaming white veneer to her flawless skin. I wondered if she'd had some "work" done. Or maybe her California good looks were the result of healthy living. After all, she had lost a huge amount of weight, all on her own.

"I'm so glad you agreed to be a script consultant," she said. "Just between us, some of my scenes are real clunkers. The dialogue is forced and I think the writers are pretty clue-less about forensic psychology." She paused with her fork in midair. "That's the writing team over there. I guess you'll be meeting with them eventually."

She gestured at two young men at the end of the table. They were wearing *Death Watch* T-shirts and baseball caps and looked about sixteen years old. One of them was playing air guitar, with his head thrown back like a rock star while his friend thumped an imaginary drum on the table-top.

"Wow, they look . . . young," I said. "Almost like they should be out skateboarding."

Sandra scrunched up her face into a frown. "And they have five Emmys between them. Can you believe it?"

I nodded. "It's a youth-driven business."

"I'll say. This is probably the last movie I'll do," she added.

"Really? I thought I read somewhere that you loved acting."

"I love performing," she corrected me. "But after a certain age, the roles dry up. I don't want to end up like Mia Farrow, playing someone's grandmother when I hit fifty. I'm lucky that I've got some other irons in the fire."

"Really? Like what?"

"Well, I'm not supposed to talk about it yet, but I guess I can tell you." She gave a girlish giggle. "I've got a deal with the Style Network for my own health and beauty show."

"That's wonderful, Sandra."

"Yes, it is, isn't it?" She sighed happily and shot me a grin. "My agent thinks that the book deal will drive the TV show and they'll work off each other. Synergy, he said. That's pretty cool, right?"

"Very cool."

"I probably need a manager, as well as an agent. I'm going to look into that."

"I'm sure you'll find the right person to guide your career," I told her.

After playing with her food for a couple of minutes, Sandra glanced at her watch. "Oh, I promised to give that cute guy from the *Gazette* equal time. Nick somebody or other; you don't mind, do you?"

"Of course not; go ahead. Nick's a friend of mine. We can catch up with each other tomorrow. I'll be back here in the morning before I do my show."

"Make sure you ask Maisie for a copy of the script." She wrinkled her nose, pulling back her chair. I noticed she had hardly touched her lunch and wondered if extreme calorie restriction was the secret to her weight loss. She stood up and patted her flat stomach. She was wearing tight white pants that were practically spray-painted on her and a yellow ribbed tank top. Not a ripple of flab or bulge anywhere. "Wait till you see the dialogue. I don't think anyone would talk like that," she confided in a whisper. "Especially not a forensic psychologist."

I nodded. "How will I find Maisie?"

"She's the continuity girl, so she always sits next to Hank during the shooting. But it would be better to catch her now, at lunchtime. Once she gets on the set, you won't be able to talk to her." Sandra shielded her eyes from the bright sunshine and then pointed to a model-thin girl at a neighboring table. "Look, there she is. She's the one with the red hair and that cute Boho top. She always has extra copies of the script and I know she'll be glad to give you one. You'll have to see some of that dialogue to believe it."

"It's that bad?" I said mildly.

Sandra rolled her eyes and gave a little shudder. "I can't even describe it to you; I know I couldn't do it justice." She reached over and gave my arm a friendly squeeze and the half-dozen thin gold bracelets she was wearing clanked together. "You've gotta help us with this, Maggie. I'm counting on you."

"I'll get a copy and read it tonight," I promised.

Chapter 5

I caught up with Maisie, the continuity girl, and introduced myself just as they started to clear the tables. She was pretty, with a sprinkling of freckles across her nose, and like most of the female cast and crew, she was wearing tight designer jeans. "A script? Sure, no problem." She pointed to a trailer that was being used as the production office. "Tell them I said it's okay. Anything else you need, just let me know." She snared a bottle of Crystal Geyser from the lunch table and grabbed a clipboard off the table. "I thought you were media, but somebody said you're also a psychologist, right?"

"Guilty as charged. I used to have a practice back in Manhattan before I moved down to Florida. Now I have a radio show on WYME." Word travels fast on a movie set, I decided. Maybe Lola had been bragging to Hank? I doubted Adriana would bother talking about me; her whole focus was always on herself.

"We're shooting a big scene in a few minutes," she said. "It's the finale scene when Adriana finally meets up with the killer. Would you like to watch? I can sneak in another folding chair next to mine. You have to promise not to make a sound, though."

"Thanks, I'd love to. And I'll be quiet as a mouse; shrinks are really good at that."

She pulled a headset over her glossy auburn hair, mumbled some words into it, and looked serious. "Are you saying Jesse is ready to go on the pond scene?" She glanced at her watch and her eyebrows shot up. "Right now?" A short pause and then, "Okay, I'll be there in three minutes. Set up an extra chair next to mine. We have company."

"Jesse is the AD, the assistant director," she explained, yanking off the headset and looping it around her neck. "I'm afraid we've got to hustle. Hank goes nuts if anyone is late when we start shooting."

"Why are you shooting a big finale scene now?" I asked breathlessly. She was making tracks past the picnic area and I was scrambling to keep up with her, my kitten heels sinking into the spongy soil. "I thought the movie was just starting?"

"Oh, we always shoot scenes out of sequence." She tossed a grin over her shoulder. "You get used to it after a while. It makes it tough on these New York method actors who have to spend hours gearing themselves up emotionally for a scene. You know, they have to 'find their motivation,' whatever that is. So pretentious! Those kind of people drive Hank crazy," she confided. "Hank thinks that all you need to do is know your lines and not trip over the furniture."

"That's what Laurence Olivier used to say," I told her.

"Yeah?" She looked doubtful and I wondered if she'd even heard of the great British actor. "Well, here we are." She scurried onto a roped-off area at the edge of a small beach. The sun was glinting off the still waters of Branscom Pond and Adriana was standing at the edge of the shoreline, looking impatient. She was fanning herself with a huge straw sun hat while a makeup girl flitted around her, touching up her lipstick.

Adriana was inspecting her work in a small hand mirror and shaking her head in dismay. "You know I hate this color lipstick," she whined. "What is it? Old-lady red?" She grabbed the tube and looked at the bottom. "Even my grandmother wouldn't wear this color. It's going to add ten years to my face. Why can't I have something bronze instead? We need to get Marlene back doing my makeup."

Her voice was shrill, the undertone deadly. I could tell this was an old argument and the makeup girl calmly took the tube away from Adriana and returned to her work.

Maisie slid into a canvas-backed chair next to Hank and patted an empty chair beside her. She immediately picked up her copy of the script and I noticed it was full of hand-written notations. "Have a seat, Maggie. This should be a good scene. Adriana confronts the killer and he takes a shot at her." She leaned over and smiled. "Don't worry; he's a lousy shot and he misses."

"You certainly made a lot of notes," I said, pointing to her script.

Maisie nodded. "Some of these are wardrobe details and hair and makeup descriptions. Everything has to look exactly the same from shot to shot. You know, continuous. The actors and the props have to be identical to where we left off shooting. So if Adriana was wearing a white scarf during the last frame of the last bit of footage, she has to be wearing the same scarf in this scene." She paused and held up her index finger. "And it has to be tied the same way. Plus her hair has to look exactly the same. You'd be surprised how easy it is to miss little things like that."

"I can see that." Mom had already told me all about continuity, but I could see that Maisie was proud of her job and seemed to enjoy talking about it.

We both watched while Hank conferred with the deeply tanned lighting director who'd argued with Adriana earlier, and then there were several sound checks. When Hank was finally satisfied, he waved to the AD. I heard a soft click as a camera slid up next to me, sidling into position.

"That's Jeff Walker," Maisie said, pointing to a fortyish actor standing a few yards down the beach. "He's plays the killer. We're going to open with a tight close-up on Adriana, and then Jeff is going to walk right into the frame for their dialogue."

"Stand by, quiet everyone," Jesse, the AD, yelled through a bullhorn. He glanced at the group of extras who were watching the filming from behind the rope. It was surprising how many people were on the set. Maybe fifty or sixty, I guessed, including all the techies and the wardrobe mistress, plus the hair and makeup artists. And I knew there were a couple of dozen administrative types, toiling away back in the production office.

Funny, but I didn't see Mom anywhere. I knew she wasn't in this scene, so I figured she must be checking out her wardrobe or catching up with old friends. There was a low buzz of conversation that suddenly wound down, and now the only sound was the humming of cicadas, signaling another hot day in south Florida.

"Looks like we're ready to go," Maisie said to me.

"Stand by to cue Jeff," Hank said.

"Uh-oh," she suddenly muttered under her breath. "Wait a minute. We've got a tiny problemo." She leaned over and whispered something to Hank Watson.

He nodded, his lips twitching with annoyance. "Adriana, we need to have you tuck your hair behind your left ear, not your right. That's the way it was where we left off after the restaurant scene." He glanced down at a notation in blue Magic Marker written in Maisie's script. "You were driving to the pond and your hair was tucked behind your left ear."

"Oh honestly," Adriana grumbled. She sighed dramatically and flipped her hair behind her left ear as directed. "Can't these people get anything right?" A young girl in jeans rushed up to Adriana and whipped a hairbrush out of her back pocket. She made a tiny adjustment to the actress's hair and then scampered out of the shot.

"Good work," Hank said in a low voice to Maisie. "Glad you caught that."

"And I'm sweating like a pig," Adriana continued in a loud voice. "What is it, a hundred and fifty degrees out here?"

Like magic, two techies dragged a long cable across the sand and a gigantic fan materialized, as powerful as a wind machine, sending a cooling breeze over Adriana. The techies glanced back at Hank Watson, ready to cut the fan the moment they began filming.

"Quiet on the set, everyone." The AD admonished an extra who had picked that moment to tear open a bag of potato chips. "No noise, no talking, no cell phones." Once again, a hush fell over the crowd; they seemed to be caught up in the excitement of the moment.

"Pond scene, take one!" I nearly jumped as a production assistant moved into the shot and snapped the clapboard just a few feet away from us.

I watched Jeff Walker and decided he was handsome in a square-jawed Hollywood sort of way. I'd seen him in some B movies, all forgettable, all straight-to-video. I knew he was getting himself psyched up for the scene. He'd closed his eyes, and he was shaking his hands at his sides and blowing out small puffs of air, as if he was trying to throw off some muscle tension. I'd seen Lola do exactly the same thing before her scenes.

"A-n-n-nd . . . action!" Hank Watson shouted.

"I didn't think you'd show up," Adriana said, moving slowly toward Jeff, who'd begun walking down the beach at the same moment. A cameraman was tracking her, gliding along beside her with his camera mounted on a little miniature railway track.

A myriad of emotions crossed her face—anger, uncertainty, and a touch of malevolence. "In fact, I was convinced that you'd had second thoughts and that—"

"Cut, cut!" Hank shouted, leaping out of his chair. "Adriana, you're moving *way* too slowly. Jeff hit the mark and you didn't. You're gonna have to speed it up, so you both hit the mark at the exact same time." His expression was tight and his tone brittle.

For the first time, I noticed someone had scratched a giant X on the sand. Apparently that was the mark Hank was talking about, and Adriana was at least six feet away from it.

"Why shouldn't Jeff be the one to speed it up?" Adriana retorted, her expression stony. She put her hands on her hips, her body language challenging. "Do you know how tough it is to walk with my damn high heels sinking into the sand at every step? I almost fell on my ass."

Maisie snickered next to me, and quickly covered it with a fake cough.

"Look, Adriana, if Jeff walks too fast, it ruins the scene," Hank said with heavy patience. "You just have to walk faster, just pick up the pace a little. Let's try it again, okay? From the top."

Hank sat back down and whispered to Maisie, "If she moved any slower, you could harvest her organs. I think she's doing it deliberately."

"This is par for the course," Maisie said quietly. "Typical Adriana behavior."

"I know. I must have been out of my mind to hire her," Hank muttered, running his hand through his silvering hair. He saw me watching him and managed a grin. "Oops; you didn't hear that, Maggie. Dealing with actresses is giving me gray hairs. You'd think after all these years, I'd be used to it." I knew he was putting a good spin on things because I was there; he didn't want me to go back to WYME and talk about trouble on the set.

"Don't worry; I didn't hear it." I smiled to reassure him.

During the next take, both Adriana and Jeff hit the mark at the same time.

"Thank God," Maisie whispered under her breath. I noticed she was following the dialogue, running her index finger under each line. I glanced down and saw some stage directions coming up at the bottom of the page: *Jeff pulls out a gun*. Maisie had hilighted that line in blue and underlined it several times.

Adriana was mouthing some lines about money, and I gathered that her character had been blackmailing Jeff. She jabbed him in the chest to emphasize a point and then her eyes widened with fear when he pulled out a gun he'd tucked into the waistband of his pants.

"No!" she screamed. "Jeff, don't do it!! We can work this out." She took a step backward, lifting her hands in front of her, palms up, her expression pleading.

It looked like Jeff was wielding a Beretta from where I sat, but of course, I knew it was only a harmless prop gun, designed to look lethal. He wouldn't be shooting real bullets. In fact, a prop gun wouldn't even take a real bullet. Instead, a harmless wad would be expelled from the gun followed by a sharp retort, just like the sound of a real gunshot.

Mom has acted in a lot of thrillers and she told me that if the prop gun didn't sound right, they would simply add a gunshot to the audio track after the filming was completed. The magic of Hollywood.

Jeff was mouthing some cliché dialogue like, "Can it, Adriana. I've had enough of your silly games and I'm never going to pay you another penny." He gave a maniacal laugh, pointed the gun at Adriana, and fired at point-blank range. The noise was surprisingly realistic and I flinched. I thought I smelled a faint scent of powder in the air, but maybe that was just my overactive imagination at work.

Adriana reacted perfectly; she clutched her chest, her eyes rolled back convincingly in her head, and she collapsed on the sand. *Interesting.* She was a much better actress than I'd thought. She'd managed to fall like a rag doll and her legs were splayed out at odd angles. Adriana is so vain I would have expected her to fall in a more graceful pose, but maybe I'd misjudged her. She played the scene convincingly, like a pro.

"A-n-n-nd . . . cut!" Hank yelled. "Nice work, guys." He turned to Maisie. "Let's get rolling on the party scene. Jesse needs to get about twenty extras in dressy clothes. Or maybe fifteen, if we shoot around them. I think the best way is to—"

"Hank," Maisie said urgently, clutching his arm. "What's going on down there?" She pointed to the water's edge where Adriana was lying still motionless. Jeff had started to walk away, but turned back, puzzled, when he realized Adriana wasn't making any move to get up.

"Hey, Adriana," Hank called. "Quit playing possum. Didn't you hear me yell 'cut'?" He started to laugh but the sound caught in his throat.

Jeff peered at Adriana and bent down to touch her neck. He yanked his hand back as if he'd been tasered. "Hank! Get an ambulance. There's something wrong. She's unconscious. I'm not even sure she's breathing."

Chapter 6

"What the devil—" Hank began, but Maisie leapt out of the chair before any of us could react and raced down to the water's edge. By the time Hank and I reached her, Maisie had grabbed Adriana's wrist and then placed two fingers on her throat. She kept her fingers there for a long time and then slowly looked up at us, her face pale in the harsh sunlight.

I noticed that a dark red patch was spreading from Adriana's chest to her collarbone—a concealed packet of fake blood, I decided. They call them squibs in the movie business. The actor presses her hand to her chest and the thin plastic packet explodes, leaking blood everywhere. The blood looked frighteningly real as it trickled down her neck and then spilled onto the grayish sand around the pond.

"Hank—" Maisie said, as he knelt down next to Adriana in the sand. I noticed her eyes were blurring with tears and her voice was trembling. "She's unconscious. I think . . . I think she's dead."

For a moment, no one moved.

All of us just stood there, frozen in place, like a freeze-frame from one of Hank's movies. Then everything seemed to happen at once. Maisie yanked out her cell phone and dialed 911, the AD came rushing over with a beach towel, which he insisted on putting under Adriana's head, and Hank Watson turned an unflattering shade of ash gray. He was still kneeling on the beach, and he covered his eyes with his hand for a moment.

"They're on their way," Maisie said, resting her hand on his shoulder. "We should probably put up a screen, or at least keep people from gawking."

Hank looked up then, just as the extras and techies were edging forward, caught up in the real-life drama playing out on the shoreline. "You're right, Maisie." He stood up, suddenly back in control. "Jesse," he yelled to the AD, "get some rope lines set up and keep everyone as far back as possible." He turned to a pair of production assistants. "Take my Jeep," he said, throwing them the keys. "Go to the north entrance to the pond, where we came in. Watch for the ambulance, so you can wave them over here."

I was surprised at how cool he was under pressure.

"The blood," I whispered to Maisie. "That's fake blood, it comes in one of those little packets, right?" I realized that I hadn't seen Adriana press her hand to her chest to break open the packet. Either she had done it surreptitiously, or the packet had exploded when she fell to the sand.

Maisie bit her lip and shook her head. "No," she said in a strangled voice. "We didn't bother using squibs in this scene because we were going to use a long shot. The audience would see Adriana's face in a tight close-up and then a long shot of two figures from a distance, and then it would . . . fade to black."

Fade to black. How ironic.

Adriana already looked very dead, even though only a few minutes had passed. Her skin had taken on a telltale bluish-gray tinge and her jaw looked slack.

"So it's real blood?" I was struggling to keep my voice on an even keel. I felt a lump the size of a walnut moving slowly up my throat and I swallowed hard. My nerves were jangled and my thoughts were scattering in a million directions. I'd run into a lot of unsettling things in my practice, but seeing death up close is always unnerving.

"I'm afraid so," she said quietly. "Adriana was shot. But how?"

She stared up at Jeff, who looked shell-shocked, still holding the gun, his right arm hanging limply at his side.

"I think you should put the gun down," I said quickly. Hank started to reach for it, and I stopped him. "Evidence," I reminded him. "The fewer people who touch it, the better."

"It can't be loaded," Jeff said slowly. "That's impossible. It's a prop gun." He stared at the shiny barrel, bewildered. "I've used these a dozen times." His voice was flat, robotic, like that of someone playing an android in a sci-fi flick. *Shock*, I decided.

He laid the gun carefully on the beach towel, just as an ambulance came tearing across the beach followed by two black-and-whites with lights flashing and sirens screaming. Half of Cypress Grove would know something had happened at Branscom Pond today. The other half would find out tonight on the six o'clock news. Cyrus would be over the moon; Adriana's death would be a ratings bonanza.

I wondered if Nick Harrison had already left the set and headed back to the Gazette offices. He must have, I decided, or he'd be here with his notebook, angling for an exclusive. And where was Mom?

"They didn't know the gun was loaded," Mom said in a cheesy, movie-trailer voice, "until the star ended up dead!"

It was half an hour later, and all of us were on edge. Cops were swarming over the set, just like this was an episode of *CSI*; crime scene tape had been put up; and Adriana's lifeless body had been whisked away by the medical examiner.

Mom waited a beat (perhaps expecting a smattering of

applause) and then looked around the makeup trailer where the Cypress Grove PD had gathered us for interrogations. They had immediately divided us up into groups, and I was sitting with Maisie, Mom, and Jesse, the AD. I glanced at my watch. I had to leave the set in exactly forty-five minutes, or I'd be late for my afternoon radio show.

I knew that Hank Watson and Jeff were stashed away somewhere in another trailer. And no one was allowed to leave the set. All the grips, the principals, the extras, and the crew members had to be interviewed. The police would record their names and addresses along with their whereabouts at the time of Adriana's death.

And of course the Big Question: who had a reason to kill her? This was the time for all the professional jealousies, petty feuds, and long-standing grudges to float to the surface, like the algae on the surface of Branscom Pond.

A monumental task, but I knew this was standard police procedure and I wondered which detective would be assigned to see us.

I caught myself wondering if it would be Detective Rafe Martino, and my heart did an annoying little flip-flop. Rafe and I have had an on-again, off-again relationship since I solved a murder case a couple of months ago. A New Age guru was poisoned after he appeared on my WYME talk show, and I had to step in to clear my roommate's name.

Rafe and I have an ongoing argument whether forensic psychology (which he calls psychobabble) trumps good solid detective work. Our relationship is like a rubber band, sometimes stretching far apart, sometimes springing back together, always quivering with tension. Maybe that's what keeps it so exciting.

"Lola, please," Maisie said imploringly. "Maybe it would be better if we don't talk at all." She looked pale and shaken as she sat twisting her hands nervously in her lap.

"Accident . . . or murder?" Lola continued in a sepulchral tone. "You decide." She paused. "I think I like that one better, actually. I can see that line scrolling across the screen before the opening credits, can't you? As the great John Gielgud used to say, 'less is more.'"

I sighed. Mom is incorrigible. She can never resist being the center of attention, even when she's in the middle of a murder investigation. Less than an hour had passed since Adriana's death and she was already caught up in the drama of it all.

"Maybe that nice young man will be assigned to us," she said with an overly bright smile. As usual, her uncanny mental radar was kicking in, and she seemed to be reading my mind. "Detective Martino. Maggie solved a crime for him once before. He's handsome enough to be a film star," she said to no one in particular. "With the right agent and the right property, he could go far. Look at Dennis Farina. One day he's a Chicago cop and the next day he's a movie star."

At that very moment, the nice young man appeared in person. All six feet of hunky detective, looking like a million bucks. He was wearing a crisp white shirt that showed off his Florida tan, and his dark hair was boyishly falling over one eye. He wears it a little long, at least compared with other cops I've known, but maybe detectives have more leeway.

He closed the trailer door behind him and scanned the room. A little smile played around the corners of his mouth when he saw me, softening his chiseled features and adding to his attractiveness.

"Dr. Walsh," he said formally. "Ms. Walsh," he added, spotting Lola.

"Detective," Lola chirped, flashing a saucy smile.

Rafe had just finished introducing himself and explaining that he and his colleague were going to ask a few questions when there was a timid knock on the metal door. Opie walked in. He banged his head on the low door frame and instantly turned beet red. I glanced at Rafe's exasperated face and stifled a laugh.

Opie is my nickname for Officer Duane Brown, a fresh-faced, gangly cop who looks about twelve years old in his blue serge uniform. He could have stepped straight off of Aunt Bea's front porch in Mayberry.

"Officer Brown will interview"—Rafe paused to look at his notes—"Maisie Curtis. Along with Jesse Hamilton." He turned to Opie. "Miss Curtis is the script supervisor. She saw the shooting. Mr. Hamilton is the assistant director. You can interview them both next door at the production office. Room B is available. Just get the background information. I'll be with you in a few minutes."

Rafe waited until they were gone before he pulled up a chair and sat down facing us. "Okay, Maggie, what's going on here?" He whipped out a notebook, pen poised, a cool look of appraisal on his face. For a moment, I was distracted by the golden flecks in his dark eyes and the sexy curve of his mouth.

"It was awful!" Mom interjected. "To think of such a young life being cut short like that. It's a tragedy, that's what it is. Poor Adriana. She had her whole career ahead of her." She paused theatrically. "Do you think I should offer to write her eulogy for *Access Hollywood*? Nancy O'Dell can't possibly know all the inside details I do about Adriana's life and career. I need to get Edgar on this right away. Edgar is my new agent." She shot another flirty smile at Rafe.

"Did you happen to see the shooting, Ms. Walsh?" Rafe cut in smoothly. If he let Mom trip down memory lane, talking about the glory days in Hollywood, we'd be here all day.

Mom hedged, crossing and uncrossing her legs, just like Sharon Stone in *Basic Instinct*. At age fifty-eight, she has remarkably good legs and knows it. "Well, not exactly. Not up close, I mean."

"How close were you to the shooting?" Rafe asked. "A few feet away? A few yards away?"

"Well, I'm not very good at judging distances," she began but I jumped in.

"Mom, for heaven's sake, you were back in Wardrobe; you said so yourself." I looked at Rafe. "She didn't see the shooting, but I did," I said quickly. "I saw the whole thing. I was sitting right next to Maisie and Hank Watson when it happened. It took place while they were filming, you know. So at least there's a record of it."

Rafe nodded. "We've already requisitioned all the dailies to be turned in to us." The dailies are the raw footage that's shot every day, before any editing is done. "Okay, let's start over." He leaned forward, resting his forearms on his knees, and locked eyes with me. "From the top."

There was a coiled readiness in his posture and a watchful, alert look in his dark eyes. You could practically feel the tension rippling off him. He reminded me of a panther, ready to spring. I never could decide if that was because he was a cop or it was just part of his personality style.

"You said you were watching the filming, Maggie. Were you expecting the actor who was the shooter—" He paused, riffling through his notes.

"Jeff Walker," Mom volunteered.

Rafe blinked at the interruption. "Jeff Walker. Were you expecting him to discharge a firearm?"

"Well, I suppose I was. It was written right in the stage directions. Jeff pulls out a gun. You can see it in Maisie's copy of the script." Rafe leaned back to make a note.

"Had you seen the gun prior to the actor drawing it and firing it?"

"No, never. I think he had it tucked into the waistband of his slacks."

He glanced at Mom. "Did you see the gun? Anywhere on the set before the shooting?"

She shook her head. "I never go near the props. They keep them locked up, you know; they don't want anyone tampering with them." She put her hand to her mouth, her blue eyes wide with shock. "Ohmigod, is that what happened? Someone tampered with the prop gun? But how could that be? They don't even shoot bullets."

"That's what we're investigating," Rafe said. "We're sending it to ballistics for analysis."

"Lola, I need to know something. What was your relationship with the deceased?"

"My relationship with her was complicated," she said primly. I nearly giggled. *Complicated? Think of a mongoose and a snake.* "We go back a long way," she admitted. "But I suppose that's true of everyone on the set. Hank tends to use the same actors over and over, so most of us had worked with Adriana in the past."

"Interesting." Rafe made a note. I tried to lean over to read it, but he was too fast for me, and quickly moved the notebook out of my line of vision.

"Maggie? How about you?"

"I just met her for the first time today. No, wait," I corrected myself. "That's not quite true. Adriana said she remembered meeting me in Hollywood. Years ago."

"But you had no real relationship with her? No reason to dislike her?"

I hesitated. Everyone disliked Adriana. "I didn't have any feelings toward her, one way or the other."

We answered all the standard questions for the next few minutes, and when Rafe realized we really didn't have anything valuable to contribute, he let us go. I bounded out of the trailer, eager to get back to WYME, and nearly collided with a dead ringer for Silvio Dante, the character Steven Van Zandt plays on *The Sopranos*. He was wearing a pinstripe suit, his hair was styled in a heavily lacquered pompadour, and he sported a pinkie ring. I almost hit him with the trailer door, but he brushed aside my apology.

"Don't worry about it, doll." He eyed me up and down in what I always think of as the "Manhattan once-over." I must have passed the test, because he suddenly bared his teeth in a smile. "You have a nice day."

I nodded and hurried to my car, wondering how a Mafia extra would fit into the *Death Watch* script. I'd have to ask Maisie another time. Right now, time was of the essence. I had a show to do!

Chapter 7

There was just time enough for a cup of coffee and some breath mints before hitting the studio.

"Holy buckets!" Vera Mae said. "You're cutting it close, girl. Heard about the murder on the set. Were you there when it happened?"

I nodded. "Front and center. I'll tell you all about it after the show." I threw my purse on the console and grabbed the press kit Vera Mae had left out for me.

I knew my guest had already checked in, because I'd spotted Dr. Lois Knudsen, a serious-looking woman in a boxy navy blazer and white skirt, sitting in the reception area. She looked exactly like her publicity photo, except that on the cover of her new book, she was talking to a bemused-looking ferret.

Dr. Knudsen is a "pet psychologist" who has managed to snare some media attention with her new book, *How to Talk to Anything with Four Legs*. I have no idea if she's actually a licensed psychologist, or if her "doctorate" was awarded by a diploma mill. In any case, her book is getting a lot of buzz, and Vera Mae, a big-time animal lover, seemed excited that she was going to be on the show.

Vera Mae is the guardian of Tweetie Bird, a listless blue

parakeet, who accompanies her to the studio every day. Cyrus tried to block Tweetie Bird from WYME on health grounds, but relented when Vera Mae threatened to quit on the spot. She's strictly a love-me-love-my-bird person, and besides, she knew Cyrus would never find another radio producer willing to work for the low salary he pays her.

I make it a point never to chat with my guests before the show. Instead, Irina takes them to the Green Room, where they can relax and have bottled water and snacks before hitting the studio. I find it makes for a better show that way. Somehow, the dialogue seems more spontaneous if I meet the guest at the same time the listeners do.

"Live in ten!" Vera Mae yelled, as I took my seat at the console. Irina whisked Dr. Knudsen into the studio, handed her a pair of headphones, and darted out the door.

"I'm Maggie Walsh, Dr. Knudsen. Glad to have you on the show." I stuck out my hand before slapping on my own headphones and was rewarded with a limp handshake. It felt like I was grasping a damp tilapia. Dr. Knudsen nodded vaguely at me, then slipped her headphones over her tightly coiled gray hair, and stared blankly at the console. Maybe I imagined it, but I think she heaved a bored sigh.

Uh-oh. My Deadly-Dull Guest radar was in overdrive. Maybe Lois Knudsen was tired from a long book tour? Or maybe she was just a lousy conversationalist? I can usually tell in the first thirty seconds whether a guest is going to be interesting and dynamic on the air, or a complete dud.

I was getting very bad vibes from She Who Speaks to Our Four-Legged Friends.

Was it possible that the good doctor was only comfortable talking to four-legged critters and not to humans? Hardly an encouraging thought. I wished I'd taken more time to read her book last night; I'd only skimmed the first couple of chapters.

This might be a long two hours.

I gave a slightly gushing introduction. (Freud would probably say I was overcompensating for my really not liking the guest. Reaction formation, he called it. It means you go overboard being nice to someone you secretly loathe.)

And then Vera Mae opened the lines for questions, and to my surprise, all the buttons were flashing. Her Marge Simpson hairdo tipped precariously as she bent toward the mike. "Dr. Maggie, we have Doris, on line three. Doris is from Hollywood Beach, and she has a question about her parrot, Hercules."

"A parrot?" I said slowly. "I'm not certain that birds fall within Dr. Knudsen's area of expertise . . ."

"Of course they do," my guest snapped. "I'll be glad to take the question," she said testily. "Go ahead, Doris." I noticed she used the caller's name, so maybe she was more media savvy than I'd originally thought.

"Well, Dr. Knudsen, let me start my saying I just loved your book," Doris began. "I have four cats, two dogs, and an African Grey Parrot. It's the parrot I'm calling about."

"Ah, yes, the Congo African Grey. Is he one of the Timneh subspecies?"

"Um, I'm not real sure. He's seven years old and I inherited him from my uncle. He's blue and gold and he's been talking a mile a minute since the day I got him."

Dr. Knudsen whipped out a pad of paper and began taking notes.

"So Hercules is a talker," she said thoughtfully. "Are you his primary caregiver?"

"Why, yes, I am. Herb, my husband, gives him some dried corn from time to time, but when it comes to cleaning out the birdcage, it seems to be my job. Herb thinks everything is my job. You should see the cat boxes." She gave a sardonic laugh.

"And does Hercules talk to all the members in your family, or just to you?" Apparently Dr. Knudsen knew her limits and wisely decided not to play marriage counselor.

"Well, mainly to me, come to think of it. But I figured that's because I'm home with him all day long. I had a part-time job down at the Winn-Dixie but then I got laid off."

I glanced up at Vera in the control room, who was rolling her eyes, her finger on the CALL button. She made a speed-it-up gesture; she was probably as bored as our listeners. She added a quack-quack motion with her right hand, meaning we were going to a commercial shortly.

"And your question is, Doris?" I cut in.

"Oh, well here's the thing: this bird is driving me crazy. Absolutely nuts."

"Really?" Lois stopped writing and pressed her thin lips together disapprovingly. "He sounds perfectly adorable; what's wrong with him?"

"He's boring!" Doris exclaimed. "That's what's wrong with him. That dang bird talks all day about nothing. He's just like my sister-in-law. He talks nonstop and he's as dumb as a brick. Sometimes I throw a towel over his cage to shut him up and then he starts humming. Show tunes, but mostly ABBA. I wish I had a dollar for every time I had to listen to 'Dancing Queen.' He knows that song drives me crazy. Crazier than his stupid talking."

A faint flush had crept up Lois Knudsen's cheeks. "Doris, what you call his 'stupid talking' is his vocalization. This is the only way he has of communicating with you. He obviously can't text message you." She chuckled at her own wit. *Move over, Kathy Griffin!* "Hercules sounds like an extremely intelligent, sociable bird and I really don't understand your point. Are you annoyed because he's talking too much—"

"No, that's not it. I told you; he's boring. I don't know how to say it any clearer. He's duller than dirt."

Lois Knudsen stiffened in her chair and squared her shoulders. "All right, Doris, I'm going to give you a straight answer, but you may not like it."

"Right on!" Vera Mae mouthed from the control room.

My guest licked her lips and took a deep breath. "Here is my professional opinion. Hercules is probably not getting enough intellectual stimulation from your company."

"What?" Doris squealed. "Are you saying I'm boring, too? Or dumb?"

I saw Vera Mae's finger hovering over to the boot button. We have a seven-second delay and if necessary she can cut off a caller in mid-sentence.

"No, I'm not saying that at all," Dr. Knudsen answered, her voice hard as granite. "What I am saying is that Hercules has nothing to say because he doesn't get enough sensory input. For example, do you read to him?"

"Read to him? Are you nuts, lady?"

Vera Mae made a throat-slitting motion, but I shook my head. I was enjoying this too much to have her hit the MUTE button.

"I would suggest you start reading to him every day. You can start with the newspaper, if you like, and then move slowly into fiction and even poetry. My own mynah bird, Themopolous, is fond of Emily Dickinson. Something about the iambic pentameter really appeals to him. He bobs his head and weaves when I start reading poetry to him."

"Are you for real?" Doris shrieked.

"I'm afraid we have to go to a commercial—" I began, but my guest cut me off.

"And one more thing. CNN."

"What? CNN?"

"Yes, CNN. Leave the television tuned to CNN. Hercules will appreciate some adult conversation and won't have to resort to small town gossip if he's exposed to world events and politics."

"Small town gossip?" Doris was practically squawking in indignation. "Listen, you crazy b—"

This time Vera Mae slammed the MUTE button and I broke in, "We'll be right back after this message from Wanda's House of Beauty." Vera Mae shoved a cassette into the machine and motioned for me to read a promo sitting at the console. "Remember, ladies," I began, "beauty is only skin deep but men have little tiny pea brains and that's what they go for. Beauty and big boobies—"

Ohmigod! I sat still, my own brain scrambling in a million directions. *Had I really said that?* Vera Mae immediately switched to another commercial and the rockabilly theme of Lemuel's Body Shop filled the studio.

Vera Mae came tearing in from the control room and grabbed the ad copy. "Cheese n'crackers! That Irina, she's done it again." Vera Mae glanced at the ad copy, crunched it into a ball, and tossed it into the wastebasket.

"What just happened?" Dr. Knudsen looked appalled. "Was that supposed to be a joke? About men and their little pea brains? And you actually said 'boobies' on the air. Are you allowed to do that?" She sniffed disapprovingly.

"It's not a joke," I said, licking my lips nervously. *Damn.* Note to self: *always read the promos before doing them live on the air.* "Irina writes our ad copy for us. She's director of promotions."

"Irina? You mean that ditzy blonde at the front desk? She can barely speak English. I thought she was the receptionist."

"She's a multitasker," Vera Mae told her. "She manages the front desk, writes the ad copy, and keeps the traffic logs. It's Cyrus's way of saving money. I'll have a chat with him, Maggie. He's just gonna have to bite the bullet and hire a copywriter, and that's all there is to it. We can't have you saying stuff like this on the air. It's not professional."

"I'll say," Dr. Knudsen tsk-ed. "You'll probably be getting calls from the Men's Anti-Defamation League. They might even try to take you off the air."

Her lips curled in a self-satisfied smirk. The Bird Woman of Alcatraz wasn't a very nice person, after all. As Vera Mae says, "Always go with your first impressions. It saves a lot of time."

"Ohmigod I hadn't thought of that. Vera Mae, do you think we could be fined by the FCC?" I wondered if I should retract my boobie comment or come up with some sort of apology. Or would that just draw attention to it and make things worse? I could feel my jaw clenching in frustration, just thinking about it.

"After all the stuff Howard Stern got away with on the air? I doubt it." Vera Mae patted me on the shoulder, with one eye on the clock. In another ten seconds, we'd be live again. "Don't worry about it, sugar," she said, her voice soft as silk. She shot a dark look at Dr. Knudsen. "Probably no one was tuning in today anyway."

Big Jim Wilcox was waiting for me outside the studio and stepped in front of me as I ducked my head and barreled down the hall to my office.

"Heard about the murder at Branscom Pond today, Maggie." His squinty eyes were glittering with excitement and he was breathing hard, the way he does when he's announcing a Hail Mary pass for the Cypress Grove Spoilers.

"Yes, it was quite a shock. My mother knew Adriana from years ago." I tried to move past him down the narrow corridor but it was impossible. His considerable bulk practically touched both walls. I noticed his jacket had fallen open, revealing an enormous gut threatening to explode from under his belt, like a muffin top. Big Jim played football in college, but now he's gone to flab. "Marathon Man" has turned into "Michelin Man."

He moved closer, and I nearly choked on a cloud of Drakkar Noir. "So, tell me, Maggie, why did you do it?" He lowered his voice to a reedy whisper and I practically had to read his lips to make out what he was saying.

"Why did I do what?" He raised one hand and splayed his stubby fingers flat against the wall. Short of ducking under his armpit, I couldn't see any way to get around him. It was like being hemmed in by a Subaru Forester SUV.

"The murder." He paused, looking at me. "Was it something you planned for a long time, or was it a crime of passion? Did you know you were going to kill Adriana when you went to the set today, or did you just snap? I've heard that happens a lot with shrinks. They just go looney tunes." He whirled his index finger in circles next to his left ear, the classic shorthand for craziness.

"What?" I shrieked. "Are you insane? Of course I didn't kill her."

Big Jim nodded slowly, a knowing look on his fleshy face. "We'll talk again, Maggie. You won't be able to keep the secret forever. And when you're finally ready to confess, I'm your guy. I'd want an exclusive, of course. 'Docs Who Kill: A Big Jim Wilcox Investigative Report.' Tonight at ten." He stabbed his beefy chest with his thumb for emphasis. "I might get an Emmy for this."

"You're out of your mind."

"Trust me, Maggie, your crime will eat away at you," he said, edging even closer. "You won't be able to eat or sleep; you'll think about the murder night and day. Eventually you'll have to tell someone or you'll die or go crazy."

I finally put my hands flat against his chest and pushed hard. "You're the one who's crazy, Big Jim."

He wagged his finger at me in mock reproach. "You'll be

just like that guy in the story—remember, the guilt ate away at him so much, he finally had to confess."

The guy in the story? "You mean Raskolnikov?" I couldn't imagine Big Jim slogging through Dostoyevsky's *Crime and Punishment*, but that's the only name that came to mind.

"Who? Rasko-what? Sounds like some Russian commie pinko." Big Jim shook his head. "Nah, that wasn't it. This was a guy I saw on a *Monk* rerun last night. Did you happen to catch it?"

"A *Monk* rerun? Afraid I missed that one." I pushed past him, my brain blanking on a snappy retort. Why was I letting this guy get to me? As Vera Mae says, you can't win an argument with an ignoranus. An ignoranus, in case you're wondering, is a person who's both stupid and an asshole. I rest my case.

I sprinted down the hall and made a quick stop in the production office to drop off some time sheets. Irina was sashaying out on four-inch heels, her yellow silk Ann Taylor blouse and black pencil skirt molded to her Barbie-like figure.

It seems that Cyrus had asked Irina to put together a series of teasers about Adriana's death. He planned to run them throughout the day, sticking them between PSAs (public service announcements) and spots (paid commercials). All in the spirit of boosting the ratings.

Interesting. The first WYME report on Adriana's death was going to be a brief announcement on the six o'clock news, coming up in less than an hour. I figured it was going to be a pretty thin piece because the Cypress Grove PD had refused to issue a statement and I was sure no one on the *Death Watch* set was willing to talk.

No wonder the station was trying to hype the news with half-hour bulletins. I riffled through a pile of promos that Cyrus was rushing into production. I noticed the WYME news team was calling it a "death," not a murder. Irina had done her best, but all the teasers sounded like they were straight out of a Lifetime Movie.

"Live at Five, Dead at Six—the Adriana St. James Story!"

"A Role to Die For—the Adriana St. James Story!"

Vera Mae came in just as I was reading my personal favorite. "Death on the High Seas—the Adriana St. James Story?" I raised an eyebrow. "The high seas? This is a joke, right?"

Vera Mae rolled her eyes and snatched the paper out of my hand. "Oh lordy, I'm glad you caught that one, hon. I told Irina it was just a little ole pond. She thought 'high seas' sounded more dramatic, bless her heart." My lips twitched.

Whenever Vera Mae says "bless her heart," about Irina, it's code for "I want to wring her gosh darn neck."

Chapter 8

I made tracks to my cubicle, my heart sinking at the mountain of press packets on my desk. It always amazes me that half of south Florida wants to be on my show. I can only guess they haven't seen the ratings.

I hadn't had a second to check in with Rafe, but Nick Harrison called at five to tell me that the Cypress Grove PD was privately calling it "foul play." They had no plans to go public with it. Still no word on how Adriana died, and whether a live bullet was involved. I wondered how much they knew and how much they were holding back.

"I don't see how it could have been an accident," I said, chewing on the end of my pencil. "Someone must have tampered with the prop gun. The real problem will be winnowing down the list of suspects."

"I figured the same thing." I could hear a steady tapping in the background. Nick never has a spare moment and it's not unusual for him to multitask; he works on stories and checks e-mail while he's on the phone. Like most reporters, he's constantly "on deadline," a crazy-making aspect of his job. "I can't believe I missed the shooting. I did the interview with Sandra Michaels and then headed right back to my desk."

"How did the interview turn out?" I know he was annoyed that he'd missed the biggest scoop of his career.

"A puff piece. She spent most of the time hawking her book deal, her movie deal, her television deal. I felt like I was talking to Suzanne Somers about the ThighMaster. I only have a few paragraphs I can use; I'll pad the rest with some material from the press packet." He paused. "Any leads on the shooting?"

"Not on this end. How about you?"

"Nothing credible enough to print." He lowered his voice. "There's a rumor that Hank Watson wanted to get rid of Adriana but I don't know too many details. Keep your ears open, okay?"

"I will, but don't leave me hanging. What was the problem between Hank and Adriana?"

"I heard he has a girlfriend waiting in the wings. A very *young* girlfriend."

"And she's an actress and looking for her big break into show business, right?"

"You got it. She figured the lead in *Death Watch* would look great on her resume. She'd be all wrong for the part, but I heard she was pressuring Hank to put her in the lead. And Adriana had a pay-or-play contract, so he couldn't dump her. Not with an indie budget."

"Wow, that changes things."

Nick gave a soft chuckle. "Yeah, it sure does. In the immortal words of Madonna, 'money changes everything.'"

"Anything else?"

"Maybe something funny about the backers, but nothing definite."

"Funny as in . . ."

"Fugeddaboutit." Nick's Brooklyn accent made me smile, and then I remembered the Steven Van Zandt look-alike.

Could there be a mob connection with Hank Watson and the production? Were they financing the production?

I flipped my phone shut and sat at my desk for a few minutes, mulling over the dilemma of the pay-or-play contract. It meant that Hank was stuck; he'd have to pay Adriana her full salary whether or not she acted in the movie. The backers would never agree to a replacement if it was going to cost them cold hard cash. Hank had seemed genuinely upset at her death, but I remembered Mom saying he'd started out as an actor, all those years ago in Hollywood. So maybe the grieving-director act was just a sham?

I glanced at my watch and made tracks to the parking lot. It was my turn to make dinner, which meant I'd get some quick take-out at Charlie Chan's and head back to the condo where Mom and Lark would be waiting. Along with Pugsley, of course.

Pugsley's a big fan of Chinese food, and I allow him one steamed dumpling as a special treat. I always order from the "Heart-Healthy" (no fat, no MSG) side of the menu for Pugsley and from the "Happy Family Feasts" section for myself. That probably explains why Pugsley's cholesterol level is better than mine.

It was a beautiful evening; the air was soft and balmy, the sky streaked with rust and gold paint-box colors. I was just about to get into my little red Honda Accord when I heard someone behind me. I whirled around in full attack mode, weight on the back foot, semicrouched position, left arm blocking my face, right fist ready to land a serious upper cut on my attacker.

Uh-oh. Suddenly, I relaxed, my heart melting. It wasn't an attacker, after all.

It was Rafe Martino.

I felt a little white-hot dash of excitement go through me.

"Easy there," he said, smiling at me. He was standing just

inches away, his dark hair falling boyishly over one eye, his teeth very white against his Florida tan. And that smile! The sexy grin was my undoing. Vera Mae was right. The man was catnip to women, no doubt about it. He could give Simon Baker a run for his money.

"Sorry, I just—" I felt myself flushing. "You know, all those years living in New York." I gave a sheepish smile. "I think they took a toll on me." A toll? Who was I kidding? I was so hypervigilant, I practically qualified for a diagnosis of full-blown PTSD.

"And I see you've had a few Krav Maga classes along the way?" Krav Maga is a self-defense technique used by the Israeli fighting forces. Rafe was letting his eyes skim over my body and I felt a little thrill inside, even though I told myself his interest was strictly professional.

"A few," I admitted. "I'm surprised you picked up on that."

"I'm a cop, remember? I notice everything. Let me give you some advice, Maggie."

"Uh, okay." I had to stop myself from screaming, *Anything!! I'll do anything you say.*

"You need to relax," he said, his voice low and husky. "You're not in Manhattan anymore. Cypress Grove is one of the safest cities in the country."

"I *am* relaxed," I said, jutting my chin. I made a conscious effort to lower my shoulders, which seemed to be hovering somewhere in the vicinity of my ears. I forced myself to take a deep calming breath, but my pulse was still racing along at a good clip.

"Really? Then what's this all about?" Rafe leaned over and gently rubbed my hand. His touch was warm and powerful; my whole body was pricking with anticipation. "Are you planning to gouge someone's eyes out?"

"What?" I said, not wanting the delicious physical contact with his fingertips to end so abruptly. I wanted more, more.

"Look at your hand," Rafe said softly. "Does that look re-laxed to you?"

I looked down, and as if by magic, the spell was broken. I hadn't even realized that I was holding my car keys and house keys between my fingers, jagged edge out, clasping them like a lethal weapon.

The good news was that all that self-defense training had really taken root! I had immediately gone into combat mode.

The bad news was that I felt like a total idiot.

"Sorry; it's silly, I know."

"It's not silly," he said softly. "It's good to be cautious; just don't overdo it." He paused. "I wondered if anything else occurred to you about today."

"Occurred to me?" *Besides the fact I want to jump your bones*? I nearly added. I don't think that's what he had in mind, because he whipped out his notebook.

He nodded, pen poised. "You were on the set for a couple of hours. I heard you had lunch with the cast and crew. Who did you talk to?"

"Sandra Michaels, mostly. She's playing a forensic psychologist in the movie. Or at least she was. She asked me a lot of questions about the forensic work I did in my practice back in Manhattan. And then, as you know, I sat with Maisie and Hank and watched the shooting." *Oh God, I literally watched the shooting; no pun intended.*

My mind flew back to the movie set. I suddenly realized I had no idea what was going to happen to *Death Watch*, Mom's role, and my job as a consultant. It sounds callous, but if there was a significant amount of money tied up in the production, the show would have to go on. With or without Adriana. Maybe it was early enough in the filming that she could be replaced.

If anyone knew, Rafe would. "Do you know what's going to happen to the film? Did Hank Watson say anything to you?"

Rafe looked up, squinting against the light from the setting sun. A golden haze had settled over the WYME building, and I remembered this was the time of day that photographers loved. "He's closed down production for two days, that's all. As far as I know, everything's going to start back up midweek. The CSIs will be out by then, and we can clear the area around the pond."

I shuddered, thinking of Adriana lying on the beach, her blood seeping into the sand. Who would ever want to go back there to shoot more scenes? Just the thought gave me goose bumps. And who would play the lead? Hank's teenybopper girlfriend? Or someone else? It wasn't like the theater, where an understudy is ready to jump into a part at a moment's notice. I wondered if there would be casting calls and auditions, or if Hank had already worked all this out.

"What's your take on Marion Summers?" he asked, interrupting my train of thought.

"Marion Summers?" I shook my head. "I didn't meet her." I struggled to remember what Nick had said about her and what I remembered from a *Vanity Fair* piece on Hank. "I've heard a lot about her, though. She's supposed to be the driving force behind Hank's company. He's in creative control, but she keeps the money flowing and the movies made. The power behind the throne."

I suddenly thought of Jean Doumanian. She was Woody Allen's producer for decades, until they had a falling out over money and the case went to court. Could the same thing have happened with Marion and Hank?

"Anything else?" Rafe was busily scribbling notes.

"This is probably a stab in the dark, but was there trouble brewing between Marion Summers and Hank Watson? Any sort of a falling out?"

"Not that I know about. We're going to have to dig hard on this one." He paused to flip through his notes. "We're just at square one—no idea about means, motive, and opportunity. It's going to take a lot of manpower doing interviews. There were over a hundred people on the set today."

"And one of them was the killer." I fell silent, a little chill passing through me. "No strong leads?"

"I'm not at liberty to say." Rafe was in Joe Friday mode, playing his cards close to his vest, as usual. It's annoying, but he's so heartbreakingly handsome I decided to forgive him for shutting me out.

"You know you can always call on me for deep psychological insights, right?" I said, half teasing. "I did my doctoral dissertation on forensic interviewing. It's all about asking open-ended questions to elicit the most information from respondents."

"Really? That sounds fascinating. I'll bet it was a real page-turner," Rafe said dryly. "I'll be sure to keep your offer in mind." Rafe has a low opinion of forensic psychology, which he usually refers to as psychobabble. It's a standing joke between us, except occasionally Rafe's digs get to me.

"You will? Do you mean that?" I knew Rafe was probably mocking me but I couldn't keep the eagerness out of my voice. I was as shameless as Pugsley salivating over a liver treat; I wanted to work side by side with Rafe, damn it!

Rafe's lips twitched as he dashed my hopes once and for all. "I think all we need is good solid detective skills, Maggie. That's what will solve the case in the end. Police work. Not psychoanalyzing."

At least he hadn't said "psychobabble"! "Sure, I understand."

"But thanks for the offer." He snapped the notebook closed and put on his Ray-Ban aviator sunglasses, channeling Horatio Caine. "If you think of anything else, you know where to find me." He turned and walked toward his unmarked car, a mud-colored Crown Vic that looked like it dated to the Pleistocene era.

He'd only gone a few feet when I suddenly remembered the *Sopranos* guy lounging outside the makeup trailer. "Wait! There was something else I meant to tell you." Rafe turned and ambled back to me, his dark eyes questioning. "I saw someone who looked a little out of place today."

"Out of place?" He frowned, scratching his chin. He had just the beginnings of a five o'clock stubble, but on him, it looked sexy, not scruffy. Think John Abraham on the cover of *GQ*. Or Hugh Jackman, *People* magazine's sexiest man alive. "You mean someone who looked suspicious?"

"Not suspicious exactly, but he just didn't look like he belonged on the set. He didn't look like anyone from the cast or crew and I'm sure he wasn't a reporter. It's probably nothing." I flapped my arms in a dismissive gesture, wondering if I was making too much out of the whole thing.

"Tell me." Out came the notebook.

So I told him all about the Steven Van Zandt look-alike and was surprised when he nodded in recognition. "A guy who looks like he's straight out of *The Godfather*? That was Frankie Domino. He tried to slip through the police lines and hightail it out of there, but we nailed him." Rafe gave a mirthless laugh.

"That's his name? Frankie Domino?" I raised my eyebrows. He really did sound like a Hollywood version of a mafioso.

"His real name's Francis Domenici."

"And is he . . . what I think he is?"

Rafe grinned. "A mafioso? He's got a string of arrests in New York, mostly small-time stuff—running numbers, assault and battery, a few shakedowns doing collections. I haven't figured out what he was doing on the set, and Hank Watson's not talking. I think something's up between them, but I'm not sure what. Just a gut instinct."

He jammed his notebook back in his pocket and then surprised me by touching my upper arm very lightly. Just one finger tracing a white-hot path over my skin. I stayed motionless, wondering what was going to happen next. Was it a caress, a warning, a friendly good-bye?

"Watch yourself, Maggie, okay?" He locked eyes with me, looking very intent and serious. "I know you're going to be spending a lot of time on the set. And—"

"And let's be careful out there?" The words came out in a whoosh; I didn't even realize I'd been holding my breath. It was a line that Sergeant Phil Esterhaus of *Hill Street Blues* used to say when he finished roll call and I knew Rafe would get the reference.

Rafe laughed, flashing his killer smile. "You got it." He dropped his hand to his side and reached for his car keys.

Okay, I got the message. Mood broken, back to reality time. No heavy relationship; we're just pals.

I guess.

We left it on that note, Rafe heading back to the station to do some paperwork, while I zoomed toward Charlie Chan's. A veggie stir-fry was waiting for me, a soft breeze was ruffling the palm trees, and the sweet scent of bougainvillea lingered in the air.

Life was good, and I tried very hard not to think about the little buzz I'd gotten from Rafe's touch.

Chapter 9

"So it all worked out for the best," Mom said over dinner. Lark quirked an eyebrow and Mom quickly amended, "Well, except for poor Adriana, I mean." She clasped her hand to her bosom, bowed her head, and was silent for a beat, eyes shut. I nearly expected her to deliver a eulogy. After a moment, her grieving heart magically healed; she looked up and reached for a hefty portion of veggie lo mein. Never underestimate the restorative powers of carbs.

"Worked out for the best in what sense?" I asked.

"Well, Hank has a new leading lady, the cameras will start rolling again, and things will be more"—she paused delicately—"harmonious on the set. And who knows, Adriana will be more popular with the public than ever. She might even be up for an Emmy!"

"Really? I don't think she's in the same league as Meryl Streep or Helen Mirren." *And I'm not sure she'll be thrilled to get an award from beyond the grave.*

"She might get the sympathy vote," Lola confided. "That's the way these things work. Everyone knows you always score extra points if you're dead." She paused, twirling lo mein on the end of her fork and her face brightened. "I just had a fabulous idea. Do you think I should accept the award for her? I have the perfect dress to wear. It's a cross between Bob Mackie and Michael Kors. Cobalt blue and very classic. It's a little low cut but I think I can pull it off."

Bob Mackie? I bet it had feathers, sequins, or both. *And low cut?* I tried not to picture Mom in a Jennifer Lopez gown that plunged to her belly button, because I knew the visual would stay with me for days.

"I think you're getting a little ahead of yourself," I said firmly.

Pugsley was doing his starving dog imitation and I gave him a tiny nibble of my egg roll. He had already polished off his heart-healthy dumpling, but he begged for more, his little feet tap-dancing on the polished floor.

"I suppose you're right. We all have to concentrate on *Death Watch* and make sure it's the best film it can be." She heaved a sigh as if she wasn't really sure how good *Death Watch* would be, even with everyone rooting for it.

"How's it going?" Lark asked.

"Pretty well, I guess. I was chatting with the producer right before I left the set today. She's trying to be optimistic, but of course she has to be. That's practically part of her job description, you know." She gave a low chuckle. "Keep everyone's spirits up and keep the money flowing in. A lot's riding on how well it does at the box office. I think Hank's had trouble getting backers lately, and if this show is a bomb—phfft! It could all be over for Marion."

My ears perked up. "Marion Summers?" I remembered what I'd read in *Vanity Fair* about Hank's production chief.

"She's all business," Lola said, wrinkling her nose. "I don't really think she's into the artistic side of film. But you have to hand it to her; Hank has done very well with her at the helm. She handles all the boring production details for him and I think she's very good at it."

"Do they get along?" Lark asked. "Sometimes it's hard to

work with someone night and day, especially if they have very different auras." Lark is into all things New Age: chakras, karma, auras, and I-Ching. She believes that we're destined to meet every single person we encounter in life, either to learn something from them or to teach them something.

I wondered how Big Jim Wilcox would fit into her view of the cosmos.

"A good point, my dear. There's been some talk on the set about a few bitter rows in the past, but I think they're going to put their differences behind them now. After all, we have to pull together for the good of the movie. And God knows, Tammilynne is going to need all the help she can get. The poor thing doesn't even know her lines."

"Tammilynne?" I stared at her.

"Tammilynne Cole," Lola said smoothly. "The new star of the show." She gave me a knowing look. "She's never acted a day in her life, but she has a special relationship with Hank Watson, if you know what I mean."

I knew exactly what she meant. It was special all right. The kind of relationship a fifty-something man has with a girl barely out of her teens.

"So they're not going to bother auditioning anyone else? Tammilynne is stepping into Adriana's part, and everything else is just the same?"

"Yes, dear, it's just the same. They may change a few lines here and there, since Tammilynne is so much younger than Adriana, but it won't be any big deal. They have the writers on the set right now, churning out new pages for tomorrow. Hank's going to hand out the new sides so people can start memorizing them." I remembered the two young guys in jeans, wearing baseball caps backward as they played air guitar.

"And Hank still wants me there, as a consultant?

"Yes, I know he does," Lola said warmly. "He said he's very happy you're on board. Having a psychologist as a consultant will bring a lot of credibility to the movie, you know. They're really going to play that up with the media. And he wants you back at work first thing tomorrow."

"I thought the production was closed down for forty-eight hours."

"The actual filming is, but there's still plenty of behind-the-scenes work to be done. Hank's expecting you there at nine sharp, actually both of us. I have a wardrobe fitting so I thought we could ride over there together, if that's okay."

"So the show must go on," Lark said, reaching down to pull Pugsley onto her lap.

"Oh heavens, yes." Mom nodded her head. "The show *always* goes on."

Marion Summer's pale eyes flicked over me, like a lizard's. She was tall and thin, a bony woman in tailored beige pants and a long-sleeved white blouse, rolled up to the elbows. No frills or color anywhere on her. She was mid-fifties with wispy blond hair pulled back in a silver clip, and she sported smart-girl glasses with black frames on a chain around her neck. Her burnished leather loafers were expensive, Dolce and Gabbana, her only nod to fashion.

"Hank's been called into town," she said abruptly, "but I can get you started right away. He'd like you to meet with Sandra and then spend some time with the writers. Follow me, please." I could see she wasn't going to waste any time on social niceties.

Mom had been whisked away to Wardrobe and I'd knocked on the door of the production trailer, hoping to find Hank. Most of the area around Branscom Pond was still considered a crime scene, but they'd set up a few extra trailers at the entrance to the park, marked with hand-lettered signs, Production, Wardrobe, Cast and Crew. I glanced over to the lake where CSIs were milling around on the beach and idly wondered if Rafe was there with them.

Sandra was waiting by some long picnic tables set up under a canopy. I hadn't seen her since Adriana's death and I wondered how she had taken the news. Very well, considering the bright smile on her face.

"Let's sit out here, okay?" she said. She wrinkled her nose. "The air-conditioning inside the trailer isn't very good." She was wearing a sunny yellow tunic top over tight white jeans, which showed off her terrific figure. No doubt about it, her personal diet and exercise plan was certainly working. "I grabbed some iced tea and cookies for us; thank God they still have the craft services tables set up. I think we're going to be stuck here all day, even though there's not that much to do. The van picked us up at the B and B this morning at eight a.m. and the driver's not coming back until five."

"Thanks." I nibbled on a sugar cookie. "You're staying at a B and B?"

"Yes, it's a cute little place, the Seabreeze—do you know it?"

"I live right next door. And the manager, Ted Rollins, is a good friend of mine." I didn't bother telling her that Ted would like to be more than friends. He's the proverbial "nice guy," but for some reason, I'm always drawn to "bad boys," the kind the nuns warned me about. You know, the ones who play havoc with your emotions and always keep you guessing.

Think Rafe Martino.

Sandra was prattling on, her voice light and breezy. She sounded like she didn't have a care in the world, so obviously Adriana's death hadn't impacted her very much. "Oh, wow. It must be fun living here. It's such a quaint little place, like something out of a movie set, you know?"

"Sometimes it seems that way to me, too." I remembered

that I'd gone through some serious culture shock when I'd first closed up my Manhattan office and moved to Cypress Grove. Everything was so laid-back and slow paced, it took some getting used to. For the first month, I felt like everyone was talking to me under water.

And sometimes the locals still ask me if all New Yorkers talk as fast as I do. For the most part, though, I've settled in and have made some good friends.

We sat down side by side at the picnic table and Sandra pulled out a script. "I'd love to just chat with you about your job, but we better look busy, in case the Bitch-on-Wheels comes by." She opened the script and pretended to be reading it, her forehead furrowed in concentration, one hand shading her eyes. I must have looked surprised, because she whispered, "I hope you weren't taken in by that cow. She's friendly to your face but she can knife you in the back in two seconds flat."

I smiled. "If you mean Marion, she wasn't even friendly to my face."

"She's probably jealous," she said promptly.

"Of me? Why?"

Sandra popped a wad of gum from one side of her mouth to the other. She looked very young and pretty in the bright sunlight, her sleek hair swept back in a ponytail. "She's jealous of anyone who Hank admires. I think she has a thing for him, ya know?"

"She has a thing for Hank? It's hard to imagine them as a couple."

Sandra shrugged. "I heard they were an item a long time ago. There aren't any secrets on a movie set, you know. Hank and Marion shared a room once when they were on location in Mexico. Everybody knew about it, but no one said anything. It probably meant a lot more to Marion than it did to Hank."

I must have looked unconvinced because Sandra laughed "Marion was a lot younger back then." She sipped her iced tea. "And the moment you came on the set, Hank was telling everyone about you, how smart you are, and how you had this big private practice in Manhattan."

I groaned inwardly. Lola must have been bragging about me again.

"That's my mom's doing," I said.

Sandra grinned. "You can't blame her for being proud. It must be cool being a psychologist."

"I'm a radio talk show host now," I reminded her.

"But you still know all this psychology stuff, right?" She riffled through the script until she came to a courtroom scene. "Take a look at this scene. Is this really what you would say to the lawyer if you were on the stand?"

I scanned the page and my heart sank. The dialogue was wooden, and the tone was all wrong. Sandra's character came off as harsh and shrewish, not calm and composed, and worst of all, she was spouting psychobabble. "Not exactly." I whipped out a pen. "Let's see if we can tighten up this dialogue a little."

"What's wrong with it?" Sandra leaned forward, interested.

"Well, lots of things, I'm afraid. You see this part about schizophrenia? Your character, Dr. Tilden, is telling the jury it means someone has a split personality."

"Isn't that right?"

"No, it's all wrong. I'm afraid the writers didn't do their homework. Schizophrenia is a thought disorder. It's characterized by delusions and hallucinations, disorganized thinking. It has nothing to do with a split personality; that's a popular misconception. Someone who's schizophrenic has seriously disordered thinking. Your character needs to make the jury understand that, if she's trying to get a reduced sentence for this guy." I hesitated. "Is it okay if I mark up the script?"

"Sure, go ahead," Sandra said. "They can type some new sides with your revisions."

I worked steadily for the next half hour, trying not to get annoyed at Sandra who periodically snapped her gum in my ear. Marion Summers wandered by a few times, giving us a suspicious glance each time before moving on.

"Marion's not really well liked, is she?" I asked Sandra.

"Hah, that's the understatement of the year. None of us can stand her. Sometimes I wonder why Hank puts up with her, but there's obviously more to the story." Sandra gave an arch smile. "I think she has something on him. Maybe a deep dark secret."

"Really?" I wondered if Sandra knew something or was just repeating idle gossip.

She nodded vigorously, her blond ponytail bobbing up and down. "There's a lot of skeletons in this business, you know? And you don't really get to the top without stepping on some people along the way." She gave me a dark look. "I think maybe there's more to Hank than meets the eye and that Marion knows the real story on him. They've been together like forever, but I get the feeling he'd like to dump her if he could." She paused. "Same as Adriana."

I quirked an eyebrow. Who would have thought little Sandra would have so much information? "He wanted to get rid of her, too?"

"Of course." She leaned closer. "You know about Tammilynne, don't you?"

"I know she's the new star of *Death Watch*. That and the fact that she looks like she's in high school."

Sandra snorted with laughter. "She's barely twenty. Not that age means anything, Mischa Barton started on *The O.C.* when she was eighteen. But Tammilynne is different; she's never had an acting lesson, never had a vocal coach. Nothing."

"Nothing?"

"Nothing except Hank Watson and a lot of promises." She paused. "You know what I think?" I had the feeling Sandra was going to tell me whether I nodded my head or not. "I think that things came to a head with Tammilynne. She was going to tell wifey back in L.A. that she's been Hank's main squeeze for the past two years. And up till now, all she's gotten from Hank have been promises."

"You're not suggesting that Hank did something to the gun, are you?"

Sandra gave me a sly look, tucking her chin and looking up at me under her long dark lashes. "Who am I to say what happened?" She widened her eyes and gave a little shrug. I noticed her arms were tanned and very toned in her clingy tunic top. I reminded myself to ask her about her miracle diet and exercise plan sometime. She took out a root-beer-flavored lip gloss and swiped it across her lips. "But look at it this way, Maggie. Whoever fooled around with that gun knew what they were doing. It's really hard to kill someone with one of those things. They don't even take bullets."

"That's certainly something to consider," I said, thinking. I wondered how many people on the set had the technical ability to tamper with the prop gun, and what the report from ballistics would say.

"If ever you want to know anything about what's going on around here, just ask me. I'd like to help the investigation. I'm into all that *CSI* stuff; I watch a lot of television. I bet I could help out."

"Oh, I'm not really part of the investigation, Sandra, but I'll remember that. At the moment, the Cypress Grove PD is handling the case. They seem to have everything under control."

Sandra gave a lascivious wink. "Did you see that hottie they sent over to interview us? Detective Martino? Wow! He could handle me anytime—maybe even do a strip search!" She let out a raucous chuckle.

I was tempted to say something scathing, but instead I gave a little sniff, pursed my lips in disapproval, and went back to work.

Detective Martino. It was hard to ignore the little tug of affection I felt just hearing Rafe's name, the buzz of excitement I felt remembering those smoldering dark eyes and sexy smile. Like the song says, "zing went my heartstrings."

I wasn't thrilled at the idea that other women's heartstrings were zinging too, but what did I expect? As Sandra said, he's a hottie.

Chapter 10

"Hi there! I'm Carla. Can I join you?" A middle-aged woman with hennaed hair swooped down on me, pulling an extra folding chair up to the long table set up under the trees. It was midday and I was having a quick lunch with Lola and a few of the cast and crew members.

Hank was still MIA, but Marion had ordered a nice selection of sandwiches and pastries from Joey's, my favorite deli in Cypress Grove. I'd just finished a cheese and tomato panini, and was doing my best to ignore the double-fudge brownies that were calling to me with their little sugary voices.

Carla looked vaguely familiar. She was in her early fifties, wearing a Tommy Bahamas tropical print blouse and stretchy white pants. The pants were practically plastic-wrapped over her thighs, making them look like a pair of country hams. I gave her a polite smile and tried to scoot my chair to one side so she could squeeze in. It was a tight fit, though, and her chair was teetering dangerously close to mine—another minute and she'd be sitting in my lap.

"Here, you can have my seat. I'm finished." I tried to get up but she laid a restraining hand on my arm. She had Dragon Lady bloodred nails, worn very long with a squared off tip. She also had a surprisingly strong grip.

"Oh, now don't go running off, honey. You're the person I want to see." She had a hawklike nose and little beady eyes, giving her an uncanny resemblance to a bird of prey. "Well, you and Lola, that is." She flashed my mom a broad smile, an expectant look in her eyes. Were they old friends? Carla seemed to think so.

"Hello, Carla," Lola said smoothly. I tried to read her expression and couldn't. Like most actresses, Lola is so expressive she can't help telegraphing her impressions of people, but this time she was giving nothing away. I watched and waited, intrigued.

"Long time no see." Carla's tone was cheery. She waved her hand in the air and nearly knocked over my iced tea. "Let's see; how long has it been? Seven or eight years, right? Some sort of shindig out on the Coast?"

Lola gave a thin smile. "Yes, it must have been ten years ago. I think it might have been Swifty Lazar's Oscar party."

Carla nodded. "Such a terrific soiree, and what a shame he's gone now. A great man. He knew how to entertain." She looked around hopefully. "And this is your daughter," she said, her eyes skimming over me.

"Maggie Walsh," I said, offering my hand.

"My, oh my. You're all grown up now. An actress, I suppose?"

"Not exactly." I gave her a pleasant smile and didn't offer any details.

She stared at me for a long moment and then glanced at Lola, a sly look creeping over her face. "Well, I've met your daughter. Aren't you going to introduce me to your friends?"

Lola tightened her lips for a microsecond, a telltale sign that she was irritated. On *Lie to Me*, they'd call this an illustrator, a subtle change in body language that reveals emotion.

"This is Carla Townsend, everyone. She's an entertainment reporter," Lola said flatly. Okay, now I was getting negative vibes from Lola. Everyone at the table had stopped eating and was watching us with unabashed interest. "Carla and I knew each other back in Manhattan several years ago—"

"I wrote for Page Six!" Carla interjected. "I covered the record industry. I nearly wrote an unauthorized biography of Madonna!" *No false modesty here*, I thought, covering a smile.

"—and we both moved out to California at the same time." Mom was determined to get the last word.

"Except you went into acting and I stuck with journalism," Carla said, eyeing the sandwiches. "Of course, I almost went into the book biz. Remember when I was going to write a big Hollywood exposé, Lola? That was years ago." Her mouth twisted into a scowl. "Random House was interested, but I got the short end of the stick that time."

"I remember. The deal fell through, didn't it?"

"Only because Adriana decided to beat me to it. I never should have opened my mouth. She took my idea and ran with it. She even used some of my best stories." Carla grabbed a tuna on rye, an egg salad on whole wheat, and a cream cheese on a bagel. Either she'd missed breakfast or she had a "hoarding" disorder.

Since I tend to overanalyze everything, I decided she was just hungry, and judging from her white pants, she had a good appetite. She was giving the brownies a thoughtful look, as if she hoped one or two might jump onto her plate. "Wonder what the calorie count is on these things?" she said, speculating.

"Oh, they're practically calorie free," Lola gushed. "No fat, no sugar, and hardly any carbs. Plus they're high fiber, so that cancels everything out. Go ahead, indulge yourself; you don't even have to feel guilty."

"Well, in that case—" Carla, said, loading three brownies onto her plate. Lola winked at me and I realized my first impression was correct. I was right; she was no fan of Carla Townsend.

Mom methodically went around the table introducing everyone to Carla, who whipped out a notebook and started jotting down their names.

"Jeff Walker?" Carla pursed her lips. "You're the shooter, right?" she said carelessly.

"Carla—" Mom said, a warning note in her voice.

Carla made a little dismissive motion. "Oh, for heaven's sake, I didn't mean to make it sound like Columbine." She turned to Jeff, who'd already pushed his plate away and stood up so abruptly he nearly knocked over his chair. A hot flush had crept from his collarbone up to his neck and his face was tight with anger. "Relax, sweetie, it was an accident; we all know that." She flashed him a high-beam smile and he shot her a flinty look. "I'm hoping we can talk privately later, Jeff. Maybe you can explain to me how a prop gun works."

"I don't think so," Jeff said coldly. He tossed his napkin on his empty paper plate and stalked away.

"Hmm. A little bit touchy, isn't he?" Carla looked around the table, flashing an amped-up Hollywood smile. "These creative types always have a dark side, don't they? Now, who else saw the shooting? I'd love to get a firsthand account." There was dead silence while she glanced at her notes and then people began clearing the table and drifting away.

In less than a minute, Mom and I found ourselves alone at the table with Carla. We exchanged a long look. "And I can't forget Maisie, the script girl," Carla continued under her breath as if nothing had happened. She was ticking off names in her notebook, seemingly oblivious to the fact that everyone had deserted us. "Now there's someone I really need to see."

"She's not here," Mom piped up. "I think she's going over some script changes with Marion."

"Too bad; I bet she'd have some tales to tell." She paused and looked up. "I wonder how long Hank will be? The cops must still be grilling him right this minute. I bet the whole thing just seems a little too coincidental to them, you know?"

"Coincidental? What exactly do you mean, Carla?" Mom's voice had an edge to it. "And what's this about the police grilling Hank? I thought he'd gone into town to pick up supplies."

"Oh please." Carla sat back, drumming her fingers on the paper tablecloth. "That's just a story Marion made up. Of course they're grilling Hank; he's been down at the station all morning. The backers are trying to keep the questioning quiet and discreet, but I've heard he's the lead suspect."

"What?" Mom's voice wobbled. "That's impossible."

"He's got motive, means, and opportunity," Carla said.

"But what's his motive?" I asked. I immediately wondered how much Rafe knew and what he'd tell me.

"Easy." Carla gave a little self-satisfied smirk. "Here's what happened. Or at least, here's the theory. Hank wanted to dump Adriana and put Malibu Barbie in the lead, and now it's all going to work out perfectly for him. Funny how the universe suddenly tilted his way, isn't it?" She gave a wry laugh.

"Is that what you think happened?" Mom asked.

"You bet I do!! If he's innocent, he must be thanking his lucky stars that someone knocked off Adriana. The movie's going to go forward, and his bimbo girlfriend will have a starring role. Of course, if he's guilty, that's another story." She flipped through her notebook. "My biggest problem is trying to figure out what to go with for the lead. This story is going to be bigger than I thought. I doubt Hank will talk to me, so I'll have to go the 'confidential sources' route."

"Your story? You mean you're here on assignment?" I asked, surprised. I didn't think Hank and Marion would allow journalists on the set while Adriana's death was still being investigated. Nick had told me he'd called earlier that day for an interview and been politely given the brush-off.

And how did Carla know that Hank was down at the Cypress Grove PD? Was he a suspect? A person of interest? My mind was exploding with possibilities. I'd have to call Nick as soon as I could get away from the set.

"It's more like an undercover assignment," Carla said, lowering her voice. "I told Marion I was doing a piece on the problems associated with on-location shooting." I raised my eyebrows. "I think she must have been preoccupied, because she actually believed me. Either that, or she thinks I'm an idiot." She gave a little chortle. "On-location shooting. That would be a snooze, wouldn't it? But at least it got me on the set. And now I can write whatever I want."

"You're writing this piece for an entertainment magazine?" I asked.

"Maybe, maybe not. This could be a lot bigger. We're talking a major murder investigation; this has national interest." She glanced at her watch and looked at Mom. "We need to go someplace private to talk. Are you free for a while?"

"Just for half an hour," Mom said hesitantly. "Then I have to go back to Wardrobe." Mom and I exchanged a look. Her eyes looked troubled; I knew she was thinking about Hank Watson. They go back a long time and I'm sure she was shocked that he was being interrogated by the police. I wondered if he really was the number one suspect, or if Carla was just trying to put together a good story.

I finished the last of my iced tea and stood up. "I need to go back to the production office and find Sandra," I said. "I'll catch up with you later, Mom."

Mom nodded, distracted by Carla, who had already pulled her close for a private conversation. Carla was talking a mile a minute, clutching Mom's arm, probably urging her to say something inflammatory about Hank. Mom was an old pro at dealing with reporters so I wasn't really worried about her. I knew she'd be careful about what she said, especially with a buzzard like Carla Townsend who would clearly do anything for a good story.

I had every intention of finding Sandra, but as I crossed the grassy area to the production trailer, my eye spotted a familiar figure walking along the shoreline. His arms were folded across his chest, and he was staring out at the sunlight glinting on the greenish waters of Branscom Pond.

Rafe! I felt a little bullet of emotion go through me. He turned at that moment and our eyes locked. It was like a freeze-frame; time stood still. The sun was high in the sky; the air, warm and moist. I could feel his eyes on me as I made my way over the narrow expanse of gray sandy beach toward him.

"I thought you were in town this morning," I said.

A tiny smile flickered over his lips, but his dark eyes were steady, unreadable. "I'm going back to the station in a few minutes. I thought you were holed up with the Guitar Heroes."

"The Guitar Heroes?" I echoed. "Oh, you mean the writers, those kids in the baseball caps." I gave a wry laugh. "I haven't gotten up with them yet. I've done some rewrites on the script but I need Hank's approval before they type up the new version."

"I'm sure he'll be glad to get your input."

"Maybe not. I pretty much gutted the scene and started over from scratch."

Rafe raised his eyebrows. "It was that bad?"

I nodded. "It was awful. Bad dialogue, full of clichés and out-of-date expressions. A few lines were just so silly, I had to cross them out completely."

I nearly told him that they'd gotten the courtroom scene all wrong, and stopped at the last minute. It would leave me open to being lectured by him on the idiocy of forensic psychology and I wasn't up to it. I already knew Rafe's views on the subject and I had something more important on my mind.

"I heard something at lunch that really worries me," I began.

"Yeah? What's that?" He moved a little closer and gently took my arm. "But first, let's get out of the sun." The heat was scorching; it felt like we were pushing against a solid wall of hot air and it was hard to draw a breath. We headed back toward the production office and stopped under a canopy that was set up over the drinks table. "So what's bothering you, Maggie?" Rafe's tone was measured, even.

"Hank Watson. That's what's bothering me." I waited, and in true cop fashion, Rafe didn't react. He could be a sphinx when he wanted to be, I reminded myself. His black eyes were shuttered, his mouth tightening slightly. There was a long beat between us and finally I couldn't stand the suspense. "So is it true? Is he really a suspect in Adriana's death? He's your main suspect?"

"Who told you that?" Another cop trick. Answer a question with a question. His cell chirped. He pulled it out, looked at the display and jammed it back into his pocket.

"There's a reporter on the set," I said in a rush. "I don't know if she's just trying to create a good story or if she really knows something, but she seems to think that Hank is the only person you're looking at. As the murderer, I mean."

"That would be Carla Townsend," Rafe said flatly.

"You know her?"

"She tried to interview me half an hour ago. I told her she was contaminating a crime scene and if she took one more step, I'd arrest her for obstruction of justice."

"Oh no," I said, nearly giggling at the idea. "What happened?"

"She backed off in a huff. I came down to the beach to escape her." A wry smile crossed Rafe's face at the memory. "It's not a crime scene anymore, but she fell for it."

"I wish I'd seen that." I smiled back. "She can be pretty irritating."

"Very irritating. Even for a reporter."

"She knew Mom in the old days, in Manhattan and Hollywood." I paused. "Mom thinks the world of Hank, you know. She'd hate to think he was being grilled as a suspect."

"What do *you* know about him?" Rafe was looking at me very intently.

I thought for a moment. "Well, I don't know him well, but he's certainly likable. Actually he's pretty darn charming and the actors seem to respect him." I remembered the way Hank had swept Lola off her feet and had seemed genuinely glad to see her. And I knew she was thrilled to be included in his movie, even if it was just a small part. "He's loyal to his friends and goes out of his way to stay in touch with them and do them favors," I pointed out. "He seems to be a good guy in a business that's full of players and sharks. So all in all, it's really difficult for me to imagine him as a murder suspect."

Rafe's lips twitched in a sardonic smile. "What a ringing endorsement. And that's your professional opinion, Dr. Maggie?" There was a sharp edge to his tone.

I knew something was up because Rafe only calls me Dr. Maggie when he wants to annoy me. Uh-oh, I was clearly venturing into dangerous territory here. "Well, maybe not my professional opinion as a psychologist," I said, backpedaling quickly. "But I think I'm a pretty good judge of people. And Hank just doesn't seem like a murderer to me." I shrugged. "He seems like a nice guy."

"A nice guy," Rafe repeated slowly. "That's interesting." He spoke slowly and precisely as if I'd just said something incredibly stupid. He was about to say something else when suddenly he reached for his phone again, flipped the lid, and barked "Martino." He listened for a long moment with his eyes narrowed. "Got it; I'll be there in ten." He pocketed the phone and faced me. "Look, Maggie, something's come up. I have to head back to the station right away." His face was closed, his voice tense. Rafe was back in cop mode. He speed-walked back toward the parking lot and I scurried to keep up with him.

"But wait a minute; what about Hank Watson?" I said. "I'd like to know if he's really your key suspect." It was the completely the wrong time to ask him anything, but I couldn't help myself. My mind was starting to twitch and thoughts were sparking around my head like fireworks.

If the Cypress Grove PD was concentrating on Hank Watson as the killer, wouldn't the real killer get away? It could have been that *Sopranos* character who murdered Adriana, Frankie Domino, or maybe someone who was on the set that day and was never interrogated. There were so many possibilities, why were the cops narrowing it down to one person? And why was that one person Hank Watson?

"Please, just tell me what you think," I persisted. Rafe was hurrying down the row of cars in the Branscom Pond parking lot and I was still trotting along at his heels like a well-trained Labrador.

This time, he didn't even bother making eye contact with me until he unlocked the car and leaned against it for a second. A flicker of amusement passed briefly over his face. "You don't need to hear any police theories on Hank Watson; you've already got it all figured out. Nice guys don't commit murders, Maggie, you said so yourself." He waited a beat. "Unless they're Ted Bundy, of course."

And with that, he jumped into his geriatric Crown Vic, gunned the engine, and left me standing in a cloud of dust. *Ted Bundy. Ted Bundy?* That was Rafe, as enigmatic and infuriating as ever. And to think I'd let him drive away without coming up with the perfect zinger!

Chapter 11

Things were "hopping" (as Vera Mae would say) back at the station, and I dashed into the studio just in time for my show. The day's topic was relationships, a subject that's usually popular with my mostly female audience.

"Holy shit on a stick! You do believe in living on the edge, don't you girl?" Vera Mae jumped up and slapped on her headphones. "I was all set to run a retrospective of your best shows. You know, the ones Cyrus calls 'Dr. Maggie's Top Ten Audience Picks.' I was going to play just a few clips from each."

"You were?" I tried to think what shows she was talking about; I couldn't imagine any of my shows being particularly memorable. I settled myself at the console, taking a few deep breaths to compose myself. My face was flushed and my brain was still skittering back to Rafe and the scene at Branscom Pond. "What are my Top Ten shows?"

"Well, the beauty pageant one you did was real popular," Vera Mae said. "People always like it when a local girl makes good, and you had that sweet little Thelma Ann Hopkins as a guest."

"Thelma Ann Hopkins?" I squinted to remember, finally bringing up the image of a teenybopper wearing a sequined blue bathing suit with white go-go boots and a dime-store tiara. It wasn't a good visual. "Isn't that the time a half-dozen ceiling tiles came crashing down while we were live on the air?"

Vera Mae grinned. "Yeah, that's the one. I suppose we shouldn't have asked her to demonstrate the talent portion of the competition for our listeners. Who knew her specialty was baton twirling? That sure didn't come across very well on the radio, did it? Something like country music singing, or maybe reciting a patriotic poem, now that would have been real nice."

"I do remember Thelma Ann," I said, cringing a little. The show had been a train wreck from start to finish and the teen queen had hit the ceiling with her damn baton—twice— in her grand finale. On the double toss, the baton had lodged firmly in the acoustic tiles and a shower of white plaster dust had drifted down onto my head. "She was Miss Fire Prevention of Bartholomew County, wasn't she?"

"No, that was her sister, Ruth Ann. They were identical twins, remember? You had a dickens of a time remembering which was which, if I recall correctly. Thelma Ann was Miss Sweet Potato Queen." Vera Mae chortled. "Of course the folks listening at home had no idea. I held up those signs over those girls' heads so you could keep them straight."

Vera Mae holds up hand-lettered signs when the spirit moves her, during my show. If she agrees with my advice to a caller, she might hold up a sign with the word Yes! on it, followed by another sign that reads Damn Straight!

Vera Mae has an infinite number of these signs and I like to think of her as a Dixie version of a Greek chorus. One of her favorite signs is KHATTC, which translates as: Kick His Ass To The Curb, Vera Mae's solution for wayward husbands.

The phone rang in the recording booth and Vera Mae

held up an index finger while she grabbed it. She kept the receiver clamped tightly to her ear, nodding vigorously as she darted a nervous glance at the oversized, schoolhouse clock mounted on the studio wall. "I got it. No problemo. Check, check, and check. Will do!" she said finally, slamming the phone down, her face flush with excitement.

"What's up?" I suddenly felt a prickling of apprehension.

"Well, hell's a-poppin'; there's a big change of plans!" Vera Mae was grinning from ear to ear. "Cyrus has a surprise in store for us today. That man has outdone himself! You know how he's been wantin' to boost the ratings?"

"Yes, but—"

"Listen up, Maggie. He decided to do a simulcast. He set the whole thing up himself, just a few minutes ago. A WYME exclusive. It's gonna be the talk of south Florida. Mark my words, the man's a creative genius. And you heard it here first," she said, using Big Jim's favorite tagline and grinning.

"Wait a minute!" I yelled. It's always hard to interrupt Vera Mae when she's on a roll. "A WYME exclusive *what*?" I don't like surprises, especially ones Cyrus might spring on me. I felt a prickle of apprehension inching up my spine.

"Now, don't you worry about a thing, hon; it's all set up for you. We're patched through and ready to go. We've got remote access out there at Branscom Pond." She took another quick peek at the clock; the second hand was winding inexorably toward the hour.

"Branscom Pond? You mean the movie set?"

"I sure do, sweetie. Here's the setup. We've got Lola out there, live on the scene, and you here in the studio." My mind was reeling, but Vera Mae didn't seem to notice. "This is going to be one doozy of a show!" She held up three fingers. "Stand by in three, sugar; I just have to run a promo and two spots before we go live."

Three minutes. Okay, the prickle of apprehension had morphed into a full-blown panic attack. Lola at Branscom Pond. Me, here in the studio. Cohosting a live show.

This. Will. Never Work. The words went charging through my brain like a locomotive.

A commercial for the Last End Funeral Home came blasting through the studio and I jumped in alarm. "Celebrating twenty-five years of fantastic funerals!"

A sepulchral voice accompanied by a Mantovani string quartet offered a midweek special in honor of their anniversary. Apparently you could save a bundle if you could arrange to die any time between Tuesday and Thursday. *Fulfilling all your funeral fantasies*, the voice droned on.

Irina strikes again. She loves alliteration. *Call today; your dead ones will thank you.*

I shook my head in disbelief and tore into the control room.

Vera Mae looked up, startled, and turned down the volume control knob on the board. "What's wrong?"

"What's wrong? How could Cyrus spring this on me at the last minute? I saw Mom on the set today and she didn't say a word. I feel like I've been blindsided by the two of them."

The truth is, it was more than the element of surprise that bothered me. I wasn't at all sure I wanted Mom horning in on my show. Call me mean-spirited, but the last time she was on the air with me, she was a huge hit with the listeners and I could barely get a word in edgewise.

"Now, don't go gettin' your panties in a twist, Maggie," Vera said, her voice low and soothing. "Why, Lola didn't know a thing about it till a few minutes ago. Cyrus drove out there himself to set it up. He had to talk to that director—"

"Hank Watson?" I stared at her in disbelief. As far as I

knew, Hank was still downtown at the station, being "grilled" by the Cypress Grove PD.

"That's the one. Cyrus figured he'd have to sweet-talk him to get permission but Hank loved the idea right from the start. He said it would be great publicity for the movie and so he gave Cyrus the go-ahead. But he insisted that you and Lola can't mention anything about the murder. So remember, not a word." Vera Mae put a finger to her lips.

"We can't mention the murder? But that's insane! That's the one thing people are going to ask about." I shook my head in disbelief. "They're going to want to hear every grisly detail about the murder and about the latest in the investigation."

"But we don't always have to give the listeners what they want, do we? All we have to do is entertain them. And you know you can do that. When you and Lola did that show together the last time, the ratings were through the roof. Cyrus was practically beside himself with joy."

Yeah, right. I winced. Big Jim Wilcox had never let me forget that my mom is a bigger draw than I am. "So today, the topic is—"

"Moviemaking! Cyrus wants you and Lola to talk about the fun parts of the movie business; you know, the clothes, the makeup, the personalities . . ."

"The bodies," I added glumly.

"Now Maggie, you've got to think positive. "Isn't that what you're always telling your listeners?"

"Yeah, but I never really believe it."

"Stand by," she said, pushing me through the door into the studio. "Live in five, sugar!"

"This is Lola Walsh, and I'm reporting to you live from Branscom Pond," Lola warbled seconds later. "I'm right smack in the middle of a movie set. When they say lights, camera, action, this is what it's all about. I've spent most of my life on film sets, but I have to tell you, I get a rush of excitement each time. How I wish you could see it, Maggie!"

She wishes I could see it? Am I supposed to pretend I haven't visited the set?

I could tell Lola was flashing a big Hollywood smile, even though it was wasted on the radio audience. I was stymied for a moment, wondering how to play this.

Vera Mae scowled at me from the studio and made a quack-quack motion with her hands. Talk-talk. Oh yeah, I had to say something fast before the silence went on too long. The last thing Cyrus—or any station manager wants—is dead air.

"And this is Maggie Walsh, live from"—I was so rattled I nearly stumbled over the call letters—"WYME Radio." I waited a beat. "We're doing a joint show today. I'm here in the studio, Lola is out on the set, and we're both eager to take your calls." I glanced at the phone lines. All the lights were flashing. "I see that we have a lot of callers, so let's get—"

"I'm ready to answer all your questions about the movie business," Lola interrupted smoothly. "As your listeners probably know, I've been a film star for"— she hesitated—"well, for quite a number of years." She gave a girlish giggle.

Please don't say you started out as a child.

"I started out as a child, of course."

Oh no, nostalgia alert! Mom was tripping down memory lane. She was all set to turn this into the Lola Walsh Lifetime Achievement Show, chronicling her years in show biz. I knew I had to act fast. But how?

"I learned pretty quickly that being a child star isn't what it's cracked up to be." Her voice was like warm molasses, smooth and comforting. She was giving the listeners an inside look into her star-studded life. She knows they love this stuff; they eat it up with a spoon.

Hollywood gossip trumps psychological insights any day. Trust me.

"There's the excitement and glamour of being around celebrities, but of course there's also a lot of pressure." She dropped her voice half an octave, sounding an appropriately somber note. "The pressure of knowing your lines, the pressure of spending long hours on the set—"

I took a deep breath and plunged in. "Yes, I'm sure it was quite an—"

"You have to hit the ground running, as they say."

"But—"

Lola skidded right over me, like my Honda fishtailing on dark ice. "I got my start when I played the second female lead in *Corazones Quebradros*, or *Broken Hearts*. I had to memorize ten pages of dialogue every single night." She paused to catch a breath and I jumped in.

"Oh yes, *Broken Hearts*. I remember that film. What year was that released?"

Hah. That stopped her cold in her tracks.

"Well, it was back in the uh, eighties, I think." *Eighties? Think seventies.*

"Let's open the phone lines," I said briskly. "Vera Mae, who's our first caller?"

"It's Stacey, from Dania," Vera Mae piped up. "And she has a question for Lola."

"Lola, I love all your movies," Stacey gushed. "Can you tell me more about your role in *Broken Hearts*? Is it out on video? I'd like to rent it."

"Well, aren't you just the sweetest thing?" Lola said. "It might be available in video, I'm not sure." *Hah. It went straight to video, and Mom knew it.* "You might have trouble finding it at Blockbuster, though, because it wasn't really a commercial film. It was more of an artistic film."

"Really? What does that mean?" Stacey asked.

"Well, let's just say it received wide critical acclaim, but it had rather a limited distribution in movie theaters." *Limited distribution? Oh yeah. She must be referring to those three people in Kentucky who happened to catch it at a drive-in.*

"Wow, I've never talked to a real-live movie star before." Stacey sounded awed. "I've always wondered if I should take acting lessons, myself. I do impressions for the folks down at the Senior Center, and I've won some local talent competitions for my singing. But maybe it's time to go pro. What do you think my chances would be? Wait; let me do an impression for you. I'll sing a few lines."

"Go ahead," Lola urged. "Let's see what you've got, Stacey!"

A nasal drone filled the studio, starting off slow and building to a caterwauling shriek. "If I could turn back ti-i-i-me, if I could find a wa-a-a-ay . . ." I found myself mouthing the rest of the familiar verse when I caught a glimpse of Vera Mae frantically twirling the volume control. Stacey's grating voice had probably slammed the meter far into the red zone.

"Very nice," Lola said, making little applause sounds. "You have a real talent for impressions, my dear. That throaty voice, the elongated vowels, I have to congratulate you. You've really captured Cher."

"That was supposed to be Celine Dion."

"Oh." A long beat. "I'm so sorry. It's probably a bad, um, connection. Over the radio, I mean." *Nice save, Mom!*

Vera Mae rolled her eyes at me as Lola segued into her standard monologue on the vicissitudes of show business ("too many actors, so few parts"). The conversation was moving along at a snail's pace and I saw Vera Mae heave a sigh.

"But if you really feel the passion, and you have that fire in the belly, I truly think you do have a chance," Mom said, winding up.

Vera Mae was giving elaborate yawns followed by a throat-slitting motion. Any minute now, she'd get out her MIAS sign, which translates as Move It Along, Sister! This was my cue to jump in.

"Thanks for calling, Stacey. And who do we have next, Vera Mae?"

"Jennifer from Hallandale," she piped up. "She says she wants to know what's really going on at Branscom Pond?" She gave me a warning glance. I knew my lips had to be sealed about the investigation so I'd have to soft-pedal this one.

I was debating what to tell her, when Mom jumped in ahead of me. "Jennifer!" she bubbled. "There's just loads of exciting things going on out here. I'm so glad you asked. As you know, we're filming *Death Watch*, a Hank Watson production. I've worked with Hank before, and I've got to say, I think this movie is going to be his best one ever. We're talking Oscar material."

Jennifer didn't take the bait. "I really meant, what's going on with the police investigation? Is it true that Adriana St. James was really murdered? That's what folks around town are saying, but there's not much in the paper about it. I'm sure the gun didn't go off by itself. I figured you'd have the inside scoop on it."

I glanced at Vera Mae. She had her finger poised over the MUTE button, ready to propel the inquisitive Jennifer into radio silence.

"Well, my dear, I do have the inside scoop . . . on a lot of things," Lola added hastily. "But I think we should focus on the positive, happy parts of the movie business. That's what makes our hearts sing and the world go 'round." Dear God, now she was channeling Julie Andrews. In a minute she'd be talking about raindrops on roses, whiskers on kittens and a few of her favorite things.

"Yes, but I really want to know—"

"Oh, I'm sure you want to know all about the fabulous costumes the wardrobe mistress whipped up for us. You know what I always say is the first lesson of survival on the set: make friends with the wardrobe mistress. Your future could be in her hands!" Mom gave a lilting laugh. "Now, Hank Watson always uses Rhonda Patterson, and let me tell you, she's dressed all the A-list stars."

Mom prattled on about the wonders of wardrobe design, and I glanced over at Vera Mae. She'd turned the volume all the way down to zero on the call line, so that explained Jennifer's silence. I smiled and gave her a thumbs-up.

A few more callers asked about the murder but Lola deflected them, always drawing the listener back into the spicy world of Hollywood gossip. After the first half hour, I could hardly believe that there really was a murder investigation going on.

Lola had managed to captivate the audience with tales of anorexic starlets ("I've known her for five years, and I've never seen her eat anything except romaine lettuce and Tic Tacs"), working with animals ("never get close to a chimp wearing a diaper!"), and Hank Watson ("he's not appreciated in the U.S. It's sort of like Jerry Lewis. Only the French really understand his genius").

When the show was over, Vera Mae scooted around to the studio and gave me a high-five. "Nice work, girl! I think this is the most calls we've ever gotten; Cyrus is going to be beside himself. And you didn't give away anything about the murder investigation." The phone rang and Vera Mae grabbed it. "You did a real nice job today, sugar. You boosted the ratings big-time." She put her hand over the receiver. "It's your momma. She needs a ride home from the set."

"Tell her I'm on my way," I said. I grinned. I put on my best Desi Arnez voice. "And make sure she knows she's got some 'splaining to do."

Chapter 12

"Really, I didn't mean to hijack your show, Maggie," Lola said, a touch of humor in her voice. "Cyrus came out here and pitched the idea to Hank, and he just ate it up. There wasn't time to check and see what you thought about it. One minute Hank handed me a headset and the next minute I was on the air." She flashed me an unrepentant grin.

"I know. I was just teasing you. You were great, Mom, really. You kept things going and the listeners really loved you."

Things were quiet on the set and most of the cast and crew had headed into town for dinner. Mom was collecting her things from the Wardrobe trailer and showed me the outfits she'd be wearing once filming resumed.

Each outfit was hung in a plastic see-through garment bag with accessories—belts, scarves, and jewelry—stashed in a separate bag on the same hanger. Every bag had "Lola Walsh" written on it, along with the date she'd be wearing the outfit and the scene number. Her shoes were neatly bagged and tagged the same way. The whole setup was so perfect, it reminded me of a Martha Stewart display.

"Very nice," I said. I was thrilled to see that there were no Lindsay Lohan thigh-high minis or skintight knits. Lola would be wearing mostly simple cotton skirts and colorful tops with huaraches, very south Florida.

"It's okay, I suppose." Mom wrinkled her nose. "If you like 'age appropriate.' This is the kind of thing you might wear to an Early Bird Special at Applebee's. I'm surprised they didn't throw in a pair of Dr. Scholl's bunion plasters."

"Oh Lola, thank God you're still here!" Carla Townsend bustled into the trailer and then stopped dead in her tracks when she saw me. "And your darling daughter is here as well. How's it going, Maggie? I came here to congratulate you. Heard the two of you did a killer radio show today, no pun intended." She guffawed.

Mom's gaze briefly met mine, then flicked away again. "You're putting in a long day, Carla." Her voice was as impassive as her face. I knew she didn't like the gossip columnist, and made a mental note to ask her about it later.

"Oh well, you know what they say, a reporter's work is never done," Carla said airily. "I figured I might get in some face time with Hank"—she lowered her voice—"now that the police have finally released him." She paused, a sly look creeping over her face. "I never thought he had what it took to be a killer. Do you? Of course, that's what people always say in these situations." She made a dismissive hand gesture. "You never know what's going on beneath the surface, do you? Still waters run deep."

"That's nonsense, Carla," Lola said sharply. "Hank had nothing to do with Adriana's death. And for all we know, it was an accident—"

"Oh, please. It was no accident," Carla jeered. "Didn't you hear about the ballistics report?"

I felt like I'd been sucker-punched. "The report is back from ballistics? How did you have access to it?"

"Oh, I have my sources," Carla said with a smug smile. "Anyway, it's going to hit the news network tonight. It went up on TMZ and Gawker this morning. And Maria Menounos is doing a big feature on *Access Hollywood* at seven o'clock. So, believe me, the secret's out."

"So it's true? Someone tampered with the prop gun?" There was a wince in Mom's voice. Her loyalty to Hank ran deep and I knew she was worried about her old friend.

"I'll say. Somebody really did a number on it. They took out the wadding, glued a BB pellet to it, and then stuffed it back in. Pretty clever, huh?"

"Carla, are you sure about this? It was definitely murder, then?" A bubble of disbelief was rising in me. Adriana would never win the Miss Congeniality Award, but who hated her enough to kill her? And who would know enough about prop guns to tamper with one?

"I'm as sure as I can be." Carla nodded sagely. "There's no way it was a joke. A pellet being expelled with that kind of velocity could easily kill someone. Especially at close range. Boom! Blunt force head trauma and you go straight to that big movie set in the sky." She giggled at her own wit.

"The whole thing is just baffling," Mom said, looking shattered. She sat down on a battered sofa and fanned herself with a take-out menu. It was crushingly hot in the trailer and I was eager to escape, but first I had to find out what else Carla knew. Her sources were clearly better than mine; she seemed to be a gold mine of information, and so far, I'd come up with nothing.

"Baffling?" Carla said archly. "Maybe, maybe not." She paused for effect. "Do you remember how Hank got his start in the business, Lola? Those early days out on the West Coast?"

"Of course I do," Lola snapped. "I was there, remember? I left New York a few months after Hank did, and by the time I got to Hollywood, he was already making a name for himself."

"He managed to get a job on a movie set," Carla said

snidely. "I'd hardly call it making a name for himself. His very first job with Don Bellisario. And do you know what he was hired to do?"

"Lighting design, I think," Mom said, frowning. "Or maybe he was a gaffer."

"Wrong!" Carla chortled. She popped open a bottle of Crystal Geyser, took a hefty swig, and stared at us. "He started out in props for *Magnum P.I.* and then he parlayed that into a job with Rudy DiSabatino. You know who Rudy is, don't you Lola?" Carla's voice was soft and wheedling. She turned to me, pinning me with her steely blue eyes. "In case you're not up on Hollywood trivia, Maggie, Rudy is one of the best special effects guys in the business. Isn't that right, Lola?"

Mom's face took on an unhealthy hue. "I don't recall that," she said stiffly. She shifted slightly on her chair as if she was bracing herself for an attack.

Carla inspected a bloodred fingernail, drawing the moment out. "Rudy was a genius at special effects and his real area of expertise was ballistics."

Ballistics. The word hung in the air for a moment like a thought balloon over my head. My synapses finally connected and my stomach flipped over at the word.

"That doesn't mean anything," Lola said quickly. "If you're trying to suggest that Hank had some kind of technical knowledge that would help him tamper with a prop gun, well, you're on the wrong track, that's all."

She struggled to sit upright on the sagging couch that was so low, it practically dragged on the trailer floor. She licked her lips and gave a nervous blink. This kind of tic is called a "tell," an automatic response to strong emotion. I could see Lola was shocked by Carla's news and trying not to show it.

Carla had probably studied up on body language because her eyes widened and she gave a smirk. "I think it's pretty significant, Lola. Maybe Hank isn't what you think he is and

you're letting friendship get in the way of your judgment."
She let the silence draw out for a moment.

"That's ridiculous," Mom said tightly.

"Is it?" Carla started ticking off items on her plump fingers. "Let's see; we have a movie director who wants to get rid of his leading lady. Why?" She struck a pose, pretending to be deep in thought like the Rodin masterpiece. "Oh, wait, I know! He wants to get rid of her because she's a pain in the ass, and he has his hottie waiting in the wings. The hottie wants a chance at stardom. In fact, she's insisting on her chance at stardom or she's threatening to tell wifey about the whole sordid affair."

"All of this is just conjecture," Mom sputtered, but Carla held up a warning finger.

"If you think that, you've got your head buried in the sand, Lola. Facts are facts. The movie director happens to be a whiz at ballistics. He would know exactly how to rig a prop gun and not leave any evidence."

"Is that true?" I blurted out. "Are you saying there weren't any fingerprints on the gun?"

"No trace evidence; no fingerprints. The barrel of the gun was wiped clean, sweetie. Naturally Jeff Walker's prints were on the trigger, because he's the one who fired the gun. But is he the one who rigged the gun? I don't think so." She looked at me carefully. "Really, for someone in the media, you seem to be out of the loop. Maybe you need to develop some new sources."

"Maybe so," I said with gritted teeth.

"Where did you get *your* news from, Carla?" Mom snapped. "The *National Enquirer*?"

"I've got credible sources, Lola." She peered at Mom's flushed face. "It's nice to be loyal, Lola, but even loyalty has its limits. You're going to have to face facts about Hank eventually, and if the police think he's the guy, they must have something to go on." She picked up her oversized tote bag and flashed a self-satisfied smirk. "So, we're talking motive, means, and opportunity. Remember, ladies, you heard it here first."

"That loathsome woman!" Lola said, the minute Carla had left the trailer. "I always knew she was mean-spirited, but this is just over-the-top." She looked at me searchingly. "I don't know why the police have focused on Hank, do you? Could you ask that nice detective friend what's going on?"

"Rafe? I can ask, but I'm not sure how far I'll get." I thought of Nick Harrison. "There's someone else I can talk to, though. Let's get out of here, and I'll make a phone call after dinner."

It was a lovely south Florida evening, soft and balmy, the air scented with honeysuckle, but my mind was ricocheting with ideas. Traffic was heavy on I-95, and Mom and I were quiet, lost in our own thoughts.

I'd hoped to have a word with Hank Watson before we left the set, but he was closeted in his trailer with Marion Summers and I didn't dare interrupt them. The future of *Death Watch* hung in the balance—it all depended on what happened to Hank. This was a white-knuckle time for both of them.

I still hadn't seen Tammilynne Cole, his main squeeze, and I wondered if Hank was deliberately keeping her out of sight. If Carla knew about his fling with the young actress, that meant other reporters knew and it was only a matter of time before his affair became public knowledge. Carla didn't seem like the type who would keep a secret. Any minute now, the rumor mills would be going into overdrive and Hank's marriage would be in a crash-and-burn mode. Or maybe Hank's wife already knew and the "secret" wasn't a secret after all?

There were so many pieces to the puzzle and I tried to put them together, my mind buzzing with possibilities. I fiddled with the radio and finally found an oldies station, one of Mom's favorites. The mellow sounds of Phil Collins swirled around us, but nothing could soothe my jangled nerves.

I thought about Frankie Domino, the mafioso I'd seen wandering around the set, and I wondered if the mob was somehow involved in the production. It seemed like a pretty far-fetched idea, but this was a crazy business and nothing would surprise me. I hadn't seen the mobster on the set again, but he could be staying somewhere in town and maybe he was even having private meetings with Hank. Note to self: find a way to check this out.

And what role did Marion Summers play in all this? According to Nick, she and Adriana had a "history." But how would Marion benefit from the movie star's death? As far as I could see, she wouldn't. There was no way Adriana's death was a good thing for Marion or for the production. Having a leading lady shot to death on the set could only cause headaches for Hank and Marion and maybe even financial disaster for the movie company.

Plus a ton of bad publicity, and Marion had enough problems without that. Too much bad press and the backers might pull out. And then what? The movie would be in "turnaround hell" while Hank and Marion scrambled to find a new source of funding.

"I still can't get over what Carla said about the prop gun," Mom said, breaking into my thoughts. "It sounds a lot more complicated than I thought. It wasn't just a matter of jamming real bullets into the gun. It must have taken some planning and technical know-how."

"Exactly. I was thinking the same thing." I was still pondering the shooting when we pulled up in front of my condo. I live on a leafy street in a quiet, residential neighborhood that's carpeted by banyan trees. My thoughts were still swirl-ing. Whoever had killed Adriana had planned it carefully. So that meant it couldn't have been a crime of passion. There was nothing spontaneous about Adriana's murder. Someone had methodically removed the wadding and tampered with the gun to turn it into a lethal weapon. I wondered if most people who spent a lot of time on movie sets would have the know-how to do that?

"What's going on tomorrow out at the set?" I asked Mom. "Are you shooting any scenes?"

"They're taking it day by day. I wonder if anyone really knows how long the production will be shut down? Marion must know, but she's not talking." She heaved a little sigh of dis-appointment. "She wouldn't win the Miss Congeniality prize."

I nodded. The area near the lake was still barricaded with sawhorses, and a few officers patrolled the beach during the day. Nick had said the production would be back in business in forty-eight hours, but maybe he was being overly optimis-tic?

Every day lost was an added expense. Hank had to pay the cast and crew whether or not they worked, and from what I'd heard, some of them were looking on it as a paid vaca-tion, running up tabs at local bars and restaurants. You could hardly blame them. Without the cameras rolling, the set was like a ghost town.

The moment we walked in the door, Pugsley threw him-self at us, barking joyfully, as if we'd been gone for months. That's the nice thing about pugs; they get excited over the little things in life. Forget moonwalks or presidential elec-tions. My coming home is a major event in Pugsley's doggie life. His feet were tapping the polished wood floor like tiny castanets, and Mom scooped him up for a giant hug while I checked for phone messages. Nick had called a couple of times; nothing urgent.

"I'm making dinner tonight," Lark called from the kitchen. "Veggie pot pie, but it won't be ready for half an hour. Is that okay?"

"That's perfect. I need to make a quick trip next door to the Seabreeze."

Lark nodded, and Mom didn't hear me. A Latino radio station was pounding out the pulsating rhythms of Juan Carlos Caceres and Mom was teaching Pugsley to tango. She was executing a progressive side step, holding Pugsley firmly in her arms while he looked up at her adoringly and tried to lick her chin. If they ever decide to have a canine version of *Dancing with the Stars*, Pugsley could be a contender. He might not have the dance steps, but he has the style and charisma. *Ole.*

Chapter 13

I zipped through an opening in the hedge of fragrant gardenia bushes that separates our condo building from the Seabreeze. Ted Rollins, the owner and general manager, was serving mimosas on the front porch and chatting with the guests. I figured this was the perfect time to mingle and pick up some information from the set.

The wide-planked porch is definitely one of the major draws of Ted's bed and breakfast. With wicker gliders and cushy rocking chairs, it's the perfect place to kick back and relax during the complimentary cocktail hour.

The porch is a showplace—a tribute to Ted's attention to detail and his design skills. Baskets of lush ferns hang from the rafters and porcelain pots of primrose are artfully arranged around the chairs. The smell of night-blooming jasmine danced in the air along with the muted sounds of a Vivaldi concerto.

"Maggie!" Ted rushed forward to greet me. He gave me a brotherly hug and gestured to the drinks and snacks he'd laid out on a glass-topped table. "What can I get you? A mimosa? White wine?"

"White wine would be nice," I said. The porch was crowded with guests, and I recognized quite a few members of the *Death Watch* cast and crew. "Looks like a full house tonight."

With its pale lemon exterior and glossy white ginger-
bread trim, the big Victorian looks more like a private house
than a B and B. Only a discreet, hand-painted sign made from
white birch, announces guests are welcome. When the inn is
full, Ted simply brings the sign inside. I noticed the sign
was conspicuously absent tonight.

"It's been like this ever since the film company came
to town," he said, pouring me a hefty glass of Chardonnay.
"They're a great group, though, very enthusiastic. I've never
had movie folks as guests before; it's been quite an experience."

The truth is, Ted likes everybody. If he was hosting a serial killer convention, he'd probably find something good to
say about each one of them. Ted guided me over to the railing, away from the chatter.

"How are you, Maggie? This must be a difficult time for
you. A murder on the set; it's hard to believe." He shook his
head, his expression troubled. "And I understand that you were
there when it happened." Ted reached out and gave my upper
arm a little squeeze. "I've been worried about you. This is a
lot for you to deal with." His brown eyes were full of puppy-
dog devotion and he let his hand trail lightly down my arm.

His touch was warm and comforting, and for one crazy
moment, I felt like laying my head on his strong shoulder
for a quick cuddle, and then I came to my senses. It would
only give him false hope. I pulled back and wrapped my hands
around the stem of the wineglass.

The thing you have to understand about Ted is that he's smart,
handsome, successful, kind-hearted, and single. He's probably Cypress Grove's most eligible bachelor, and everyone—
including my mother—can't understand why I won't go out
with him. Lola always claims that someday she's going to
"pull a Demi Moore" and date him herself. I think she's only
half kidding.

Ted is everything I should be looking for in a guy, except there's a complete lack of chemistry between us. Like the song says, it's just one of those things. He doesn't make my heart go pitter-patter like a certain detective does, and I don't have X-rated fantasies about him.

Here's how I would sum it up: hugging Ted always gives me a warm, cozy feeling inside.

But then so does hugging Pugsley.

I took a sip of chilled Chardonnay; it was dry and delicious. "Yes, I saw the whole thing; it was awful. In fact, I can't get the picture out of my mind." My skin prickled when I thought of Adriana lying on the sand with a sea of dark red blood pouring out of her chest.

"I can't believe they're going to keep on filming," Ted said. "But from what I hear"—he gestured to the gaggle of guests attacking the cheese puffs—"the show must go on."

"I always wondered who came up with that slogan—" I began.

"A producer, of course! Who else?" Sandra Michaels suddenly appeared beside me, accompanied by an older actor who looked vaguely familiar. She was her usual bubbly self, but I sensed a nervous edge to her banter. She swallowed half her mimosa in one gulp. "That's what they always say, isn't it, Sidney? Actors don't have personal lives, do they? We're just paid to get up there and play our characters, no matter what. It's all about the show, all about the profits."

His brows rose a fraction and he managed a small laugh. "That may be true. But all of us love the business too much to leave it, don't we darling? If we weren't actors, what in the world would we be doing?" He smiled at me and extended his hand. "Sidney Carter. I don't think we've met."

"Maggie Walsh." I paused, taking a closer look at him. Finely chiseled features, tall with a good build, thick hair that was gray at the temples. "Your name is familiar, but I can't seem to—"

"Don't worry, no one recognizes me." He flashed a wry grin. "I'm not a star. I've always been a second-string actor; you know, the ones who turn up in minor roles in loads of films. The third male lead, the guy you never remember."

"Sidney, don't talk about yourself that way! Sidney is an amazing actor," Sandra said firmly, her cheeks high with color. "He has the best training of anyone I know, and he should be starring in films, not playing character roles." Her voice had ratcheted up a notch or two and I wondered how many mimosas she'd had. "It's just the nature of this crappy business. It grinds you up and spits you out, and we have no control over our careers—"

Sidney laid a restraining hand on her arm, his smile never wavering. "Now Sandra, we don't want to ruin the magic, do we? Civilians like to think that we have the best jobs in the world." I knew from Mom that movie and theater people always referred to the rest of the population as "civilians," meaning anyone who wasn't in show business. He turned to me. "I hear you're working as a consultant on the set. I'm afraid things are at a standstill at the moment, though."

"Yes, I wanted to ask you about that," I said quickly. "Is there any news about when Hank will resume filming?"

Sidney swirled his mimosa around and stared glumly into his glass. "I suppose whenever a suitable period of mourning for Adriana has passed," he said sardonically. He gave a humorless little laugh.

"A period of mourning for Adriana? That would only take a New York minute," Sandra piped up. Sidney shot her a warning look and she flushed. "Sorry, I shouldn't have said that. It's just that all of us are used to working and this enforced . . . vacation . . . is getting on our nerves. Not that this isn't a lovely place," she said quickly to Ted, who was hovering nearby. She glanced out at the expanse of manicured lawn, graceful palms, and colorful bougainvillea. The palms were swaying gracefully in the night air, as if they were lulling themselves to sleep. "Under different circumstances, I think I could really enjoy Cypress Grove."

"It's a charming town," Sidney offered. I had the feeling he was saying it just to be polite. He took a swig of wine, his brows knitted in concentration. "I'm afraid our nerves are a bit frazzled tonight."

"Yes, that's it!" Sandra said. "We're all so worried about the movie and what's going to happen to our careers. You understand, don't you?" she asked Ted, who had moved in closer.

"Of course." He smiled, ever the polite host. "You must feel like you're in limbo. The filming is at a standstill, yet you're stuck here in our little town. It's enough to stress anyone out. And of course, the terrible tragedy with Adriana." He noticed Sandra and Sidney both were holding empty glasses and gently took them out of their hands. "Let me get everyone another round. Things will seem much brighter, I promise you."

"Is he for real?" Sandra asked when he'd hurried away. "He's so damn nice and he's always smiling. Give him a hat and a cane and he could be Jiminy Cricket."

My eyebrows shot up. Is that how Ted came across to people—as an irritating chucklehead? Couldn't they see he was a just a genuinely friendly guy? "Ted's for real," I assured her. "He's just one of these cheerful people. He loves what he does and he enjoys making people happy."

"Then he's the polar opposite of Adriana," Sandra muttered. "She lived to make people *unhappy*. I think she thrived on it."

"Let's not speak ill of the dead," Sidney said quickly. There was a long beat of silence and Sidney was the first to rally with a change of topic. "So, what is your area of expertise, Maggie? Forensics?"

I nodded. "Yes, I did a lot of forensic work back in Manhattan. So when Hank invited me to the set to look over the script and do some consulting, I thought it might be fun. Usually it's my mom who's on the movie set. You probably know she's playing a small role in *Death Watch*."

"Oh yes, Lola Walsh. Of course. I met her the other day; charming lady."

I listened to Sidney talking about his early days in the business and suddenly something clicked. "Yes, of course I remember you!" I said. "You did some work on *Dynasty* and *Falcon Crest*. And you starred in some thrillers, some very edgy, noir stuff; you were terrific."

"Sidney was going to be the new James Bond," Sandra said. She patted his arm, her blue eyes clouding a little. "But it didn't work out the way it was supposed to," she finished, with a razor sharp edge in her voice. "It wasn't fair; it really wasn't."

"Fair"? I wondered what she was driving at, unless she was still on a rant about the vagaries of show business.

"Sometimes fate intervenes in your life," Sidney said lightly. "Things were going wonderfully for me for a while and a lot of terrific parts were coming my way. Everyone was sending me scripts; I could pick and choose the parts I wanted to play."

"They called him Hollywood's Golden Boy," Sandra interjected. "The next James Dean."

"Yes, well," Sidney murmured, "like they say, that was then and this is now." I must have looked surprised because he went on. "I guess some things just weren't meant to be." He rubbed his face with his hand as if he was trying to wake himself up from a bad dream. "Well, those days are over; no sense in dwelling on it. I'm lucky to be a working actor; I don't need to be a star."

Ted appeared with refills for everyone, and after saying my good-byes, I darted back through the hedge, like Alice.

A ruined career, a lifetime of playing second-string parts? My heart was beginning to jump and my gut feeling told me there was more to the story than Sidney and Sandra were letting on.

I knew I had to find out more. It was time to compare notes with Nick.

"Sidney Carter?" Nick's voice raced over the line. "That was a big Hollywood scandal, or I should say, a big Hollywood cover-up. It was years ago, before my time, but I can check it out for you in a sec." He paused. "How is this relevant to the murder?"

"I don't know yet." I quickly filled him in on the conversation at the Seabreeze. I was still puzzled over how furious Sandra had been but I couldn't make sense of any of it. As Rafe always says, "usually when people are pissed off, they're telling the truth." But what was the truth about Sidney Carter and how did it fit into the puzzle?

Sometimes I think psychology is like detective work; both involve puzzles and require endless patience. When I was seeing patients back in my practice back in New York, I'd listen to their stories every week and try to make sense of what they were telling me. I had to figure out how all their hopes and dreams, their fantasies and disappointments fit into the big picture. What was relevant and what wasn't? Which facts should I concentrate on, and which should I brush aside?

I finally decided that everything is relevant. Failed marriages, career problems, financial woes; everything is connected, even though the patients never realize it at the first session. The "presenting problem" is often not the real issue;

usually it's just the tip of the iceberg. It might take weeks or even months to get to the real issue, as the clock ticks by in fifty-minute hours.

It all feels like a giant jigsaw puzzle, waiting to be solved. Of course, some patients "fail to disclose" as they say in shrink-speak, and they decide to keep some of the pieces tucked away safely in their pocket. That makes the puzzle a million times harder to solve.

I have the feeling murderers do the same thing.

I kept the phone clamped to my ear as Nick tapped away. I'd just finished dinner and was sprawled on my bed, going over my notes for the next day's show. Pugsley gave a soft grunt in his sleep—he was stretched flat out on my new Laura Ashley bedspread, without a care in the world. I'd like to believe in reincarnation, because I'd be happy to come back to earth as a beloved pug.

"Okay, here's the scoop on Sidney Carter," Nick said finally, breaking into my thoughts. "His career took a nosedive because of an AIDS rumor. An AIDS rumor that Adriana started."

"That's awful. Why would she do something like that?"

"Who knows? The sad thing is, it wasn't even true. He didn't have AIDS. He *never* had AIDS. But once the word got out there, his career bombed."

"You're saying people thought he had AIDS and no one hired him?"

"That's exactly what I'm saying." Nick's voice was soft but the undertone was deadly. "This was the eighties, after all. Things were different back then and the disease was poorly understood. Do you remember when Burt Reynolds lost weight because of a TMJ problem, and everyone thought he had AIDS? Loni Anderson talks about it in her autobiography. She said her own hairdresser banned her from his Beverly Hills salon— he thought her presence there might upset the customers.

They might think that if she was married to someone with AIDS, she could be contagious herself."

"Unbelievable."

"Yes, but that's the way things were back then. It looks like Carter's last decent role was in a thriller, *Call at Midnight*. Everything after that is character roles, small parts, nothing memorable. No doubt about it. He never scored another big part."

"It's still hard to believe his career ended up in the toilet because of a rumor." I carefully edged some papers out from under Pugsley, who had started to snore, face twitching, paws racing like a greyhound's.

"Those were crazy times, Maggie," Nick said. "Even the hint of AIDS was the kiss of death for a film career. I can make a few calls tonight and find out more details. AP has cut back on their stringers, but I still have a few friends who cover entertainment on the West Coast. Want to do lunch tomorrow? Meet you at Gino's to compare notes?"

"Sure, sounds good. Gino's at twelve."

I flipped the phone shut and thought for a moment. So Sidney Carter's career was killed by a false rumor. But why didn't anyone refute it? Was it the sort of thing that once it's out there, the damage is done?

Chapter 14

"An early day on the set, sweetie. Are you up for it?"

It was barely six thirty, but Mom was already bustling around the kitchen, and the delicious smell of french vanilla coffee was wafting through the air. Lark was frying some veggie sausage and my stomach gave a happy gurgle when I spotted the Belgian-waffle maker sitting on the counter. Lark loves to cook and one of her recent discoveries is waffles made out of heart-healthy almond meal, topped with a home-made fresh blueberry sauce. Delish.

My idea of breakfast is a strawberry Pop-Tart along with a few cups of java, but Lark is determined to "educate my palate," as she calls it. I have to admit, she's winning. Her waffles are world-class, and if she ever tires of her paralegal studies, she could be a gourmet chef.

"I think with three cups of coffee, I'll be ready to go," I promised. "Just pour on those calories and caffeine." Lark placed a steaming plate of waffles and veggie sausage links in front of me along with a side dish of sliced mango and kiwi.

"I want you to eat every bite," she said, wagging her finger at me in mock reproach. "You need more than coffee,

Maggie. Remember, breakfast is the most important meal of the day."

"Yeah, and my body is my temple," I kidded right back.

"Speaking of temples," Mom cut in, "do you think this Goddess look is too mature for me?" She was holding up a gauzy pale green dress with flowing lines and thin ribbons crisscrossing the bodice. It was floaty and diaphanous, with a Grecian flair. She'd pulled it out of a Nordstrom's bag, and I wondered if she'd picked it up at Sawgrass Mills.

"Wow, Lola; that's fantastic. Is it new?" Lark stepped back from the counter and nearly tripped over Pugsley, who'd taken up a strategic spot in the middle of the kitchen floor, practicing his "Oliver Twist" routine. His roly-poly body quivering with excitement, Pugsley fixed Lark with an unwavering doggie stare. His eyes were the size of Ping-Pong balls, and his tongue was lolling out of his mouth in a trademark pug grin. *Feed me!* his body language screamed.

With Pugsley, begging for food has reached the level of performance art. It's street theater, all the way.

All he has to do is flash that bug-eyed pug stare and we cave, showering him with all sorts of delicious treats. Today was no different. Lark reached down and popped a veggie sausage link into his mouth. It was like putting a quarter into a vending machine. It disappeared instantly.

"It's not my dress," Lola said, sniffing slightly. "It's from Wardrobe but I'm not even sure it suits me. They want me to wear it in the party scene; you know, scene twenty-three?"

"Scene twenty-three? So filming has started up again?" I asked around a mouthful of Belgian waffles.

"Fingers crossed," Mom said. "Nothing is definite but the AD called late last night and said things might get rolling again this morning."

"But how did you get the dress?" Lark asked.

"Oh, Rhonda was a sweetie and let me take the dress home

a couple of days ago so I could try it on with heels and jewelry. I have to bring it back this morning and give her the verdict."

"Why didn't you just try it on for Rhonda while you were on the set yesterday? Wouldn't that have been easier?" I took my first sip of french vanilla coffee. *Perfecto*. My neurotransmitters revved into high gear, and my synapses connected. It takes caffeine for me to have a functioning brain.

"I just hate trying things on in Wardrobe you know? No privacy. I feel like I'm in the dressing room at Loehmann's! All those mirrors, the unflattering lights, people gawking at each other." She blew out an unhappy sigh and held the dress up to her chest, biting her lower lip.

I wondered if Mom felt intimidated by all the size zeros and double zeros in the Wardrobe trailer. Drop-dead gorgeous twenty-year-olds with fake tans and perfect Barbie doll bodies, all squealing happily as they wriggled into barely-there designer clothes.

True confession time: I wouldn't like to get undressed in front of them, either.

"Well, I think it's lovely and I bet it looks terrific on you." Lark was tactful, as always.

"I don't know; I think it was intended for someone, you know, older." Lola paused. "It might be a little too mother-of-the-bride, you know? Something about the pastel color and those flowing lines. I don't want to look like Queen Elizabeth inspecting the Palace Guard."

Lark and I locked eyes over Mom, who was decked out in a denim miniskirt, pink crop top, and chandelier earrings. "Mom," I said firmly, "no one would ever mistake you for a matronly type. Or for the queen, or even the mother-of-the-bride. Trust me on this one," I added as Lark smothered a giggle. "I like the dress; tell Rhonda you'll wear it."

"You're sure?"

"I'm sure."

She never suspected that I had my fingers crossed behind my back.

"Oh, Maggie, I'm so glad you're here early," Maisie said an hour later. "We need to talk." Mom and I had just arrived on the *Death Watch* set and checked the call sheet. Apparently the cameras were rolling again, because Mom was scheduled for hair and makeup followed by the party scene filming at 11:00 a.m. sharp.

She had only a few lines in that scene, but I knew that Mom would manage to steal the show. Whenever Mom's in a group shot, she figures out a way to stand out from the other actors. She's the one laughing a little too gaily, flipping her blond hair over her shoulder with abandon, or winking flirtatiously across the table. It's become a running gag with the cast and crew. They call it "The Lola Walsh Effect." Just keep the camera trained on Lola, because that's where the viewers are going to be looking, anyway.

"Toodles, sweetie." She grabbed a coffee and gave me a hurried wave before dashing across the grass toward the makeup tent. The Grecian-style dress was tucked into a garment bag under her arm, and I wondered what the final decision would be.

Maisie pulled me to the side, away from the cast members who were making a stampede for the craft services table. The big shiny catering trucks had just rolled in and the workers were unloading hot breakfasts in white Styrofoam containers along with gallons of coffee and boxed doughnuts.

"Is everything okay?" I wondered if the Guitar Heroes had objected to my script changes and was bracing myself for some possible fallout. Mom had warned me that scriptwriters are notoriously temperamental and that "the boys" wouldn't appreciate my tampering with their dialogue in the courtroom scene. I reminded myself that Hank, as the director, had the final say-so in the matter, and after all, he was paying for my expertise.

"Are you kidding? Everything's more than okay," she said, breaking into a wide smile. "Maggie, I've gotta tell you, you did a fantastic job on those revisions; you really nailed it. Hank was so pleased." Maisie was wearing her long red hair in two braids today. If I wore my hair that way, I'd look like Pippi Longstocking, but Maisie, in her black denim jeans and Boho top from Miu Miu looked very hip, very L.A.

"Really?" I felt a little frisson of relief go through me. "I'm glad he liked it. I didn't want to step on any toes"—I lowered my voice—"but there were a few things that needed to be smoothed out."

Maisie's headset made a squawking noise and she yanked it off and looped it around her neck. "Just between us, Hank isn't thrilled with the scriptwriters. Sometimes I can't believe Beavis and Butthead have actually won five Emmys between them. It just shows there's no justice in this world. They're no Einsteins; believe me. Just look at them!"

She gave a little snort and nodded toward the scriptwriters, who were playing basketball outside the production office. Someone had duct-taped a cardboard box to the outside of the trailer to make an improvised hoop and they'd managed to dredge up a battered basketball. They glanced over, gave me a blank stare, and then went back to the game.

"Are they annoyed with me?"

She grinned. "Maybe a little. But don't worry about it. Hank's the one paying your salary and he's thrilled with you. That's all that matters."

She was right. The director called the shots. Everything else was smoke and mirrors. "So what's on for today?"

Maisie consulted her clipboard as her headset squawked again. "We're shooting some exteriors and the party scene. If you want, you can just go over some dialogue with Sandra and talk to her about her character, or you can keep working on the script on your own. I know Hank's paying you by the day, so you don't have to report to anyone. Just do whatever it takes to get the job done; that's all he cares about."

"That's good to know." This was turning into a very sweet gig, as Nick would say. Maybe with *Death Watch* on my resume, I could pick up some more movie work, assuming of course that *Death Watch* did reasonably well at the box office. If it tanked in a really spectacular way (think *Waterworld*), then it would be best left off my resume and never mentioned again.

The headset squawked again. This time she glanced at her watch and blew out a little sigh. I had the feeling Maisie was always running late, that she was one of those chronically overscheduled people whose life was spinning out of control. *One Xanax away from a nervous breakdown*, I thought idly. "All the actors are at your disposal and you can go wherever you want on the set," she said in a rush. "You can watch the filming, hang out with the actors, do whatever you want."

I raised my eyebrows. "It sounds great. I guess I'd like to start by spending some time with Sandra, if I could."

"Sure, no problem. Help yourself to some coffee and doughnuts and I'll send her right over. She said she really learned a lot from talking with you the other day. She likes you."

One of the Guitar Heroes glanced over again and gave me the evil eye. I stared right back and he gave me a death glare and broke eye contact. If he thought he was going to intimidate me with his frat boy antics, he had "another think coming," as Vera Mae would say. I've gone one-on-one with murderers, rapists, and convicted felons in my forensic work. It's going to take more than a couple of twenty-something surfer-dudes in baseball caps to give me the heebie-jeebies.

I smiled at Maisie. "It's always good to have friends. You never know when you might need them."

Sandra showed up a few minutes later, talking animatedly to one of the grips. He was wearing black denim jeans and a T-shirt from Copper Canyon, a resort area south of the California border. "I'm telling you, you've gotta go back to Mexico," she was saying. "How long were you there? If you were working the whole time, you probably didn't get a chance to really look around."

He hoisted a length of cable from one shoulder to the other before nodding. "We only shot in Chihuahua for one night, and they put us up in some tourist rattrap. It had fake stucco walls and a plastic fountain, can you believe it?"

"Ohmigod, it sounds awful!" Sandra's squeal could have peeled paint off the walls.

"It was. It looked just like the Mexican Village set at Universal studios."

Sandra gave him a knowing look. "Trojan Productions, right? That's the trouble with these little indie outfits. They put you up in crappy places and they work you like a dog. Anything to save a buck, you know."

She suddenly spotted me and her features morphed into a grin. Instant personality change. It was like someone had pushed a button or she'd just swallowed a handful of mood stabilizers. "Although I really like the Seabreeze; that was a cool party last night, wasn't it?" She was talking a little too loudly, smiling at him like her life depended on it.

I had the feeling the Little Miss Sunshine act was all for my benefit, and I tucked the information away in my memory bank. Like all performers, she has a strong desire to be liked. Why else would she go into a profession where the chance of success was so small, and the odds of rejection so great?

"That it was," the grip said, edging away. "Catch you at lunch, hon."

"So what are we doing today, Maggie?" Sandra asked, widening her blue eyes, giving me a broad smile. She was dressed casually but revealingly in tiny denim shorts and a low-cut halter top. I wondered if she was going overboard on the amount of skin she was showing and then decided she was entitled. After all, she'd lost all that weight through strenuous dieting and exercise and she was eager to show off her new bod. Who could blame her? She looked terrific.

"I thought we'd work on the script some more and go over some of your dialogue. If that's okay with you."

"Cool!" She perched on the top of a picnic table and let her long, tanned legs hang over the edge. She was wearing four-inch espadrilles that made her legs look incredibly long and lean. It was hard to remember that this Gisele Bündchen look-alike used to be the "formerly fat actress."

"You're a fan of Mexico? The Copper Canyon area?"

She narrowed her eyes, just for a microsecond, and then quickly recovered. "Oh, you mean the conversation I was just having with Howie? We both love to travel. He got stuck in some tourist hellhole down there shooting a movie and I was just telling him about some attractions in the area."

"Sounds like you know the area really well." I opened up my copy of the script and pretended to be absorbed in it. I could feel a slight change in Sandra's body language, an almost imperceptible tightening of her core muscles, as she folded her arms and crossed her legs. A protective gesture, a defensive mode? Certainly a classically "closed" position.

"You must have spent a lot of time there." I smiled at her. She looked at me and her face stalled. I sensed a little wave of tension rolling off her but I acted like I was clueless. Something was definitely up; my radar was pinging. She still hadn't said a word. "I'd like to go there sometime," I continued.

"I've never been south of Tijuana." I made sure my voice was deliberately casual, smoothing out my tone. This is a trick I learned early on, dealing with anxious clients at my psychology practice.

There's a saying in psychoanalytical circles: "If there are two people in a room and one is anxious, the other one better not be." Good advice for beginning therapists. If I kept my tone easy and conversational, they'd unconsciously mimic me and their own voices would slide down a notch or two.

Except with Sandra it didn't seem to be working; her whole body was vibrating with tension.

"Well, I'm no expert," she said a little too quickly. Her eyes landed hard on me and she sounded like she was still on high alert. "But I can jot down the names of a couple of hotels for you. I can think of a few nice places down there that don't cost an arm and a leg."

"In Copper Canyon?" I made a note on a piece of scrap paper and I swear I saw Sandra flinch.

"Not just Copper Canyon, the whole area," she hedged. She blinked, licked her lips, and swallowed hard. Sandra was really feeling the heat and I had no idea why. The tiny muscles around her mouth tensed, and her eyes clouded with some negative emotion. Fear? Shame? I wasn't sure.

It was a fleeting look, totally unconscious, but I caught it anyway. It's called a microexpression, a flash of emotion that reveals what an individual is really feeling. Microexpressions can appear on their own, or sometimes they show up right in the middle of a fake expression, but they're only there for a flash. It usually takes a trained eye—or someone with really good instincts—to pick up on them. "There's Monte Alban," she said quickly. "I would definitely recommend it."

"White Mountain?" I asked, calling on my limited Spanish.

"Yes, it's very pretty; amazing scenery. And there's Palenque in the northern Chiapas; it's a famous Mayan site. And of course, the Chihuahua al Pacifico Railway."

I couldn't figure out why Sandra seemed uncomfortable when I'd asked her about Copper Canyon. Was it my imagination or was she trying to steer me away from the topic? And why did Copper Canyon sound so familiar to me? Was it a popular location for indie films? Had I read about it in *People* magazine? Or heard of it in a *Dateline* documentary? I made a mental note to ask Mom if she'd ever heard of it. The name was nibbling around the edges of my mind like a hungry squirrel and I found it hard to concentrate on anything else.

Nick, as usual, came through with the goods. A couple of hours later, I met him at Gino's for a quick lunch before heading to WYME. Gino's Trattoria is one of our favorite spots; it's a cute little place close to the station, just two blocks from the Cypress Grove Gazette building. Nick was waiting for me and had already grabbed one of the popular patio tables.

Gino's reminds me of that Billy Joel song about an Italian restaurant, with its red-and-white-checked tablecloths and photos of long-dead opera singers lining the walls. The new outdoor patio area is a winner, featuring a handful of cozy wrought-iron tables topped with striped umbrellas in the colors of the Italian flag: red, white, and green. But best of all, the food is terrific, the prices are reasonable, and the service is fast. No wonder it's a hit with the Cypress Grove business crowd.

Nick half stood up and I waved him back to his seat. He was wolfing down an antipasto tray probably designed for six people and he pushed it toward me when I sat down across from him. I raised my eyebrows at his offering. All that was left was a handful of black olives, half a marinated artichoke, and a few pieces of wilted lettuce.

"How's the movie biz?" he asked, just as a server, a cute blonde named Terri, plunked a frosty mug of draft beer in front of him. I tried not to look at it too longingly and ordered an iced tea before she darted away. The beer looked tempting but I had a show to do that afternoon.

"It's crazy making," I told him. "You know that expression, 'it's a nice place to visit but I wouldn't want to live there'? That's what a movie set is like. It's a lot of chaos followed by hours of downtime. Hurry-up-and-wait, they call it."

"Lola certainly loves it."

"She does. I was thinking about that today. She loves being on camera, loves being on the set—she practically absorbs the atmosphere through her pores. She always comes home energized, even after a fourteen- or fifteen-hour day. Maybe you have to be an actor to really get a buzz going. I have to tell you, being a script consultant just doesn't do it for me."

I filled him in about the Guitar Heroes and my work as a script doctor. "I still can't believe those yahoos got paid big bucks to write the script."

Nick's eyebrow twitched upward. "And that someone actually thought they did a good job."

"Exactly. Thank God Hank Watson has more sense."

Nick speared one of the remaining olives before he tried to catch Terri's eye as she zipped by with a pitcher of lime-colored margaritas. "I'll tell you my favorite quote about the movie business. Here's a hint; it's by William Goldman. You've heard of him, right?"

"Of course. Everyone's heard of William Goldman. He wrote the screenplays for *Butch Cassidy and the Sundance Kid* and *Marathon Man*. And he wrote *Adventures in the Screen Trade*. It's one of the best books I've ever read about the movie business."

Nick smiled. "And after decades in the business, what did he have to say?"

"He said, 'Nobody knows anything.' Mom uses that quote all the time. She loves it. It sums it up perfectly."

Sometimes Mom and I try to outdo each other, coming up with a list of the world's worst movies. To qualify for a "worst movie award," the movie has to have truly abominable acting, a weak script, bad casting, and schlock production values. You'd be surprised how many movies make the cut.

"You look at certain movies"—I shook my head helplessly—"and you wonder how they ever got made. You picture a bunch of studio execs sitting around in a Development meeting, saying, 'What a terrific idea! This will kill! Totally kill!' And then they find someone crazy enough to put up money for backing and they scramble to get A-list stars onboard, because after all, everyone knows you have to have a name star to carry a movie . . ."

"And sometimes even that doesn't help," Nick said.

I nodded. "And then you put together the bad script, the awful acting, and the cornball premise and everyone's surprised when the movie tanks." I scrunched my chair over a little. Gino's was filling up rapidly with the lunch crowd. One of the servers had dragged out another umbrella table and was struggling to set it up next to ours.

Nick gestured with his fork. "Case in point. Here's one of my choices for worst movie. See if you can top it." He locked eyes with me. *"The Waterboy."*

The Waterboy*! That god-awful Adam Sandler movie. This would be hard to beat, but I was going to give it my best shot.*

"Patch Adams."

Nick groaned. "I was going to use that as my first choice."

"But you didn't. So that means I'm winning."

"Not yet, you aren't."

Nick's eyes narrowed in thought. "How about *Battlefield*

Earth, which is a close tie with *Armageddon.* I'm giving you two for the price of one."

I thought about this for a moment. Nick was better at this than I'd thought. "*Glitter?*"

He shrugged. "The Mariah Carey epic? Yeah, that's got to be up there in the top ten. And how about *A Knight's Tale?* Do you remember the dry spaghetti shooting out of the jousting rods? The prop guy told everyone it would look really cool on film. It was supposed to look like wood splintering at the moment of impact. And of course, all it looked like was—"

"Dry spaghetti!" A beat. "I loved Keith Ledger, though."

"*Dirty Dancing?* Remember that line about putting Baby in the corner?"

"Yeah, but I loved Patrick Swayze." I always hate to pan a movie if I love the star.

"Maybe I just don't get girlie movies," Nick said finally. I figured this wasn't the time to tell him I'd worn out my DVD of *When Harry Met Sally* from playing it so many times.

I glanced at my watch. I needed to find out as much as I could about that mysterious Mexican retreat before heading back to the station. "So tell me everything you know about Copper Canyon." I fumbled in my purse for a notebook and pen.

"Planning a little Botox or a mini face-lift?" he teased. "I think you're a little young for it, but it never hurts to start early." He leaned across the table and patted me playfully under the chin. "Hmm, maybe a touch of tightening would help in the chin area. I think I see a bit of softening along the jawline."

"You do not!" I started to swat him with my menu and then stopped as his words sunk in. "Wait a minute—plastic surgery? I thought we were talking about a resort area in Mexico."

"Copper Canyon," he shot back with a grin. "They'll do the works. Anything you ask for, face-lifts, acid peels, and total body lifts. A certain star went there for implants, but not the usual kind. She wanted to have a derriere like Jennifer Lopez. They'll do anything you want there; they'd probably screw your head on backwards, if you paid enough."

"I hope you're kidding," I told him. "You mean Copper Canyon is—"

"The top cosmetic surgery center in Mexico." Terri drifted by again, and we ordered fast: chicken alfredo for him, spinach ravioli for me. "It's a mecca for the A-list types in Hollywood."

"How do you know these things?" I always am amazed at the breadth and depth of Nick's knowledge; his youthful face and boyish grin are deceiving. He may look like someone's kid brother, but behind those cool green eyes lies a first-rate mind, always on the lookout for the next big story.

"One of my pals with NBC did a piece on medical tourism last year. Mexico is one of the hottest places, with top docs, or so they say, and the price is right." He paused to spear a piece of marinated artichoke. "You haven't been living in a cave, so I suppose you've heard of all this?"

"I've heard they had some experimental treatments for serious diseases, and some new cancer treatments down in Mexico. And maybe some supplements. I think I heard about senior citizens going over the border to get cheaper meds." I scrunched up my face, trying to remember the details of an exposé I'd seen. "But I didn't hear anything about cosmetic surgery. Was there some scandal down there?"

"More than one. Quite a few. Mostly to do with phony meds being passed off as the real thing. The cosmetic surgery angle is something different."

"Tell me about it."

"It's huge. Supposedly they have world-class cosmetic

surgeons, operating in high-tech hospitals that look like spas. They do eye lifts, face-lifts, laser treatments, everything. And you can live it up during your recovery and pretend you're at Sandals. Five-star oceanfront resorts, along with twenty-four-hour nursing care. You can have mojitos and pedicures with your IV drips. At least that's what I've heard."

"Interesting." I thought about Sandra. She seemed to know a little too much about the place. Did she have some connection with a hospital or doctor down there? Maybe she'd bought some special supplements to induce weight loss and the whole I did-it-through-diet-and-exercise number was a scam?

"And of course there's bariatric surgery," he added. Nick's voice was casual, but I nearly dropped my pen.

"Bariatric surgery?" I suddenly had a mental flash. "You mean gastric bypass? Why would anyone go to Mexico? It's a big operation and we do that here. They do it all across the country at major medical centers and teaching hospitals." I shook my head, bewildered. "It has some pretty serious risk factors; it's nothing to fool around with."

"Yeah, but it's much cheaper to have it done in Mexico. It only costs seven grand or so down there. And they say they do the same techniques American doctors use; lap band, tummy tucks, and everything else you can think of."

"Wow," I said softly. "I guess I can see why some people would go there to save money. But it seems like they're taking a chance." It still sounded risky to me. Why would you want to economize on surgery?

"It's not only the bargain rates that are the big draw," Nick said. "It's the privacy. That's why they cater to celebs. You're not going to have stringers from the *National Enquirer* taking shots of you coming out of a surgery clinic if you're miles away from civilization. Think about it. If you were going to have a face-lift, would you rather have paparazzi stalking you at Cedars-Sinai in Los Angeles, or would you rather stay at a five-star hotel in Mexico and come back looking years younger? And with no one the wiser?"

"I see your point."

"So who's had a face-lift?" Nick asked.

I shook my head. "No one I can think of. Just trying to put the pieces together."

We split the bill and prepared to leave when Nick tapped me on the arm. "Hey, check out the guy in the linen suit and black shirt. Isn't that Frankie Domino?" He gestured to the mafioso type I'd seen on the set of *Death Watch* my very first day.

"Yes, I'm sure that's him." Frankie Domino had been sitting alone at a tiny table at the end of the patio and we'd never noticed him. There was an empty bottle of Heineken beer in front of him, and as we watched, he stood up, tossed a bill on the table, and exited Gino's.

"Interesting," Nick said, edging me forward. "Let's walk by that table. I want to see something. Just act natural, okay?"

"Act natural? What's with the cloak-and-dagger stuff?" I protested. "So the guy came in to have a beer on a hot day; no big deal, right? He has terrible taste in clothes, but that's not a crime."

"Just look straight ahead and keep walking," Nick ordered. As we passed the empty table, Nick looked down and gave a low whistle. "A Benjamin, just as I thought."

"A Benjamin?"

"Ben Franklin," Nick said. "He left a hundred-dollar tip."

"Wow." I was taken aback. "He must have gotten really good service." I glanced at the back of the mobster who was walking rapidly down Front Street. It suddenly dawned on me that I must be missing something. "Frankie Domino is a good tipper and this is significant—why?"

"Maggie, you should be able to figure this out." He did a small eye-roll, his mouth quirking in a smile. "He didn't wait for the check and he tosses a hundred-dollar bill on the table. That's what mobsters do. Classic wiseguy behavior. So my instincts about this guy were right."

So Frankie Domino was definitely with the mob, not exactly a news flash, since we'd already suspected as much. I wondered how this fit into the bigger picture. I wanted to ask Nick his thoughts but I glanced at my watch and my heart thumped in alarm.

No time to schmooze; I had a show to do.

Chapter 15

"What's the latest from the set, Maggie? Did you come across any big-name movie stars?" Vera Mae was poised at the control board, ready to open the lines for the afternoon show. I took a quick glance at the clock. Ten minutes to go.

"Nobody new, I'm afraid. At least the production is up and running again. Mom was in a party scene today. She just had a few lines, but she's over the moon."

"I can imagine. You know, I should have auditioned for one of those little parts, maybe an under-five or something. Is that what they call them?"

"Yes, it's an under-five if you have less than five lines. If you don't have any lines at all, you're an extra. Or sometimes they call you 'background.'"

"Background? Why's that?"

"Well, because the people with no lines are just . . . there. They don't really do anything; they're background, sort of like wallpaper. Not a very flattering term, is it? Lola did some work as an extra when she was starting out in the business. Those were tough days for her out in Hollywood; she had to take whatever she could, to make ends meet."

"I bet," Vera Mae said sympathetically. "She's so bright

and sparkly, I can't imagine her just standing there with nothing to say."

"It's a pretty thankless job, and sometimes she'd end up standing out in the rain and cold for hours on end. And for very little money. Things aren't much better now. You might make a hundred and twenty dollars a day if you're a member of SAG, but if it's an indie flick, they can pay you whatever they want. As little as twenty bucks a day, or sometimes nothing. I don't know what Hank's paying, but I don't think it's very much."

Vera Mae raised her eyebrows at me. "Who'd want to stand around in the rain and cold for twenty bucks a day?"

"You'd be surprised. They do it because they think it's their shot at the brass ring. A lot of actors think that if they start out as an extra, it will lead to something better. Maybe they have a certain look and they think they'll catch the eye of a producer or director who'll hire them for a speaking role. Or maybe they just want to get added to the client list with a casting director. They figure if they play nice and take roles as an extra, maybe they'll be sent out on auditions for speaking parts."

"That sounds like a lot of maybes. Does it ever work out that way?" Vera Mae looked dubious.

"Not usually," I admitted. "Brad Pitt was an extra in *Less Than Zero* and Jeff Goldblum was an extra in a party scene in *Annie Hall*, but those are the exceptions."

I thought about Tammilynne Cole, Hank Watson's main squeeze. I remember Sandra telling me Tammilynne had started out as an extra, and then Hank Watson had noticed her, and the rest, as they say, is fodder for the tabloids. But was she impatient with his promises of stardom? Did she wonder if she'd ever make it to the big leagues? Maybe she thought Hank was just stringing her along and that she was on her way to being replaced by yet another Hollywood wannabe.

After all, Tinseltown is full of aspiring actresses, and Hank Watson could have had his pick. He may not have been an A-list director, but he still could deliver the goods and quite a few producers were willing to invest with him.

Could Tammilynne possibly have killed Adriana, figuring it was her one shot—literally—at fame? She wasn't really suited for Adriana's role, but did that matter? The Guitar Heroes had juggled the plot and rewritten the script for a much younger woman. If you ignored that Tammilynne had no acting training and no movie credits, she was a shoo-in for the starring role.

I decided to rein in my scattered thoughts and concentrate on the show. One look at the guest folder and my spirits sank like a stone. "We're having Dr. Natasha Grayson on the show again?" I wailed. "We just had her on last month. What's going on, Vera Mae?"

"I know we did, sugar, but Lurleen Higgins from the Cypress Horticultural Society had to cancel at the last minute. It was the best I could do." She flashed an apologetic smile. "And you weren't available, you know, so I had to fill the slot any way I could. I tried to call you on your cell, but you must have had it turned off."

"Oh, you're right! My bad." After I'd worked with Sandra on her lines, I'd watched a little of the filming, and the AD had ordered everyone to turn off their cell phones. Like an idiot, I must have forgotten to turn mine back on. "Don't worry about it, I brought this on myself. Maybe I can make her sound interesting."

"And maybe pigs will fly," Vera Mae said helpfully.

Chapter 16

Dr. Grayson was a major buzz-kill.

Petite, with steel gray hair swept back off her face and a slightly feral smile, she bore an uncanny resemblance to a rat terrier. She always toted a teddy bear around with her, a sort of signature totem, to prove she was in touch with her "inner child."

"I figured you already know a lot about her, sweetie, so you should have plenty to talk about. It's not like you have to read up on her or do any research." Vera Mae glanced at the clock. "Anyway, there's no time for that. We go live in five minutes."

I nodded, shuffling through Dr. Grayson's bio, even though I knew it by heart. A doctorate in clinical psychology from an Ivy League university, followed by a couple of decades in academia writing dusty research articles for obscure publications.

Lately, she'd forged a new career for herself, giving seminars for mental health professionals all across the country. It was hard to imagine her as a mesmerizing public speaker, but maybe it didn't matter. Maybe her credentials were enough. And maybe her audiences—all clinical psychologists—had low expectations.

After all, she didn't have to be Chelsea Handler to do a six-hour PowerPoint presentation on treatment for borderline personality disorder. I've sat through enough psychology presentations myself to know that most of them are so dull they give me "butt freeze" (as Vera Mae says) after the first thirty minutes.

I tried to think of a clever hook for today's show. I knew Dr. Grayson was into dream therapy and maybe I could encourage her to talk about that. Freud always insisted that dreams were significant; he called them "the royal road to the unconscious."

He believed that all dream material should be analyzed because it opens a window into what the client is really thinking and feeling. He thought dreams represent what we fear and what we strongly desire, although sometimes the message is couched symbolically.

A good therapist should be able to tease out the psychodynamic underpinnings in dreams. At least that's Sigmund's take on it all.

I have to confess, I don't really share his enthusiasm. Whenever my clients would start to tell me about their dreams, I'd practically nod off—that's how boring they were.

The patients had a different take on them. They loved to talk about their dreams and found them endlessly fascinating. They wanted me to analyze them and they seemed disappointed if I couldn't find some hidden significance.

I scribbled a few lines on some sticky notes and slapped them on the control board at eye level. They could serve as a sort of cheat sheet during my introduction, in case my brain stalled.

Dream Analysis. What do our dreams really tell us? I decided to open with that line. Not bad. Maybe the board would light up with calls, after all. Dr. Grayson would be here in another ten seconds, and I had time for just one more quick question.

"Vera Mae, how did we do in the ratings the last time she was here? Do you happen to remember?"

"Oh I remember all right. Did you see the movie *Titanic*?" Vera Mae gave an evil grin.

"Yes, of course—"

"And Jack? Do you recall what happened to him? Remember how he was clinging to a piece of driftwood in the ocean?"

"Yeah, I know. He was holding on by his fingernails and then he slipped underwater and sank like a stone."

"Need I say more?" Vera Mae slapped on her headphones, just as Irina ushered Dr. Grayson into the studio. "Do you get it, sugar? Sank. Like. A. Stone."

Oh God. "Yes, I get it, Vera Mae. I get it. Really nice analogy. Thanks."

Okay. I was the captain of the *Titanic* and we were headed straight for a giant iceberg. You don't need to be a three-hundred-dollar-an-hour shrink to figure out how this scenario was going to play itself out.

I whizzed through Dr. Grayson's introduction and she gave me a tight nod of acknowledgment, baring tiny, pointed teeth. She certainly wouldn't win any awards for charm, I decided, because she made zero effort to be friendly or even cordial.

I checked her out as she perched on the edge of her chair, clutching her teddy bear (who was stylishly dressed in a little vest and shorts outfit from Ralph Lauren). Her hair was cut in a severe style, almost butch. A little Rachel Maddow–y, but I'm sure it wasn't deliberate. She was wearing a boxy navy blue suit, a little too heavy for the south Florida weather, with a white shell underneath.

No jewelry, no makeup. Not even lip gloss.

I thought of Wanda, owner of Wanda's House of Beauty, who once said on the show, "When I see a woman with gray hair and no makeup, Dr. Maggie, I see a woman who's just plum given up!"

I decided not to share this insight with Dr. Grayson.

I gave the standard introduction, sliding over the boring parts in Dr. Grayson's bio (practically the whole thing) and read my opening lines right off my sticky notes. Then Vera Mae opened the phone lines, and to my amazement, things were buzzing. Apparently Cypress Grove was more into dreams than I'd realized.

"We've got Lucy from Pompano on line three, Dr. Maggie," Vera Mae said.

"Welcome, Lucy. Do you have a question for our guest?"

"I sure do." A molasses voice trickled through the line. "Maybe you can tell me what it means when a black crow smashes into your windshield?"

"A black crow? That's very interesting," Dr. Grayson said. "I think first we have to address the symbolic significance associated with the color black." She edged forward, her eyes lighting up. I almost warned her not to get too close to the mike, or there would be that awful popping sound, but I didn't want to interrupt her train of thought.

"I'm not following you about the color black." Lucy sounded a trifle impatient, and I thought I heard traffic sounds in the background.

"Well, I think we have to agree that throughout history, black has connoted evil, dangerous spirits, or something sinister. Like the Black Death, which of course was the Plague. And of course, it makes you think of funerals. What do you wear to a funeral? Red? Yellow? Of course not! You wear black. Always black."

Dr. Grayson chuckled at her own cleverness. Rosie O'Donnell, watch your back. Natasha Grayson's in town!

I glanced at Vera Mae, who rolled her eyes with one finger on the mute button. She saw my look and reached for a marker pen. Uh-oh. It was time for another one of Vera Mae's famous signs.

"But this was a crow. I think they only come in black."

"Oh, but a crow is never just a crow, is it?" Dr. Grayson threw her head back and gave a tinny little laugh. There was something odd about her, something a little off-kilter. Funny, I hadn't noticed it the first time she'd come on the show. But now that I was taking a closer peek, she had the look of a glassy-eyed zealot, someone who'd be the first in line to drink poisoned Kool-Aid with Jim Jones down in Guyana.

"I beg to disagree," I cut in. "You know what Freud said: sometimes a cigar is just a cigar."

Her smile instantly faded. "You're wrong. I'm sure Freud would agree that a dead crow is a symbol of some underlying psychic problem."

"Really?" I kept my voice deliberately neutral. No sense in antagonizing the guest. Not yet, anyway.

"Yes, really." She gave me a hard look. "He'd say that there's a certain element of danger or negativity present, both from the color black and, of course, from the fact that the bird was smashed against the windshield." She waited to let this sink in. "Tell me, Lucy, are you going through a difficult time right now? Any personal problems in your life you'd like to discuss?"

"Personal problems? No, nothing like that." A pause. Another second and it would be the dreaded dead air.

I was just about to jump in but Dr. Grayson beat me to it. "Are you sure?" she prodded. "No marital problems, financial woes, work-related disputes?"

"No, nothing." Another pause. "So what do you think it means?"

"I think your dream means that you are probably in an emotionally fragile state—"

"My dream? What are you talking about?"

"Your dream, my dear," Dr. Grayson said smoothly. "Your dream about the dead crow."

"My *dream*? This isn't a dream. I'm driving down 95 South from Boca and a dang crow just smashed into my windshield. I called up to see if I was going to have bad luck all day long. Isn't this the show on superstitions and bad luck?"

"Oh honey, you've got the wrong station," Vera Mae piped up. "You're probably looking for that show over on WXVW," she added helpfully. "They have that psychic lady on today; I bet that's what you want. Her name is Sylvia Trent and she's into all that good luck—bad luck stuff."

"Yeah, Sylvia Trent! That's who I was thinking of."

"It's a bunch of hooey as far as I'm concerned, but she's real popular with some people. Get on over to twelve ten on the dial and you can hear her, sugar."

"I will, thanks! I want to find out if a dead crow means the same thing as breaking a mirror. Or walking under a ladder."

Dr. Grayson suddenly sputtered to life. "Really, these superstitions are ridiculous and not the least bit scientific. Can we please get back to the subject at hand?" She was perched on the edge of her chair, her face flushed bright pink, her voice quavering, her beady little eyes dilated in anger.

"Let's take another call," Vera Mae piped up. "How about Nadine from Briny Breezes? You're on the air with Dr. Maggie, Nadine."

"I'd like to tell your guest about my dream," Nadine began in a sultry voice. "I have this recurring dream about Hugh Jackman and Russell Crowe. The details are sort of fuzzy, though."

"I'd like to hear more," Dr. Grayson said.

"Well, here's the problem. Every time I start to think about it, it slips away. One minute it's real clear, just like watching a movie, and then the next minute, it's clouded over and foggy."

"Here is what I would recommend." Dr. Grayson lowered her voice to a hypnotic whisper. "I want you to sit very still. Now close your eyes and picture Russell Crowe and Hugh Jackman. All three of you are together in the same picture. Just like watching a movie. Everything is clear; nothing is fuzzy. The whole scene will come into focus, if you concentrate."

A pause. I heard Nadine give a breathy little sigh.

"Can you see the picture clearly?"

A long pause. "I'm doing my best. Uh, yeah, okay, I think I can see them. They're coming right into focus, just like you said."

"Stay with the image, Nadine," Dr. Grayson said. "Get right back into the picture. You're with Russell Crowe and Hugh Jackman, and you're inside. I wonder where you are?"

"It's somewhere very cold; I can feel goose bumps on my arm. It's so cold, I'm shaking a little. I have chills running up and down my spine. I may never be warm again."

"Heck, if I was out with Hugh Jackman and Russell Crowe, I'd be shaking, too," Vera Mae chortled. "That Russell Crowe is something else. Those eyes and that sexy accent. He can put his shoes under my bed anytime." I shot her a dark look and she clamped her mouth shut.

"Nadine, the fact that you have chills and a feeling that your temperature is dropping is significant. It could be from tension or excitement." Dr. Grayson leaned into the mike. "Sometimes the autonomic nervous system takes over as a form of repression."

Ouch. She was too close to the mike. The "p" sound in

"repression" bounced through the studio like someone had tossed a handful of marbles against the walls.

"Repression? What's that?" Vera Mae looked baffled, one hand on her hip.

Dr. Grayson thinned her lips and bared her teeth, reverting to rat-terrier mode. "Repression is a common defense mechanism. There are several possibilities. Perhaps Nadine doesn't want to let certain images into her conscious mind, so she is withholding them, repressing them. All on an unconscious level, of course."

"Interesting," I said. Not the world's most intelligent remark, but I couldn't think of anything else to say. I was distracted by Vera Mae, who was holding up a sign. She'd angled it toward me, so my guest wouldn't see it.

PHUDNICK. I bit my cheek to keep from laughing. Phudnick is Vera Mae's name for a really stupid person who is well educated. A nudnick with a PhD is called a Phudnick.

In other words, the esteemed Dr. Grayson was a classic Phudnick.

"Yeah, and the picture's getting real clear. It's very cold, so cold I can almost see my breath. And there's a little frost on the glass."

"Ah-ha!" Dr. Grayson licked her lips with excitement. "Frost on the glass. Do you see the imagery here?" She gave me a wild-eyed look; she was buzzing with energy. "From a psychodynamic point of view, the symbolism is quite fascinating."

"Fascinating," I echoed, only because she was staring at me, waiting for me to say something.

"What's so darn fascinating?" Vera Mae asked from the control room.

She was looking at me, but Dr. Grayson took over. "The frosted glass symbolizes Nadine's ego. The fact that it's frosted"—she allowed herself a small chuckle—"well, I hardly need to tell you what *that* means, Maggie." She raised her eyebrows in a perfect arch. "The interpretation is crystal clear."

"Oh absolutely," I chimed in. "It's as clear as . . . Crystal Geyser," I said, in a burst of inspiration. (Proving once again that I specialize in moronic comments.) Dr. Grayson's mouth twisted in a frown and her beady eyes narrowed. I took a deep breath. Okay, truth time. I had no idea what she was talking about. And from the little smirk on her face, I had the sinking feeling she was on to me.

"Well, one of you better explain it to me," Nadine piped up.

"And to me," Vera Mae added. "And do it quick, because we're going to a commercial in thirty seconds."

"I can hardly explain psychodynamic theory in thirty seconds. Maybe you'd like to tackle this one, *Dr.* Maggie?" There was a tiny edge to the word "doctor," as if she was putting air quotes around it.

Vera Mae was twirling her index finger in the air in a let's-wrap-it-up motion.

"No, you do it. Just give us the CliffsNotes version," I urged. "Please!"

"All right." She flashed a brief, triumphant smile. "The glass represents Nadine's conscious mind; the frost represents the unconscious part of her mind. The frost is blocking our view. That tells me she may be hiding her most secret desires from us, and maybe even from herself."

She waited a beat to let the significance of this sink in, and I put on my best "interested" look.

"That's intriguing," I piped up. And to be honest, it might have been intriguing if only I had some clue as to what she was talking about.

Dr. Grayson rewarded me with a thin smile before turning back to the caller. "Tell me, Nadine: is the frost covering all the characters in your dream, or just covering you?"

"The frost? Oh, it's just over the frozen vegetables," Nadine said earnestly.

Dead silence. Vera Mae and I stared at each other. *Frozen vegetables? Whoa!!*

"The frozen vegetables?" Dr. Grayson faltered. "I'm afraid I've lost you. Where exactly does this dream take place?"

"I finally recognized the location." Nadine sounded almost giddy with happiness. "I'm standing in the frozen vegetable aisle at Winn-Dixie . . ."

"Winn-Dixie? You're telling me you're in a supermarket?" Dr. Grayson's voice ratcheted up an entire octave.

"Yes, I am. And here's the exciting part. Russell Crowe and Hugh Jackman are pushing a shopping cart toward me. I'm reaching into the frozen food case for a package of frozen peas and it's all chilly and frosty in there; you know? And I'm looking at them through the frosty glass. I still have the door to the freezer open and the cold air is blasting me in the face."

"You're looking into the freezer compartment?" I asked.

"Sounds like you've got quite a dream on your hands, Nadine," Vera Mae boomed. "Just hold that thought, honey. We'll come right back to it after this word from Gus's Body Shop." *Dead crows and dreams about frozen vegetables?*

No wonder my show had a minus number in Arbitron.

Chapter 17

"Your momma called during the break, sugar," Vera Mae said. The show had just ended and the always-delightful Dr. Grayson was ushered out of the studio. From the murderous look on her face, it seemed doubtful she'd ever agree to be a guest on my show again. At least not in this lifetime.

So every cloud really does have a silver lining, as Lola always tells me.

"What's up?" I asked, taking a quick look at my listener mail. I noticed the pet psychologist had sparked some interest in animal shows and loads of listeners were angling to get their pets on the air. I decided to sort through them later, and was just about to toss them aside, when one envelope caught my eye.

My name was written in block capitals and I felt a funny little blip in the pit of my stomach as I ripped open the envelope. The message was short and sweet. Just two words.

"BACK OFF."

Back off? Someone had cut the letters out of magazines and pasted them on the page, like they'd read too many noir mystery novels. I felt a chill, almost like a breath of frost, on the back of my neck. They meant back off from the murder investigation, right? What else could it be?

"Lola wants you to pick her up at the set," Vera Mae said, breaking into my thoughts. "I really think she wants you to watch some of the filming." She must have noticed the stricken expression on my face because she put her hand on my arm. "What's wrong, sugar?"

I handed her the letter and her eyes widened as she scanned it. "This is someone's idea of a joke, right?" I gave a nervous laugh, hoping she'd agree with me.

"I'm not sure," she said slowly. "What do you think it means? Something to do with Adriana would be my guess."

"That's what I'm afraid of." I thought for a moment, my mind scrambling for a different explanation. "We haven't aired any shows lately that were really controversial, have we?"

Every once in a while we do a show that causes a rash of "negative audience feedback," as Cyrus likes to call it, and we try to analyze what went wrong. But lately all the show topics and guests had been as bland as baby oatmeal. No drama, no controversy.

Vera Mae scrunched up her face, considering. "There was that cooking show you did last month. Remember the big debate on fried okra versus sauteed tofu cubes? As I remember, that got kind of heated and there were some raised voices. Might have been some hurt feelings; that's all I can think of."

I shuddered, remembering that train wreck of a show. Cyrus had been awed by the success of *A Chef's Table*, a popular PBS radio cooking show, and he'd decided that WYME could do a copycat version. Except it hadn't turned out that way.

"I don't think anyone would get upset enough over fried okra to send me this," I said.

Vera Mae nodded, her beehive bobbing up and down. "You may be right. It's hard to imagine anyone getting all fired up over okra. Now if they were complaining about the tofu, that would be another story," she teased me. "Remember the time you wanted me to try tofu? I nearly threatened to kill you myself."

Vera Mae and I have finally reached a detente about vegetarianism. When I tried to bring her a tofu burger for lunch one day, she made the sign of the cross with her fingers and waved me away, like Father Merrin in *The Exorcist*. Since then, I've let her eat her turkey burgers in peace while I chow down on Linda McCartney frozen dinners.

She studied the note. "I think we should give this to Cyrus, just in case somebody really has it in for you. He keeps a file of letters like these. That way, if you end up in pieces in three different Hefty bags, we'll know where to start looking. Kidding!" She gave me a big grin.

"A file? You mean I'm not the only one who gets hate mail?"

Vera Mae leaned close. "Big Jim gets a bundle, because he always screws up the scores at the football games. This is just between us, but I think he takes a little nip of Jack when he's in the bleachers on cold days; you know?"

"I wouldn't be surprised." I looked at my watch. "What time does Lola want me on the set?"

"Now sugar, right now! You go on and I'll take care of this; don't you worry about a thing."

"Over here, sweetie!" Lola called to me from across the set. "I want you to meet someone special." She was standing next to a blond bombshell, early twenties, who had the kind of chiseled cheekbones and pouty lips that you see on the all the *Cosmo* covers. She even had long flowing *Cosmo* hair with caramel-colored highlights, very Sienna Miller (before Sienna Miller caught Jude Law cheating and pulled a Mia Farrow, chopping off her golden tresses).

I stepped over a tangled mass of cables and picked my

way past a throng of gawking extras to reach them. "Who is she?" someone asked in a loud whisper. "Is she an actress? Is she anybody?"

"Afraid not," I tossed over my shoulder.

I noticed that the extras were kept well away from the stars by a rope line. There's no democracy on a movie set and extras are instructed not to talk to the stars, ask them for autographs, or beg them to pose for pictures.

It's a case of the haves and the have-nots. The extras eat the same Craft Services food as the stars but they eat separately. It's pretty much a below-deck, above-deck pecking order, just like on the *Titanic*. If you're an extra, you're considered steerage.

"This is my daughter, Maggie," Lola said with a wide smile. "Maggie, meet Tammilynne Cole, the star of *Death Watch*."

Tammilynne looked supremely bored, gave me a full body scan, and then offered a limp fish handshake. She was wearing an outfit I recognized, a top and skirt from Kate Moss's new line for Topshop. Very hot, very L.A. via London. She'd paired a navy-and-white pinstriped hitched-hem skirt with an ivory silk spaghetti strap T. Just a hint of a black lace bra showed, and I had the feeling that it was deliberate.

"Isn't she gorgeous?" Mom was beaming.

"Gorgeous," I agreed.

Tammilynne had a figure to die for. She looked like she might be a size 00 with a tiny waist and impossibly long legs like a gazelle's, but she managed to look fragile and voluptuous at the same time. I could see Lola was trying not to be too envious or at least not to let it show.

A grip stopped to stare at Tammilynne with a wistful look, as if she was a slice of key lime pie and he'd just signed up for a year on Atkins. She gave him an "in your dreams" glare and he turned away.

"So . . . it must be exciting starring in your very first movie,"

I said, when it became obvious that she wasn't going to bother making small talk with me.

Tammilynne opened her mouth, popped a huge pink bubble, and snapped it shut like a turtle.

"Kind of."

Kind of? That was the best she could do? This was the opportunity that thousands of actresses in Hollywood would kill for. And all she had to do was sleep with Hank Watson. *Or kill Adriana and force Hank's hand.* Is that what really happened? I wondered.

The thought slipped into my mind unbidden. It was hard to imagine the Ice Princess having the technical know-how or the energy to rig the prop gun, though. Unless she had an accomplice? But why would she bother? She didn't even seem that interested in her starring role. I was more confused than ever, my thoughts fluttering like moths in my brain.

"It's a dream come true!" Lola gushed, as if she was Tammilynne's publicist and the young starlet was a sulky client. "Isn't that right, sweetie? This is what you've been waiting for your whole life."When Mom wants to be enthusiastic, she pulls out all the stops. I always thought she missed a great career as a Home Shopping Channel hostess. She can wax enthusiastic about anything from cheese graters to cubic zirconia and she can do it at two in the morning.

Tammilynne stared at Lola for a long moment and shifted her gum from one side of her mouth to the other. "I thought acting in a movie was pretty wicked at first," she said, letting the words roll around in her mouth like marbles, "but it's getting old real fast. You know?"

"Really?" I hadn't expected this. Isn't this why she'd stuck with Hank Watson for the past two years, all to get a crack at stardom? "I thought you'd be over the moon. What part of the movie business is"—I searched for a word and gave up—"getting old for you?"

Tammilynne heaved a sigh, and her underwire bra gave a sexy little ripple under her silk top. "All this standing around, you know." She waved her hand dismissively at the crew members, who looked like they were setting up for the next shot.

"But it's part of the job," I blurted out.

"Yeah? Well, I didn't get the memo," she said scathingly. "I thought I'd just be able to do my scenes and, you know, go home and chill. I didn't know there'd be like a zillion retakes of every scene. And the early morning calls! Why do they have to start at the crack of dawn? I'm not used to getting up until ten or eleven."

"It's always like this on a film set, honey," Mom said soothingly. "Start early and finish early, if you're lucky."

Tammilynne turned the corners of her bee-sting lips down in an unattractive pout. "Well, we're not finishing early today, are we?" she said sarcastically. "It's dinner time, the sun is setting, and we're still stuck here filming. I've had the same makeup on since six o'clock this morning," she whined. "I feel like this industrial-strength Pan-Cake crap is eating into my pores. I bet I look a wreck." She rummaged in her purse and held up a small hand mirror to inspect her perfect features.

Naturally, she looked flawless.

"You look gorgeous, Tammilynne," Mom told her. "And you'll really photograph beautifully in this light. You'll be even more of a knockout than you already are."

"The golden hour," I murmured.

Mom nodded. "Maggie's right. That's what photographers call it, the golden hour. There's something special about the lighting at this time of day. Everything has a sort of golden glow to it. It's beautiful, isn't it?"

She was right. The sun was a blood orange hanging low in the west and the ceramic blue sky was exploding into ribbons of rust, red and gold at the horizon. The water in

Branscom Pond would soon turn to violet in the setting sun. I figured Hank had time to shoot one more scene and then they'd wrap for the day.

"I'm not into lighting," Tammilynne said dismissively. "I just want to get back to my trailer, away from the bugs and the heat; you know?" She popped another big pink bubble and I winced as it splattered on her face. "This is the time of day I like to kick back and have a few margaritas." She let out a dramatic sigh and Mom and I exchanged a look.

Hmm. So the strain of a movie career was already getting to her. Hank Watson had the reputation for being a perfectionist and maybe he was finding it a challenge to get a good performance out of his Malibu Barbie star. After all, she'd had no acting training, and I wondered if she could even memorize lines? Maybe the drama coach wasn't doing enough to help her, or maybe she'd given up.

"Now, you just need to hang in there and you'll be just fine," Lola said, patting her hand. "Remember what Woody Allen said. 'Ninety percent of life is just showing up.'"

A long beat. "I guess." I wondered if she'd ever seen a Woody Allen film in her life. Probably not.

"You'll just find the rhythm of working on the set and after a while, you won't mind the early hours or the long days. It just goes with the territory, you know. We all have to put up with it."

"Whatever," Tammilynne said ungraciously. The gorgeous young actress had a way of sucking the energy out of the air around her. The set was bustling with activity but she was in the Dead Zone, wrapped up in her own self-absorbed little world.

A few minutes later, Marion Summers called her name from the production trailer and Tammilynne perked up. "Gotta go; they're gonna make me go over my lines one more time before we start shooting. If I can't remember them, they said they'd put them on cue cards. It's either that or I'll have to write them on my hand." This was the most animation I'd seen out of her. "Catch you later, Lola," she said as she darted off.

"Nice to meet you, too," I said under my breath and Lola giggled.

"Now honey, don't be mean. She's just young, that's all. The poor thing is barely out of high school."

"I know. She looks like she should be playing a troubled teen in an After-School Special." *Meow.* "How is she doing with her lines? I hope they have someone really good working with her."

"Hank didn't have time to hire a drama coach," Mom confided. "So Marion stepped in and she's trying to do her best, bless her heart, but it's slow going. The word on the set is that her acting is so bad, they're going to have to loop all her dialogue when they get back to L.A."

Mom had told me before that looping is an expensive, time-consuming process. The actor has to go into the studio and redo every line of dialogue, making sure it matches with the lip movements on the screen.

I couldn't imagine Tammilynne being up to the task. Of course, another possibility would be to hire a different actress to redo all the dialogue. If Tammilynne's acting was really hopelessly robotic, perhaps that's what they'd have to do.

"Really? That'll cost a fortune. And Hank's trying to keep costs down." I paused. "Is she really that bad?"

Lola leaned close. "Do you remember Sophia Coppola playing Mary Corleone in *The Godfather Part Three*?"

"Yes, it made me cringe. The ultimate in bad acting. And to make it worse she was playing opposite Andy Garcia, who could outact her even if he was in a coma. I heard all her lines had to be redone."

Lola grinned. "Sophie Coppola is Meryl Streep compared to Tammilynne Cole."

"Oh, no!" I giggled. "This is going to be one hell of a movie."

Lola got the high sign from Maisie, who tapped her watch and pointed in the direction of the pond. Lola immediately charged into high gear, and I could feel the energy pouring off her. "Maggie, my scene's coming up; do you want to watch?"

"Sure; which one is it?"

"Another party scene. I only have a couple of lines, but it should be fun." She smoothed her top—a pale chiffon dropped tunic—and grabbed a plastic champagne glass off the prop table. It was filled with a pale amber liquid. "I have to pretend this is Cristal," she said, making a face.

"And what is it really?"

"Take a sip, dear. Don't worry, it's not lethal."

She handed me the glass and I barely touched my lips to the rim of the glass. *It's not lethal? But that left a lot of wiggle room. Did it come from somebody's swimming pool? Or from a chemistry set?*

"This can't be champagne. And it's lukewarm." I looked at it suspiciously, wondering if I'd been poisoned.

"It's not champagne. They never use the real thing; the crew members would guzzle it down before shooting even started. It's cheaper for the prop manager to use soda or iced tea and that way he doesn't have to keep refilling the bottle. No one wants to drink this stuff, especially without ice."

"So you're telling me this is . . ."

"Diet Mountain Dew."

Chapter 18

Mom was in her element in the party scene, flirting with Sidney Carter, giggling girlishly, managing to edge herself into the frame as much as possible. It's always fascinating to watch her working; she's one part consummate professional and one part pure country ham, as Vera Mae would say.

She's a genius at making sure she's in every shot. Even if she's not talking, she's smiling, laughing, emoting, reacting.

Like most skilled actors, she's always "on," always performing. In the first run-through, she threw back her head and laughed gaily, even though Sidney hadn't said anything. The back of Sidney's head was to the camera, so the audience wouldn't know that, of course. I heard a gentle click as the camera swung softly toward her, and I wondered if they were doing a close-up shot.

Hank Watson has the reputation for shooting way more film than he really needs, which means he rarely brings a film in under budget. Or on time. He has the reputation of being a perfectionist in the industry and is more interested in getting a flawless shot than in cost control. He always does lots of establishing shots to set the scene, along with plenty of close-ups of the actors as they give their lines and, of course, "reaction shots."

It's not a quick process, but it seems to work for Hank. His movies all receive critical acclaim even though they may not be major box office hits. During the editing process, Hank sits down with the cinematographer and together they pick and choose the very best shots to use from the raw footage.

It was hard to imagine that *Death Watch* would be successful with Tammilynne in the lead. There might be a flurry of publicity because of Adriana's death, but that would quickly die down and the critics were sure to be merciless toward Hank's main squeeze.

If *Death Watch* tanked, how would Hank ever find funding for future projects? And surely his investors in this film would be outraged over losing all their money?

Nick always says to "follow the money" when you're trying to solve a crime. I wondered how this rule would apply to Adriana's death, but I was drawing a blank.

I thought of Frankie Domino and wondered again what his role could be in the production. Was he somehow involved in providing the cash flow for *Death Watch*? Why else would he be hanging around the set? Was he trying to protect his investment? Was he keeping an eye on Hank Watson? Why? I was baffled.

He certainly wasn't part of the cast and crew and he didn't seem to be a close friend of Hank's. I noticed him standing off camera, talking earnestly on his cell phone, gesturing with his hands. He seemed angry and impatient but maybe that was just his perpetually jazzed New York style.

From time to time, he glanced over at Hank Watson, and I thought I saw his upper lip curl in disgust. Finally, he snapped the phone shut, a sneering expression crossing his doughy features. He caught me looking at him, but I quickly looked away, pretending to be absorbed in the filming. There was something threatening, almost sinister about him, in spite of the cartoonish clothes (black shirt, white tie) and his Wise-guy accent.

I glanced back at the set as another burst of feminine laughter floated through the balmy air. It was Lola, of course. Emoting her little heart out. Lola really comes alive when she's performing and today she was in her element.

Hank was probably thanking the climate gods because he had perfect weather for the outdoor party scene. The last moments of sunset were streaking across the sky and the waters of Branscom Pond were lapping softly against the shore.

Mom seemed to sense whenever the cameras were on her, because she'd toss her hair over her shoulder, lift her chin to get a more flattering angle, and widen her eyes. She always said she learned this trick from Zsa Zsa Gabor, who certainly knew a thing or two about looking good on camera. Mom even tossed Sidney Carter a couple of saucy winks, and he gave a little bow and grinned back in acknowledgment.

Whenever I thought about how Adriana had ruined his career by spreading that false AIDS rumor, I shook my head in bewilderment. How could someone do something so heartless, so unfeeling? Was Adriana really that cruel, or did she have some other reason for wanting to destroy him, to publicly humiliate him?

No matter how hard I tried, I still hadn't come up with a motive for Adriana's murder that would satisfy me. A lot of people probably had wished she was no longer on the planet, but I couldn't really see any one of them having a strong enough reason to kill her.

I was sitting with Maisie and Hank Watson, watching the film when Hank suddenly yelled, "Cut!"

Instantly, there was dead silence. "Tami," he said, his voice ragged, "you were looking at the camera. Remember, we talked about that, sweetie. You have to look anyplace *but* the camera."

Tammilynne tossed her blond mane of hair. "Well, honestly, it's hard *not* to look at it," she said irritably. "I've got to remember my lines and everything. It's all too much; you know?" She glanced at her watch, an elegant Patek Philippe, the face studded with diamonds. "We should have stopped ages ago. You know I get dizzy if I don't have something to eat every three hours. I think I'm hypoglycemic."

She looked like she might have a meltdown and Maisie rushed to intervene while Hank ran his fingers through his hair.

"Tammilynne, it's okay to look in the *direction* of the camera, but just don't look at the lens. It looks really bad and it ruins the scene. Okay?" A beat and then when Tammilynne didn't bother answering her, Maisie asked suspiciously, "Tammilynne, are you chewing gum?"

"Not anymore," Tammilynne said sulkily. She removed the offending gum from her mouth as a crew member rushed over with a tissue to whisk it away. "I forgot. My bad. So shoot me."

"Yeah, right," Hank muttered under his breath. "Don't tempt me."

"Hank—" Maisie said warningly.

"I know. I know," he replied. He took a deep breath and clamped his headset back on, his expression tight. "Okay, take it from the top, everyone." He glared at Tammilynne. "And try to look happy, okay? Remember this is a party, not a wake."

"You could have fooled me," Tammilynne said.

Half an hour later, Hank called a quick break and I decided to hit the craft services table for an iced tea. I stood up and stretched for a moment, then headed across the set. I'd gone only a few feet when a loud crash followed by a sudden scream made me turn back. It sounded like a car wreck, something glass and metallic smashing on concrete.

"Ohmigod!" Maisie was staring at a heavy Klieg light that had fallen off the pole and had landed smack dab onto the chair next to her—the chair I'd been sitting in. The flimsy canvas-backed director's chair had actually collapsed under the weight of the shattered lamp and was lying in pieces on the sand. The light was ruined, the metal frame twisted, the glass bulb smashed into a zillion fragments.

My heart sped up and a chill went through me. *If I hadn't gotten up to get that glass of iced tea, I'd be toast right this minute. My brains would have been scrambled along with fifty pounds of glass and metal.* I shuddered at the thought and some tiny hairs at the back of my neck stood up at attention.

Hank jumped up, scowling. "What the devil? Who the hell's responsible for this?"

Maisie shook her head, helplessly. "I have no idea," she said, her face suddenly turning pale under her California-girl tan. "Thank God no one was hurt."

"Hank, I have no idea how this happened." Jesse, the AD, came running over, hands outstretched, palms turned up, all apologies.

Hank shook his head and pushed him brusquely aside. Hank has a reputation in the business for being a tough director and for having high standards. Like Donald Trump and Ted Turner, Hank doesn't like excuses and he can't stand incompetence. I knew heads would roll after this incident. It didn't matter if it was an accident, it shouldn't have happened and that meant someone's job was on the line.

"Maggie, are you okay?" Hank rushed to my side, his voice warm with concern. He touched my arm very lightly, his dark eyes worried. "You're bleeding—you must have been hit with a piece of flying glass."

"I am? I didn't even notice." I glanced down. Hank was right. I must have been sprayed by a shower of glass fragments, because a series of tiny red dots were sprouting on my upper arm. I took a slow breath to ease the tightness in my throat. "It's nothing, really—"

"Maisie, take her to First Aid," Hank snapped. He turned back to Jesse, who looked like he was one Valium away from a meltdown. "We're wrapping for the day. Get everyone back on the set early tomorrow. Make them check the call sheet, tell them to be on time, and no excuses. I want to get some sunrise shots." He gave the AD a long hard look. "You and I will talk about this later. I want the names of everyone who touched that light. In the meantime, get someone over here to sweep up this broken glass. I don't want anyone stepping on it."

"C'mon Maggie; over this way." Maisie steered me away from the shattered light and dabbed ineffectually at my arm with a tissue. "We've got some first aid supplies in the production office."

"But, it's nothing, just a tiny scratch. I feel really silly—"

"Hey, there's nothing silly about nearly getting brained by a piece of lighting equipment." She lowered her voice. "Let's just get some alcohol for it and a bandage, okay? Hank will be furious if you don't come with me." She locked eyes with me. "Do it for me, please?"

"Okay, but it's only a scratch. I had to admit I was a little surprised at Hank's reaction." I struggled to keep up with her as she crossed the sandy beach at a good clip, making her way to the trailers.

She let out a little sigh. "Things have been really tense today and I think Hank's coming unglued. The last thing he wants is another accident on the set."

I nodded. It would be hard not to be upset after what happened to Adriana, I decided. Maybe everyone's nerves were on edge.

"An accident? I don't think Adriana's death was an accident, sweetie," a familiar voice piped up. Carla Townsend was standing right behind us, flushed with excitement. "And maybe this wasn't an accident, either. Or didn't that thought occur to you?" she purred.

"I didn't know you were on the set today, Carla." Maisie's voice was chilly but the celebrity journalist grinned at her and didn't seem to be the least bit miffed. Maybe she was used to being persona non grata on movie sets; she had a hide like an elephant's.

"Oh, I'm everywhere," Carla said. "That's how I get all the good stories. All the exclusives. I get in first and I get the dirt." She winked at me. "That's the only way to be successful in this business. It's all about the story."

And if there isn't a story, you make one up, I caught myself thinking.

"Well, there's no story here," Maisie said flatly. She ushered me into the production office and opened a cabinet with first aid supplies. Carla trotted along with us, and I noticed she'd whipped out a notebook, ready to get down to business.

"Now, Maggie, let's start with you," she said in a conversational voice. "How did you feel when the Klieg light nearly killed you?" Her tone was friendly and low-key, and I wondered if she deliberately used a soothing tone, hoping to disarm her subjects. A nice bit of psychology, if it was deliberate. "It must have been quite a shock." She peered at me closely, standing a little too close, resting her hand on my arm. "You look a little pale, dearie; I think I'll make a note of that."

Oh yes, she was flashing a fake-concerned look at me. Another nice touch. Carla was quite a manipulator, up there with the best of them.

"Carla," I said, bewildered, "what are you talking about? It didn't nearly kill me. As you can see, I'm standing right here and I'm perfectly fine." Maisie was busily swabbing my upper arm with antiseptic and I winced as she slapped a Band-Aid on the tiny cut.

"Yes, but it was just a matter of blind luck, wasn't it? I saw what happened. Two seconds later and you would have been smashed like a bug on a windshield." Carla chortled, showing her back teeth. I winced at the image of myself splattered and bloody. I hate anything gory or gruesome; that's why I didn't go to medical school and became a psychologist instead. It's easier to play around in people's minds than in their large intestines. "So tell me why did you stand up, anyway? Did you have a premonition?" Carla had her pen poised, all set for a juicy quote.

"Hardly," I said dryly. "I felt like an iced tea, that's all."

Maybe if I stuck to the bare facts, Carla would lose interest and leave me alone. There really was no story here, no sinister plot at work here, right? I felt a funny little tingling along my spine, and willed it away. Accidents happen and I just happened to be sitting in that chair at that time. Certainly no one planned it. So why did I feel a little queasiness in the pit of my stomach?

I gave myself a mental shake. It was an accident, that's all. If I listened to Carla any longer, I'd end up completely paranoid. Time to rein in my always-too-vivid imagination.

"Maybe not, but it was certainly a lucky break for you," Carla said casually. Her beady-eyed stare was beginning to unnerve me. "That iced tea saved your life, Maggie. Another couple of seconds and you would have been sitting in the Death Chair." She paused, deep in thought and then smiled. "You know, I really need to get a shot of that chair before they clean up the broken glass. And I need to make sure I get the words Death Chair in the headlines."

"The Death Chair?" I asked. This woman was shameless!

"Yes. It has a ring to it, doesn't it?" Her smile widened; she was clearly pleased with herself. "Death Chair." She dragged the syllables out in a sepulchral tone. "It's the kind of thing that could end up on eBay. It would fetch a good price, I imagine. Of course, if you'd been killed, it would fetch even more."

"The Death Chair?" Maisie turned from the first-aid cabinet to give me a little eye-roll. "Oh Carla, please. Let's not get all dramatic here. It was an accident, that's all—a very minor accident. Things like this happen all the time on movie sets, and they don't make front page news. Even in the tabloids," she added, giving Carla a little dig.

"Is that so?" Carla was waiting with pen poised. "Are you sure about that?"

"Of course I'm sure. It was just a technical glitch. Apparently someone didn't tighten the screw enough and the light could have come slamming down from the pole at any moment—" She stopped talking suddenly and glared at Carla. "Oh God, you're not writing all this down, are you?"

"You bet I am!" Carla chuckled. "A technical glitch," she said, parroting Maisie's words. "It doesn't sound like the production company is showing much concern for the safety and well-being of the actors, does it? Sounds like carelessness to me. You know, Maisie, you're calling it an accident, but I think my editor will have quite a different take on it."

"You do?" Maisie asked.

Carla nodded, looking pleased with herself. "Oh yes, definitely. First Adriana, and now another nasty accident on the *Death Watch* set." She shook her head sadly. "Maybe the set is cursed?" She bit the end of her ballpoint pen, lost in thought.

"The set isn't cursed!" Maisie tossed her a furious look.

Carla smiled. "You know, that's another good angle to explore. Paranormal is very hot these days. That would make a good lead. I'm thinking there's enough here for a three-part special." She paused. "And I like that line about the screw not being tightened; it's kind of like someone cutting the brake lines on a car, isn't it? I've gotta remember that."

Maisie's eyes flashed, her lips tightening. "I was just guessing when I made that remark about the screw and the pole. Anyway, this isn't an interview, is it? You tagged along with us into the production office. Uninvited, I might add. I thought this whole conversation was off the record."

"Really?" Carla was unruffled. "You honestly thought that? That was very silly of you, my dear. With journalists, nothing is off the record. You should know that by now, Maisie. I need a little background, honey; you know, something to pad out the piece." She licked her index finger and flipped through her notebook. "How long have you been working with Hank? I probably have that in my notes somewhere, but it would be quicker if you could just tell me again. I want to file this story tonight." She gave us a broad smile. "And of course, I want to make sure I spell everyone's name correctly."

Chapter 19

Mom caught up with me just as Carla and I were walking out of the production trailer and heading across the set. Carla was still trying to weasel a blow-by-blow account of the Klieg light episode out of me and I was doing my damnedest to get rid of her. After all, what could I possibly have to say to her? I hadn't seen a thing. I knew that wouldn't stop her and I dreaded seeing the tabloids tomorrow.

"Honey, are you okay? I ran back to wardrobe to get another pair of shoes and I just heard there was an accident. I'm afraid I missed all the excitement." Mom gave me a quick embrace, her eyes looking teary. Thirty-two years old but I'm still her baby. Her blue eyes widened in alarm when she got a look at my bandaged arm. "Oh Maggie, you've been hurt! No one told me."

"Hurt? She was nearly killed," Carla said flatly. "And I don't think it was an accident, do you?"

"It wasn't an accident?" Mom looked baffled." I heard that one of the lights fell down, that's all. I figured it was some sort of technical problem."

"Really? Then you don't know the half of it, sweetie." She gave Mom a calculating look, her mouth twisting into her trademark sneer. "Maybe you have a comment for me,

Lola? I'm filing the story in half an hour and I just need a few good quotes to punch it up. Something from the mother of the victim would be good. Readers always like that. It tugs at the heartstrings, as my editor always says."

"The victim?" Mom's eyes widened and I rested my hand lightly on her arm. "Does she mean you, Maggie?"

"It's nothing, Mom. She doesn't know what she's talking about."

"Oh, a little mother-daughter discussion; that's good, too." Carla whisked out her notebook and pen, her eyes bright with interest. "The daughter being brave and stoic but the mother sensing the deadly game being played out." She put on a somber announcer's voice like she was doing a voice-over on the Discovery Channel. "Very protective, I like that. Just like a momma bear with her cubs."

"Carla—" I said warningly.

"This is nice, very nice." Her eyes were gleaming with excitement. "Who knows? I might even win a local Emmy for this story, especially if it's an exclusive. You're not talking to anyone else, are you?"

She gave us both a hard look and I gave her a stony glare. "Of course we're not," I said coldly.

"No? I didn't think so," she said, returning to her scribbling. "That's a relief. Now, Maggie, sweetie, let's get down to business. You need to tell me your thoughts on all this. Don't hold back; let it all out. Isn't that what you shrinks tell your clients to do? I can write it in shorthand, or if you want, I have a pocket tape recorder we can use."

"Carla, I told you I have no comment for you, none at all. I don't want to talk about this, and I certainly don't want to be quoted in some rag." I motioned to Mom to collect her things—the sooner we got out of here the better.

Carla flashed me a hard look, her eyes flat and shiny. There was something cunning, almost predatory, about her features that I hadn't noticed before. "Well, maybe you don't want to be interviewed for the story, Maggie, but I bet your mother does. She understands the value of publicity. Now, Lola," she said, softening her tone. "I need something catchy for the headline. How about: 'My Desire for Fame Nearly Killed My Daughter'!"

"Ohmigod." Lola looked stricken, her face turning pale. "I nearly *killed* you?"

"I don't believe this," I said through gritted teeth.

Carla spread her hands at eye level as if she was picturing the words in sans serif font splashed across the tabloids. "I can see that on the front page, can't you? It's a real attention-grabber. This is the kind of thing that would make it onto *Access Hollywood*. Can't you just picture Mario Lopez reporting the story, flashing those cute little dimples of his? The audience will eat it up!"

"You're insane," I said, half under my breath.

"Well, Lola, what do you think?" Carla raced on, ignoring me.

"My desire for fame nearly killed my daughter?" Mom asked, finally springing to life. "Carla, this is simply ridiculous. I don't even know what you're talking about."

"What's ridiculous about it?" Carla asked calmly. "Maggie was sitting with Maisie and Hank because you wanted her to watch you in a scene, right? I happened to overhear that little conversation you had with your daughter, so there's no point in denying it." She gave me a naughty little wink as though we were coconspirators. "So you put your own daughter in harm's way." She wagged her finger at Mom. "Not good, sweetie, not good at all."

"But I certainly never intended to," Mom said, clearly flustered. "And Maggie was on the set because she was hired by Hank Watson. She was just doing her job."

"Mom, don't say another word." I took a deep breath,

trying to calm my jangled nerves. "Anything you tell her is going to end up on the front page of one of the tabloids and it's going to be blown all out of proportion. Carla's going to twist whatever you say."

"Oh my, feeling a little defensive, are we, Maggie? I'd never twist anyone's words." She gave a nasty cackle. "I don't have to, honey. I find that people dig their own grave; all I have to do is hand them a shovel."

Mom went back to her trailer to gather up her belongings and I headed for the craft services table for a water bottle. Carla was still yipping at my heels like a persistent hound. I couldn't seem to shake her, even though I thought I'd made it clear that I had nothing to say to her.

The catering staff was packing everything up for the day and I reached for the last bottle of Crystal Geyser just as an attractive young actress did the same thing. She was tall and blond, California slim, dressed casually in jeans and a tank top. I remembered her from an earlier scene that Hank filmed.

"You go ahead and take it," she said graciously. "I have an extra water bottle in my tote bag, and I'll just grab some ice in a paper cup." She shot me a curious look. "You're Maggie Walsh, right? The one who got hit in the head with the light?" She shook her head sympathetically. "It must have been awful; I hope you're okay."

"I'm fine." I smiled at her. "And just for the record, I wasn't hit on the head. The light missed me completely and I just have a couple of scratches on my arm. A little flying glass, that's all."

She grinned back. "I'm glad you're all right. I guess somebody just got the wrong story out there—you know how it is."

"I certainly do." Movie sets were gossip mills and I knew people were going to ask me about the Klieg light incident over and over. The story was going to get bigger and bigger each time it was told. I wondered who'd started the rumor that I'd been conked on the head. For all I knew it could have been the intrepid tabloid reporter standing next to me.

"She's just being brave," Carla piped up. "It was almost a near-death experience." Carla turned to me. "I meant to ask you, Maggie, did you see a white light? Or maybe even hear a voice telling you to go to the light? That would be a great addition to the piece. Readers always like to hear stories about the afterlife." She paused. "If you happened to see some dead relatives waiting for you, that would be good, too. Just give me a few names; I can fill in the rest. I'll add a little dialogue to flesh it out."

"Carla," I said firmly, "there *was* no near death experience. And no white light or voices or dead relatives."

"Sorry to hear it," Carla said, not the least bit embarrassed. "It would have made a hell of a good story. Unless you're saving it for a book, of course."

"Look, Carla," I said, my nerves fraying, "I'm sorry to disappoint you, but you really need to give it a rest. There's no story here, really."

I gave her a hard look, but Carla just laughed and helped herself to a stale doughnut. "Oh, you have a lot to learn, my dear. There's always a story. Always." She gave the starlet a sharp look. "Say, you're Lori Taylor, right? You play the part of Tiffany Hale, don't you?"

"Yes, I do. It's a very small part. And you are—"

"Carla Townsend, entertainment reporter." She whisked out a card like an insurance salesman and pressed it into Lori's hand. "You didn't see the light crashing down by any chance? An eyewitness report is always good. I could include it in my story. I might even be able to get the editor to include a picture of you."

"No, I wasn't in that scene, I was back in my trailer studying my lines."

"And how is that incredibly sexy husband of yours?" Carla nudged me and winked. "Lori is married to one of Hollywood's most gorgeous guys, Sam Taylor."

Lori tensed, a wary look crossing her face. "He's fine. He's only here for a couple of days. He's flying back to L.A. before I am."

"Just as well," Carla said, munching on her doughnut. She brushed away some sugary crumbs that had dropped onto her polyester tunic top. "You know how people talk." She let that comment hang in the air for a moment, and when Lori didn't take the bait, she continued, "I suppose he's devastated by Adriana's death? The word on the street is that the two of them were very"—she paused delicately—"close." Carla turned to me. "You may not know this, Maggie, but Adriana was very fond of young guys." She flashed a look at Lori. "Isn't that right, Lori? Or is it true what they say? The wife is always the last to know?" She gave a sly laugh.

"I don't know what you're talking about." Lori slung her tote bag over her arm and stalked away, her face flushed with anger.

"Oh my, what a temper. It's always better to keep your cool in these situations, but I guess as a psychologist, you already know that."

"I think you provoked her, Carla. What exactly were you hinting at?"

"It was more than a hint," Carla said, licking powdered sugar off her fingers, one by one. "It's well known that if you're a struggling actor and have the right look, you can score a bigger part in the film by making nice with Adriana."

"And making nice means—"

"Exactly what you think it means, sweetie." She heaved a

sigh. "It's a tough business, Maggie, and Sam Taylor wouldn't be the first guy to be tempted. After all, a quickie affair with Adriana, and his career gets a tremendous boost. Who wouldn't jump at the chance?"

"But he has a lovely young wife." I tried not to look as shocked as I felt.

Carla shook her head. "You haven't seen much of the world, have you? I think Lola has kept you way too protected, my dear. Lori and Sam have only been married for a few months and I guarantee they won't last another year together."

"Why not?"

"She wants to move to some little podunk town in the Midwest and have kids and he wants to spread his wings in Hollywood. It's just not meant to be; you know?" She paused, raising her eyebrows. "Of course, with Adriana out of the picture, maybe that chapter of Sam's life is over and he'll be ready to settle down. Adriana was his mentor, to put it delicately. He's really not much of an actor, you know."

"I think I've seen him in a few movies," I said doubtfully.

"Adriana got him those parts. She begged the producers to find something for him, even if it was a bit part." She waited a beat, flashing me a look. "It's certainly a nice break for Lori that Adriana isn't on the set anymore, isn't it? Her death might have saved Lori's marriage. Would a woman kill to hang on to her husband? I'd say yes. Just my own opinion. You probably know more about this than I do."

"You're not going to publish this 'opinion' of yours, are you?" I was horrified. "A lot of innocent people could get hurt."

Carla elbowed me. "Oh honey, believe me, they're not that innocent. And as far as being hurt, well you know what they say, there's no such thing as bad publicity." She gave a high-pitched laugh and I winced. "As long as I spell their names right, they'll be happy!"

Chapter 20

"That dreadful woman!" Lola steamed. "I haven't seen her in years and I'd forgotten how truly odious she can be. She's much more bitter and cynical than I remembered."

We'd just finished a quick stir-fry dinner and were stashing the plates in the sink. Lark had gone out for the evening so Mom and I were alone in the town house.

The kitchen is a cozy place, with a round oak dining table, gleaming wood floors, exposed beams, and cream-colored walls. The walls are dotted with colorful canvases that Lark picks up at local flea markets along with some nice pieces of vintage wicker. She has a good eye for color and texture; if she wasn't studying to be a legal assistant, she could have a kick-ass career as an interior decorator. I feel more at home here than I ever did in my overpriced apartment on the Upper East Side of Manhattan.

"No argument there," I muttered. "She's the reporter-from-hell." I was still flummoxed over Carla's revelations about Lori and Sam Taylor. "Did you ever hear anything about Sam on the set?" I asked. "Was there ever any gossip about him and Adriana?"

"It's hard to say. Adriana always did have the reputation of being a cougar, and he's not a very good actor, I'm sorry to say. So it's very possible that Carla was right. All Sam really has going for him is his youth and good looks."

"And Adriana," I said wryly. "So you think it's possible that Hank Watson hired him because Adriana asked him to?"

Pugsley tapped his feet on the wide oak floor and I tossed him a Beggin' Strip. I knew he'd have "bacon breath" all evening, but I couldn't resist. Eating Beggin' is the doggie world's equivalent of nibbling a luscious Godiva chocolate in ours.

"I'd like to say no, but the truth is, I just don't know. Everything's changed so much. It was different when we were all starting out together in Los Angeles. It was always competitive, but now it's at a completely different level; it's really cutthroat. I don't know what Sam would do to get a part." She shrugged. "He's a good-looking guy, but hunks are a dime a dozen in Hollywood. He doesn't have any real training as an actor. I think he started out as a model and then he met Adriana." She raised her eyebrows. "And the rest, as they say, is history."

We both were silent for a moment. "Are you up for watching a movie?" Mom asked. "I saw some good ones listed on the TNT Channel for tonight." Mom and I are both fans of old movies, especially anything set in the golden days of Hollywood. I think I've seen every Gloria Swanson movie ever made. Several times.

"Hold that thought. I want to take Pugsley for a quick walk first. Maybe I'll stop by Sweet Dreams on the way back. Is there anything you'd like?" Sweet Dreams is an ice cream shop just a few blocks away. The signature dish is to die for—lemon sorbet, topped with fresh raspberry sauce and whipped cream. I thought of the Oscar Wilde quote, *I can resist anything but temptation.*

"I'd like something really decadent, but I have to fit into

my costume tomorrow." Mom sighed, patting her stomach. "If they have any of that sugar-free frozen yogurt, the coffee flavor, that would be great."

Pugsley was jazzed because he recognized the word "walk" and was dancing around the kitchen in excitement, making little yips of joy.

"You've got it. C'mon, Pugs."

I gave a low whistle and Pugsley appeared at my side with his leash in his mouth. It's the only trick he knows, unless you count running in frenzied circles when he greets us. And jumping straight up with all four feet off the floor when he spies his favorite treats. Not enough to get him on Letterman, perhaps, but he has no interest in a career in show business—he's happy being a pampered pet.

It was a lovely evening, the air soft and balmy, the cicadas humming in the trees. My brain was racing with possibilities as I thought about the events on the *Death Watch* set. Carla, in her own irritating way, had added yet another suspect to the list.

According to Carla, the young actress, Lori Taylor, might have had a motive for tampering with the prop gun. After all, she was a "woman scorned," and if Carla was correct, Lori's husband Sam was sleeping with Adriana. Lori didn't seem like the type of person to commit a murder, but then, who does?

I remembered Rafe's crack about Ted Bundy. According to the newspaper reporters, even his neighbors liked him. He volunteered at a crisis hotline with the now-famous true crime author Ann Rule. How's that for irony? He was a chameleon and could fool the most astute people.

And remember the serial killer John Wayne Gacy? He dressed up as a clown to entertain sick children at a hospital in Philadelphia. I shudder every time I think of it. No one had a clue what he was up to until they found the bodies of the murdered boys stashed underneath his house. Scott Peterson? Another supposedly great guy with a charismatic personality; generous to his friends; a great host and the life of every party, people said. No one suspected a thing.

When I think about these crimes, I'm glad I'm out of forensic psychology and doing a radio talk show.

Was Lori Taylor capable of murder? I didn't seriously think she was a killer, but I added her to the list anyway. She wasn't at the top of the list, though; I had plenty of other suspects to consider.

Sidney Carter, for one. Revenge is certainly a motive for murder. Even though Sidney had seemed outwardly calm and composed when I met him at the Seabreeze, it must have galled him that Adriana had managed to thwart his career. All because she decided to spread a false AIDS rumor about him. So cruel and unnecessary.

So perhaps seeing Adriana land a starring role in *Death Watch*, and watching her lording it over everyone on the set every single day, may have proved to be too much. Maybe it caused him to snap?

Did he have the technical knowledge to tamper with the prop gun? I made a mental note to ask Rafe about the ballistics report. How hard would it be to do? I'd never be able to figure out how to rig a gun with a pellet, but I'm very low-tech.

And there was Malibu Barbie, the ditzy actress, Tammi-lynne Cole. She was no Einstein and it was hard to picture her fooling around with the gun. But maybe she talked someone else into doing it for her? She seemed to have several admirers on the set; would one of them be smitten enough to kill for her? A long shot, perhaps, but I've seen crazier things in my forensic work.

Pugsley stopped for a moment to do his bloodhound imitation. He circled a banyan tree three times, nose to the ground, snuffling along like he was hot on the trail of an escaped convict. Of course, all he was really doing was checking out all the dogs who'd been there before. I waited quietly while he went through his evening ritual, my mind still mulling over the case.

Hank Watson was the number one suspect according to the police, but I just couldn't bring myself to believe that he'd killed Adriana. Why? I wasn't really sure. Just a gut feeling. If I tested the theory with my mental Magic 8 Ball, I was sure it would say, "Signs point to no."

And Carla Townsend. Adriana was going to coauthor a book with her and then bailed out on the deal. And to add salt to the wound, she wrote her own tell-all book, probably stealing a few of Carla's ideas along the way. Would that be enough of a motive for murder?

It seemed like a pretty thin motive, but with a woman like Carla Townsend, all bets are off. She seemed like the type of woman who'd carry a grudge into eternity—a dangerous woman to cross.

The failed book deal happened a long time ago, but as they say, "Revenge is a dish best served cold."

Speaking of cold, I was starting to get brain-freeze, just thinking about all the possibilities. Two more people sprang to mind. One was Sandra Michaels, the "formerly fat actress." She'd seemed very upset when I asked her about Copper Canyon and couldn't wait to change the subject. Was she hiding something—and how was it connected with Adriana?

Another "possible" was Marion Summers, Hank's assistant. She was certainly long-suffering, working like a dog for Hank for a couple of decades, never really getting the recognition she deserved. And she had no job security. If she ever left Hank, or if he ever fired her, what would she do?

Could she have reached the boiling point and killed Adriana? But what would her motive be? Unless she had some sort of major crush on Hank, and saw Adriana as a rival? It seemed pretty far-fetched, but I made a mental note to find out more about their relationship. Marion and Adriana had always disliked each other, and maybe there was some sort of history between them? I wondered if Nick could help me check that out; he had sources everywhere.

But what sort of history? It would have to be something buried deep in the past. A secret? A vendetta? Impossible to say. I needed real insider information, not something I could check out myself on Google.

Pugsley finally finished his endless sniffing and we moved on. A veterinarian once told me never to hurry your dog when he's sniffing around a tree or a fire hydrant. This is how he gets his daily news; it's just like you or I sitting down with a cup of coffee and the local paper.

When I think of it as a doggie version of catching the daily news, I know I can't deprive him of it. The excitement of learning about other dogs in the neighborhood is probably the highlight of his little doggie day. Love, hate, fear, revenge—a myriad of doggie emotions is right there for the taking. Pugsley doesn't need the afternoon soaps for instant access to high drama; all he has to do is sniff the base of a tree. Just ask him.

It was dusk when we finally reached Sweet Dreams. The shop was almost empty and I managed to resist the platter of half-priced eclairs and the Frisbee-sized oatmeal cookies sitting on the counter. They were calling to me with their little sugary voices, but I managed to stay strong.

Instead, I bought some low-fat spumoni ice cream for myself and a carton of coffee-flavored frozen yogurt for Mom, and the lady behind the counter gave Pugsley his own little doggie treat. A tiny scoop of vanilla Frosty Paws, on the house. Pugsley is a huge fan of the frozen concoction; it's a dog-healthy substitute for ice cream.

We'd just left the shop when a low voice at my side made me jump.

"I wonder how many calories you have in there?"

The sexy voice, the throaty laugh—it could be only one person. A guy who always seems to turn up when I least expect him to—the one guy in the world who can tug at my heartstrings and turn my life upside down at the same time.

Rafe Martino!

Chapter 21

He stepped out of the shadows, chuckling when I tightened my grip on the ice cream bag, as if I was afraid he was going to wrestle it away from me. I'd nearly jumped out of my skin like the heroine in a Freddy Krueger movie, but now I pulled in a slow, deep breath, willing myself to be calm. Had he noticed the effect he had on me? Probably. The guy doesn't miss a thing.

"Relax, Maggie, I'm not the food police. I won't ask you to step away from the ice cream, if that's what you're worried about." *Damn it!* He was enjoying this.

"I'm not worried," I snipped. "Were you doing a drive-by of the neighborhood, or did Lola tell you I was here? Or maybe you're psychic?"

Freud would say I was overcompensating. Reaction formation, a classic defense. Sounds a little crazy to you? Don't blame me, blame Sigmund; he's the one who came up with the idea in the first place.

Rafe nodded, a tiny smile playing along his sensuous lips. "Maybe all of the above. I'll let you decide; after all, you're the psychologist. This should be a really easy one for you. What do you think happened?"

He crossed his arms over his chest and looked at me,

dark eyes flashing, amused as hell. I wanted to reach out and delicately trace that strong jawline with my fingertip, but I restrained myself. It's one thing to have insane urges, and another to put them into action.

"You're the expert," he added.

Hmmm. The way he'd said "expert" with that little twist of his mouth told me he thought I knew absolutely nothing about the subject at all. This is an argument we've had many times in the past. Rafe thinks psychology is on a par with tarot cards and crystal balls and has never believed me when I say my theories are based on solid evidence and years of scientific research.

Whenever I tell him psychology is a science, he tells me it's a pseudoscience. And a snooze. When I mention criminal profiling, he dismisses it as nothing more than "good police work."

See what I mean? It's a zero-sum game with Rafe.

The guy never misses a chance to push my buttons, making it very clear that he thinks shrinks are at the bottom of the food chain. Why do I stand for it? Well, because he's drop-dead gorgeous, for one thing, and I'm a sucker for great-looking guys. And he's wildly sexy with dark, soulful eyes; and do I really need a third reason?

I feel a white-hot dash of excitement whenever I'm around him, and in my book, that's enough.

Okay, time to do a verbal mating dance with Detective Martino. "Well, I don't see that vintage Crown Vic you drive, so I assume you're on foot." Score one for me.

"Very good, Nancy Drew. That must have taken some first-rate powers of deduction. I can see why you're at the top of your game as a forensic psychologist."

Score two for Rafe.

I gritted my teeth, biting back a snarky reply. *Rafe.* He was as ruthlessly handsome as ever, and I felt my heartbeat rushing in my ears. It was exciting just standing close to him. Rafe Martino is like catnip to women and as dangerously addictive as—well, as the frozen spumoni I was carrying under my arm. I took a deep breath, willing my pulse to slow down, and tried to arrange my features into a neutral expression.

Was I successful? Probably not. His smile was slow and knowing and made me blink with heat. He was wearing black denim jeans with a black T-shirt, and both were molded to his body in all the right places. His black hair, worn on the longish side, completed the "bad boy" look. It had a tendency to curl up in the back in a very sexy way, like Simon Baker's on *The Mentalist*. I doubted it was a regulation cop-style haircut, but since he's a detective, they probably give him more leeway.

"Actually, I did stop by your condo a few minutes ago," he said easily, falling into step beside me. He bent down to pet Pugsley and give him a soft greeting, earning extra points in my book (as if he needed any!). "Lola said you'd gone out for a walk and suggested I come inside and wait for you. In fact, she even—"

"She even what?" I cut in, immediately suspicious.

"You know what? I probably shouldn't even go there." He laughed and scratched his chin. "But I've gotta tell you, Maggie, your momma is something else." His tone was teasing, his eyebrow quirked as if he'd just heard a bawdy joke.

"Go where? What happened?" I demanded. "What did Lola do?" A nervous giggle escaped from my mouth before I could repress it. "Rafe, you've got to finish the sentence because whatever Lola did to you"—I took a deep breath—"it's probably not as bad as what I'm imagining right now."

Or was it? My mental Magic 8 Ball would say: "Signs point to yes."

"Are you sure about that?" His smile was gently teasing.

"Yes. No. Actually, I'm not sure about anything at the moment."

Pugsley looked up at me and gave a questioning yip as if even he could sense the tension in the air. He knows Lola's name and was probably reacting to the strong "expressed emotion" under the words. That's shrink-speak for there's-some-serious-stuff-going-on-here. Dogs pick up on body language cues very quickly and Pugsley is surprisingly intuitive, sensing my moods before I've even identified them myself.

I reached down and tickled Pugsley quickly under his chin to reassure him. He looked up at me with his soulful dark eyes and licked my fingers.

"So I think you probably better tell me exactly what happened back at the condo." I took a deep breath of the magnolia-scented night air, bracing myself for the worst.

Rafe squinted up at the darkening sky as if he was channeling his thoughts and weighing his words carefully. Uh-oh. Lola must have done something really embarrassing, like changing into a Victoria's Secret negligee or turning on some salsa music and throwing herself into his arms for a sexy tango. Thank God we were on a dark stretch of sidewalk with no streetlights, because I think I might have been blushing.

"Your mother's full of surprises."

"Give me specifics. Hold nothing back."

I shook my head in despair. Nothing Lola does should shock me anymore. The truth is, she's a hopeless flirt and she's certainly not immune to Rafe's charms. She's made that very clear to me the first time she met him. He'd stopped by the condo on police business; very routine. She tried to monopolize the conversation until I'd finally sent her scurrying to the kitchen with one of my famous death glares.

"All right," Rafe said, spreading his hands. "Here's the honest-to-god truth, and you'll never guess it. She offered to make me a Kir Royale." He looked up at me expectantly and I swear he looked a little flushed.

"What?" This is the last thing in the world I expected.

He rubbed his jaw and gave me a sheepish grin. "And she invited me to watch a movie with her." He ran his fingers through his dark hair and locked eyes with me. "I'm still not sure what that was all about. I wonder what a shrink would make of that?" He gave me the full eye-roll and slapped his head in mock surprise. "Oh wait a minute; *you're* a shrink. How could I have forgotten that?"

I ignored the jibe, my mind racing like a squirrel. "A Kir Royale?" I was baffled. "I don't even think she knows what it is. I wonder why that popped into her head?" I sighed. Just when I think I've got her all figured out, she does something outrageous. "Oh, wait a minute. The movie—what movie are we talking about?"

"She was watching *Pulp Fiction* on TNT."

"*Pulp Fiction*? Now I get it," I said wryly. "There's that scene when Samuel Jackson and John Travolta are talking about a Kir Royale. Do you know the one I'm talking about?"

"Sure, I remember that scene," he said slowly, "but I'm not sure I get the connection with your mother." His dark eyes turned thoughtful, as if he wanted to say more, but was holding back.

Here's something you have to understand about Lola. It's just a crazy little personality quirk, but if she sees food in a movie, she suddenly gets a craving for whatever the character is eating. She simply has to have it. Cherry cheesecake, lobster bisque, or pineapple pizza. It doesn't matter; she has this irresistible urge to have some. I've seen her pick up the phone and order fish tacos at midnight, and believe me, those are an acquired taste.

Remember *When Harry Met Sally*? She's still trying to figure out what Meg Ryan was eating in the restaurant or-

gasm scene with Billy Crystal. I thought of renting the movie
again and telling her, but why spoil the suspense.

"So you really did turn her down when she invited you
inside?" *Ouch; that must have stung.* My mind was reeling,
trying to take it all in. I pictured Rafe standing at the condo
door, and Mom giving him a big welcoming smile, maybe a
little flustered but managing to be as flirtatious as hell at the
same time. Maybe even leaning forward slightly, pushing
the girls out as far as they would go (Mom's a big fan of low-
cut tops) or maybe giving a sexy twitch to her hips and—

Stop it, stop it! I gave myself a mental head-slap and
stopped in mid-thought, wincing at the visual.

"I told her that I was there on official police business but
that I'd be happy to take a rain check."

"You *told* her that? Oh God, that would just encourage
her. If you told her you were taking a rain check, that means
you'll be back. Don't you get that?" For a guy who seems
to know a lot about women, Rafe can be amazingly obtuse
about my mom.

"What did you want me to say?"

"Nothing, I mean . . . it was very gentlemanly of you. I
guess." I glanced at him and we fell into step together with
Pugsley trotting happily between us, very "and doggie made
three." I waited a beat. "So are you really here on official
business? Or was that just a story you invented for my
mother?"

"No, it's true. I'd never joke about police work." Rafe
frowned, and I felt a little ping of guilt. Even though Rafe is
drop-dead sexy with movie-star good looks, he's a cop through
and through. He's as straight arrow as they come. "I heard
about what happened on the set today," he said quietly," so I
thought maybe I should stop by and check on you."

"You heard," I said softly. "News travels fast in our little
town."

His tone had suddenly turned serious, and his eyes were dark and intense, the shadows playing across his finely chiseled features. "The Klieg light." He shook his head. "I still can't believe it happened. You could have been killed."

"But I wasn't in any danger at all; it was nothing, a non-event." A sudden thought hit me. "How in the world did you manage to find out about it?"

"Maggie, I'm a cop. I have my sources. Why would that surprise you?"

"I guess it shouldn't." I was silent for a moment. "But it was no big deal, honestly. Really, Carla *tried* to make a big deal of it—" I stopped, hit by a sudden idea. "Wait a minute. Did Carla Townsend call you? Is that how you heard about it?"

"Guilty as charged," he admitted. "She wanted to quote me for a story she was filing tonight. She said it should hit the TV news late tonight or early tomorrow."

"The evening news? You mean the network news?" I groaned in dismay. "This is worse than I thought. I figured she meant one of the tabloids." I remembered Carla's ghoulish delight in describing the Death Chair and I wondered if I'd end up on *Access Hollywood*. "What did you tell her?"

"Are you kidding me? I didn't tell her anything. I told her the captain would have my badge if I talked to a reporter and I put her in touch with the community relations officer. Of course, Carla got nowhere with her, either, so eventually she threatened to go to the mayor. She's an amazingly persistent woman, you know."

"Do I ever! If she really does have a piece on the ten o'clock news, we can still catch it." I glanced at my watch and picked up the pace, urging Pugsley to walk faster.

Chapter 22

"Thank God, you're back! Maggie, you're going to be on television, right after the commercial break."

"So they really *are* actually doing a feature on the accident with the Klieg light?"

"Of course they are. You're big news, honey." Mom amped her smile to the nth degree when she spotted Rafe trailing behind me. "And you brought company home; how nice." She gave Rafe a saucy wink as I handed her the freezer bag and shot her a meaningful look. "I'll just stow this away and be right with you." She darted into the kitchen and I noticed she couldn't resist giving a seductive little swivel to her hips.

The hip roll was presumably for Rafe's benefit. He locked eyes with me and shot me a see-what-I-mean? look. What can I tell you? Lola is incorrigible.

I let Pugsley off the leash and he trotted after Mom, skidding on the oak floor in his excitement, hot on the trail of ice cream. I thought of telling her that's he'd already had his Frosty Paws treat, but then I decided a tiny taste of Mom's frozen yogurt wouldn't kill him.

"I can't believe this," I said, sinking down onto the beige IKEA sofa. "Carla certainly didn't waste any time, did she?"

"She figured she had an exclusive—a breaking story," Rafe said.

I was appalled. Carla had actually followed through on her threat to get the maximum coverage for something that was a nonevent. The woman was shameless. If the incident with the Klieg light was making the network news, I knew it would be blown all out of proportion. I wondered if Hank Watson was watching and what his reaction would be. Note to self: remember to let Hank know I had nothing to do with this unwelcome PR blitz.

"They've already played the teaser for it," Lark piped up. "They had a picture of something they called the Death Chair."

"Oh no," I groaned.

"They had a nice shot of you, though. I think it was your headshot from WYME. Someone had Photoshopped your teeth. They were dazzling."

"I wonder how Carla got my picture. She probably stole it." *Had Carla stopped by the station after she left the* Death Watch *set? I'd have to check with Cyrus.*

"Well, maybe something good will still come of all this."

Lark is an incurable optimist and believes in cosmic harmony, yin and yang, and the notion that the universe bestows blessings disguised as disasters. I don't share her beliefs, but she's such a gentle soul that I never try to force my more cynical, hard-boiled views of life on her. I've seen more of the dark side of life than she has, and as Lark is fond of telling me, I'm an "old soul."

We're polar opposites. As I said before, I love Woody Allen flicks; her favorite movie is *Forrest Gump*. Need I say more?

She smiled at Rafe, who settled himself in a wicker swivel chair and then she flashed me a he's-as-gorgeous-as-ever look. At one time she and Rafe had been at odds, because Lark was the prime suspect in a murder case. But that was all cleared up, and now she thinks he'd be the ideal boyfriend for me, if only we both didn't have so much "cosmic baggage."

According to Lark, I'm a mercurial Pisces, dreamy, impulsive and never able to settle down with one man, one job, or in one town. After all, as she reminds me, Pisces is a water sign and my symbol is two fish, eternally swimming in opposite directions.

And Rafe—can you guess?—is a Leo. If you've ever read up on astrology, you'll see that we're practically doomed to fail, right out of the gate. Whenever a Leo and a Pisces get together, there's plenty of fireworks and sizzle, but never a solid future.

Lark blames it on the stars, but I think there's more than astrology going on here. I think it's *characterological*—another five-dollar shrink word, meaning a deeply held personality trait, highly resistant to change. I have some hard evidence about Bad Boy Rafe from the Cypress Grove gossip mill (thanks to Vera Mae and her friend Wanda, from the House of Beauty).

The word on the street about Rafe is that he never gets too involved with anyone—he's had a string of girlfriends, but he makes sure he can walk away at a moment's notice. Rafe always has an exit strategy. Doesn't give a girl a warm, fuzzy feeling inside to hear that, does it?

So I hold back a little, too, knowing that Rafe isn't the kind of guy who plays for keeps. I have the sneaky feeling that with Rafe it's all about the thrill of the hunt. On some level—even unconsciously—I tend to cool my jets when I'm around him. Why should I put my heart on the chopping block and let Rafe do an Emeril Lagasse (Bam!) on it?

"Shhh, here it is, everyone!" Lola gave an impatient flip of her hand. She squeezed between us on the sofa and pulled

Pugsley onto her lap. His breath smelled like coffee frozen yogurt; what a surprise. "Lark, turn up the volume, sweetie; I don't want to miss a word."

I recognized the newscaster, Laura Tremaine, a sleek blonde with model-perfect features and a Julia Roberts smile.

"Has someone put a curse on *Death Watch*, the Hank Watson flick being filmed here in south Florida? Sounds like something out of a Stephen King novel, doesn't it?" Laura managed to talk and show all of her teeth at the same time, as she zipped through the cheesy introduction. *"Death Watch."* She drew out the syllables, and threw in a sexy little chuckle, letting the viewers in on the play on words. Nudge. Wink.

"Stephen King? What is she talking about? This is ridiculous." I could feel a little bubble of anger rising inside my chest and my jaw muscles were clenching.

"There's already been one death connected with the film, the actress Adriana St. James, and today there was a near-fatal accident on the set. Let's take a look." She lowered her voice to a somber pitch and swiveled to look at the monitor behind her.

A crumpled director's chair filled the screen. Was it staged? No, it looked exactly as I remembered it.

The shot was slightly out of focus but it was still pretty dramatic, with the smashed chair, broken glass, and twisted metal lying on the sand. A few grips were standing in the background, but none of the principal actors appeared in the shot. The picture had very bad resolution and I wondered if Carla had taken it with her cell phone as soon as she left the production office.

"Oh, Maggie," Lark said, grasping my hand. "That's where you were sitting?" Her eyes filled with tears. "I didn't realize how awful it was. You really had a close call—you could have been killed."

Lola held up her hand for silence. She was sitting on the edge of the sofa, raptly watching the feature, her lips parted. "Maggie, honey, look at you! You are absolutely gorgeous."

Suddenly my WYME head shot filled the screen. Lark was right, my teeth were so white they were practically fluorescent; I bet they'd glow in the dark. And they used a tight close-up, which made my head look ridiculously large. Gorgeous? I didn't look gorgeous; I looked like I'd just dropped in from Roswell.

The head that ate Miami.

"Nice teeth," Rafe said, his lips twitching.

"Dr. Maggie Walsh is probably thanking her lucky stars tonight, because she could have been killed today. She was sitting in the Death Chair when a fifty-pound Klieg light came crashing down on her."

"But I wasn't sitting in the chair, you idiot," I muttered. "At least get your facts right." I practically shot off the sofa and Lark put out a restraining hand to stop me.

"A narrow escape for the former psychologist who now hosts her own radio show right here in south Florida. In the picturesque town of"—she took a quick peek at her notes— "Cypress Grove."

Laura paused, staring straight into the lens, a fake-thoughtful expression on her face. She looked so serious you'd think she was pondering global warming or the mysteries of sub-prime lending. "Will this near-death experience have a profound effect on her? Was it a coincidence or a curse? We've asked Dr. Heinrich Smoot from the Okaloosa County Psycho-analytic Society for his take on all this." She flashed another toothy grin at the camera, as it panned to a tiny bearded man who bore a passing resemblance to Toulouse-Lautrec. He'd been staring blankly at the desktop, but magically sprang to life when he realized the camera was focused on him. He widened his eyes and bared his lips in a grin, showing a mouthful of yellowed teeth that really did need some serious Photoshopping.

"Welcome, Dr. Smoot. I know you've been following this incredible story out of Cypress Grove."

"Ya, is very interesting. Really incredible."

Then he stopped talking abruptly and looked at Laura. Uh-oh. She raised her eyebrows, her glossy lips pursed in pained surprise. Actually shock was more like it. I could almost see a thought bubble drifting above her head: *Hey, didn't anyone tell this guy he's on live television? So say something! Anything!*

He was from the psychoanalytic society so I assumed he was a Freudian. Maybe he gives his patients the silent treatment (as Freud recommended) but I could have told him it doesn't go over well on camera. He'd better lose the mute act fast or they'd have to cut away to a commercial.

"You said you find it, um, interesting," Laura said, tripping over the words. "Would that be because you believe the set might actually be cursed? Would that be an apt description?"

"Cursed? Nah, that is kooky conspiracy theory." He wagged a finger at her playfully. "No curse. There is no curse. Who would believe such nonsense?"

Again, total silence. Dead air.

Dr. Smoot reminded me of a Tickle Me Elmo doll whose triple A batteries needed recharging. He had only enough energy to spew out a few words before slamming to a quivering halt.

Apparently, he'd never mastered the art of the sound bite, which involves using a few well-crafted sentences to make your point in a way that's succinct and compelling. The trick is to talk about the issue in a way that viewers can immediately grasp. Instead, he just sat there and stared at Laura who stared right back at him; it was painful to watch. She looked flustered and he appeared eerily calm.

The tension was palpable and I caught Laura gnawing her lower lip when the camera panned to her unexpectedly. A thin sheen of perspiration had popped up on her forehead and her eyes had that distinctive deer-in-the-headlights look, the telltale sign that signals: full panic attack dead ahead.

I wondered if anyone had bothered to do a "preinterview" with Dr. Smoot. If they had, they would have known he'd be a disaster on the air. In a preinterview, the producer asks you to come up with three interesting stories about the topic and then you "deliver" them, in a way that's entertaining, or at the very least informative.

Entertaining? Informative? Dr. Smoot failed on both counts. I wondered how he'd ever made the cut.

Laura's eyes flickered nervously to the left as if she was getting instructions from the IFB (interruptible frequency broadcast) monitor device tucked behind her ear. I bet her producer was pulling a Vera Mae on her, urging her to pick up the pace, pleading with her to get this guy talking.

Some performers, like Rosie O'Donnell, refuse to use an IFB, saying it's too distracting to have a flood of instructions pouring into your ear when you're live on camera. You're bombarded with suggestions from the producer and at the same time, you're trying to listen to the guest and come up with your next question.

I know what it's like to have dead air on my radio show, and I felt a little twinge of compassion for her.

"So, tell me. Do you believe in coincidence, Dr. Smoot?" Her words tumbled out in a rush as if she was trying to make up for lost time.

"Coincidence?" He looked suspicious, as if it was a trick question.

"Do you think Maggie Walsh just happened to be in the wrong place at the wrong time?"

Just a touch of desperation in her tone, but who could blame her. He scratched his beard for a full five seconds. My Magic 8 Ball is more entertaining than this guy!

"It could be." A long beat. "Or maybe not."

"And what do you think the aftereffects of this, uh, accident might be?"

"Could be very serious," he said, looking profound, and then gave a little shrug. "I think maybe evaluate her for PTSD."

"PTSD?" Laura said brightly. "We just did a feature on that. It's posttraumatic stress disorder," she said, showing off for the viewers. "But I thought it only happened to combat veterans?"

"Nah, can happen to anyone. Any place, any time. Someone has big shock and then boom—they end up with PTSD. Nightmares, racing thoughts, big-time anxiety." He paused, and Laura leaned in, eager to catch every word. "It could happen," he said, stroking his jowly chin. "Not fun stuff."

"Not fun stuff?" Rafe hooted. "Is this guy for real?"

"Shhh," Lola said, taking in every word. "Did you hear that, Maggie? He thinks you may need help. Psychological help."

Funny, that's what Rafe had told me earlier that evening. Looks like Mom and Rafe are on the same team.

A couple of more minutes of psychobabble and Laura neatly wrapped up the interview. When they cut to a commercial, Lark said, "Well, they certainly didn't say much, did they? We're not any closer to understanding why the light fell."

"There's no mystery about it," I countered. "Carla's trying to make this into a big story and it just isn't there. It will all be forgotten by tomorrow, I promise you."

Chapter 23

Mom and Lark went to the kitchen to make coffee and Rafe shot me a questioning look, his dark eyes flickering with concern. "You really don't believe that light was intended for you."

"Of course I don't."

"I wouldn't be so quick to say that. Maybe it's someone's way of telling you to back off."

Back Off. My mind lurched with a new sickening thought. That's what the note had said.

Rafe must have seen my expression change because he said quickly, "Maggie, is there something you're not telling me?"

Back Off. I licked my lips, my mouth went dry, and my stomach gave a nervous little flutter and then dropped straight to my feet.

Rafe narrowed his eyes, giving me a hard look. "You haven't had any threatening phone calls or anything like that, have you?"

"Of course not. Well, not exactly," I hedged. "Okay, there was a note that came into the station." I waved my hand in a little dismissive flip. "I suppose it depends on how you interpret it, and maybe it could be called threatening. But I think that's stretching it a little; I prefer to think it was nothing. A harmless prank, that's all. Maybe some disgruntled listener."

Rafe's eyes were penetrating, locked on mine. "You think it's nothing? What exactly did it say?"

"The same thing you just did." My thoughts scrambled and I let out my breath in a soft sigh. "Two words: back off."

"The two words were written on a sheet of paper? That's it?"

"They weren't handwritten; the letters were cut out of magazines. Very retro, like something out of a cornball film noir. Pretty over-the-top, right?" I smiled, to show how amusing the whole thing was.

Rafe didn't smile back and I noticed he was wearing his stony cop-face, with his mouth drawn into a thin line of disapproval.

"Where's the note now? You didn't throw it out, did you? And I hope to God you saved the envelope." His voice was harsh, the words shooting out of his mouth like bullets. I'd hate to be a suspect being grilled by Rafe Martino; I think I'd cave at the first question.

"Of course I didn't throw it out," I said, stung. "It's tucked away in a folder somewhere at work, and I'm sure Vera Mae saved the envelope. She told me Cyrus keeps a whole file of hate mail." *Whoa. Hate mail. A big slip of the tongue. That was a little strong, wasn't it? Too late to take it back now.* Rafe looked like he was ready to jump out of his chair, his hands balled into fists.

"Hate mail." He gave me a scathing look, shaking his head in disbelief. "You get a threatening note, and you were just going to ignore it; you didn't even think of calling the police? You don't worry about putting yourself in jeopardy, do you?"

Hmmm. He had a point. Rafe has always told me to stay

out of police business, insisting that I was putting myself at risk with my sleuthing.

I was feeling a little defensive, so what did I do? Like an idiot, I overcorrected, and came across as way too strident and argumentative. Now I was stuck. I'd been operating on the theory that Rafe was wrong, that there was no danger, nothing to worry about. How could I back down now without looking like a total wuss?

I remembered Vera Mae saying the best defense is a good offense.

"Hey, I'm not the only one who gets these kinds of letters, you know." My voice was getting a little shrill, and I made a conscious effort to rein it in. "I'm sure it was just a prank, really. This sort of thing happens all the time in broadcasting. It goes with the territory, you know."

"Does it?"

"Yes, it does." I deliberately made my tone very cool and casual, even though I had a funny little flip in the pit of my stomach. "I probably offended someone by something I said on my show and they decided to write me an anonymous note. No big deal. Or maybe they were angling to be a guest on the show and Vera Mae didn't invite them. There are a zillion possibilities, Rafe. You can't take these things too seriously, can you?" I tried for another smile, but I could feel it dying on my lips under Rafe's harsh glare.

"Maybe you can't take it seriously, Maggie," he said, the words dropping like stones, "but I can." Heavy pause, just like Horatio Caine when he nails a suspect in CSI Miami and shoots his trademark badass stare.

"And you can be sure that I will."

Yowsers. Rafe's protective instincts were kicking in bigtime. Well, that's what cops do, right? Protect and serve. That's what it says on all the black-and-whites patrolling Cypress

Grove. But was Rafe just being a good cop or was his interest in the case personal?

Rafe left a few minutes later, leaving Lark and Mom sharing the Sweet Dreams treats with Pugsley in the kitchen. I was dead on my feet and tumbled into bed at eleven thirty, still pondering the characters on my suspect list. Who really wanted to kill Adriana, and why? I pulled my lavender Laura Ashley quilt up to my chin and stared at the ceiling, my thoughts racing in a million directions while I reviewed everyone's MMO. I still hadn't reached any conclusions by midnight, when Pugsley bounded into bed next to me, and I fell into a dreamless sleep.

An early morning phone call from Vera Mae the next day jolted me awake.

"Maggie, are you up, girl?" Her honeysuckle tones melted over the line and I heard a commercial for Wanda's House of Beauty playing softly in the background. She and Irina start the day very early.

"I am now," I said wryly. "What's up?"

Okay, the truth is out: I'm not an early morning person and no one would ever accuse me of being "perky" before I've had my daily caffeine infusion. Vera Mae knows this, so I figured something major had happened. She wasn't calling just to chic-chat about the latest episode of *Dancing with the Stars*, but I knew there was no way to hurry her. Vera Mae would tell me in her own good time.

"Just thought you'd like to know that Sonny Crockett stopped by the station. I think he's got it bad for you, honey. I really do." She laughed, pleased with herself. "It doesn't take a shrink or a psychic to figure that one out."

Sonny Crockett? Oh yeah. Vera Mae collects *Miami Vice* memorabilia and is a huge fan of Detective James ("Sonny") Crockett, the character that Don Johnson played in the police drama. Rafe doesn't even look like Don Johnson, although he does have bedroom eyes and a sexy swagger. I can't dissuade Vera Mae, though. She's convinced that there's a striking resemblance, as if Rafe and Don Johnson were separated at birth.

She even reminds me that Rafe has the same cute little dimple when he smiles (as if I needed reminding!).

If anyone "has it bad," it's Vera Mae, who has the major crush, but I figured this wasn't the time to tell her.

"We're talking about Rafe Martino, right?"

I bit back a yawn. The bright sunlight was streaming through the wooden blinds and I heard cicadas buzzing in the bougainvillea outside my window. It was going to be another south Florida scorcher. I glanced at the outfit I'd laid out the night before. White capri pants, espadrilles, and a sleeveless green silk top. It would work for the set and then later for my afternoon show.

My hair was another matter. With ninety percent humidity, I'd turn into a fuzz ball. I'd have to pull it back off my shoulders and fasten it with a tortoiseshell clip. I keep one in the glove box just for bad hair days. And in south Florida, there are a lot of them.

"Of course; who else?" Vera Mae gave a lustful if-only-I-were-twenty-years-younger sigh. "He's real worried about you; any fool can see that."

"He is." I felt a warm little buzz inside me when I thought of Rafe and his bone-melting smile. His long lanky frame, those chiseled features—I quickly snapped back to reality when I heard Vera Mae laughing. "I mean, he is?" I made sure my voice spiraled up in a question, as if I really didn't know the answer. I don't think Vera Mae was fooled for a second, but she played along with me.

"You bet he is. You must have told him about that nasty letter you got. He got here bright and early, asked to see it, and he ended up taking it back to the police station with him. I guess they're gonna analyze it or something."

"Wow." I was impressed. "Do you mean for fingerprints? What did he have to say about it?"

"The look on his face said it all, honey. He put on some rubber gloves and he put the letter in one of those little plastic evidence bags, just like they do on *CSI*. My heart was beating like a rabbit's; believe me. This is the closest I've come to a real crime scene investigation. I wanted to ask him about trace evidence, fingerprint whorls, too. I've always had a question about those, but he seemed like he was in a big hurry to get out of here."

I grinned. *Trace evidence? Fingerprint whorls?* Vera Mae is a great fan of TV crime shows, and if she misses one because she's working at the station, she TiVos them to watch later.

"I don't think he's going to be able to do much with that note. Just those two words. *Back Off.* Anyone could have sent that, and it isn't really like a death threat, is it?"

There was a long pause and I wondered if Vera Mae had put the phone down to run another commercial. "Well, honey, the note that you saw might not have been so bad, but the second one, that's a lot worse."

The second one?

"Vera Mae—" I began, but she cut me off.

"Honey, a second note was delivered by hand sometime last night. Somebody must have slipped it under the front door to the station. Irina found it when she unlocked the glass doors this morning. She about flipped out, let me tell you." She paused while my thoughts zigzagged around my head. "Rafe took that one with him, too."

"A second note," I said slowly. This was a surprise and I sat straight up in bed, disturbing Pugsley, who woke up with an annoyed yip. "Was it like the first? Did Rafe think it came from the same person?"

"He wasn't sure." A long beat. "I hate to tell you, sugar, but this one was worse, sugar, much worse."

I bit my lip in frustration. What a way to start the day. "So Rafe has the note with him right now? Damn, I'd like to see it."

"I figured that, honey, so I made a copy to show you. I wasn't sure if I should, but I figured you'd want to see it. What time are you coming in today?"

I glanced at the clock. Seven oh five and my day was already in shreds. "I've got to be on the set for a few hours this morning, but I'll see you right after lunch."

"Be careful, sugar," Vera Mae said, signing off. "Especially out at Branscom Pond."

I decided not to tell Mom or Lark about the second note, and after dressing hurriedly, I headed out to the set. Mom didn't have to be there until early afternoon, so we decided to take two cars instead of driving together.

My mind was reeling with this new information from Vera Mae as I drove down 95 South. I jammed my Phil Collins CD into the player and asked myself: how did all this fit into the bigger picture? Were the notes really relevant to Adriana's death or was it just a coincidence? If someone was bothering to threaten me, that meant they really thought I was on to something. But what?

Time to take stock, Maggie.

A shooting death, a near accident, and two threatening notes.

Could it be that Rafe was right? Was I setting myself up to be the next victim—was someone going to silence me for good? Had I put myself in harm's way by investigating the case? I felt like my head was going to explode and I knew I had some tough decisions to make before it would all be too late.

Chapter 24

The Guitar Heroes were up to their usual antics when I parked in the far lot at Branscom Pond and hoofed my way to the set. They were passing a football back and forth and glanced up briefly when I passed them, gave me a blank look, and then went right back to their game. Not even a nod of recognition.

Either they didn't remember me or they had nothing to say to me. That was okay; I had nothing to say to them, either. As Maisie reminded me, Hank Watson had hired me and he seemed pleased with my work on the script. I didn't have to win a popularity contest with these two yahoos.

I was happy with the way the script was turning out and I hoped to catch up with Sandra Michaels for another talk about her lines and delivery this morning. She seemed much more confident since we'd been working together and I knew she'd give a powerful performance in the courtroom scene. She was an excellent actress and just needed a little direction.

I thought about what Nick had told me about Copper Canyon—the secret getaway for stars who needed a nip and tuck—and I wondered how I could delicately bring up the subject with her. Unless I'd been imagining it, Sandra had seemed uncomfortable when I'd asked her about the popular resort area in Mexico. It might be worth bringing it up again to see what sort of reaction I got.

The set was buzzing with activity: the caterers from the craft services truck were setting out a not-so-healthy breakfast spread of doughnuts and pastries, gaffers were trailing loops of electrical cable between the cameras, and Tammilynne Cole was having a meltdown in front of the Wardrobe trailer.

It was like a gory traffic accident on I-95, the kind you don't want to watch, but can't bring yourself to turn away from. Tammilynne was holding a flowered dress on a hanger, haranguing Hank and Maisie, who looked tense and unhappy. A small group of extras stood by, listening avidly and trying their damnedest to pretend they weren't.

I saw someone take out a camera phone and try to take a surreptitious picture of the trio. I wondered if it would make it into the *Enquirer*. I could picture the headline: *"Tempers Explode on the* Death Watch *Set! Star and Director in a No-Holds-Barred Battle of Wills!"*

"I'm telling you, this is not what my character would wear!" Tammilynne was shrieking at Hank, who looked pale and distracted, as if the events of the past few days had finally caught up with him. "No one in their right mind would wear this piece of crap!"

"I'm not sure what you don't like about it," Maisie said, unable to keep the hostility out of her tone. She gave a world-weary sigh, along with a small eye-roll. I had the feeling this discussion had been going on for some time.

"You're not? Well, open your eyes and take a look at it. Don't you get it? I'll look like a fat housewife in a Tide commercial. Who do I need to talk to around here to get another outfit? Something that my character would actually wear!"

Maisie shifted uncomfortably and cast a worried glance at Hank. After all, he was the director of the film and everyone knew that the buck stopped right here. Right now. With him.

If anyone could order a wardrobe change, it was Hank. One word from him and the dress would be history. The same as with script changes, lighting changes and crew changes, and of course cast changes. One minute Adriana was in the lead, and now Tammilynne was the star.

The director calls the shots on a film set, and that's no pun intended.

But I knew enough about Hank to realize that he doesn't like to override other people's decisions. And dealing with Tammilynne was a touchy subject. Everyone on the set either knew, or suspected, that he was sleeping with her. So I suppose he had to bend over backward to give the appearance of being impartial.

"Tami, I told you to take it up with Wardrobe," Hank said, looking hollow-eyed and weary. He had a faint stubble on his chin and looked like he hadn't slept for days. He was still the lead suspect in the investigation of Adriana's murder, even though Rafe had admitted there was no indictment in the works. But just being under the cloud of suspicion must have been taking a toll on him.

"Wardrobe won't do anything about it!" Tammilynne's voice quavered as if she was close to tears. "They think the dress is right for the scene. Hah," she added, flicking her blond hair over her shoulder, "what do they know? They're morons."

"They know what they're doing; that's why I hired them. They're the best in the business and I've worked with them for years." Hank glared at her, his features stony.

Hank glanced at Maisie, who had turned away from the conversation and was making some notes on the script with a Magic Marker. I bet Tammilynne had interrupted them right in the middle of a story conference. Hank let his eyes stray back to the script as if he longed to go back to it and not be forced to deal with Tammilynne's wardrobe malfunction. But Tammilynne had center stage at the moment and from the looks of things, she wasn't going to go away.

"I'm telling you, Hank, they don't know what they're doing. They're clueless. Look, I'll prove it." Tammilynne grabbed a rail-thin extra strolling by and held her by the elbow. "Let's get an unbiased opinion, shall we? Will you give me a minute here?"

Maisie rolled her eyes, drumming her long fingernails against the script pages, but Hank gave a heavy sigh and turned to Tammilynne.

"Okay, you've got my full attention, Tami, but make it fast." Hank put down the script and crossed his arms over his chest. I saw him take a quick peek at his watch and a look of annoyance crossed his face—everyone knows time is money on a movie set.

Round one was going to Tammilynne. A sly look crossed her perfect features; she knew she'd won just by getting his attention. "Well, that's better," she said snidely.

"Please just get on with it," Maisie pleaded. "We're going to lose the morning light." She shaded her eyes and looked up at the bright ball of orange that was slipping behind a cloud bank. They'd predicted a hot and hazy day today, not ideal for filming.

Tammilynne gave her a cold stare. "Okay, here's the thing. You want fast, you've got fast. We can settle this in two minutes."

She smiled at the extra she'd plucked out of the crowd. Tammilyne was still holding her by the elbow and the girl was smiling back uncertainly at her. The girl was pretty but lanky, like an anorexic greyhound with silky blond hair and a lean body. She was wearing a gauzy apricot-colored smock top and white linen pants, probably the kind of outfit Tammilynne would have picked out for herself.

"What's your name, sweetie?"

"Sherry. My name is Sherry Hawkins, Miss Cole." Her voice quavered a little as if she wasn't quite sure why she'd been plucked out of the crowd. "I'm in the party scene."

"Oh honey, everyone's in the party scene," Tammilynne said with heavy patience. "Look, I need you to tell the truth. Can you do that? All I want is your honest opinion."

"Yes, of course. I'll be glad to tell you what I think." She brightened a little and glanced at the extras behind her. Maybe she was happy to be singled out, thinking a little attention from the lead actress might lead to a speaking part. She unconsciously touched her hand to her heart like she was taking a solemn oath.

"Okay, Sherry, it's truth time. What do you think of when you see this dress?"

Tammilyne held up a floral wraparound dress; the skirt was a little long, what they used to call "tea length." It wasn't anything you'd see Julianna Rancic wearing on the red carpet, but it wasn't the worst dress in the world, either. The color wasn't my favorite, a mixture of sky blue and royal blue on a white background.

It was a little retro, something like the iconic Diane Von Furstenberg wrap dress from the seventies. It's what they call "figure flattering" but with a knockout figure like Tammilynne's, you don't need any extra help. Tammilynne wanted to flaunt her body, not hide it.

The truth is, the dress was a little "old" for Tammilynne, who could look fifteen with the right lighting and makeup.

"What do I think of it?" Sherry gave a nervous giggle.

"Yes, just say the first thing that comes into your mind."

"Really, Tammilynne, we need to get these scenes nailed

down—" Maisie began, but Hank raised a hand in the air to silence her.

"Give her a minute. I want to hear what she has to say," Hank said, his expression grim.

I had the feeling he was used to dealing with temperamental actresses and he probably knew damn well that Tammilynne being his mistress made the whole situation much more complicated. The only sign that he was annoyed was a muscle twitching lightly in his lower jaw and his right hand clenching and unclenching lightly at his side.

Interesting. I raised my eyebrows, but I doubt anyone else noticed these giveaways, these "tells." Funny how body language can be your undoing, even if you're a trained actor.

To paraphrase Freud, the unconscious gives you away every time. (Okay, Freud didn't say it exactly that way, but do you really want to plow through *The Psychopathology of Everyday Life* or *The Complete Introductory Lectures on Psychoanalysis*? Hah. I thought not. That's why I'm giving you the CliffsNotes version.)

"You want to hear what I think?" Sherry asked. Her voice was soft with a slight Georgia accent.

"You bet. We're standing here waiting for it," Maisie said tartly. She glanced at the sky and frowned. The sun had already slipped behind the clouds and all the magic had disappeared from the scenery. No more sun-dappled water and vivid colors; now it was just a cloudy, humid day at a south Florida pond.

Sherry ran her hand lightly over the fabric of the dress, picked up one of the long sleeves, and let it fall back in place. "It reminds me of my aunt Vivian," she said slowly.

"Your aunt Vivian?" Tammilynne hooted. "This dress reminds you of your aunt Vivian?" She turned to Hank Watson. "What did I tell you? This looks like something Aunt Bea would wear to a gardening club luncheon back in Mayberry."

"Yes, it does," Sherry agreed, not aware that she was fueling the fire. "In fact, my aunt Vivian has a dress a lot like this, except it's in lime green and white." She brightened suddenly, turning a high-beam smile on Tammilynne. "And she wears it to church socials—"

"Church socials?" Even Maisie looked aghast.

"Or maybe potluck suppers. But I think it might be a little dressy for a potluck supper," she added. She cocked her head to one side like Tim Roth playing Dr. Cal Lightman on *Lie to Me*.

"And how old is your aunt Vivian?" Tammilynne asked, her chest thrust out, one hand on her bony hip.

"Oh, I'd say early sixties. Somewhere around there. Maybe sixty-two."

Chapter 25

"Wow, that was a little awkward, wasn't it?"

I whirled around to see my reporter friend Nick Harrison standing behind me, rubbing the back of his neck. He was dressed in a Cypress Grove casual outfit—a white golfing shirt, khakis, and loafers with no socks.

"I didn't know you were on the set today," I said in a low voice. "How much did you hear?"

Tammilynne had won her argument over the wrap dress and had flounced away to wardrobe with a triumphant smile plastered on her perfect features. Hank Watson and Maisie were bent over the script, presumably still working out the kinks in a scene.

"Only the tail end, but that was enough," Nick admitted. He edged over to the craft services table and I tagged along next to him. "I don't know how Hank deals with these people every day. I was afraid he might take a swing at her; did you notice he had his fists clenched?"

"You picked up on that? I'm impressed."

"You've taught me well, master." Nick gave me a mock bow. "I try to watch for body language clues now. And judging from that murderous look I saw on his face, it seems like Hank isn't as laid-back as I'd thought." *But is he capable of violence?* I wondered. *Being uptight is one thing. Being capable of murder is something else.*

"You're suggesting that he was actually angry enough with Adriana to kill her?"

"According to the Cypress Grove PD, he's still the number one suspect," Nick said easily. "They can't seem to finger anyone else for it, even though she pissed off a lot of people."

"This wasn't a crime of anger, though," I said slowly. "It doesn't have any of the earmarks of a crime of passion. It certainly wasn't impulsive—it took a lot of thought and planning to rig that prop gun."

"That's true." His eyes scanned the breakfast spread laid out on the long table. I smelled bacon cooking somewhere but they hadn't put it out yet. "This place is a hotbed of intrigue, isn't it?"

"Tammilynne is making things much worse," I said. "Adriana was bad enough, but everyone was used to her and knew what to expect. Tammilynne is like a tornado; she's volatile and unpredictable. She's making Hank's life a living hell. He's probably regretting giving her the lead role, but now it's too late."

"Funny," Nick said thoughtfully, "I thought she was gorgeous when I first saw her, but now I don't even find her attractive."

I quirked an eyebrow. Was he kidding me? Even a celibate monk would find Tammilynne attractive. "Really? You're probably the only man in America who isn't salivating over her. She's a supermodel—that blond hair and knockout body compensates for a lousy personality."

Nick shook his head. "Not for me, it doesn't. She's either a diva or a certified nut case, in my book." He reached for an iced coffee and looped his pinky finger through two doughnuts. "Or maybe she's both."

I watched, fascinated, as Nick spread a paper napkin on top of his coffee cup, balanced the doughnuts on top, and then reached for a bear claw. Reporters and free food go together like corned beef and sauerkraut, but Nick raises mooching to an art form. I've seen him make a whole dinner out of crab cakes, Vienna sausages, and chocolate-covered strawberries. And do it while juggling a glass of wine in one hand and a notebook in the other. I always threaten to secretly film him and put the video up on YouTube.

"Do you have any idea what all that saturated fat is doing to your arteries?"

"Probably clogging them," he admitted through a mouthful of a glazed jelly doughnut. "I'll worry about it later."

"Later?"

"When I'm forty. You know, when I hit middle age, somewhere around your age, Maggie." He flashed me a boyish grin and went right on scarfing down the pastries.

Nick knows very well that I'm only thirty-two, but he likes to tease me about being over-the-hill. Nick is only a couple of years out of college, and there's enough of an age difference between us that he thinks of me as a big sister. Definitely not girlfriend material. So I guess snide remarks and friendly teasing go with the territory.

And of course I tease him right back and pretend I see an imaginary bald spot on the back of his head. It's amazing how sensitive guys are to things like that. I've caught Nick touching the back of his head worriedly a couple of times, when he doesn't know I'm watching.

"You're here on assignment, I guess. But I thought you'd already wrapped up the 'Live on the Set' series?" There's been so much interest in the *Death Watch* production that Nick's editor told him to extend his original "Live on the Set" piece into a four part series, featuring interviews with Hank Watson, the principals, the tech crew, and even the extras.

He nodded carefully, trying not to make any sudden movements. One false move and his Eiffel Tower of sugary treats would come crashing down. "I did, but I want to tie up a few loose ends with Sandra Michaels. Are you seeing her today?"

"I hope to. I was going to look for her this morning and see if we can work on the script a little more."

"You're really getting into it, aren't you? Being a script consultant."

"I am. It's just one of those opportunities that came out of nowhere and I'm enjoying every minute. Who knows, I may never visit a movie set again, so I may as well make the most of it."

I looked around the bustling set. Jesse, the AD, was busily herding a dozen extras into a gazebo down by the pond, Tammilynne was prancing out of Wardrobe in a traffic-stopping red minidress, and Marion Summers was barking into her cell phone.

It was giving me a little chill to think that the murderer was probably right here on the set with us. It had to be someone connected with the *Death Watch* production, didn't it? So many possibilities. I'd narrowed them down in my mind, turning them over and over, and outside of Frankie Domino—who still was the mystery man—all of them had a motive for killing Adriana. Sidney Carter had Adriana to thank for his ruined career. There was no love lost between Sandra Michaels and Adriana, that much was clear. Carla hated Adriana, and blamed her for the loss of a lucrative book deal. And Hank Watson? Adriana's death certainly paved the way for his young girlfriend, Tammilynne, to step into the starring role. And if Adriana really had been having an affair with Lori's husband, maybe the actress would have been angry enough to kill her. My head was reeling, and Nick interrupted my jumbled thoughts.

"You know, Maggie, there's one possibility standing right over there," Nick said, as if he had read my mind. "I bet you didn't even consider her as a suspect, did you?"

Her? I gulped in surprise. He was looking straight at Marion Summers. "Marion?" I whispered. "Did you find out anything else about her?"

Nick moved away from the table, which was buzzing with hungry extras. "She has a thing for Hank Watson, but then, that's no surprise, is it?"

"I'd figured as much. She's supposed to be one of the best in the business, yet she's stayed with Hank all these years, and she's never really gotten the money or the recognition she deserves. So I figured she had to have another reason for staying—she must be in love with the guy."

"Bingo."

"But that still doesn't give her a reason for killing Adriana. She wasn't jealous of Adriana, and her death hurt the production. So that makes it unlikely that Marion would kill her. Marion wouldn't want to do anything that would hurt Hank."

"Marion owes Hank, trust me, but they have a complicated relationship," Nick said. "It has nothing to do with a romantic connection; it's something else. Something that goes back a long way. I just heard about it last night."

"What is it?" We edged under a banyan tree, trying to catch a little shade. The sun had come out in full force and now that the cloud cover had drifted away; the day had turned into a scorcher. I could feel my hair sticking to the back of my neck and my low ponytail turning to frizz.

"There was an accident a long time ago, a traffic accident. Hank and Marion were in the car, along with Steve, Marion's teenage nephew, and they were driving back from doing some location scouting in Kentucky. They were out in the boondocks and a jogger appeared out of nowhere. The

car hit him, and he was injured very badly. The police were
called in. The jogger had a head injury and wasn't sure who
he saw behind the wheel. He thought it was Hank—"

"And it was?"

"Yes, Hank was the driver. But here's the interesting part
of the story." Nick ducked his head and leaned close to me.
He smelled like a doughnut factory. "Steve, Marion's nephew,
took the blame for the accident."

"Why would he do that?"

"Because Hank was into alcohol back then and already
had some DUIs on his record. Marion told Steve to take the
blame because she knew the judge would go easy on him.
After all, he was just a kid and he'd only had his license a
few months."

I shook my head. "So she sacrificed her nephew for Hank?
What happened next? I assume the whole thing was covered
up."

"Absolutely. The judge did go easy on him, just as Marion
predicted, and the cops wanted the case wrapped up so they
didn't do a thorough investigation. It was a clumsy cover-up
but it worked. The nephew's records were expunged, so no
one was the wiser. It took some digging to get this. I had a
friend in L.A. working on it."

"Why did the cops play along with it? Usually the cops
are hard on celebrities." I remembered that awful mug shot
of Nick Nolte that went viral—he looked wild-eyed and dis-
heveled, an image that could never be erased.

Nick shook his head. "Not this time. The DA's brother was
the mayor and the movie company was bringing in a lot of
money to this little backwoods town. They wanted to play
nice and keep the production company happy."

"Makes you cynical, doesn't it?" I asked after a moment.

"I'm already cynical," Nick replied.

We went our own ways then, Nick hoping to nail down

Jesse, the AD, for a quick interview while I tracked down Sandra, the "formerly fat actress." I found her in Wardrobe, trying on a clingy halter dress and twirling in front of a three-way mirror.

She smiled and greeted me with a big hug. "Do you like this? I think it's really hot. A nice change from the suits I have to wear in the courtroom scenes."

"It's gorgeous," I said, sinking down on a low couch. "And you have the right body to show it off. All your dieting and exercise paid off."

"Yes, it was tough going for a while, but in the end it was all worth it," she said, her smile fading a little.

"And think how many people you'll be inspiring with your book and your talk show."

Sandra nodded, but her neck flushed crimson. *Maybe she's one of these people who can't take a compliment?* "That's what I keep telling myself." Funny, but she didn't seem enthused; her voice was flat and robotic. "I love to motivate people and show them that anyone can do what I did. All it takes is knowledge about how the body works and some self-discipline. I'm going to have exercise and nutrition experts on the show. They'll provide the knowledge and I'll provide the motivation."

"You're certainly the perfect role model," I agreed.

I stared at her, expecting to see a look of pride or maybe even satisfaction on her face, but it wasn't there. Mental note: *what's going on here?*

Just for a second, I thought I saw something else flicker across her face, an emotion I couldn't identify. The bodily clues were there. A tightening at the edge of her lips and a quick downward glance to the side. That downward look was significant.

Was it fear? No, something else. Shame? I was puzzled. Why would she be ashamed of losing weight and looking great in a dress? Sometimes people who lose a lot of weight still think of themselves as "fat," and I wondered if this could be the case.

Back in my Manhattan practice, I had a few patients with body dysmorphic disorder. They were rail thin, but when they looked in the mirror, they saw a fat person staring back. It's a complicated disorder, and difficult to treat. Could Sandra have BDD? Or was I simply seeing something that wasn't there, overanalyzing everything, as Nick says I tend to do.

"Do you need me to work on the script with you?" Sandra asked. Unless I was mistaken, she was eager to get the focus off of her weight loss. "I can change out of this dress in a flash and meet you outside. Or we can just grab an iced tea and sit here and work together. They've finally got the AC working in the trailer." She gave a rueful smile and pushed a golden lock of hair out of her face. "I guess you noticed."

"I did. No more sweat box." I pulled out a copy of the script, with my notes, from my tote bag. "Let's go over a few things right here; it will only take half an hour."

I never got the chance to ask her about Copper Canyon, and before I knew it, time slipped away and I was heading back to WYME. I made sure I was there early enough to talk to Vera Mae before doing the show. She had the most recent hate note ready for me, and I wanted to give myself time to "process" it, as the shrinks say. She said it was "worse than the last one," but what exactly did she mean? It couldn't be that bad, could it?

It could, and it was.

Chapter 26

"I wasn't sure I should show it to you, sugar," Vera Mae said, all apologies, "but I figured you'd want to see it. If I was in your shoes, I know I would."

"You did the right thing, Vera Mae."

I took a deep breath and looked at the piece of paper lying on my desk.

And then my heart slammed into my rib cage and a trail of goose bumps popped up on my bare arms.

It was a montage, and a grisly one at that.

Someone had taken pictures of me—most were publicity shots, including my WYME headshot—and glued them to the paper in neat columns across the page. Then they'd mutilated my face in every gruesome way you can imagine. Some of the pictures were slashed, leaving a split-open smile and bleeding eyeballs, some had a devil's face with horns, and a few of them had obscene words scrawled across my features.

You get the idea.

This was a copy, of course. I knew that Rafe had taken the original to the Cypress Grove PD and it was probably being analyzed right this minute. I looked away for a moment to compose myself, looked back, and shuddered, my nerves jangled. This was more than a prank, wasn't it? It practically reeked of evil. It was full of rage, cruelty, a demonic desire to wound, to kill. And especially to shock.

Someone hates me enough to do this, but who?

"Rafe wanted to talk to you this morning, honey, but I said you'd be tied up on the set, and then you'd be dashing in here to do your show." She glanced at the clock. Fifteen minutes till air time.

"Maybe I should give him a ring."

"He said he was working on another case today, but I wouldn't be surprised if he drops by anyway. You could always talk to him during the commercial break, or during the news segment."

I nodded and stared silently at the photos. It was shocking to think that someone wanted me dead. Or mutilated. *What sort of warped mind would create this?*

The same kind of warped mind who plans a murder, a little inner voice reminded me.

"This is all that was inside the envelope? No message, just these awful pictures?"

Vera Mae nodded. "This is it—except for the message at the bottom right." She tapped the paper with her magenta-colored fingernail. "Looks like he couldn't resist getting in another little dig."

I followed her eyes and saw the tiny words block-printed at the bottom of the paper, where an artist would place his signature. A chill danced down my spine. *Back Off. Or Lola won't like what she gets.*

"It's him," I breathed softly. The lines from the old song buzzed through my head. Whatever Lola wants, Lola gets. "And now he's threatening Lola."

"Or her," Vera Mae corrected me. "It could be a woman, you know."

It was hard to concentrate on my work that afternoon. My

scheduled guest was Shirley Dawson, a motivational speaker from Dania. She was hawking her new book, *Open Your Heart to Magic*, and she was getting an amazing amount of local buzz.

It was one of those "feel good" books, the kind of psychobabble that clogs the media with its nutty message. Perfect health, unlimited wealth, and lusty sexuality, it's all there for the asking. Knock and the door shall be opened. Ask and the universe will tilt your way.

"Hey, sign me up!" I muttered under my breath. I'm never a fan of "magical thinking" and I certainly wasn't in the mood for this nonsense today.

I took a peek at the back cover copy. It was annoyingly optimistic—almost to the point of being delusional. Did the author really believe this tripe, or was she giving the public the quick fix, the magical solution that they craved? I'd soon find out when we opened the lines and started taking questions from the listeners.

I tried not to groan as I forced myself to flip through the pages and skim through the press packet her publicist had thoughtfully provided. Are you looking for the secret to finding money, sex, and happiness? All you have to do is tap into your inner "heartsongs" and the rest is easy.

Heartsongs. Huh? Who knew!

I checked out the table of contents and the first chapter jumped out at me. "Stick a rose between your teeth and have an awesome day!"

The last time I saw someone walking around with a rose between her teeth, she was snowed on Haldol and committed to a locked psych unit.

And I don't think she was having an awesome day.

I found myself wondering who would buy a book like this ($24.95 and available only in hardcover from Shirley Dawson Enterprises). Maybe it was self-published and Shirley

Dawson bought all the copies herself? That was the only possible explanation.

I raised my eyebrows, tilted back in my Aeron chair, and tossed Vera Mae a speculative look. Call me cynical but I bet Shirley Dawson had some strong financial ties to Cypress Grove and maybe even to the station.

"Did you look at this?" I held up the cover, which was plastered with a giant sunflower.

"Yeah, it's pretty cheesy, I know. I tried to read a little last night, but I gave up."

"It's more than cheesy; it's insane. It says all you have to do is tap into your heartsongs, and all good things will come to you. What in the world is a heartsong?"

"A heartsong? You got me, sweetie. I don't know; maybe it's something like whale songs." She'd opened the mike to talk to me and her liquid caramel voice trickled into the studio.

"Whale songs?" I asked incredulously.

"Whales make music, you know. People record them and everything. Do you suppose it's something like that?" She was thumbing through the commercial log for that afternoon and she sneaked a quick look at the clock. Vera Mae is the ultimate multitasker. She stopped and stared at the ceiling, her face scrunched up in thought. "Or, wait a minute. Maybe I'm thinking of dolphin sounds. Yeah, that could be it. They make those squeaky noises, but I guess you could call them sounds."

"Dolphin squeaks? I don't think that's what she has in mind."

"Did you know that dolphins are the only animals who commit suicide?" Vera Mae continued in a conversational tone. I learned early on that Vera Mae is an expert on trivia and little-known facts. "Although I can't imagine why a dolphin would want to kill himself, can you?"

"Only if someone forced him to read this book. Then he'd so depressed, he'd swim right down to the ocean floor and never resurface."

"Now you be nice, girl," Vera Mae teased. "This show might turn out better than you think."

"I doubt it," I groused. "It's going to be a train wreck, I just know it."

I looked at the author page. With her big hair, big smile, and veneered teeth, Shirley Dawson could be a contestant on *American Idol*. "I'm not at all happy about this guest, Vera Mae." I lowered my voice even though the studio was sound-proof. "This woman sounds like a wack job. Who invited her on the show—and why? That's what I'd like to know."

"Here's the thing. Her daddy is a real good friend of Cyrus's family and they all play golf together over at the Parson's Creek club."

Vera Mae's shoulders heaved as she blew out a little sigh. She shot me a sympathetic look as she made her last-minute preparations from the control room. Just minutes till air time, and I still didn't have a handle on my guest. What in the world would I find to talk about?

"And—" I persisted.

"And we just had to have her on the show; there was no getting out of it sugar. You see what I mean? Besides, her daddy's thinking of taking out some prime-time radio spots advertising her book. We're talking big bucks here. You should have seen Cyrus, his eyes lit up like a pinball machine when he heard what their advertising budget was."

"That would impress him, all right."

"So you just do the best you can. You can make her sound interesting; I know you can. You always bring out the best in the everyone, Maggie."

"Flattery will get you everywhere, Vera Mae."

"It has so far, sugar; it has so far."

Irina ushered my guest in right before showtime. Shirley Dawson reminded me of a real estate agent, well dressed in a pale green linen suit with a lacy white shell underneath. She extended a manicured hand to me (French, squared-off tips, buffed, no polish) and flashed me her veneers. I had the feeling she drove an immaculate, late-model car, maybe a Lexus or a BMW.

"I am a *huge* fan of your show," she gushed. "Huge! And I brought you an autographed copy of my book."

Shirley presented the book with another blinding smile and looked deeply into my eyes. She was attractive, mid-thirties, with long chestnut hair and green eyes, but there was something vaguely unsettling about her gaze. It seemed a bit practiced, as if the "eye lock" was something she'd picked up in a competing self-help book.

"Thanks, but your publicist already sent me a copy." I held up my copy to show her, and hoped she didn't suspect that I had only looked at the cover.

"Oh, you can give that one to someone on your staff, or maybe even have a radio promotion giveaway. Do you ever do contests?"

"Well, no, actually. At least we haven't so far."

I suppose we could have some sort of contest to promote her book, but why should we? The lines would be clogged with callers, and it would be a giant headache for the staff. I hoped Cyrus hadn't promised her anything except the guest spot on my show. That was bad enough.

She settled herself in the visitor's chair next to me and crossed her legs. Uh-oh. She reached into her bag and pulled out a grande latte from Starbucks. I never allow anyone to bring food or drinks into the studio, but now that she'd already plunked down the coffee cup on the console, what could I do? It would be a little awkward to snatch it away.

Luckily, Vera Mae saw the problem and came bustling in

from the control room. "I'll just leave this for you over here," she said, whisking away the offending coffee and settling it on a low table by the door. "I'm Vera Mae Atkins, the producer," she added by way of introduction.

"Oh, yes, we spoke on the phone. I just have to tell you, I am *such* a fan of the show," Shirley said. "You have the *most* exciting guests. Here, I brought a personalized copy for you, too." She reached into her seemingly bottomless Coach tote bag, and pulled out another copy. "This book will change your life!" She gave a triumphant smile, as if she'd done something impossible—like David Copperfield levitating over the Grand Canyon, or making the Statue of Liberty disappear.

"Well, now that's really sweet of you." Vera Mae looked a little startled. "I'll get right down to reading this tonight."

"And be sure to call me if you have any questions, or if you just want to talk," Shirley said, oozing sincerity. "I put my unlisted phone number on the card, and you can always reach me on my cell, my BlackBerry, or my landline. And of course, I'm on Twitter, Facebook, MySpace, Gather, and LinkedIn. All my online contact information is on the back, including my Web site, my publicist's private line, and my five blogs."

This was a woman who was clearly in love with herself. Narcissistic personality disorder, I decided. Like the mythical figure Narcissus, she was entranced by her own reflection and thought we should be, too.

"Vera Mae, look at the time!" I said urgently. The second hand was winding down to 12; we'd be live in a heartbeat. *Enough with the love fest!*

"Oh lordy," Vera Mae squealed, making tracks for the control room. She jammed her headphones over her ears, twirled a dial, and pointed at me. "Go!" she mouthed.

The lines were jammed with callers, and to my surprise, Shirley did a good job on the air, even if her answers sounded a bit practiced. Her speech had a certain robotic effect. It was as if someone had implanted a Chatty Cathy chip in her memory storage banks, allowing her to give the right answer to any question.

Were there a finite number of comments on the chip? What if she encountered something unfamiliar, something she hadn't been programmed to handle? Would she suddenly come to a squeaking halt like the esteemed psychiatrist Dr. Smoot? Luckily no one surprised her with any trick questions and I felt myself begin to relax. I let my mind roll downstream as she peppered her remarks with personal vignettes and feel-good stories.

They were inspirational, often straining credibility, but the listeners ate them up. ("I told her to visualize a pile of money coming her way. Just as she was going to be evicted from her house, a mysterious stranger came to her front door with a million dollars!")

Still, the time passed quickly, and since I didn't have to concentrate on the show, I could think more about the case. There were so many troubling aspects, so many loose ends. It was depressing to think that all I had were leads, no solid suspects, and I wasn't close to finding the killer. I had the nagging feeling I was overlooking something important; but what?

And now there was a new element to be considered—the threatening notes I'd received. Were they real, were they pranks, or were they connected to Adriana's murder? Was I really in danger, and had my "sleuthing" caught up with me? Rafe had always warned me that my "detective work" would be the death of me, no pun intended.

I knew Rafe would have an opinion on the notes and he wouldn't be afraid to mince words.

Rafe. I caught myself smiling, just thinking about him. In spite of the craziness, the emotional turmoil, and the gut-wrenching stress of a murder investigation, Rafe was always a bright spot in my life. He was exciting, dangerous, and had enough sex appeal to melt my bones.

I glanced at my watch. Another half hour and I'd call him.

Chapter 27

Nick called just as I was saying my good-byes to Shirley Dawson and promising to "do lunch" with her sometime soon. I put him on hold, and told him I'd be right back.

Shirley passed out a half-dozen more promotional copies of her book to the WYME staff, including Irina, who was intrigued by the idea that you could attract money just by visualizing it. Just make a wish, and you would be wealthy beyond your wildest dreams.

"But this is, how you say, amazing, really good stuff," Irina said, flipping through the pages. She stared at Shirley, who was beaming at her in the reception area. "You mean, just by thinking many good thoughts about money, dollars will come to me. Is that simple?"

"It sure is, sweetie," Shirley said. "It's a secret, but I'm happy to share it. I'm revealing it to the whole world! Life as we know it will never be the same."

Hmm. Another insight into the wacky mind of Shirley Dawson.

Shirley believes she holds the key to a world-shattering secret that will change the future of mankind. *Ooo-kay.* Grandiosity, anyone? Check your *DSM* for details. (The *DSM* is the *Diagnostic and Statistical Manual of Mental Disorders*,

every clinician's bible.) We're talking serious bipolar disorder here, and we'll keep the narcissistic personality disorder
as well.

"In my country, many people do not have money to
spend, not on food, not on clothes, not on nothing. Sad, very
sad." A cloud passed over Irina's model-perfect features,
and she tapped her fingernails thoughtfully on the book
cover. "Maybe I mail this book home to my cousin Sergei;
he reads a little English. This maybe help him do better in
life."

"Oh, that's a wonderful idea, Irina," Shirley said, her eyes
moist. "What a touching story. I love the idea that I can
reach out to people across the world!" She took Irina's hand
and squeezed it, her face radiant. "I promise you that this book
will change your cousin's life, and the lives of his whole
family."

"I think so, too," Irina said, her face lighting up in a smile.
"If Sergei has money, he will be happy. So is good news for
everyone."

"Yes, money will bring him happiness and security," Shirley
agreed. "And most important of all, it will bring him freedom. Don't forget, Irina, freedom's just—"

Another word for nothin' left to lose? No, wait, that's
Janis Joplin.

"—the key to a happy life," Shirley finished.

"Yes, freedom." Irina repeated the word slowly, rolling it
around her mouth, her tone hushed and reverent. "You are
right, very right. If Sergei has money, his life will change for
good." She nodded her head up and down several times, her
blond tresses bobbing against her neck.

"That's true." Shirley clasped her hands together in front
of her chest, steepled her fingers, and looked pleased with
herself. She'd just brought another follower into Camp
Shirley.

"And you know best part of all this?" Irina asked. Her shoulders heaved in a happy little sigh.

"What's that?" Shirley's green eyes glowed with pride. I bet she was already planning on how to incorporate this touching story into her next media appearance.

Irina smiled. "With money, Sergei not have to rob no more liquor stores, or sell no more drugs on street. As you say, dollars will just fall in lap. My mother and sister will be so happy, no more prison time for him. Whole village will celebrate."

Prison time? Selling drugs on the street? Whoa there, missy, too much information! Shirley's eyebrows knotted together in disapproval. *Uh-oh.* I guess she won't be using Irina's touching story in her next media appearance, after all.

"Er, yes, quite right," Shirley said, straightening up and backing away from the reception desk. She was moving at a good clip, heading for the double glass doors that exited onto the parking lot. "Thanks again, Maggie!" She flashed another Hollywood smile at me along with a cheery wave as I scooted back to my office to take Nick's call.

"Hey, you kept me on hold long enough," he protested. I heard his fingers tapping away in the background.

"Sorry, I was saying good-bye to a guest." I figured I'd save the Shirley Dawson story for the next time Nick and I met for lunch at Gino's. "What's up?"

"My L.A. contact did a little more research and something interesting came up on that actress, Lori Taylor. You talked with her on the set, right?"

"Yes, but it was just for a couple of minutes. She seemed very sweet. Of course, Carla Townsend couldn't resist making a sniping remark about Lori's husband having an affair with Adriana, and Lori walked away in a huff. Carla's always ready to dig up dirt on someone; that's her stock-in-trade as a sleazoid journalist, I guess. The sad thing is, it's

probably true in this case. It seems that Adriana liked to sam
ple the talent, and Lori's husband is a good-looking guy."

"Did Lori seem angry?"

"More hurt than angry, I'd say." I paused. "I can't believe
Lori would have what it takes to kill someone, even if she
did want Adriana out of the way."

"There's more to Lori than meets the eye."

"Meaning what?" I pictured the pretty young actress chatting with me on the set. There was something vulnerable about
her, something that went beyond her delicate features and
soft voice.

"Did you know she used to live in Utah?"

"No, it never came up. Why's that important, anyway?"

"She was part of a survivalist group out there." Nick
waited a beat to let this new information sink in. "We're
talking a David Koresh type of compound."

"Yikes. Survivalist?" I couldn't imagine Lori ever being
part of a group like the Branch Davidians.

"Yeah, it surprised me, too. Appearances can be deceiving. She could be a steel magnolia; you know?"

"I can't believe it. She looks so fragile, so innocent. She'd
have to be brainwashed."

"Look what happened to Patty Hearst."

I flashed on that iconic photo of Patty Hearst holding
a submachine gun. "You're right. Anyone can break under
pressure." I thought of the young girl's heart-shaped face
and silky blond hair. "Poor Lori; she seems as delicate as a
flower."

"She's into firearms and she's an expert marksman. That
little tidbit was buried in a TMZ piece about her."

My brain finally kicked into high gear; there was no way
I could ignore the latest intel. Fact number one: Lori Taylor
was a whiz with firearms. Fact number two: she might have
a good reason for wanting Adriana out of the picture. "So

you're saying, she'd have the technical know-how to rig the prop gun with the pellet? She wouldn't have any problem doing that?"

"That's exactly what I'm saying."

My mind was reeling with this new information. I was so shocked, I could hardly take it all in. I wasn't sure what to do next, and made a mental note to find out more about Lori.

Nick and I promised to touch base later that day, and as I hung up, I noticed the message light blinking. Oh, no! I'd missed a call from Rafe when I'd been ushering Shirley Dawson out of the studio.

Rafe's message was characteristically short and to the point.

"Maggie, some new information has come up. Do not do anything further on the case; got it? Don't do anything until we talk." He hesitated as if he wanted to say something else and I heard people talking in the background, station house noises and phones ringing. *Had he come up with a new lead? Had he nailed a suspect?* "Gotta run. Talk to you later," he signed off brusquely.

I was going to be in the dark until I managed to talk to Rafe again.

But that didn't mean I couldn't continue my own investigation, did it? I was about to leave for home, when I saw the light blinking with another message: Lola.

Her voice was the opposite of Rafe's, breathy and excited. She told me not to bother with dinner because she was on her way to Miami for another movie audition. *A movie audition in Miami?* Mom's new agent, Edgar Dumont, must be more on the ball than I'd thought. She hadn't given any details, just that she knew this was her "big break."

Since Lola has been talking about her big break for the past thirty years, I hoped she hadn't gotten her hopes up too high. With Lola, it's all about catching the shiny brass ring, even if it means riding the merry-go-round a few million times hoping for the big payoff..

Live in hope, die in despair, as Vera Mae always says.

Luckily Lola believes only the first half of that sentence.

Chapter 28

"Was Lola excited about the audition?"

"Excited? That's an understatement. She was over the moon. I don't think I've ever seen her so jazzed about anything. It sounds like a big deal, the second female lead, with loads of dialogue. The kind of role she can really get her teeth into."

Lark and I were having an after-dinner cappuccino on the tiny balcony of our condo. It was a lovely evening. The setting sun was casting an orange glow over the garden below, the bougainvillea were full of scarlet blooms, and a hint of honeysuckle wafted over us.

It's a peaceful place, and we could look down at a pretty little fountain spilling into a pond. This is my favorite place to relax, and Lark, a yoga freak, does her early morning Salute to the Sun out here. Pugsley even has his own little canvas doggie bed on the balcony, although naturally he prefers to sit with us.

Lark was sitting on one of the navy canvas deck chairs I'd picked up at Target, her legs tucked up under her. "You should see her bedroom. It looks like it was ransacked; she must have tried on a dozen outfits before she went flying out of here."

"Wardrobe malfunction?"

"More like a wardrobe meltdown. She couldn't find anything that was just the right match for the role."

"Oh, no." I pictured Lola dressed as a geriatric version of Hannah Montana. Not a pretty picture and I blinked to erase it. I watched the copper-green metal dolphins twirling in the spray of the fountain. "How bad was it?" I asked, trying not to wince. "Tell me the truth, don't try to spare me."

Lark smiled. "It's not as bad as you think. Or what you're probably picturing in your mind's eye." Lark knows I have an all-too-vivid imagination and visuals tend to get locked in my head forever. Once they take up residence in my memory bank, I can't seem to shake them. "She was all set to wear that bright yellow halter top that you hate—"

"The really plunging one? The one Lindsay Lohan wore on MTV?"

"Yeah, that's the one." Lark made a face. "I finally told her that it showed up her tan lines; it's the only way I could talk her out of it. She finally settled on a nice tropical print blouse from Ann Taylor with white capri pants. Pretty conservative, actually. Especially for Lola."

"I'm glad to hear it." I felt a happy little whoosh of relief. Not that I expected Mom to dress like she was going to a Junior League luncheon, but I was glad that she wasn't dressed too outrageously. "It sounds like Edgar is doing a better job for her than I thought."

"Edgar?" Lark swept Pugsley onto her lap and nuzzled her face in his soft fur. "What do you mean?"

"Edgar Dumont, you know, her new agent. He's the one who must have set up the audition for her today. Funny, I guess I had him pegged all wrong. I figured he was going to sign her up with the agency and then just ignore her and concentrate on his younger clients."

"Wait a second; that can't be right." Lark turned to me,

her eyes troubled. "I don't think Edgar had anything to do with this audition today. Lola got a phone call from some Florida producer and he told her to be in South Beach at four this afternoon. It's some sort of private audition for an indie film."

"An indie film?"

"She said she'd never heard of him or the production company. I think she left a message with Edgar's secretary but no one got back to her."

My heartbeat ratcheted up a notch. An unknown producer calls her out of the blue to audition for an indie film? And of course Lola, being Lola, took off like a rocket to get there. Why should that surprise me? Mom has always been impulsive; acting quickly and intuitively is part of her personality style. Usually her shoot-ready-aim philosophy pays off for her. But this time I had my doubts.

"Do you remember the name of the company?"

"No, I don't think she mentioned it. I know she tried to google it but nothing showed up."

"Really?" Alarm bells were clanging in my head.

Lark must have caught my frown because she put Pugsley down and stood up, twisting her hands in front of her. "Lola didn't seem too upset over it. She said sometimes producers come into town and rent space for a few days to hold auditions. So if you try to google them, you don't get any hits, because it isn't a permanent address. That would explain it, wouldn't it?"

"Maybe, maybe not."

A horrible thought slammed in my brain. Would someone actually threaten Lola to get to me? It seemed unlikely, and I tried to quell the little twinges of paranoia nibbling at the edges of my mind.

I told myself there was nothing to worry about.

But what about the Klieg light and the two threatening notes I'd received? I flashed on the mutilated photos that were sent to the station—they were enough to make anyone paranoid. My stomach churned just thinking about them.

"Lark, do you happen to know where Lola went in South Beach? Was her appointment in the Art Deco section?" As long as Mom was surrounded by plenty of tourists and activity, I knew she'd be safe. After all, four o'clock was broad daylight and there would be people jamming the sidewalks, having coffees and taking in the sights.

"No, I know it wasn't in the historic district. She said it was somewhere south of that. What's wrong?"

I bit my lip. "Nothing, I just wondered what time she'd be back." I glanced at my watch. "I guess she didn't say, did she?"

"Afraid not." A little flicker of fear crossed Lark's face; she'd picked up on the distress signals in my voice. "Why didn't I ask her? What was I thinking? I never should have let her drive to Miami alone."

"Hey, Lark, don't be silly." I forced a little chuckle into my voice. "Why should you sit on a folding chair for three hours while Mom waits her turn to say four lines? That's usually how these things turn out. She's probably on her way home by now, anyway." But Lola hadn't called and left a message here at the condo. She always lets us know if she's going to be home for dinner, so what was different about today? "She probably got tied up in traffic on A1A coming back from the studio. That's always a possibility. "

"The audition wasn't in a studio," Lark said slowly. "I think she said it was in a warehouse."

A warehouse? Okay, now I was in full-throttle panic mode. A tangle of fear and anxiety gripped my mind and I drew in a deep breath.

Lark gave me the briefest of sideways glances. "Do you think we should call Rafe?"

I nodded. "You read my mind."

I had my cell phone with me, out on the balcony. I flipped it open and at that very moment, it gave a shrill ring. I was so startled I nearly dropped it.

"Maggie, thank God I reached you!" It was Mom, clearly on the edge of hysteria, her voice coming in ragged gasps.

"Where are you?" I was already on my feet. "Are you all right?" A silly question. She was clearly not all right. Pugsley began running in nervous circles around my ankles. Even he sensed the tension in the air and he gave a series of nervous yips, his eyes bulging.

"Yes. No. I don't know; I'm not making sense, am I?" She gave a high-pitched laugh that ended in a sob. She sounded as though she was on the brink of hysteria.

"Mom, calm down. Take a deep breath." I forced my own voice down an octave, like I used to do with my patients when they were in crisis. I walked into the living room and grabbed a notepad. "Just give me an address and I'll be there. Are you hurt?"

"No, I'm okay," she said, her voice quavering. "But it's a miracle I'm still alive. I was nearly killed today."

"Nearly killed?"

"Maggie, someone shot at me! I was just lucky they missed. Why would anyone do that to me?" The question ended in another gut-wrenching sob and my heart went out to her.

"Tell me exactly where you are, and I'll tell you what to do," I said grimly. With a trembling hand, I copied down the address she gave me. It was in south Miami. My worst fears had come true. Whoever had told me to "back off" clearly meant business. This was no prank. My heart felt like I'd just completed the last leg of a triathlon and my palms were slick.

I forced myself to take another deep breath and put down the phone while I clicked on Google satellite maps. I found Lola's location immediately. I didn't like the looks of the area. She needed to get to a safe location—fast.

"Mom, this is what I want you to do." I ordered her to lock her car doors and told her to drive three miles north. That would bring her back into the southernmost edge of the historic district where there would be plenty of people. "You're pretty close to Dolce Vita; remember that gelato place we went to?"

"Yes, I remember." Her voice was still strained, but she seemed a little calmer.

"I'll meet you there. I'm leaving now and I'll be there as fast as I can."

"Maggie, this is silly. I think I'm probably okay to drive home—"

I cut her off. "Drive back home? No way. It's too far and you're going to have to be available when the police check out the warehouse." I paused, thinking . . . "Mom, the main thing right now is for you to be safe. I want you to get away from the warehouse, do you understand me?"

In a little-girl voice, she assured me that she would do exactly as I asked her. Lola, who prided herself on being a "tough old broad," sounded frightened, and more than a little vulnerable.

I guess being shot at will have that effect on you.

I whirled around to Lark, who was standing in the doorway to the balcony, looking stunned. "What happened? What can I do? Do you want me to go with you?"

"I'll explain it all later, but right now I need you to stay here. Call Rafe, and give him this information." I scribbled the address for Dolce Vita and grabbed my car keys. Goggle maps was still up on the screen. "Tell him to meet us at the gelato place and to alert the Miami Police to go there." I pointed to the computer. "I'll call you as soon as I get there."

"I feel terrible," she began. "This is all my fault."

"Lark, don't be silly." I smiled with more confidence than I felt. "Lola will be fine, but make that call now, okay?"

Chapter 29

I took a gamble and decided I-95 was the quickest way to get to Miami. For once, the traffic gods were with me—it seemed everyone was driving north out of the city at four thirty in the afternoon, and I made good time.

I zipped along in the left lane, with the radio tuned to an oldies station, concentrating on the words to a Robert Palmer song and willing myself to be calm. *Addicted to love, addicted to love.* I was repeating the lyrics over and over, softly under my breath, like a mantra. This was no time to fall apart, and I wished I'd learned some of Lark's meditation techniques. She swears meditation "calms the mind" but she's had years of practice. It's not something you can just call on in a crisis and expect instant nirvana.

Stay cool, Maggie. I knew I had to be in control of my jangled nerves and I had no idea what was waiting for me in South Beach.

When I walked into Dolce Vita, my pulse jumped for a second—and then I saw her. A big whoosh of relief poured out of me. I hadn't even realized I'd been holding my breath.

Lola was sitting at a back booth facing the door, looking pale and tired, but otherwise unscathed by her adventure. At least there were no obvious scrapes or bruises. She gave a wobbly smile when she saw me and managed a brave little wave. I hurried past the customers lining up for rainbow-colored gelato and pulled her close to me for a tight hug.

A wave of emotion body-slammed me.

"Thank God you're all right," I murmured. I slid into the booth, sitting across from her, my eyes focused on her face. Now that I was close to her, I saw that her blue eyes were red rimmed as if she'd been crying and she was clutching a wadded-up tissue in her hand. "Rafe is going to meet us here any minute. But in the meantime, tell me everything that happened. Lark said someone called you about an audition?"

"Yes, that's how it all started." She paused to dab at her eyes. "Well, what a surprise, there wasn't any audition." Her voice was a little shaky and she swallowed a couple of times. "I was such an idiot, Maggie. This guy called me out of the blue. He said he was a Hollywood producer, and you know me, I thought it was my big break."

I couldn't help but smile. It's true. Lola thinks everything is going to be her big break.

"And he lured you to this—warehouse? Tell me exactly what he said."

Lola nodded. "He said they were auditioning actresses for speaking roles in an indie film, a horror flick. He told me it was a lot like *Death Watch* and that I'd be a shoo-in for a major role."

"He said that?" I was half listening, watching the street outside for any sign of Rafe. Something was nagging at the edges of my brain but I couldn't quite bring it into focus.

"Yes, he did. He said he was planning on shooting in south Florida even though his company is based out in L.A. He made it sound like I'd be up for other parts, maybe even the lead role, in future productions. But it was very important that I come in today, because they had to make a decision by tonight. And he didn't want to go through Edgar. He was quite insistent about that."

Okay, now I knew what was wrong. "Wait a minute. Back up. Why didn't he want to go through Edgar?"

She looked puzzled, biting her lower lip. "I don't know. He said that everything with Edgar was a big deal, that he was too slow to close a deal. Now that you mention it, it does seem a little strange."

"It's more than strange. It's very suspicious."

"Yes, you're right; I should have picked up on that." She shook her head, her eyes starting to tear up a little. "The timing was perfect. Hank told me this afternoon that he'd probably wind up filming in Cypress Grove in a day or two, so I figured it would be good to get another job lined up as soon as possible. And I can only rely on Edgar to do so much. He's got over a hundred clients, so he can't spend every minute thinking about me or my acting career."

She paused while I ordered a couple of coffees from a waitress who'd materialized next to us.

"It makes sense to me, Mom. I can see why you fell for it."

I glanced at my watch, wishing Rafe would show up and hoping he'd have the entire Miami PD with him. Or maybe a SWAT team.

I still didn't have any concrete information about what happened to Mom, but I knew Rafe would ask all the right questions. We needed to get back to that warehouse, but we didn't dare set foot in that place without the cops.

"No, really, what I did was inexcusable. It was incredibly stupid of me, wasn't it?" Mom broke into my thoughts. "I can't believe I didn't take the time to check it out."

"Well, you thought it was legit. You can't blame yourself; you're not psychic."

"I was an idiot, Maggie." She gave a derisive little snort. "You don't have to sugarcoat it; I know I messed up."

"Well, you're okay; that's the main thing." I reached across the table and squeezed her hand. She looked haggard and washed-out under the harsh fluorescent lighting. "That's what we should focus on, because that's the only thing that matters. I know how excited you get when you hear about an audition." I smiled at her. "You used to be the first one in line at those cattle calls, back in New York."

It was true. And she used to drag me along with her. Funny, I vowed never to go after a career in show business and yet here I was, a talk show host at a tiny south Florida radio station. The bottom rung of the entertainment ladder, but I was still in show business, when all was said and done.

Maybe you can't fight genetics, after all.

Lola gave a wistful smile. "Cattle calls. That's exactly what they were. We were all young and hopeful, jammed together into a big room, waiting to do a three-minute reading for a producer. All of us were convinced this would be our big break, our entry into show business. Sometimes I wonder why I did it. Those were some crazy times."

Mom seemed calmer, and I figured it was time to redirect her to the present before she tripped down memory lane. If you give her a chance, Mom will start talking about Woodstock and the Summer of Love and how she nearly met Jerry Garcia. (Then she'll catch herself and tell you she was a toddler at the time.) "I bet you never ran into anything like this, though."

"Oh, never. Absolutely not." She rested her chin on her hand and looked lost in thought for a moment. Was she thinking about tie-dyes and flower children? Or was she reliving the scene in the warehouse?

On the phone, Mom had said that someone had tried to shoot her. That's pretty black-and-white, not the kind of thing she would invent. But could she have been mistaken?

I wanted to hear about what happened in the warehouse, but I knew Mom needed to tell me in her own good time. There was no sense in rushing her; she'd been traumatized by the event and she needed time to process it.

"I wonder if I've gotten more careless lately?" She gave a wry little laugh. "All those years ago back in Manhattan"— she gave an impatient little flip of her hand—"I never would have fallen for something like this. This is the kind of mistake that only a newbie would make. Somebody really green and naive. So what does this say about me?" she asked ruefully. "That I'm not as smart and streetwise as I used to be? I hope I'm not getting old and foolish."

"Old and foolish? Never."

She grinned to let me know she didn't believe it, either. "Well, maybe old and foolish is too harsh. How about 'in her prime and ready for anything'?"

"Works for me," I told her. *Especially the part about being ready for anything.*

"You'll have to take the coffee with you," a familiar male voice said. "We need to get moving right now and head back to the warehouse."

Rafe. My heart did a grateful little flip-flop when I saw him. He was standing next to the booth, jiggling his car keys in his hand, tight-lipped, his expression grim. He had his cop face on, I decided, taking in his dark eyes and the muscle jumping in his tense jaw.

He looked poised like a panther, ready to spring. I realized I still hadn't gotten any details from Mom, but now that Rafe was here, he could take over. I felt a surge of relief, knowing he could handle everything from here on in, dealing with the Miami police and checking out the warehouse. It was all in his hands.

"Are you okay, Lola?" His tone was brusque but I knew from the look on his face that he was concerned about her.

"I'm fine. I don't know how I get myself into these things."

"Did you get the guy's name? It's probably an alias, but we can check it out."

"I'll write it down for you." She scribbled something on a napkin and handed it to him. Her face flushed with embarrassment. She was all set to launch into a major apology, but I stood up and grabbed my purse, signaling it was time to go.

"I have my car right outside, Rafe. I'll take Mom with me and we can follow you."

"Good, the Miami PD is already over there. That was smart to give the address from Lark. They sent a couple of patrol cars to the warehouse right away so they've probably had a chance to check things out. Let's go and see what turned up. It should be interesting."

"I can't believe we're going back there." Mom gave a little shudder, and shot me an imploring look as we got into my Honda.

"If you want, you can stay in the car, but I really think Rafe needs you inside, okay? You're going to have to tell him exactly what happened. Especially the part about being shot at. Just saying the word "shot" made me wince. "Do you think you'll be able to do that?"

She bit her lip and fastened her seat belt. "I'll do my best. This is no time to wuss out."

Mom and I followed Rafe, and a few minutes later, we pulled up outside a boxy structure with a filthy gray facade and a flat cement roof. It looked like an abandoned chop shop and I raised my eyebrows. I couldn't believe Mom actually had gone in here. *What was she thinking?*

"This is it?" I asked incredulously.

There were four windows facing the street. They were covered with years of grime, and like many buildings in that part of town, they had black security grilles over them. Security grilles? How could there be anything in there worth stealing? The place looked like it had been deserted for years. A broken cement sidewalk snaked up to the battered front door and the dusty front yard was littered with beer bottles and debris.

I spotted an empty Miami PD black-and-white pulled up at the curb and saw two cops coming out of the building. I wondered if I should get the okay from Rafe before getting out of my car.

"Mom, it looks like a crack house."

"It looks a little better inside." She cast me a sideways glance, her tone defensive.

"I'm not even sure we *should* go inside," I muttered. "I can't believe you went in there alone." I'd warned myself not to sound judgmental, but it was hard not to, after seeing the place.

"Maggie, I've been to loads of auditions in bad areas. I figured it must be a low-budget outfit, that's all. It didn't look dangerous to me, just run-down."

I bit my tongue; there was no point in lecturing her. I was shocked, though. No one in their right mind would go into a place like this, even in the daytime.

Then I spotted Rafe talking to a couple of uniformed officers who were pointing and shaking their heads. I got out slowly, wondering what to do next when Rafe saw me and signaled me to join him. He introduced us to the two officers, Jiminez and Conrad, who stared at us with frank curiosity. I wondered what Rafe had told them about the situation.

"Okay, here's the thing," Rafe began. "They've already checked out the building and didn't find anything. Lola, how about if you and I do a walk-through and you tell me exactly what happened?"

The three of us headed inside, with the Miami officers trailing along behind us. One of them was talking into a mike on his shoulder and I had the feeling they were winding things up, getting ready to leave.

The building looked deserted. The main room had a concrete floor and was nearly empty, containing only a couple of battered desks and an old file cabinet. There was a dingy hallway off to the right. It was paneled in some cheap imitation-wood material and the floor was covered with dirty linoleum.

"What's down there?" Rafe asked, pointing to the hallway.

"The john," Officer Jiminez said, making a face. "Believe me, you don't want to go in there."

"I'll take your word for it."

"A back door?"

"Yeah, but it's double locked from the inside. It looks like it hasn't been opened in years." Jiminez took a quick peek at his watch. From the look on his face, he was dying to get out of here and get back to some real police work. Or maybe he just wanted to get a burger at Big Pink on Collins Avenue.

Rafe was right; there was nothing here. Had they even dusted for fingerprints? The whole place was so filthy it was hard to tell. I didn't see any telltale white powder sprinkled anywhere. I glanced at Jiminez and Conrad, who were talking in low voices—it was obvious they'd given up on doing any real investigation here. There was no crime scene tape in place and none of those little cones they use on *CSI* to mark evidence.

"Was the front door open when you got here?" Rafe asked the two cops.

"Yeah, it was unlocked, open about three feet."

"I left it *like that*," Mom offered. "I went flying out of here, and didn't look back." She turned to the officers. "Are you sure you didn't see anyone inside or maybe running out the back?" Mom couldn't resist launching her own investigation.

The two officers exchanged a look. "No, ma'am, we didn't."
She stared them down and Jiminez continued, "We walked
through the whole place. Nothing. Nada." He threw an apologetic glance at Rafe. "Do you want us to stick around?"

"Just for a minute." He turned to Lola. "Show me what
happened. You were standing where?"

"Right about here." She walked forward a few feet. "I
called out the producer's name and there was dead silence.
It was a little creepy. I wondered if I'd gotten the address
wrong but I checked my notes and this is where he told me
to come. I was just about to leave"—she gave a little gasp—
"when a shot rang out. It went whizzing by my right ear. It
was really loud."

"You're sure it was a gunshot, ma'am?" Jiminez asked.

"Of course, I'm sure." Mom's tone was haughty. "I've
been in dozens of action movies and I know what a gunshot
sounds like. Once I even auditioned for a Chuck Norris movie.
I would have gotten the part, but they wanted someone who
could ride a horse."

"Mom—"

"Another inch and that bullet would have blown my brains
out," she said dramatically. "Or at least blown my ear off."
She touched her hand to her ear as if to reassure herself that
she hadn't ended up like Van Gogh.

"And you never saw anyone, or heard anyone?" Rafe
asked.

"No one." Mom sighed. "The moment I heard that shot,
I hightailed it out of here. I locked myself in the car and
called Maggie. I was shaking like a leaf. I certainly wasn't
going to stick around to get shot at again. I took a few deep
breaths to calm down and Maggie told me to drive straight
to Dolce Vita." I squeezed her arm in sympathy. "I figured it
would be safe there, and it would be a good place to meet up."

"Show me where you think the shot came from. If you

were standing here, and it went past your right ear, I'm thinking it came from—there." Rafe whirled around and pointed to a pile of wooden fruit crates in the corner. They were easily tall enough to hide an attacker. "And that means the bullet would be lodged somewhere over here."

He inspected a section of drywall on the far side of the room; it was riddled with graffiti, and suspicious-looking brown smears. I didn't want to look too closely, but Rafe took out a penknife and poked around in a few spots.

"We've already checked that wall," Officer Conrad said. "We didn't see anything. No bullet holes, no shell casings, nothing."

"Was there just one shot?" Rafe asked Mom.

"That's all I stuck around for. So yes, I think so." She scrunched her eyebrows together. "But I can't be a hundred percent sure."

Rafe shook his head, frowning at the wall for several minutes while Conrad and Jiminez stood by, their arms folded in front of their chests. Finally Conrad cleared his throat.

"Ma'am, is it true that you're an actress?"

"Why yes, I am." Mom smiled, thinking she'd found a fan. "Have you seen any of my movies?" She looked delighted. "I've done a lot of theater work, but people always seem to recognize me from my movie roles. Oh, and I did a Hallmark Hall of Fame television drama. I played a young social worker in Minnesota who broke up with her fiancé and moved to Guatemala to open an orphanage where she found a half sister she never knew she had. She ended up marrying a journalist who wrote a story about her experience." She paused to take a break. "Maybe you caught that one."

I raised my eyebrows. Officer Conrad was probably three years old when that show aired.

"No, I'm afraid I didn't." He shifted uneasily and stared

at his feet for a moment "I was just wondering, you being an actress and all, if maybe you could have imagined that someone shot at you?" He spread his hands out in front of my Mom apologetically. "No offense, ma'am, but the thought crossed my mind; you know?"

"You think I imagined it? Well, I certainly did not!" Mom was outraged.

"Sorry, ma'am," Conrad offered, "but you know, sometimes creative people . . ." He let his voice trail off and stared at the floor.

"See things that aren't there," Jiminez, his partner, finished for him. "The lighting is pretty bad in here." He was right. The greasy windows didn't let in much ambient light and the only illumination came from a low-wattage ceiling light dangling above us on a chain.

"What does lighting have to do with anything? I'm telling you, I *heard* the gunshot!"

"Could have been a car backfiring," Jiminez offered.

"Ridiculous!" Mom muttered. "They don't sound anything alike."

"Did you find anything?" I asked Rafe, who was still staring at the wall, as if willing a bullet hole to magically appear.

A long moment passed. He crossed the room and looked around, presumably for a shell casing. "No, nothing at all." He looked at Lola. "Whatever happened here, Lola, there's no trace of it. I'm afraid we don't have much to go on."

Chapter 30

"Maggie, someone really did try to shoot at me. I didn't imagine it. You believe me, right?"

It was nine o'clock that evening and Mom and I were sitting at the kitchen table with a plate of Lark's wheat germ–walnut brownies in front of us. They're loaded with iron-rich blackstrap molasses and taste far too good to be healthy, but trust me, they are. Lark had brewed a pot of chamomile tea, and I held the cup to my lips, enjoying the soothing fragrance and the delicate herbal flavor.

"Of course, I believe you. If you say it happened, it happened. You walked into the warehouse and someone took a shot at you."

I remembered how shattered Mom had looked at Dolce Vita just a few hours earlier and how she'd tried so hard to be brave. She'd insisted on driving her own car back to Cypress Grove even though Rafe had offered to send someone to get it for her.

Now that we were safely back in the condo, I made a conscious effort to unwind, pushing the disturbing picture of the warehouse to the back corners of my mind. My thoughts were whirling in a million directions and it seemed pretty clear that someone wanted me to stop investigating Adriana's murder.

As Freud said, "there are no coincidences." The attack on Lola was directed at me. And somehow it was all related to the murder on the *Death Watch* set. But how to connect the dots? That was the problem. It was like a giant jigsaw puzzle, but I was missing a few key pieces.

"So what's the next step? Is the Miami PD going to do anything?"

I shrugged. "Rafe said they'll make a formal report but they don't have much information to go on. Apparently they can't find the tenant; the building was rented out to a guy who paid cash. And he paid in advance for six months, so there's no paper trail at all. The people in the neighborhood say it's been vacant for the past few weeks. The cops tried to follow up on the name you gave them, but I guess it was phony."

"Cal Silverman. He said he had offices in New York and L.A. Cal Silverman Productions. It really sounded legit."

"No such person, I'm afraid. Either here or on the West Coast."

"It seems hopeless, then. There's nothing for them to go on." She looked crestfallen, finishing the last of her tea and rubbing her eyes.

I was silent for a moment, thinking. "The only concrete evidence is that phone call you got here at the condo. They can try to figure out where it originated, but that may be a dead end, too. Rafe said he'd call or stop by tonight, if he had any new information."

Mom nodded and stood up slowly, stifling a jaw-cracking yawn. Mom is like the Energizer Bunny, always operating at full throttle, but tonight she looked like she'd finally run down.

"You know, Maggie, I think I'm ready to call it a night." She glanced at her watch. "I haven't gone to bed this early since I was twelve years old," she said wryly," but I've got to be on the set bright and early tomorrow. Hank gave me a couple more lines of dialogue and he put me in another scene."

"That's good." I smiled. I knew having some extra lines made her happy and I wondered if Hank had gone out of his way to beef up the role for her. He'd sounded genuinely upset when we'd called him about the fake audition down in Miami and he'd asked if he could do anything to help. I told him the best thing would be for Mom to get right back to work and try to put the whole incident out of her mind.

Good advice, but I wondered if I could do the same thing?

I was ready to call it a night myself half an hour later when there was a quiet tap on the front door. Pugsley gave a soft little yip and trotted to the front hall with me. When I swung open the door, my breath caught in my throat.

"Is it too late to stop by?"

Rafe, looking a little rumpled but sexy as hell, was standing on my doorstep, his jacket slung over his shoulder.

"Of course not; c'mon in."

I pulled the door back, but he shook his head. "I've only got a second. Just wanted to fill you in on the latest."

"Okay, then I'll join you out here." I stepped outside, closing the door softly behind me. Mom was probably dead to the world and I didn't want to disturb her. I knew the incident at the warehouse had taken a terrible toll on her, even though she'd tried to make light of it.

It was a gorgeous evening, and I took a deep breath of the night-blooming jasmine Lark had planted next to the front walk. The fragrance was intoxicating. Rafe leaned against the wrought-iron railing, his eyes dark and intense. He was

always watchful, even when he tried to look relaxed. It's as
though all his senses are always on high alert, and his mind
is always sizing up the situation. I never can decide if it's
personality style or learned behavior. He's a cop so maybe it
just goes with the territory.

"So what's up?"

"Nothing substantial. The call to your condo is the only
thing we really have, and the guy used a phone card."

"I was afraid of that." I paused, thinking. "And nothing
turned up in the warehouse, did it? I don't think the cops
believed a word Lola said. They think that because she's an
actress she has a vivid imagination. They probably think she's
a drama queen."

Rafe grinned. "She's pretty dramatic all right, but I know
she didn't make this up. Something happened but it might
not be what she thought it was. I went over the warehouse
again, after you left. I used a Maglite and went over it inch
by inch—there was nothing there, Maggie, no bullet hole.
Nothing. I'd bet my badge on it."

"Then I don't know where this leaves us." I bit my lip in
frustration. "Mom's not delusional; she really heard a gunshot. I believe her."

"I know she thinks she heard a gunshot, but it could have
been something else. A car backfiring, or maybe some kids
had a cap gun; I don't know—"

A cap gun. That's when it hit me, the thought that had
been playing around the edges of my mind for hours. It
had tickled my brain cells, tantalizing me, and now it finally
drifted to the surface. *Bingo*. My pulse glitched in excitement.

"Rafe, I think I know what happened," I said, cutting him
off. "What if it was a prop gun? Could that be what she heard
in the warehouse? They sound very realistic. That would explain everything, wouldn't it? Someone wanted to threaten

Lola, to intimidate her, but not kill her, so they shot a prop gun."

He scratched his chin; he had just a faint hint of stubble. "That's an interesting theory," he said slowly. "It's certainly possible."

"And remember, whoever called her knew that Edgar Dumont was her agent. And he deliberately wanted to keep Edgar out of the loop. Someone decided to play this cruel prank—or whatever it was—to lure her down to Miami and then nearly scare her to death."

My mind was racing with possibilities and I could hear the words tumbling out too fast. Pressured speech, the shrinks call it. It didn't matter. I couldn't seem to rein in my thoughts or my words and they bubbled up under their own power.

I was sure I had the key to what happened and I wanted Rafe to agree with me.

"There wasn't any gunpowder smell in the warehouse," he said thoughtfully. He was obviously turning the idea over and over in his mind, realizing it was the only way to explain what had happened. "So that would go along with your theory," he admitted.

"I'm telling you it was a prop gun; I know it." I grabbed his arm in my excitement, and he locked eyes with me for a moment. We were standing very close and I felt the hard muscle ripple under my fingertips. I flushed and let my hand drop back to my side. "Anyway," I hurried on, "this the best explanation we have so far."

"You realize you're playing with fire, don't you? Whoever set this up went to a lot of trouble. First the notes at the station and now the threat against Lola."

"I know. It's awful to think I might be responsible for what happened today." I stared at the street for a moment, lost in thought. It was shrouded in shadows and the fronds on the palm trees were dancing in the evening breeze. I pulled my thoughts back to the unpleasant truth I couldn't escape. I couldn't believe I'd put Lola in harm's way, but that's exactly what I'd done.

"You're not responsible, Maggie," he said, touching me lightly under the chin, forcing me to look up at him. "But this has to end, right? It has to end right here, right now. You've got to let us do our work, and you do your work. We're the cops and you're—"

"Nancy Drew?" This is one of Rafe's not-so-affectionate nicknames for me and it never fails to annoy me. I'm sure that's why he does it.

"Wrong. As usual, you're jumping to conclusions. I was going to say 'you're a talk show host.'" His cell phone chirped and he pulled it out to look at the screen. "Gotta run, Maggie. Promise me you won't do anything foolish," he added, heading down the steps to his car.

Foolish? Rafe has an uncanny ability to push my buttons and I felt a little bubble of anger start to rise in my chest.

"I won't do anything *foolish*," I echoed. Just a touch of sarcasm in my tone, to let him know I'm not a pushover.

He stopped dead in his tracks on the middle step and whirled around to glare at me. "I mean it, Maggie. This guy isn't kidding; he's playing hardball, whoever he is. Remember what the notes said: Back off. That's two warnings, and now there's this incident with Lola. Here's exactly what I want you to do—"

"Yes?"

"Nothing." His voice was flat with a steely edge to it. "I want you to do nothing. We'll solve this crime without your help, and you're just putting yourself and your mother in danger by meddling. You're making our job tougher, not easier. Got it?"

Wow, no subtlety here. Rafe can lay it on the line when he wants to. Sometimes he talks to me like I'm one of his suspects, I thought with a flash of intuition.

"Got it." I gave him a mock salute but his back was to me; he already was getting into his Crown Vic with his cell phone jammed to his ear. Rafe was back in his cop world, moving on to the next problem, another pressing case, and our conversation was no longer center stage.

I sighed and went back inside. For a really hot guy, Rafe can be an incredible pain in the ass sometimes.

Chapter 31

I sat down at the kitchen table, too jazzed to even think about going to bed after my conversation with Rafe. I grabbed a piece of paper and started to make a list of all the suspects in Adriana's murder, hoping something would jump out at me, some key fact that I'd missed or maybe a subtle clue that I'd managed to overlook.

Writing has always been soothing for me, offering me a shot of clarity when my thoughts are hopelessly deadlocked. I used to jot down all my impressions when I was dealing with a particularly troubling patient back in Manhattan. Somehow, just the act of putting pen to paper gave me a new perspective on the case—it seemed to jolt my brain into problem-solving mode.

I started by writing my patient's name in the center of a piece of paper and then I listed the names of all his friends and family members in a big circle. Then I drew a line from my patient to each of the main characters in her life, connecting them, like the spokes of a wheel.

It's a sort of visual shorthand. A straight line means a harmonious relationship, a jagged line indicates some tension or troubling issues, and a broken line tells me the relationship has been severed.

Would my write-it-out technique help me this time? My mental Magic 8 ball said: Signs point to yes.

So I wrote *Adriana* in the middle of a circle and surrounded her with everyone who was involved in her life. I knew that at least one of them was involved in her death.

The names in the outer circle included Hank Watson. Did I really consider him a suspect? The Cypress Grove PD did, but was that just by default? They didn't seem to have a key suspect and Hank was on their radar screen because he certainly had the technical ability to rig the prop gun. Plus, he'd had some difficulties with Adriana in the past, but I still couldn't imagine him as a murderer. I was ready to rule him out.

Right next to Hank was Tammilynne Cole, his main squeeze. Adriana's death was a stroke of luck for her, because the bimbo actress found herself in a starring role. But could Tammilynne really mastermind a murder? I had the feeling she had trouble deciding which lip gloss to wear every day (mocha glaze or sun-kissed bronze?). I put a question mark next to her name.

Was she a murderer? If so, she was the ditziest one I'd ever come across.

Sidney Carter was something of a wild card, and I didn't really know much about him, except what I'd learned at that wine and cheese mixer at the Seabreeze. Adriana had certainly treated him badly, and starting that AIDS rumor had effectively sabotaged his career. Sidney acted like it had all been a long time ago, though, and seemed to have made peace with the situation.

Sandra Michaels had always been a bitter rival of Adriana's, but was there really anything there to kill over? It seems like Sandra was moving ahead with her life and career and was full of plans for the future. She had a book deal and a television show in the works. Why kill Adriana when things were going so well in her life?

Marion Summers was probably resentful at always being the second-in-command, stuck in a perpetual "bridesmaid" role with Hank. But they seemed to have a good working relationship and I couldn't imagine her risking the success of the movie to settle some personal grudge. She wasn't getting a fair shake in the relationship, but I had the feeling she'd come to terms with it, years ago. I couldn't see any reason for her to rock the boat.

Lori Taylor had a very good reason to resent Adriana, if her husband, Sam, was really sleeping with the leading lady. And there was that nagging comment from Nick—he'd said Lori had been part of a survivalist group in Utah and was very good with firearms. That gave me pause for a moment. Still, Lori had her plans all laid out—she wanted to move to the Midwest and start a family. As long as Sam acquiesced with her dream, why kill Adriana? It made no sense to me.

Jeff Walker was the person who actually shot the prop gun that killed Adriana. He'd seemed genuinely horrified at what he'd done and I couldn't come up with a reason why he would want Adriana dead.

Carla Townsend, the Queen of Mean tabloid journalist, certainly had a reason to dislike Adriana. When Adriana decided to jettison her tell-all book, Carla lost her job as co-writer and probably a hefty chunk of change. But plans change and book deals fall through all the time. Was it really worth killing Adriana over a failed book deal? I didn't think so.

Frankie Domino, the mobster type, was still something of an enigma to me. He had business dealings with Hank, possibly shady, but I didn't see any connection with Adriana. Whatever Frankie was up to, it had something to do with Hank Watson and the *Death Watch* production.

I looked through the list again and shook my head in dismay. Adriana's "circle" consisted of all jagged lines, indicating failed relationships, fractured friendships, and long-standing grudges.

It all added up to one dead actress.

Who killed Adriana? I was ready to eliminate Frankie Domino, the mafioso, and Jeff Walker, who had shot the prop gun. Ditto for Marion Summers, his longtime producer, and the two actresses, Lori Taylor and Tammilynne Cole. I dismissed the idea that Hank Watson could have killed Adriana. Her death had thrown the production into a turmoil.

I had three main contenders at the moment: Carla Townsend, who had a long-standing grudge against Adriana; Sidney Carter, who might have been out for revenge over his ruined career; and Sandra Michaels. Why Sandra Michaels? Call it a gut instinct, but there was something about the "formerly fat actress" that just didn't ring true.

I zipped through my show the next day ("Monica Morgan: Stress-Busting Secrets from the Herb Lady") and stayed at my desk through dinnertime, catching up on paperwork. Mom had called earlier in the day to say she'd be tied up at the set for an evening shoot, so there was no point in rushing back to the condo.

Vera Mae was working late, too, so around seven o'clock, we decided to share a pizza.

"I still can't believe what happened to your momma," Vera Mae said sympathetically. "I'd like to have died if that had happened to me, and the scary thing is they still don't know who did it."

"No, they don't have a clue." I told her my own theory about the gunshot, and that someone had used a prop gun to frighten Lola, but they never had the intention to kill her.

"What does Rafe have to say about all this?" She finished off the last piece of pizza and reached for a breadstick. Cinnamon buns were also included as freebies. An odd combination. Six months' worth of sugar, salt, and artery-clogging trans fat, all on one plate. I resolved to eat salads for the rest of the week.

"He didn't have much to say," I admitted. "In fact, he told me that I was hindering the police investigation." I made a little face to let her know what I thought of that remark.

"Oh, now sugar, I'm sure he didn't mean that. At least not the way it sounded," she added, catching my eye roll. Vera Mae has a soft spot for Rafe, and believes that you just have to make a few allowances for guys who are so drop-dead gorgeous. Cut them a little slack; you know? Hopelessly antifeminist thinking, but I've never been able to talk her out of it.

"I think he meant it."

We were silent for a moment, and Vera Mae produced two cans of Arizona iced tea. "Maggie, what do you want me to tell that Townsend woman if she calls you again?" She glanced at her watch. "It's only four thirty on the Coast and she said she's going to try to talk to you before she leaves the office. I can keep stalling her, if you want. She's persistent, I'll say that for her."

"She's a tabloid reporter; I think it goes with the territory."

Carla had tried to reach me earlier in the day and I'd refused to take her call. I was still smarting over that "Death Chair" feature on the TV news and I had nothing to say to her. She'd left a vague message about leaving the tabloids and starting her own talent management company, but I couldn't imagine what that had to do with me.

"I think she wants to offer an olive branch," Vera Mae said thoughtfully. "Maybe she knows her behavior was out of line? Wants to mend a few fences?"

"Carla?" I snorted. "Never. She has skin like an armadillo; she's lacking an empathy gene. She doesn't have the sensitivity to realize how badly she treats people."

Vera Mae considered this. "Well, then I guess she must want something from you."

"I can't imagine what it could be."

As if on cue, Irina appeared. She was working late and came trotting into my office, weaving a little on her five-inch platform stilettos. They were Jimmy Choo knockoffs that she'd scored at a street fair and she looked like she was walking on stilts.

"There is a very rude woman on line three. Carla Townsend. She says she is journalist, and I say you are not journalist, you write tabloid smut. You are not nice person."

Vera Mae chuckled. "Good for you, girl."

"So I tell her you are making busy. Then she says she is good friend and needs to talk to you. So I put her on hold." Irina spotted one lonely cinnamon roll left in the box. "Ah, gravkelaches. I have not seen these since childhood. Very delicious." She smiled and grabbed the roll before tottering back to the reception area.

"Gravkelaches?" Vera Mae asked.

I shook my head. "No idea." I punched the button for line three and was greeted with Carla's nasal whine.

"Maggie, sweetie, how are you?" Carla's voice was pumped with energy; she seemed to be summoning every ounce of warmth in her black soul. You'd think we were best buds and had exchanged string bracelets.

"I'm fine, Carla," I said crisply. "What can I do for you?"

"Maggie, honey, you've got it all wrong. I can do something for *you*. Did you read *USA Today* this morning?"

"Afraid not, what did I miss?"

"A big piece in the entertainment section on my new career move. I'm not writing for the tabloids anymore. I've joined Simon Sheckleberg Entertainment. You'd heard of them, I assume. We have offices in New York, Beverly Hills,

and London. And we're planning to open a new branch in
South Beach."

"How nice for you."

"It could also be nice for *you*, my darling."

"How's that?" Vera Mae shot me an interested look as
she scooped up the empty pizza boxes and napkins.

"Do you really want to spend your life in that little back-
water burg? I'm in a position to help you. As you know, we
represent some of the biggest names in the business. We can
take your career to the next level, Maggie."

A sales pitch. I knew something was coming, but I hadn't
expected this.

"And we do a lot of packaging, so we can work on some
projects together, as well. You can be a triple threat—a talk
show host, a celebrity shrink, and a best-selling author."

"A best-selling author?" I raised my eyebrows and Vera
Mae pointed to her ear. I punched the button for speaker, and
Vera Mae smiled and sat back down. I knew she'd enjoy hear-
ing whatever crazy plan Carla had concocted.

"That's right, sweetie. I'm fielding offers right now from
five major publishing houses. They want me to write a creative nonfiction book for them. Do you know what that is?"

"Something like a memoir." It suddenly occurred to me
that if Carla wrote a memoir, she could blow the lid off Hollywood. She knew where all the bodies were buried. "So
they want you to write a memoir. What does this have to do
with me?"

"Well, here's the thing, Maggie. This will probably surprise you, but I'm not much of a writer." She gave a little
self-deprecating laugh. "Oh, I'm okay at knocking out some
quick columns and celeb pieces but I don't have the stamina
for the long haul. I can't churn out three hundred and fifty
pages without some help. So I need a coauthor. Someone

with some credentials. The book is going to be more than a memoir. It's going to be more of an inspirational book for women, based on my own life and the people I've known."

"Sounds like quite an undertaking," I said mildly. "But it's not anything I'd be interested in pursuing."

"Now, Maggie, don't say no without hearing me out. I'll make you a deal. You know how you're always looking for guests for your show?"

"Yes, but—"

"There's a private party at the Delano tonight. The big hotel in South Beach; you know it, right?"

"Of course I know it."

"It's going to be fabulous, packed with A-list celebs. The Hilton girls will be there, of course, both Paris and Nicki, are flying down from the Hamptons. And rumor has it that Brad Pitt will be there, without Angie. Possibly Nicole Kidman and definitely Hugh Jackman. Is that enough to get you interested?"

"Wow. I'm interested, all right." It slipped out before I could stop myself.

"I thought so," she said smugly. "Patrick McMullan is taking photos and I can get you interviews with all the hot stars. Everyone's in town doing promo for the Fall television season. Bring a tape recorder and do a few minutes of stand-up with them. You can use them as teasers for *On the Couch* and then I'll schedule them for a whole hour on your show. Your listeners will eat it up."

It was a tempting offer. I had to hand it to her. Carla, for all her annoying habits, is a genius at self-promotion and at getting A-list actors to talk to her. Vera Mae was nodding her head up and down, her towering beehive waving from side to side. This would be a ratings bonanza.

"SAY YES," Vera Mae scribbled on a piece of paper.

"All these actors are really going to be there tonight?"

Carla laughed, a tinny sound that sounded like a gargle. "Of course they are." She rattled off a half-dozen more names that made my pulse quicken. When she mentioned Simon Baker of *The Mentalist*, Vera Mae leaned back, clutching her chest as if she was in the early stages of a coronary.

They were all major celebs, people I would love to have on the show, guests who would bump me up in the ratings.

"And all I'm asking is that you let me fax you some notes for my book next week. Take a look and see if you want to be involved with the project. If you decide you don't want to do it, no hard feelings, Maggie. This is a win-win situation. You'll have a fabulous time at the Delano tonight and you'll have access to some A-list guests for your show. From what I've been hearing, you could really use them, sweetie."

I thought of today's guest, *Monica Morgan, the Herb Lady*. Maybe it was time for a change, and after all, I wasn't really committing myself to anything. Just a celeb event at the Delano with movie stars and mojitos. What's not to like?

I glanced at Vera Mae, who had shot out of her chair and was doing the happy dance around my cluttered office, waving her arms above her head like a televangelist.

Carla was right; this was a no-brainer.

"You're on, Carla." I glanced over at Vera Mae and had a sudden inspiration. "Can you make that invitation for two guests? I'd like to bring my producer."

"No problem, sweetie. I'll fax you two invitations right now and I'll call the people hosting the party."

Chapter 32

The sun had set and night was closing in on us as we zipped along A1A toward South Beach. Vera Mae had changed from her work shoes (she has an infinite number of pairs of snowy white Reeboks) into some dress sandals she keeps in her desk drawer for "fashion emergencies." I'd run a brush through my hair and added a coat of lip gloss. My tan linen pencil skirt and jungle print Ann Taylor blouse would have to do. I switched from my comfy sandals into a pair of cream-colored stiletto sling-backs and hoped I could walk in them without wobbling too much.

Vera Mae had fretted that there was no time to change into party clothes, but I convinced her it really didn't matter. We wouldn't be able to compete with the "beautiful people" at the Delano party anyway, so why should we worry about it? We didn't have to be glam; we were members of the working press. Vera Mae had grabbed a couple of official-looking press passes out of Cyrus's desk drawer before we headed out.

"Just in case Carla forgot to call the organizers and the bouncers try to stop us," she explained. "Oh, and I brought batteries for your tape recorder, Maggie," she said, cramming some triple A's into the pocket-sized recorder I usually forget in my office. "I really like Carla's idea of taping some teasers with the celebs. We'll run them as promos throughout the week. It'll get the listeners really jazzed, knowing you're going to have some big Hollywood celebs on the show. Just be sure to keep the sound bites short and snappy."

"Will do," I said, cranking down the window to let the soft night air in. I loved driving along A1A, the coast road. The moon sparkled on the glassy Atlantic Ocean to the left of us, and I felt a little thrill of excitement at the sound of the surf pounding on the shore.

"Cyrus will be over the moon when he hears about this," Vera Mae said happily. "We really do need a boost for this quarter's ratings, sugar, and this will put us over the top."

"Just so we come out ahead of Bob Figgs and *The Swine Report*," I said wryly. It still galled me that the Hogmaster and I were tied for last place, according to the Nielsens.

"We will, sugar, we will. We can't let a passel of pigs outrank us."

"Damn straight," I said, borrowing one of Vera Mae's favorite expressions.

"Although pigs are actually very intelligent animals," Vera Mae continued, touching her hand to her towering beehive. Amazingly, the evening breeze pouring in the windows didn't ruffle it; she must have shellacked it into place. "Some folks believe pigs are smarter than dogs." She gave a throaty chuckle. "It wouldn't surprise me if they're smarter than Big Jim Wilcox, but I wouldn't want to be quoted on that."

"Your secret's safe with me," I told her.

We passed two very grand hotels as we approached Miami; the Eden Roc and the Fontainebleau. Vera Mae chatted about all the celebrities that had performed there in the days when everyone drank scotch on the rocks and could name the members of the Rat Pack.

Night had fallen when we approached the northern end

of South Beach, but the city was alive with color and lights. South Beach has a continental feel to it, with outdoor cafés, trendy nightspots, and luxurious watering holes. No wonder they call it the playground of the rich and famous.

I started to pull into the circular drive leading to the De-lano and slowed to a crawl. It was jammed with cars. Uni-formed valets were doing their best, but I figured it would be a good half-hour wait before we could hand over the car and get inside.

"Vera Mae, how about if I drop you off right here? You can get us signed in for the party and I'll leave the car some-where close. There's that public garage I always use. It's just a block or two away."

"Well, I don't know," Vera Mae said, looking flustered. "You're really the one Carla invited; I'm just tagging along."

"Don't be silly. Get in there and wow them. Look," I said, pointing past her out the car window. "Isn't that Matt Damon over there?"

"Oh land sakes, do you think it is? I can't see with all these people." Vera Mae squinted into the crowd milling around in front of the entrance.

"If you want to say hello, you better get in there fast."

"I'll sign us in and I'll wait for you in the lobby," she said, scrambling to get out of the car.

"Wait a minute!" I reached into the glove box and handed her the invitations Carla had faxed to the station. They didn't look elegant but they'd get us in the door, and at the mo-ment, that's all I cared about.

"Oh Lordy, where's my brain?" Vera Mae said, grabbing the invitations. "See you in a bit, hon."

I pulled into the parking garage and my mind was buzz-ing with possibilities. Funny how one connection could lead to something interesting, proving once again the power of networking. I couldn't imagine getting involved with Carla and her "creative nonfiction project" but I appreciated the chance to mingle with celebs at the Delano. Vera Mae was right; Cyrus would be thrilled.

I drove up to the fourth level to find a space, locked the car, and headed toward the exit to Collins Avenue. It was dark in the garage and my too-high heels were tapping a little staccato on the concrete floor. Funny, but I felt a tiny shiver of anxiety crawling up my spine. Why was I worried about a celeb party? I've met enough A-list celebrities that they don't impress me, and anyway, it was all about work tonight.

My mind was playing over possible interview questions when a car came tearing out of the blackness, rounding the corner like it was at the Daytona 500 tryouts. *Are they drunk? Are they nuts?* A big warning light flashed like a strobe in my brain when I realized the car was headed straight toward me.

My brain seized and I flashed back to a college Physics class. I was seeing the second law of thermodynamics in action. Also known as the Pauli exclusion principle. Two objects can't occupy the same space at the same time.

What did that mean for me? Simple. Either the car was going to be a hunk of twisted metal, or I was going to be roadkill. Realistically, I'd put my money on the latter.

I have to tell you, no matter what Sylvia Browne says, my whole life didn't flash in front of me. There was no blurry montage of my first day in kindergarten or my first kiss with Harold Feddermarker, a dweeb I dated in junior high. Trust me, there are some life memories you *want* to forget.

What was going on here? I was pissed off. Big-time. I jumped to the side just as the car whizzed past me. I tried to send a death glare to the driver, but the windows were tinted so I contented myself with shaking my fist in the air.

I decided it would be a good idea to get out of there ASAP, just in case some other Mario Andretti types were lurking around. That's when I heard it. The screech of brakes, followed by the sound of an engine revving up, pushed to the max. It suddenly dawned on me.

The driver was coming back to take another pass at me.

The good news is that I wasn't mad anymore. I didn't have time to be. I was scared out of my wits, and I started running blindly, tripping along in my silly heels. An odd image fluttered in my brain. I thought of a line from a spaghetti western: "He died with his boots on." In my case, they'd say, "She died with her stilettos on."

Either way, I'd be dead.

I yanked off the shoes and finally came to my senses. If someone was out to run me over, why was I making their job easier by staying in the center of the aisle?

I ducked back between the parked cars, hoping I could stay out of sight until the maniac driver gave up the chase. I had a better look at the car as it whizzed past again; it looked like a late-model Mercedes. My heart took a painful lurch and a cold knot formed in my stomach. Was this personal or was it some new street game? Kill the pedestrian?

I knew I had to keep my wits about me. After all, I had the edge, I decided, hunkering down next to a navy blue BMW. I was on foot, and my attacker—whoever it was—was stuck in a car. As long as I stayed out of the aisle and out of sight, the game would be over. So eventually, they'd give up and leave the garage.

At least that's what I was telling myself.

Then there was another sickening screech of brakes and the Mercedes shimmied to a halt, rocking slightly. *Uh-oh.* My heart was hammering in my chest and the skin was tingling on the back of my neck. I hunkered down even lower and watched as the driver's door opened. I knew I had to stay calm even though my heart was thumping like a rabbit's.

The driver was getting out. It was a woman, but the garage was far too shadowy for me to make out anything else.

She left the motor running and the driver's door open. Then she advanced on me.

"Come out, come out, wherever you are," she said softly. This was beginning to have a *Hush . . . Hush, Sweet Charlotte* feel to it and I could feel my heart pounding in my ears. A very bad sign. Was this some lunatic, an act of random violence, or was this personal?

"Maggie, I know you're there," the voice went on.

Maggie? Okay, now I finally got the message. This was personal.

"There's no point in hiding because I'm going to ge-e-e-e-t you. One way or the o-o-o-other." The voice slithered through my brain, reminding me of every B horror movie I've ever seen. She was half singing to herself; clearly she was a wack job. Something was familiar about her voice, but I couldn't quite place it. An idea bubbled in the back of my brain and suddenly broke the surface. Suddenly I got it. This was a trained voice, a cultivated voice.

An actor's voice. But whose?

I didn't have time to ponder my own question, because when I took another peek, the woman was just a few yards away, moving slowly toward the BMW. I still couldn't make out who she was, but suddenly that didn't matter anymore, because something else grabbed my attention.

She was holding a big, shiny gun.

Chapter 33

Time for evasive action before this Joan Crawford wannabe blew my brains out. Very quietly, I dropped to my knees and slithered under the BMW. I stayed perfectly still, listening as her footsteps echoed in the parking garage bouncing off the cement block walls.

She wouldn't think to look under a parked car, would she? I turned my head to the side and nearly gasped. I'd left my shoes, the killer stilettos, next to the BMW. I could have cried in frustration. Instead, I carefully inched one hand out and grabbed the offending shoes, being careful not to scratch them on the concrete floor and laid them on top of my chest.

Success. For the moment at least.

Mommie Dearest was still out prowling around the parking garage, and from the sound of her footsteps, I decided that she'd moved further down the aisle. Should I try to make a break for it?

A tempting idea, but I decided against it. After all, I was perfectly safe where I was, and she'd left her car door open with the motor running. That told me she'd be giving up the search at any moment and exiting the garage. Then I could make my getaway, presumably with my head and brains still intact.

I breathed a sigh of relief. For some reason, I thought of Lark and her theories about cosmic harmony and yin and yang. According to Lark, if the universe gives you a gift (providing me with a cozy refuge under the BMW), it immediately tilts the other way, giving you a challenge or major test. Or maybe even a disaster.

I smiled to myself. Sometimes you have to take things at face value and I didn't believe any cosmic disaster would happen to me in the next five seconds.

Except it could and it did.

A loud chirp, enough to wake the dead. My cell phone!

I nearly jumped out of my skin, half sitting up and banging my head on the chassis. Why hadn't I put it on mute? No time to worry about that at the moment, because now I was front and center in Miss Wack Job's scopes.

"There you are, sweetie!" I heard her heels tap-tapping as she hurried over. She reached under the car and gave my arm a vicious tug. "Do you want to come out, or shall I shoot you right where you are?" A high-pitched cackle, almost maniacal.

"Maybe we could talk about this," I gasped, wriggling out from the under the car. Hey, I'm a psychologist and I've had crisis intervention training. There was a slim chance I could talk Ms. Crazy out of killing me. It was odd that she knew my name, but maybe I could figure out what she wanted, and find a way to talk her out of cold-blooded murder.

"Come out slowly and put your back against the car," she barked, as I scrambled out.

I wriggled out from under the car, and slowly stood up to face my unknown assailant.

Except she wasn't unknown.

It was Sandra Michaels, the "formerly fat actress."

"Sandra?" I said, as if my eyes were deceiving me. "What are you doing here?"

"I came here to kill you," she said, a wide smile spreading across her face. She leveled the gun at me.

So much for my crisis intervention training. I couldn't think of any deep psychological insights to offer. I could ask her why she wanted to kill me, but I figured that might annoy her, and she might shoot me on the spot. Maybe a diversionary tactic? Could I stall for time?

"You know, a gunshot is going to make a hell of a noise in this enclosed space," I pointed out. "The sound will go ricocheting off the walls and you'll be surrounded by security guys."

"Ya think?" she asked sarcastically. She reached into her bag and pulled out something that looked like a scope. "That's why I brought a silencer."

"Good thinking," I said weakly. "You must have been a Girl Scout." It's always a good idea to reinforce a patient's ego strengths, but maybe I was taking psychoanalytic theory a little too far. "And you're shooting me because—"

"Because it's the only way to shut you up."

"Ah-hah." I hate it when murderers make perfect sense. It's so hard to come up with a really good comeback. "Here's a thought. I could just be quiet, I could promise not to speak again for the rest of my life. I could take a vow of silence like one of those Carmelite nuns. Do you remember Audrey Hepburn in *A Nun's Story*? She had to have her head shaved, and all that beautiful chestnut hair was falling around her—"

"Shut up!" Sandra yelled. "This is the problem with you shrinks—you talk all the time. I was so sick of listening to you on the set. I had to pretend to eat up all that psychobabble crap you were dishing out."

"I thought you found it interesting," I replied, feeling a little miffed.

"I had to play the game, sweetie. I knew it was only a matter of time before you realized I killed Adriana."

"You killed Adriana?" So my gut instinct had been right; my jaw dropped.

"I thought the game was up," she said, faltering for a second. "I figured that hot cop of yours was only a few days away from arresting me."

"Rafe?" I laughed. "He didn't have any idea; you kept everyone in the dark." Maybe I could string her along and play this out a little. "You know, he's already given Hank Watson the green light to take the production company back to Hollywood." I gave her a knowing look. "You could go with them. We can just pretend this never happened. Adriana's death will end up in a cold case file somewhere."

"Hah. Fat chance; you'd never keep your big mouth shut." She pointed the gun squarely at my chest.

"Wait!" I pleaded. "I just have two questions. You can grant a dying wish, can't you?"

"This better be quick." She was releasing the safety on the gun.

"How did you know I was here tonight?"

"That's easy. I signed up with Carla's new management company. She was looking for talent and I wanted to change agencies anyway. She mentioned you'd be at this party at the Delano and I was invited, too. So I followed you from the radio station. It was a no-brainer, Sherlock. You made my job easier when you decided to park here, instead of at the hotel."

"Ah, I see." She leveled the gun at me again.

"And you killed Adriana, why?" I said, talking quickly.

"You really don't know? She was going to blab to the world that I'd had lap band surgery in Copper Canyon, the silly bitch."

"She was going to spread a rumor—" I widened my eyes, remembering how Adriana had killed Sidney Carter's career with a rumor.

"Oh, it was more than a rumor, sweetie. It was the truth.

She was suspicious when I lost the weight so fast so she hired an investigator to do some digging around. He hacked into my credit card charges, and he found out I'd flown down to Mexico and hired a car to take me to the clinic. Once he had that information, it was easy to bribe a staff member to talk about the surgery. Money talks." She gave a little snort. "Adriana would have done anything to ruin my book deal and my television show. The networks and my publisher thought I did it all with diet and exercise."

"So you really did have bariatric surgery," I said slowly. "I should have figured that one out. You didn't want to talk about Copper Canyon when I asked you about it."

"You're not much of a detective, are you?" she said, giving a harsh laugh. "Well, none of that matters now," she said taking a step closer to me.

And that's when I moved. Still holding the stilettos at my side, I swung them in a wide arc, connecting solidly with her head. They made a soft whumping sound against her skull, and I thought she was going to go down for the count. But she was stronger than I thought, and instead, she lunged at me, gun in hand.

"Stop right there, sister!" someone shouted. Sandra turned her head just for a moment, and Vera Mae rushed out of the shadows, heading right toward her.

"Vera Mae, no! Stay back, she's got a gun!" I screamed. The gun wavered as a wild-eyed Sandra couldn't decide which one of us to shoot first. Then Vera Mae stretched her right arm straight out in front of her, and Sandra was enveloped in a cloud of noxious fumes. She shrieked as she sank to the garage floor, her hands covering her eyes.

Vera Mae was staring in surprise at the canister of pepper spray in her hand. "Wow. I was afraid this stuff might have evaporated. I've been carrying it around for at least five years. Looks like it did the trick, though."

"Vera Mae," I said, panting in fright, "do you have something to tie her up with? A belt, anything?"

"We'll take care of that, ma'am." A male voice, low and assured, came from behind me.

I looked up to see Officers Jiminez and Conrad from the Miami PD moving swiftly toward Sandra, who was trying to scramble to her feet. You'd think they were Crockett and Tubbs, I was so glad to see them. I turned to Vera Mae in surprise.

"You called them? But how?"

"I had one of my premonitions," Vera Mae said. "I started to register us for the Delano party and suddenly I had a real bad feeling that something was going on back here. So I hightailed it back, just in time to see you cornered like a raccoon. I called the Miami PD on my cell, and then I came right over to help you."

She smiled at the officers, who had handcuffed a dazed-looking Sandra and were guiding her into the backseat of a cruiser.

"These two fine young officers happened to be doing crowd control at the Delano. That's how they got here so fast." She stared at Officer Conrad, looking tall and rugged in his perfectly pressed uniform. A wistful look passed over her face. "I'm telling you, Maggie, if I were twenty years younger . . ."

She let her voice trail off and I leaned weakly back against the BMW. "Vera Mae, you're the best," I said simply. "You risked your life for me."

"Well, we gals have to stick together, hon. WYME just wouldn't be the same without you, now would it? Who would I have to talk to and make jokes with?" She playfully punched me on the arm, but I noticed that her eyes were misty.

"Ma'am? Dr. Maggie?" Officer Jiminez said. "Can you come down to the station to make a statement? We need you, too, Miss Vera Mae."

"You bet we can, sugar. And don't forget to call Rafe Martino, up in Cypress Grove," she added. "After all, this is sort of his case."

"I think he already knows," I said, checking my cell phone. It was still turned on, and that meant Sandra's whole confession must have been caught on tape.

And there was Rafe's number on the display screen.

"Rafe, are you there?"

"Always, baby. I called the Miami PD, too. Who's there with you?"

"Jiminez and Conrad," I said. There was a squeal of tires and four more squad cars came racing up next to us. "Oh, wait a minute. A few more cruisers just showed up; there's probably a dozen cops on the scene now. Hey, it looks like *CSI Miami* down here. You must have been worried about me."

Rafe laughed. "I always have your back, Maggie. Don't you know that?"

Chapter 34

"So let me get this straight," Lola said. "Frankie Domino never had anything to do with this?"

It was after midnight and I was sitting at the round oak table in the kitchen with Vera Mae, Lark, Rafe, and Lola. Vera Mae and I had given our statements to the Miami PD a couple of hours earlier and Sandra Michaels was safely in custody. She was charged with Adriana's death, plus attempted homicide because of her attack on me in the South Beach parking garage.

"Who's Frankie Domino?" Vera Mae asked.

"He's just a low-level mobster from New York," I piped up. "Like somebody you'd see on *The Sopranos*."

"Yes, but you said he was hanging around the set a lot." She watched as Lark sliced a homemade banana-walnut loaf and helped herself to a piece. "I wonder what he was up to?"

"I can answer that one," Rafe said. "It seems that Hank Watson's production company was about to go under last year and Hank borrowed a big sum of money from the mob to keep it afloat. Not the smartest thing to do but he was desperate. He figured he could pay it all back if *Death Watch* was a success. That's what he was counting on. Frankie Domino was hanging around the set to make sure that the film stayed on schedule; he was trying to protect the mob's investment."

"What's going to happen to Hank's movie now?" Lark asked.

"Who knows?" I shrugged. "Sandra's arrest will create a lot of buzz about *Death Watch* and Hank may finally have a hit movie. All of Sandra's scenes have already been shot, so the production can go on without her."

"I still can't get over that girl," Vera Mae said with a shudder. "She was such a sweet-looking thing; who'd think she was a cold-blooded murderer?"

"She felt she was going to lose everything if Adriana told the press about her bariatric surgery," I said. "She saw her whole life going down the tubes—the TV show, the book deal, her chance at big money and a huge career. And Adriana was so jealous and such a mean-spirited person, I can picture her telling the world how Sandra really lost the weight."

"Why would anyone take such delight in hurting someone?" Lark asked.

I shook my head. "You'd have to know Adriana to understand. There was something twisted deep inside her. It would take years of analysis to figure out."

"It would be quicker to hire an exorcist," Vera Mae suggested. "Some people are just plain evil through and through."

I thought about Sidney Carter. Adriana's treatment of him had certainly been diabolical. She'd delighted in spreading a false rumor about him that had ruined his career. I remembered being surprised at how outraged Sandra had seemed on Sidney's behalf that night at the Seabreeze. Now it made sense to me. Adriana had already ruined one career and Sandra knew she wouldn't hesitate to do it again. And this time she'd be the one in the crosshairs.

"And everything Sandra said to you in the parking garage was caught on tape?" Mom asked.

"Every word." Rafe gave a satisfied smile. "She decided to come clean with the Miami PD and she's already signed a written confession. She admitted to everything—Adriana's murder, the attack on Maggie in the parking garage, and those threatening notes to WYME. And one other thing—she really did shoot a prop gun at Lola in the warehouse. The best she can hope for now is a plea bargain."

I suddenly thought of something. "Did Sandra tamper with that Klieg light?"

"Not as far as we can tell. She denied doing it and I think she's telling the truth." Rafe leaned back in his chair, shooting me an intense look with those dark, sexy eyes. "That was just an accident. It was a lucky break that you stood up to get an iced tea when you did. Another second and you might not be sitting here with us." He reached over and laid his hand on my thigh, just for an instant. It was so fast it was practically subliminal, but a wave of heat went through me.

Lark quirked an eyebrow and smiled at me. She was sure that blind luck had nothing to do with my narrow escape. She prefers to think that positive energy and good karma saved me from being brained that day. We all were silent for a moment, sipping cappuccino and musing over the night's events until Mom spoke up.

"Tell me again about Carla Townsend." Her eyes looked troubled. "She wasn't trying to set you up tonight, was she?"

"No," Vera Mae answered swiftly, "the party at the Delano was legit. Carla really did join a talent management company out on the Coast and she'd signed up Sandra as one of her first clients. It was just a stroke of luck for Sandra when she heard that Maggie was going to be at the Delano party tonight."

"Does Carla know what happened tonight?" Lola asked.

Vera Mae nodded. "She sure does. As soon as she heard the news on the wire service, she called me on my cell to see what was going on."

I remembered the Death Chair TV feature and frowned. "That means we'll be seeing another Carla Townsend exclusive splashed over the network news."

"I'm afraid so, sugar. It will be her last one, though; she really has quit the tabloid business."

"So what does this mean for all of us?" Lola pondered.

"Well, I guess it means I'm never going to meet Matt Damon," Vera Mae said. "Or Brad Pitt, for that matter."

"And my work on the set is obviously finished," I offered. "How about you, Mom? You don't have any more scenes to do, right?"

She shook her head. "No, I'm done." Her tone was vague, as if she had something more pressing on her mind. She glanced at her watch. "You know, if it's one o'clock in the morning here, that means it's only ten in the evening out in L.A."

"And your point is?" I said, baffled.

She stood up, picking up her cell and heading for her bedroom. "I'm thinking of giving Carla a call. You know, I'm really not happy with Edgar Dumont as my agent." She pursed her lips in disapproval. "And all his clients seem to be in their teens. So I think it's time for new representation, someone out in Hollywood."

That's when I finally got it. "Mom, you can't be serious. You're actually thinking of asking Carla Townsend to represent you? You said she was despicable."

"Well, she might be despicable," Mom said, flushing a little, "but she's joined that big talent agency on Wilshire Boulevard and she has really good connections. She knows all the A-list directors and producers in L.A." She paused.

"You don't think I'm too terrible, do you? You know what they say, 'business is business.'"

"I say, go for it, sister!" Vera Mae cheered.

A few minutes later, I walked Rafe to the front landing. It had been a tough night for both of us and Rafe had to be at work in just five hours. He looked pale and drawn as he turned to face me on the step but he still had a sexy smile that made my heart go pitter-patter.

"You look beautiful, Maggie," he said, touching my hair. "It's hard to believe you can look this good after everything you've been through tonight." I knew that was a stretch; my hair was as fuzzy as a Brillo pad and my face was shiny—the light foundation I'd put on that morning had worn off hours ago.

"Well, land sakes, Detective Martino, you do know how to turn a girl's head," I said, doing a spot-on imitation of Vera Mae. "If I didn't know better, I'd say you were courtin' me."

Rafe laughed, a deep husky sound that made my nerve endings buzz. "Maybe I am." He reached out his hand, and for one crazy moment, I thought he was going to draw me into a hot embrace. Instead, he touched my nose with his index finger, big brother style.

"Really?" I quavered. "You could have fooled me."

His expression was seductive but his touch was playful, as chaste as a hug from Ted Rollins next door. He stared at me for a long moment. "If I ever decide to court you, Maggie, I promise you one thing." He pretended to cross his heart, his expression intent, his dark eyes serious.

"What's that?"

"You'll be the first to know."

I'll be the first to know? The words crashed into my brain but I couldn't really absorb what he was saying. I was drowning in his sexy eyes and killer smile, and a white-hot dash of excitement went through me. I felt like I was falling into a void, and then suddenly it didn't matter anymore because he leaned forward and kissed me.

A light kiss that sizzled on my lips and sent my pulse thrumming with desire.

I stared into those dark eyes flecked with gold, heat rising fast as a wave of pure (or not so pure!) animal attraction body-slammed me. What was going to happen next? He brushed the back of his fingers against my cheek, letting them linger there for a heart-stopping moment. I tried to move closer to him, but he was already backing away, moving down the steps.

"Sleep tight, baby." He tossed the line over his shoulder, and followed it with that heart-stopping smile and a sexy wink. *Sleep tight?* My mind tried to make sense of what had just happened.

A quick kiss on the lips and a fleeting caress?

It could mean everything. Or nothing.

And with that, Rafe Martino, man of mystery, blended into the Florida night.

Read on for a sneak peek at
Mary Kennedy's next Talk Radio Mystery,

TALKING CAN BE DEADLY

coming from Obsidian in January 2011.

You would assume that people who talk to the dead would be pale as vampires, their luminous eyes filled with unspoken secrets and timeless wisdom. You would expect them to speak in hushed tones, their voices floating like whispers on a tropical breeze as they invoke spirits from the beyond. You'd probably picture them as quiet and introspective, pondering the mysteries of life and what lies beyond the grave.

You would be wrong. Dead wrong.

Chantel Carrington, the new "psychic sensation" in Cypress Grove, is none of the above. Everything about Chantel is larger than life, strictly va-va-voom. Think of one of those giant Macy's Thanksgiving Day Parade balloons bobbing over Broadway.

Big. Brash. Garish. Inescapable.

Oh, yes. And full of hot air.

From her booming "Hello, dahlings!" as she rolls down the WYME corridors to her eye-popping Hawaiian muumuus, Chantel steals the spotlight every time.

Today she was the featured guest on my afternoon radio talk show, *On the Couch with Maggie Walsh*. She's been on the show four times in the past two weeks, and I hate to admit it, but each time the ratings have skyrocketed.

It seems that my entire listening audience is jonesing to communicate with the dearly departed, and Chantel does her best to accommodate them. Cyrus, the station manager, is so thrilled with her otherworldly chats that I'm sure he salivates just thinking about all that extra advertising revenue pouring into WYME.

Vera Mae, my producer, and I are less happy with the arrangement.

When I first arrived in Cypress Grove a few months ago to host my own radio show, I'd been pretty naive about the topics I'd be covering. A former clinical psychologist with a cushy Manhattan practice, I'd gained quite a following for my work in what the shrinks call "behavioral medicine."

Behavioral medicine is based on the idea that if you change your thinking, you can change your behavior, leading to a more positive mental outlook. No Freudian claptrap, no endless discussions of your dreams or Jungian archetypes.

But after a few brutal winters in the Big Apple, I'd become sick of the city, frustrated by the skyrocketing real estate prices, and worst of all, I discovered I was tired of listening to people's problems all day long. Yes, tired of listening to people's problems.

Some days I felt like I was trapped in a Jerry Springer marathon.

A shocking revelation, right? Practically career suicide to say it publicly, but there you have it. I was whipped, emotionally drained, with nothing left to give.

I had total burn-out.

So what did I do? I diagnosed the problem and wrote my own prescription. I made an executive decision as the Donald would say. I knew I needed a complete change of pace, and I made it happen. I closed up shop, transferred my patients to a trusted colleague, sold my IKEA furniture and moved to a sleepy Florida town.

Dr. Maggie, heal thyself.

At least, that was what I thought I was doing. I picked a town that's more like Mayberry than Manhattan, a place that's north of Boca, not too far from Palm Beach and a pleasant ride to Ft. Lauderdale. As the chamber of commerce says, "Cypress Grove. We're near every place else you'd rather be!"

I figured I'd use my clinical expertise and introduce my listening audience to the hottest topics in behavioral medicine, featuring the latest news in mental-health issues. I'd select a topic and take calls myself on Mondays, Wednesdays and Fridays. On Tuesdays and Thursdays, I'd invite a fascinating guest expert to join me on the airwaves.

Except for one tiny problem. Where was I going to find a bunch of fascinating guests? It never occurred to me that we'd have trouble persuading A-list experts to make the trek to Cypress Grove to appear on my show. We don't pay our guests, so unless they're hawking a book or a tape, there's really not much in it for them, except for the proverbial fifteen minutes of fame. And all the stale glazed doughnuts they can scarf down in the break room.

When Chantel Carrington blew into town last month to promote her latest book, *I Talk to Dead People—and You Can Too!* I invited her to do a guest spot on my show. It was against my better judgment, but I knew Cyrus would be pleased, and frankly, my ratings needed a bit of a boost.

During the last Nielsen ratings, *On the Couch with Maggie Walsh* tied for last place, right up there with *Bob Figgs and the Swine Report.* I was running neck and neck with a show that features pigs!

I had no idea Chantel would be such a huge success and, worse, that she would pick Cypress Grove as the perfect place to work on her next book. Before you could say woowoo, she'd rented an apartment near Branscom Pond and was hosting séances in town.

So there I was, entertaining her as a guest on my show and making the best of a bad situation. I was making lemonade out of lemons.

Ironic, really, because this is the same annoying bit of advice I used to give my patients. Funny how our bromides come back to haunt us.

Chantel was carrying a cup of Starbucks coffee as she breezed into the studio and collapsed into a chair next to me at the control board. Chantel is a large woman in her late forties, with violet eyes (colored contacts?) and a mane of black curls trailing Gypsy-style down her back.

She favors bright red lipstick and odd-looking z-coil shoes that make her look like she might levitate up to the ceiling or spring into the netherworld without warning. Today she was wearing a peekaboo lacy white shawl over a yellow muumuu festooned with bright blue parrots.

"Two minutes till airtime," Vera Me yelled from the control room. She glanced at me and made a two-fingered peace sign. I nodded back. Then Vera Mae spotted Chantel's coffee, shook her head and thinned her lips in disapproval. Uh-oh. No one is allowed to have food or drinks in the studio, but Chantel seems to be a law unto herself. I knew Vera Mae would dart in at the first commercial break and whisk the coffee away.

Chantel fanned herself with a copy of the daily traffic log. She had a thin layer of perspiration on her upper lip and her face was flushed a sickly shade of Pepto-Bismol pink.

"I should have worn something cooler today," she confided. "You'd think the weather guys would get it right for once." She tugged at the shawl, which she wore Martha Washington—style, fastened in front with a tortoiseshell brooch.

I bit back a smile. Why would a psychic need the Weather Channel?

"Live in thirty seconds." Vera Mae slapped her headphones

on and pointed to the board. It was already lit up with call
crs. We'd been running "talk to the dead" promos for the last
three days. We usually don't get this many callers unless we're
giving away tickets to a Reba McIntire show or offering a
free style and cut at Wanda's House of Beauty.

"Showtime," I said to Chantel, who licked her lips and
squiggled her hips a little in her chair, gearing herself up for
her big performance. I grabbed my headphones just as Vera
Mae pointed at me and mouthed the word *Go*.

Vera Mae's towering beehive quivered with excitement as
she leaned over the board. I've tried to get Vera Mae to ditch
her Marge Simpson volcano of carrot-colored hair, but she
believes, "The higher the hairdo, the closer to God."

There's always that electric moment when the phone
lines open, and I feel a little rush of adrenaline thumping in
my chest. Okay, this was it. We were live on the air in south
Florida.

"You're *On the Couch with Maggie Walsh*," I said, sliding
into my trademark introduction. "Today, we have the renowned
psychic and bestselling author Chantel Carrington with us.
Welcome to the show, Chantel. It looks like the lines are
flooded with calls. Are you ready to get started?" This question, of course, was strictly a formality. I could see that Chantel
was more than ready; she was practically quivering with anticipation, like Sea Biscuit at the starting gate.

"Ready!" Chantel sang out, looking giddy with excitement.

"So, Vera Mae, who do we have first?"

"We have Sylvia on line one, Maggie. She's calling from
Boca and she wants to communicate with Barney, who passed
recently. It was just last week, in fact—"

"So sorry for your loss, Sylvia," Chantel cut in smoothly,
talking over the tail end of Vera Mae's comment. "Can you
tell me a little bit about Barney? I'm getting some strong

vibes that you were lifelong partners." She pursed her lips, staring up at the ceiling for a moment, as if seeking inspiration.

I followed her gaze. All I saw were some loose sound-proofing tiles, so I turned my attention back to the control board.

"We were together for eight years," Sylvia sniffled. It sounded like she was biting back a sob. Interesting she used the word *together*; she didn't say *husband*. I immediately wondered, was Barney a boyfriend? Fiancé? Friend with benefits?

"Eight wonderful years," she went on. "My bed is so lonely at night, I cry myself to sleep without Barney there. I just can't believe he's gone."

I watched as Chantel whipped out a notepad and scribbled: *Eight years. Cries herself to sleep. Guilt? Unresolved issues?* Then she scrunched up her face in a fake-sympathetic look, her forehead creased in concern.

"But he's not really gone," she interjected. "You know that, don't you, Sylvia? He's watching over you this very minute. I can feel his love, can't you?" Chantel was making notes as she talked, spouting the familiar lines by rote.

The idea of the dead watching over us is one of her favorite themes. The dead aren't really gone on Planet Chantel. They are just out of sight, like the sun when a cloud passes in front of it. They're still with us, we just can't see them.

Sylvia tried to rally. "Well, I know you say that in your book, Chantel, and I really do try to believe it, but sometimes I wonder—"

"There's nothing to wonder about." There was a steely edge to Chantel's voice. "You *must* stay positive and believe that you'll see Barney again. Remember, our lives here on earth are short, ephemeral," she said, warming to her subject.

She lifted her right hand for emphasis and a half dozen little gold bracelets clanked together. Vera Mae winced as the mike amplified the sound and the arrow on the volume meter flipped into the red. I pointed to the bracelets and Chantel, ever the media pro, slapped her left hand over her wrist to stop the jangling sound.

"If you've read my book, *I Talk to Dead People*, you should have a good understanding of my views on mortality, Sylvia. There is no room in your heart for doubt. You must choose love and optimism over doubt and despair."

I glanced into the control room and saw Vera Mae give me a little eye roll. We'd been forced to listen to Chantel's spiel over and over, and it was getting old. Plus, Chantel never misses a chance to mention the title of her book. Once or twice is okay, but her shameless self-promotion was beginning to grate on my nerves.

Yesterday Vera Mae threatened to hang a Chinese gong in the control room and give it a good whack every time Chantel plugged *I Talk to Dead People*. I caught myself drumming my fingertips on the console and made a conscious effort to stop. I glanced over at Chantel as she mouthed her all too familiar clichés. They were so cloying they made my teeth ache.

I stared hard, narrowed my eyes and tried to send her a psychic message. *Chantel, please don't say our time here is like a drop of water in the ocean. Please, I'm begging you.*

"Our time on earth is like a drop of water in the ocean," she said.

So much for thought transference. Or maybe she'd heard me and had decided to tune me out. I watched as she leaned forward, her bloodred lips aiming for the mike like a heat-seeking missile.

Not the grain of sand analogy again . . .

"We're like a grain of sand on the beach."

Ouch. I knew what was coming next. Think eye. Blink. Millisecond. Here it comes.

"Believe me, Sylvia, our life on earth is over in the blink of an eye."

Hmm. I glanced at the clock. Life might be over in the blink of an eye but this show felt like it was stretching into tomorrow. We were two minutes into the first hour so that meant it was time for her to plug one of her books. Again.

"In chapter three of my sequel, *Dead People Talk to Me*, I'll be covering this topic in some detail."

Aha, right on schedule. And now she's hawking the sequel to *I Talk to Dead People*, a book that isn't even in print yet! Genius, right? Chantel glanced up just in time to catch Vera Mae making a throat-slitting gesture. She glared at Vera Mae for a long moment, while I ducked my head and pretended to be studying my notes.

"Yes, but to answer Sylvia's question," I prodded. I looked up and plastered an innocent-looking smile on my face.

"I was *getting* to that," Chantel said testily. "I want you to know I'm feeling very strong vibes from Barney right this minute, Sylvia. In fact, he's here in the studio." She looked past me and gave a faint smile. "I can practically reach out and touch him. Do you see him, Maggie? He's right behind you."

Wh-a-a- a-t? He's here in the studio? Standing behind me? Yowsers!

Vera Mae gave a startled yelp and dropped all her show notes on the floor. As she scrambled to pick them up, my heart thumped in my chest and my pulse zoomed into overdrive. A little rash of goose bumps sprang up on my arm, and I willed them away. I thought I felt a cool breeze fluttering somewhere behind my left shoulder, or was I imagining it? I refused to turn around; I wasn't going to play into her silly game.

I forced myself to maintain eye contact with Chantel. She

was obviously a master manipulator and was playing tricks with my head, making me doubt my own perceptions. I hated to admit it, but she was good, very good.

I don't believe in ghosts. Again, there was another little puff of cool air behind me, and the papers ruffled slightly on the console. It was my imagination. *It had to be.* Or maybe the always temperamental air-conditioning unit was pumping out erratic blasts of icy air. That was why the papers were moving ever so slightly on the countertop.

No way was it a sign from the dearly departed Barney!

Was it?

I don't believe in ghosts.

Do I?

"Yes, he's here," Chantel continued, her voice low and silky. "I feel his presence. Don't you feel it, Maggie?"

"Well, um, actually—"

"You *would* feel it if you were more open to it." *You mean I'd feel it if I were open to mass hysteria like your crazy followers. Call me Galileo, but I believe in science, not superstition. There is no way I'm going to fall for this, as a psychologist, I know all about the power of suggestion and—*

"Barney is standing right next to you, practically screaming to be heard."

He is?

I'm sure pure shock registered on my face because she added, "I'm speaking metaphorically, of course. His spirit, his aura, is in the room, not his corporeal form. I'll send you an advance copy of my next book, Maggie, and you'll learn how to tune into the spirit world."

See what I mean? Chantel has an uncanny ability to steal the show, put me down with a snide remark and draw the conversation back to herself. Who could compete with her "I see a dead guy in the studio" schtick? Ghosts trump psychological insights with the audience every time. Trust me.

"Ohmigod, Barney's in the studio? Is he all right?" Sylvia shrieked through the headphones. I jumped in surprise, my right elbow slipping off the console. I'd been so caught up in the saga of Barney the Friendly Ghost, I'd completely forgotten about poor grieving Sylvia, waiting patiently on the other end of the line.

"Ask him if he needs anything! Does he look good? Is he happy?" Sylvia was so excited, she was almost hyperventilating.

"He's very happy, Sylvia," Chantel said warmly. "He has everything he needs. And he looks fine to me." Chantel gave me a sly smile. "How does he look to you, Maggie?"

Ah, a trick question. How would a dead person look? I thought for a minute and drew a blank.

"Well, I guess he looks—" *Dead?* I wanted to say. I started to sweat a little, even though the AC was cranked up to the max. I thought I heard a faint cough sound behind me. *Do ghosts cough?*

This time I really had to force myself not to look around. I was developing a nervous tic in my left shoulder, and I was stammering a little, which is also something I do when I get nervous. "I mean, I think he looks—"

"Maggie thinks he looks fine, too, Sylvia," Chantel interjected. Then she waited a beat, lowering her voice to a funereal tone. "But he's worried about you, dear. He doesn't want you to be sad or unhappy at his passing."

"But I miss him!" Sylvia wailed. "Of course I'm sad and unhappy."

"Barney wants you to know that you didn't do anything wrong," Chantel said firmly, her forehead wrinkling in thought. "There's nothing you could have done differently. He knows you feel troubled about something. It seems like he left this earth very quickly. That is correct, is he not?"

Chantel always tries to get "those left behind" to agree with her as part of her schtick. Then she builds on what they say, or changes tack if she thinks she's veering off course.

Dead air for a beat. "No, not really." Sylvia sounded confused.

Chantel frowned. "He passed unexpectedly, did he not?" Her tone was wheedling, argumentative, like Sam Waterston's when he's grilling a witness on *Law & Order*.

"Well, no—"

"One minute he was here, and the next he was not? That is correct, is it not?" Chantel was in rare form. She could give James Van Praggh a run for his money any day.

"I suppose so—"

"Then that's *unexpected*, right?" She gave a derisive little snort, very unladylike. "Here one moment and gone the next. You can't *get* much more unexpected than that, sweetie." She snapped her fingers for emphasis and all the bracelets jangled together again.

"Yes, if you put it that way."

Chantel closed her eyes for a moment and put her fingertips to the bridge of her nose, as if lost in thought. "I'm sensing there was a problem with his heart, or it might have been cancer."

Heart disease or cancer. A safe choice. Don't most people die of those things?

I mean, she could have gone out on a limb and said "leprosy" or "malaria" but why should she? Nothing like hedging your bets. I found myself hoping that Barney had died in a bizarre way.

Maybe an avalanche? Admittedly, an avalanche would have been a rarity in southern Florida, but I'd love to see Chantel try to talk her way out of that one.

Or maybe a hang-gliding accident. That would certainly

throw Chantel for a loop. Or maybe he was eaten by a shark or—

"But he didn't have heart trouble, and his blood sugar was fine." *Uh-oh.* A doubtful note was creeping into Sylvia's voice. Grief-stricken or not, she wasn't falling for what Vera Mae calls Chantel's phony-baloney.

So now what? It looked like Chantel was way off target, and that meant it was time for a quick backpedal.

"Of course he had heart trouble! When he died, his heart *stopped*, didn't it?"

"Yes, that's true, but—"

"There are no buts about it. He died because his heart stopped. That means he had heart trouble. Period." Chantel sat back in her chair and folded her arms over her chest, looking smug and vindicated. Chantel Carrington, the psychic cardiologist.

Dr. Oz, eat your heart out.

Vera Mae and I locked eyes as she gave a little shrug. *But doesn't everyone die because their heart stops? Isn't that the definition of dying?* I bet our thoughts were chugging along the same track because she gave me a tiny eye roll.

Chantel took a quick peek at her notes. Better get off the details of Barney's passing and jump into something else fast.

"Is he still there in the studio?" Sylvia asked.

"Yes, he is. In fact, Barney is telling me right this minute that you were his soul mate, the love of his life," she said slowly into the mike. "But you already know that, right?" Her tone was as treacly as molasses.

Sylvia gave a tremulous laugh. Chantel was winning her back. "Oh, yes, I do know that." A pause. "I hope he realizes it was his time. At least that's what Dr. Harper said."

Dr. Harper? Chantel hesitated, looking blank for a moment. She opened her mouth like a guppie, snapped it shut and then took a deep breath through her nose. "Barney knows that Dr. Harper made the right decision." She spoke slowly, the way people do when they're not quite sure of what they're saying.

Had Barney been on life support? I wondered. Maybe Sylvia felt guilty about pulling the plug. I couldn't think of any tactful way to ask, so I remained silent.

Luckily Chantel talks enough for both of us.

"Barney tells me his loved ones were all with him when he passed," Chantel continued. "That must be a comfort to you."

"But that's impossible. Barney didn't have any relatives. They all died years ago."

Chantel blinked. She was off her game today. "Well, when I said they were *with* him, I meant they were *waiting* for him on the other side. You know, after he went into the white light and crossed the Rainbow Bridge."

Nice save, Chantel.

"Oh, I see what you mean."

Out of the corner of my eye, I saw Vera Mae making a quack-quack motion with her hands, a sign that a commercial was coming up. Time to wrap this up till the next segment.

"I'm afraid we have to take a break now—" I ventured.

"Wait!" Sylvia pleaded. "I have to ask one more question. Does Barney know about Harold?"

Harold? It's awful when a caller says something out of left field, and I saw a flash of panic in Chantel's eyes. She bit her lip uncertainly and some of her flame red lipstick smeared onto her front teeth.

Who was Harold? An illegitimate son? A business partner? A new romantic interest?

"I think he does," Chantel told her. "Yes, he's nodding his

head." I resisted a ridiculous impulse to look around and see if the ghostly Barney really was nodding in approval.

"And he's okay with that?" Sylvia asked breathlessly. "Because Harold's sleeping with me now. I know it seems a little soon, but it was just one of those things."

Harold is sleeping with her and Barney just passed last week? I felt like I was caught up in an episode of *The Young and the Restless*. Or maybe *One Tree Hill*.

"I . . . Yes, I believe Barney is okay with that," Chantel said. She swallowed, clearly flustered. "Barney seems to be drifting away now, so I'm afraid I can't be more specific. . . ."

"I never thought I'd get another Pomeranian, but I bought Harold from the same breeder that Barney came from." Sylvia was talking in a rush. Pressured speech, the shrinks call it. "He's got papers and everything. I may show him at Westminster next year."

Same breeder, Westminster? Suddenly it all made sense.

"Barney's a *dog*?" I blurted out.

"Of course he's a dog," Sylvia huffed. "A prizewinning Pomeranian. What did you think he was? I had to have him euthanized last week, his kidneys went. Dr. Harper said it was time. I just wanted to see if he was doing okay and to tell him about Harold."

I was speechless but Vera Mae took up the slack. "And so the circle of life continues," she muttered into her mike. "We're coming up on a break, and we just have time for a quick word from our sponsor, Wanda's House of Beauty."

The moment we went to break, Chantel and I whipped our headphones off and stared at each other in stunned silence.

ABOUT THE AUTHOR

Mary Kennedy is a former radio copywriter and the award-winning author of forty novels. A clinical psychologist in private practice, she lives on the East Coast with her husband and eight eccentric cats. Both husband and cats have resisted all her attempts to psychoanalyze them, but she remains optimistic. Visit her Web site at www.marykennedy.net

<u>Also Available</u>

Mary Kennedy

Dead Air
A Talk Radio Mystery

Maggie left her clinical practice in Manhattan and moved to sunny Cypress Grove, Florida, where she became host of WYME's *On the Couch with Maggie Walsh*. From co-dependent wives to fetish fiends, all the local crazies love her show.

Then threats start pouring in against one of the station's special guests: self-styled new age prophet Guru Sanjay Gingii. When one of the threats becomes a deadly reality, Maggie's new roommate, Lark, is surprisingly the prime suspect. Now, Maggie has to prove Lark innocent while dealing with a killer who needs more than just therapy...

**Available wherever books are sold or
at penguin.com**

The **Crime of Fashion** Mysteries
by Ellen Byerrum

Killer Hair

An up-and-coming stylist, Angie Woods had a reputation
for rescuing down-and-out looks—and careers—all with
a pair of scissors. But when Angie is found with a
drastic haircut and a razor in her hand, the police
assume she committed suicide. Lacey knew the stylist
and suspects something more sinister—that the story
may lie with Angie's star client, a White House staffer
with a salacious website. With the help of a hunky
ex-cop, Lacey must root out the truth...

Hostile Makeover

As makeover madness sweeps the nation's capital,
reporter Lacey Smithsonian interviews TV show makeover success story Amanda Manville. But with Amanda's
beauty comes a beast in the form of a stalker with
vicious intentions—and Lacey may be the only one who
can stop him.

<u>Also in the **Crime of Fashion** series:</u>
Designer Knockoff
Raiders of the Lost Corset
Grave Apparel
Armed and Glamorous

**Available wherever books are sold or at
penguin.com**